THE RAVENS

THE RAVENS

KASS MORGAN
DANIELLE PAIGE

HOUGHTON MIFFLIN HARCOURT
boston new york

hmhbooks.com

alloyentertainment

Produced by Alloy Entertainment
30 Hudson Yards
New York, NY 10001

The text was set in Bembo Book MT Std.

Library of Congress Cataloging-in-Publication Data
Names: Morgan, Kass, author. | Paige, Danielle (Novelist), author.
Title: The Ravens / by Kass Morgan and Danielle Paige.
Description: Boston; New York: Houghton Mifflin Harcourt, [2021] |
Audience: Ages 14 and up. | Audience: Grades 10–12. |
Summary: Loner Vivi Deveraux is thrilled to join Westerly College's Kappas, who are secretly witches, until she meets perfect, polished Scarlett Winter, who will stop at nothing to be the sorority's next president.
Identifiers: LCCN 2019052298 (print) | LCCN 2019052299 (ebook) |
ISBN 9780358098232 (hardcover) | ISBN 9780358098195 (ebook)
Subjects: CYAC: Witchcraft—Fiction. | Magic—Fiction. |
Greek letter societies—Fiction. | Colleges and universities—Fiction.
Classification: LCC PZ7.M8249 Rav 2021 (print) | LCC PZ7.M8249 (ebook) |
DDC [Fic]—dc23
LC record available at https://lccn.loc.gov/2019052298
LC ebook record available at https://lccn.loc.gov/2019052299

Manufactured in the United States of America
DOC 10 9 8 7 6 5 4 3 2 1
4500811977

For my mother, Marcia Bloom, who taught me the best kind of witchcraft—how to see beauty all around and find magic in unexpected places

—Kass

For Andrea, Sienna, Fiona, and the rest of my coven. And for my mother, Shirley Paige, whose magic will always be with me

—Danielle

PROLOGUE

The witch looked at the blond girl cowering on the ground, her eyes wide with fear.

"Don't look at me that way. I told you, I don't want to do this," the witch said as she drew the circle, lit the candles, and checked the contents of the bubbling cauldron. The knife, already sharpened, glinted on the altar next to her offering.

The girl moaned in response, tears streaking down her face. Her mouth was bound, but her words rang crystal-clear in the witch's head.

Remember who I am. Remember who you are. Remember the Ravens.

The witch hardened her heart. No doubt the girl thought she sensed an opportunity in her captor's apologetic tone. A chance to persuade her to stop. A chance to hope. A chance to live.

It was too late for that. Magic didn't preach. It gave and took. This was the gift. This was the cost.

The witch knelt beside the girl and tested the bonds one last time. Tight, though not enough to cut off her circulation. She wasn't a monster.

The girl's screams began again, piercing through the gag stuffed in her mouth.

The witch gritted her teeth. She'd much prefer the girl to be unconscious. But the rite she'd dug up had been very specific. If this was going to work, she needed to do it perfectly. If it didn't . . .

She shut her eyes. She couldn't think about that possibility. It *had* to work. There was no other way.

She picked up the knife and began to chant.

In the end, she was surprised at how easy it was. A slash and a shower of red, followed by the unmistakable electric crackle of magic bleeding into the air . . .

Magic that was now all hers.

CHAPTER ONE

Vivi

"Vivian." Daphne Devereaux stood in her daughter's doorway, her face twisted in exaggerated anguish. Even in the unforgiving Reno heat, she wore a floor-length black housecoat edged in gold tassels and had wrapped a velvet scarf around her dark, unruly hair. "You can't go. I've had a premonition."

Vivi glanced at her mother, suppressed a sigh, and returned to her packing. She was leaving for Westerly College in Savannah that afternoon and was trying to fit her entire life into two suitcases and a backpack. Luckily, Vivi had had a lifetime of practice. Whenever Daphne Devereaux got one of her "premonitions," they tended to leave the next morning, unpaid rent and unpacked belongings be damned. "It's healthy to start fresh, sugar snap," Daphne said once when eight-year-old Vivi begged to go back for her stuffed hippo, Philip. "You don't want to carry that bad energy with you."

"Let me guess," Vivi said now, shoving several books into her backpack. Daphne was moving too, trading Reno for Louisville, and Vivi didn't trust her mom to take her library. "You've seen a powerful darkness headed my way."

"It's not safe for you at that . . . *place*."

Vivi closed her eyes and took what she hoped would be a

calming breath. Her mother hadn't been able to bring herself to say the word *college* for months. "It's called Westerly. It's not a curse word."

Far from it. Westerly was Vivi's lifeline. She'd been shocked when she received a full scholarship to Westerly, a school she'd considered to be way out of her league. Vivi had always been a strong student, but she'd attended three different high schools—two of which she'd started midyear—and her transcript contained nearly as many incompletes as it did As.

Daphne, however, had been adamantly against it. "You'll hate Westerly," she'd said with surprising conviction. "I'd never set foot on that campus."

That was what sealed the deal for Vivi. If her mom hated it that much, it was clearly the perfect place for Vivi to start a brand-new life.

As Daphne stood mournfully in the doorway, Vivi looked at the Westerly calendar she'd tacked to the yellowing wall, the only decoration she'd bothered with this time around. Of all the places they'd lived over the years, this apartment was her least favorite. It was a stucco-filled two-bedroom above a pawnshop in Reno, and the whole place reeked of cigarettes and desperation. Much like the whole dusty state of Nevada. The calendar's photos, glossy odes to ivy-covered buildings and mossy live oaks, had become a beacon of hope. They were a reminder of something better, a future she could carve out for herself—away from her mother and her portents of evil.

But then she saw the tears in her mother's eyes and Vivi felt her frustration relent, just a little. Although Daphne was a supremely accomplished actress—a necessity when your livelihood depended on parting strangers from their money—she'd never been able to fake tears.

Vivi abandoned her packing and took a few steps across her cramped bedroom toward her mother. "It's going to be okay, Mom," Vivi said. "I won't be gone long. Thanksgiving will be here before you know it."

Her mother sniffed and extended her pale arm. Vivi shared her mother's fair coloring, which meant that she burned after fifteen minutes in the desert sun. "Look what I drew as your cross card."

It was a tarot card. Daphne made a living "reading the fortunes" of all the sad, wretched people who sought her out and forked over good money in exchange for bullshit platitudes: *Yes, your lazy husband will find work soon; no, your deadbeat dad doesn't hate you—in fact, he's trying to find you too . . .*

As a child, Vivi had loved watching her beautiful mother dazzle the customers with her wisdom and glamour. But as she grew older, seeing her mother profiting from their pain began to set Vivi's teeth on edge. She couldn't bear to watch people being taken advantage of, yet there was nothing she could do about it. Daphne's readings were their one source of income, the only way to pay for their shitty apartments and discount groceries.

But not anymore. Vivi had finally found a way out. A new beginning, far from her mother's impulsive behaviors. The kind that had led them to uproot their whole lives time and again based on nothing more than Daphne's "premonitions."

"Let me guess," Vivi said, raising an eyebrow at the tarot card in her mother's hand. "Death?"

Her mother's face darkened, and when Daphne spoke, her normally melodic voice was chillingly sharp and quiet. "Vivi, I know you don't believe in tarot, but for once, just listen to me."

Vivi took the card and turned it over. Sure enough, a skeleton carrying a scythe glared up from the card. Its eyes were hollowed-out gouges and its mouth curved up in an almost gleeful leer. Disembodied hands and feet pushed up from the loamy earth as the sun sank in a blood-red sky. Vivi felt an odd tremor of vertigo, like she was standing at the edge of a great precipice and looking down into a vast nothingness instead of standing in her bedroom, where the only view was the neon-yellow WE BUY GOLD sign across the street.

"I told you. Westerly isn't a safe place, not for people like you," Daphne whispered. "You have an ability to see beyond the veil. It makes you a target for dark forces."

"Beyond the veil?" Vivi repeated wearily. "I thought you weren't going to say stuff like that anymore." Throughout Vivi's childhood, Daphne had tried to draw her into her world of tarot and séances and crystals, claiming that Vivi had "special powers" waiting to be unlocked. She'd even trained Vivi to do simple readings for clients, who'd been mesmerized by the sight of a small child communing with the spirits. But eventually, Vivi had realized the truth—she didn't have any power; she was just another pawn in her mother's game.

"I can't control which card I draw. It's foolish to ignore a warning like this."

A horn honked outside and someone yelled an expletive. Vivi sighed and shook her head. "But you taught me yourself that Death is a symbol of transformation." Vivi tried to hand the card back to her mother, but Daphne's arms remained resolutely at her sides. "Obviously that's what it means. College is my fresh start."

No more random midnight moves to new cities; no uprooting themselves every time Vivi was about to finally form a real friendship. For the next four years, she could reinvent herself as a normal college student. She'd make friends, have a social life, maybe sign up for a few extracurricular activities—or, at the very least, figure out what activities she enjoyed. They'd moved around so much that she hadn't had the chance to get good at anything. She'd been forced to quit the flute after three months and abandon softball midseason, and she'd given up Intro to French so many times that all she knew how to reliably say was *Bonjour, je m'appelle Vivian. Je suis nouvelle.*

Her mother shook her head. "In the reading, Death was accompanied by the Ten of Swords and the Tower. Betrayal and sudden violence. Vivian, I have a terrible feeling—"

Vivi gave up and tucked the card into her suitcase, then reached up and took Daphne's hands in hers. "This is a big change for both of us. It's okay to be upset. Just tell me you're going to miss me, like a normal parent would, instead of turning this into some sign from the spirit world."

Her mother squeezed her hands tightly. "I know I can't make this decision for you—"

"Then stop trying to. Please." Vivi laced her fingers through her mother's the way she used to when she was little. "I don't want to spend our last day fighting."

Daphne's shoulders slumped as if she'd finally realized this was a losing battle. "Promise me you'll be careful. Remember, things aren't always as they appear. Even something that seems good can be dangerous."

"Is this your way of telling me I'm secretly evil?"

Her mother gave her a withering look. "Just be smart, Viv."

"That I can definitely do." Vivi's smile widened enough to make Daphne roll her eyes.

"I've raised an egomaniac." But her mother leaned in to hug her all the same.

"I blame you for all the 'you're magic and you can do anything' talks," Vivi said, letting go of her hands to finish zipping the suitcase shut. "I'll be careful, I promise."

And she would be. She knew bad things could happen in college. Bad things happened everywhere, but Daphne was fooling herself if she thought some silly tarot reading meant anything. There was no such thing as magic.

Or so Vivi thought.

CHAPTER TWO

Scarlett

You don't choose your sisters. The magic does, Scarlett Winter's nanny, Minnie, had told her years before Scarlett joined Kappa Rho Nu. The words came back to Scarlett now as her mother drove through the wrought-iron gates of Westerly College's campus, passing clusters of girls. Some clutched suitcases, looking nervous and young; others gazed at the campus with a hungry look, as if they were ready to conquer it. Somewhere in this sea of girls was the new class of Kappa recruits. A new class of Ravens, as the sisters called themselves, who, if everything went according to her plan—and if the magic was willing—would look up to Scarlett as their leader in just one year's time.

Once they passed through the gates, she felt freer and stronger. As if she were stepping out of her family's shadow and into the light. It made no sense, really, because Marjorie, her mother, and Eugenie, her older sister, were everywhere in Kappa House. Their pictures were in the group photos on the wall. Their names were on the lips of the older sorority sisters. They had made their mark here before her. But as much as the expectation weighed on her, Scarlett was determined to show everyone that the best Winter was yet to come. She would be president, as they had, but she would be better, brighter, stronger, and more unforgettable than they had been. That was the beauty of coming after: she could still exceed them. Or so she told herself.

"You really should have worn the red dress," Marjorie said, frowning at her daughter in the rearview mirror. "It's more presidential. You need to convey power, taste, leadership capability . . ."

Scarlett caught her reflection behind her mother's in the rearview mirror. Scarlett, Eugenie, and Marjorie were different shades of brown. Each was objectively striking, but Eugenie was the spitting image of their mother while Scarlett's look was all her own, distinguished by a sharp nose and wide-set eyes. Growing up, Scarlett had always envied her mother and Eugenie for sharing so much, right down to their perfect noses.

Scarlett smoothed down her green A-line dress. "Mama, I doubt Dahlia is going to name the next Kappa president based on her dress the first day of school. And wearing red when your name is Scarlett is a little on the nose."

Marjorie's expression went deadly serious. "Scarlett, *everything* goes into consideration."

"She's right, you know," Eugenie put in from the front seat.

"Listen to your sister. She was president two years in a row," Marjorie said proudly. "And now it's your turn to carry on the family tradition."

Eugenie smirked. "Unless, of course, you're content with just sitting on the sidelines."

"Of course not. I'm a Winter, aren't I?" Scarlett straightened her spine and glared at her sister. She wasn't sure why Eugenie had insisted on coming to drop her off at Westerly; she was always going on about how busy she was as a junior associate at their mother's law firm. Then again, Eugenie took every opportunity she could to put Scarlett in her place. Including managing to ride shotgun on Scarlett's first day back while Scarlett herself was relegated to the back seat.

Her mother nodded sharply. "Don't ever forget it, my dear."

She shifted to look back at Scarlett, and Scarlett caught a whiff of her perfume, a light jasmine scent that reminded her of the way her mother used to sneak into her room after a long night at the firm and plant a kiss on her forehead. Scarlett always pretended to be sleeping, because her mother tried so hard not to wake her. But she didn't mind being woken. It reminded her how much her mother cared, something that Scarlett didn't always feel during her waking hours.

And what her mother cared most about was each of her two daughters following in her footsteps and becoming president of Kappa. Scarlett grew up hearing, *A Kappa president cannot be just one thing, Scarlett. She must be everything. Smart, stylish, kind. The type of girl who inspires envy and respect in equal measure. The type of girl who puts her sisters first—and is powerful enough to change the world.*

Scarlett had known for as long as she could remember that she was a witch and that Kappa was her destiny. To be accepted into its ranks was a necessity; to become president in her own right was the most basic expectation. Which was why Minnie, who had been Scarlett's mother's nanny before she was hers, had spent the better part of her golden years training Scarlett in the ways of their magic, just as she had done with her sister and mother before her.

Every witch was born with her own magic: Cups, the Water sign; Pentacles, the Earth sign; Swords, the Air sign; and Wands, the Fire sign. Each sign was aligned with a suit in the tarot cards, which always amused Scarlett. Naysayers dismissed tarot as the tool of charlatans and fakes, but, really, they had no idea how close to the truth tarot came.

Scarlett was a Cups, which meant she was strongest working with water elements. She'd learned from Minnie that if she held the right symbol and said the right words, she could perform magic that made the world a bigger and brighter place.

Minnie hadn't been a Raven herself; her family had come to witchcraft on its own, with secrets and spells passed down through the generations. But she'd known the Winters her entire life and she understood the pressure Scarlett's family put on Scarlett better than anyone did. Minnie was the one who had always believed in her—who'd reassured her when she felt her mother's disappointment or Eugenie's disdain. Minnie was the one who told Scarlett she could be the most powerful witch in the world if she believed in herself and trusted the magic.

When Minnie died of old age last spring, Scarlett had cried so hard that all around her, it began to rain. She still felt an emptiness in her heart when she thought of Minnie, but Scarlett knew that what Minnie wanted more than anything was for Scarlett to be happy, which was why Scarlett was more determined than ever to prove to her family—and all the Ravens—that she was powerful enough to be the sorority's next president.

Failure was not an option.

Marjorie pulled up in front of Kappa House, and Scarlett's heart skipped a beat. The sorority house was a beautiful, dove-gray French revival, complete with wrought-iron balconies on every level and a widow's walk on the roof where the sisters sometimes did their spellcasting. Sisters were streaming into the house, carrying suitcases and lamps and hugging each other after a long summer away. There was Hazel Kim, a sophomore who was a star on the school's track team; Juliet Simms, a senior who was a brilliant chemist and potion-maker; and Mei Okada, a fellow junior who could change her looks as easily as she could change her outfits.

Marjorie turned off the engine and surveyed the scene like a commanding officer might survey a battlefield. "Where's Mason? I wanted to hear all about his travels."

"He's not getting in until tomorrow," Scarlett said, trying to contain her giddy smile.

She hadn't seen Mason in almost two months. It was the longest they'd been apart since they'd started dating two years ago. On a whim, Mason had decided to backpack through Europe after attending a family friend's wedding in Italy. He'd skipped out on his internship at his father's law firm—and all the plans Scarlett had made for them. While Scarlett interned at her mother's firm, toiling over briefs and planning the Ravens' social calendar with her sorority sisters, she'd waited for his short, sporadic texts and pictures filling her in on his travels—Just swam in Lake Como—wish you were here; You have to see the water in Capri—I'm taking you here after you graduate. It wasn't like Mason to shirk his family duties or keep her waiting all summer to see him. As a general rule, Scarlett didn't wait for anything or anyone, but Mason was worth it.

"Bring him by the house as soon as you can," Marjorie urged, her voice as warm as it ever got. Eugenie shifted in her seat and began to aggressively scroll through her work emails.

Scarlett hid a smug smile. Mason was the one place Scarlett had Eugenie beat. Mason was a *complement*. That was the word the sisters used to describe those worthy of a Raven. And there was an incredibly high bar for who qualified as a complementary. Only the best would do, and Mason was the best. He not only had the right past—he was the son of Georgia's second-most-prominent lawyer, after Marjorie, of course, and the president of their brother frat—he also had a future. He was at the top of his class, athletic, dead sexy—and all hers. The icing on top: her mother absolutely loved him.

"Thanks for the ride, Mama," Scarlett said, her hand on the door of the car.

"Oh, here," her mother said as if she were remembering something suddenly. She handed a wrapped box over the back seat.

Scarlett felt herself brighten as she took the box—she didn't remember her mother giving Eugenie a back-to-school present on her first day of junior year—and she had to stop herself from ripping the paper as she opened it.

It was a deck of tarot cards, beautifully rendered. A woman with a knowing smile wearing a dress made of feathers practically winked out at her on the back of each card.

"Were these yours?" Scarlett asked, wondering if these were the cards her mother and Eugenie had used when they'd been voted in as president and, if so, touched to be included in the family tradition.

"They're brand-new. I ordered them from a powerful Cups who is very high up in the Senate. She painted them herself," she boasted.

Disappointment tightened Scarlett's chest. As much as Scarlett loved political royalty, how could her mother give her these now? "These are lovely, Mama, but I already have Minnie's cards." Scarlett didn't understand how her mother could know so little about her. She would never replace Minnie's deck with a shiny new set of cards.

"New year, new start," her mother said. "I know Minnie meant the world to you; she meant the world to me, too. But I can see that you're still grieving, and Minnie wouldn't want you carrying that sadness into the new year. You being a Raven—you becoming president—that meant the world to her."

You mean it means the world to you. Scarlett pocketed the cards, bent over the seat, and gave her mother a kiss on the cheek. "Of course, Mama. Thank you," she murmured, though she had no intention of ever using them.

After a dutiful kiss for Eugenie and another for her mother, Scarlett popped the trunk and grabbed her two bags, which she'd spelled earlier to feel light as air. She waved, watching until the car disappeared down the street. When she took a step back onto the sidewalk, she collided with a solid, muscular body. "Hey. Watch it!" she huffed.

An indignant voice sounded behind her. "You're the one who ran into me."

Scarlett turned to see Jackson Carter, who'd been in her philosophy class last year, slightly out of breath and wearing jogging shorts and headphones. Sweat beaded on his dark brown skin, and a soaked shirt stuck to his muscular frame. His lips turned down in a frown. "But I suppose I shouldn't be surprised. You Kappas act like you own this place."

"We *do* own it," Scarlett said without missing a beat. This was their first exchange that had nothing to do with dead philosophers and it seemed like downright bad manners for him to begin the conversation with an insult. "You're standing in front of our house."

Jackson wasn't from Savannah. Not even close. She could tell by his lack of manners and basic lack of deference—not to mention his lack of a drawl. His consonants just sat there stubbornly, unlike hers, which she stretched out for effect. A gentleman would offer to take the suitcases from her. Then again, a gentleman wouldn't have reprimanded her for standing on her own sidewalk in the first place.

Jackson leaned closer to her. "So, do Kappas lose their souls a little bit at a time or does it happen all at once, like ripping off a Band-Aid?"

Scarlett's hackles rose. She knew how he saw her, and she knew why. There were a million movies that depicted sorority girls as vapid, exclusive witches, and she didn't mean the magical kind. And unfortunately, there were way too many real videos and stories that backed up that image. Scarlett cringed thinking about a YouTube video that had recently gone viral about a sorority girl who wrote an open letter to her sisters detailing every single thing she hated about them. But Scarlett was sure that for every one of those awful stories, there were dozens more about sorority girls who were there for good reasons, who were in it for the sisterhood. And Kappa offered more than just sisterhood; the house provided protection, a safe place where the coven could learn and practice their magic. Not that she could explain that to Jackson.

"All at once," Scarlett said. "I'm surprised that you couldn't see that from your position looking down at us poor, morally bereft sorority girls."

"At least we agree on one thing." Jackson crossed his arms, his brown eyes flashing.

"If you have such a problem with us," Scarlett said, picking up steam, "maybe you should be a little more careful where you go running."

"Is that a threat?" He arched a single eyebrow, seeming to consider her anew. "Because from what I hear—"

Suddenly, his gaze went fuzzy and blank, and his eyes fixed on something slightly above her. It was like she'd just vanished from his world. His head snapped to the side, and without another word, he resumed his jog.

Scarlett turned toward Kappa. Coming down the front walk of the house were Dahlia Everly, the Kappa president, and Tiffany Beckett, Scarlett's best friend. They walked arm in arm, Dahlia's blond ponytail a shade darker than Tiffany's platinum one. Dahlia winked, making it clear who had just enchanted the boy.

"Thanks for that." Scarlett dropped her suitcases and shot one last glare at Jackson's retreating form. She had no idea what was wrong with him or why he seemed to hate Kappas so much. A sister had probably rejected him last spring. Some guys could be so fragile and petty.

"What's with the drama? You looked like you were this close to whipping up a category three," Dahlia said.

"Hardly. A boy like that certainly isn't worth getting soaked over."

"Why were you even talking to him in the first place?" Dahlia's nose wrinkled. Dahlia was the consummate imperious sorority president; anyone who wasn't part of the Greek system wasn't worth her time.

"I wasn't. He ran into me—literally."

Tiffany just laughed and held out her arms.

Scarlett sank into her best friend's hug, squeezing her hard—though not hard enough to wrinkle the silk blouse Tiff was wearing. "I missed you."

"Same." Tiffany turned to give her a peck on the cheek. Her dark red lipstick didn't leave a single mark. Ravens' makeup never smudged.

"How's your mom?" Scarlett asked.

A shadow crossed Tiffany's face. Dahlia shifted uncomfortably. "We're trying a new treatment. We'll know more soon."

Scarlett gave Tiffany another hug. Her friend had spent the summer in Charleston with her mom, who was battling cancer. Last year Tiffany had asked Dahlia to do an all-hands healing spell for her mom; every Raven was a witch in her own right, but together, the coven was far stronger than any individual. As president, Dahlia chose what spells the group would take on, a role she unabashedly relished. A Houston debutante, Dahlia loved being in charge, being the one whom all the other sisters looked to. Her confidence made her a great president, but there were times that Scarlett felt Dahlia prioritized her authority or her legacy over the needs of other girls in the house. And according to Dahlia, Kappa's history was riddled with failed healing rituals of this magnitude. "Some things just aren't within our power," Dahlia had said.

Tiffany had never forgiven Dahlia for shutting her down, suspecting that Dahlia was more worried about the optics of such a spell and its possible risks than about Tiffany's mom. Scarlett, who'd seen the fear in her usually fearless bestie's blue eyes, wasn't satisfied with Dahlia's ruling either and had asked Minnie about it. What Scarlett didn't know at the time was that Minnie was close to death herself.

"If there were a cure for dying, we wouldn't be witches—we'd be immortal . . . The only spells that touch death touch back in equal measure," Minnie had warned with a sad smile.

Now Tiffany pulled back from the hug with a bright smile Scarlett knew was fake. She blinked fast, clearly willing away the tears Scarlett sensed were always just beneath the surface, even though Tiffany was a Swords, not a Cups.

"How are preparations for rush going?" Scarlett pivoted, letting Tiffany off the emotional hook and looking up at the house.

"Hazel and Jess are glamouring the house right now," Tiffany said, clearly grateful to have all eyes off her.

Scarlett nodded. Tradition dictated that the sophomore sisters decorated the house for recruitment. This year was speakeasy-themed; she couldn't wait to see what her sisters had come up with.

"Did you bring the sparklers?" Dahlia asked.

"They're right here," Scarlett said, tapping one of her suitcases. "I enchanted them last night."

Minnie always said that the magic did the real choosing, and she was right—mostly. All girls grew up with magic in them whether they knew it or not. The strength of the magic was what mattered. While magic was only a whisper in some, barely present, others could summon winds with the force of a tornado. The sparklers the Kappas gave out at their recruitment party showed who had the baseline of power required to be a Raven. But it wasn't *just* about ability. The Ravens had to be exemplary. It was about personality, pedigree, intelligence, and sophistication. And above all, it was about being a good sister.

"I can't wait to meet our latest round of potentials," Tiffany said, tapping her fingers together with a smile.

"Only the best will do, of course," Scarlett said. Finding powerful witches among Westerly's froshlings was like searching for diamonds in a sea of cubic zirconias. She didn't want an unruly sophomore crop when she became president.

"Of course," Dahlia echoed, a frown marring her perfect features. "We have to protect Kappa. The last thing we want is another Harper situation."

Scarlett's stomach twisted and she carefully avoided Tiffany's eyes. *Another Harper situation.* Something dark and unspoken passed between Scarlett and Tiffany. Something Scarlett never let herself think about.

Something that could ruin everything she'd worked so hard to get.

CHAPTER THREE

Vivi

Vivi adjusted the strap of her backpack, wincing slightly as the edge of a hardcover book dug into her spine. Once she'd walked through the wrought-iron gate, Vivi let go of her larger suitcase and flexed her cramping fingers. The bus station was less than a mile from Westerly College, but lugging her bulging bags from there had taken nearly an hour and left her palms smarting. Yet, as Vivi took a deep breath of surprisingly fragrant air, a tingle of excitement chased away the fatigue. She'd made it. After eighteen exhausting hours—hell, after eighteen exhausting *years*—she was finally on her own, free to make her own choices and start her real life.

She paused to glance at the map on her phone, then up at the grass-filled quad ahead. On the far side was an ivy-covered stone building with a WELCOME, NEW STUDENTS banner hanging from the second-floor bay windows. *Almost there,* she told herself as she trudged forward, ignoring the pain in her shoulders. But as her eyes fell on the crowd of students and parents, Vivi's stomach twisted slightly. She was hardly a stranger to new situations. Having attended four elementary schools, two middle schools, and three high schools, Vivi had been the new girl for most of her life.

But now everything was different. Vivi was going to be at Westerly for four whole years, longer than she'd ever stayed anywhere before. She wouldn't automatically be the strange new girl. She could be anyone she wanted.

She just needed to figure out exactly who that was.

Vivi dragged her bags up to the folding table where volunteers were handing out orientation packets. "Welcome!" a white girl with long, straight red hair chirped as Vivi approached. "What's your last name?"

"Devereaux," Vivi said, taking in the girl's crisp pink blouse and expertly applied eyeliner. Normally, this kind of elegance struck Vivi as a rare gift, something to be admired but not necessarily envied, like the ability to touch your nose with your tongue or walk on your hands. But a glance around the quad quickly established this level of grooming as the norm. Vivi had never seen so many manicured hands or pastel shirts in her entire life, and for the first time, she began to wonder if perhaps her mother was right about this place. Maybe this wasn't the right school for Vivi after all.

"Devereaux," the red-haired girl repeated, flipping through the thick packet in front of her. "You're in Simmons Hall, room three-oh-five. Simmons is this building right here. Here's your orientation folder . . . and your ID card. It's also your key, so don't lose it."

"Thanks." Vivi reached out to take the folder. But the girl didn't let go. She was frozen in place, staring over Vivi's shoulder.

When Vivi glanced around, she realized everyone was looking in the same direction. The air in the courtyard shifted subtly, like the prickle of electricity before a storm.

Vivi turned and followed everyone's gaze. Three girls were crossing the velvety green lawn at the heart of the quad. Even from a distance, it was clear that they weren't newly arrived freshmen. It was partly their clothes; the black girl in the middle wore a mint-green sundress with a flared skirt that swirled around her long, ballerina-esque legs, and her friends—both of them white and blond—wore nearly matching tweed skirts and the type of cream-colored silk tops that, until now, Vivi had seen only on rich women in movies. But even if they'd been in ratty sweatpants, the girls would've caught her eye. They moved with languorous assurance, as if confident in their right to go wherever they wanted at whatever speed they chose. As though they weren't afraid of taking up space in the world. For someone like Vivi, who'd spent most of her life trying to blend in, there was something intoxicating about seeing girls so clearly at ease with standing out.

She watched the trio approach a red-brick building with a crowd of students waiting to get in. The moment the girls reached the building, the crowd parted; every person stood aside without protest to let the girls in.

"Those are Kappas," the redhead said, reading the question in Vivi's interested gaze. "One of the sororities on campus. Everyone calls them the Ravens. I don't know why. Maybe because they're so mysterious and secretive."

"Sorry," Vivi said, blushing, embarrassed to be caught staring.

"It's okay. They have that effect on everyone. If you want to see them in action, go to their recruitment party tonight. They'll be in rare form, scouting for potential new members." She shrugged, trying to seem nonchalant even though her eyes shone with obvious desire. "You should check it out, if only to see their sorority house. It's the only time all year they let non-Kappas inside, and that place is pretty spectacular."

"Yeah, maybe," Vivi said, secretly thrilled that someone thought she was the type of girl who could "check out" a party. No one at any of her three high schools had ever invited her to a party. She wasn't sure the Kappas' rush event was the right way to get her feet wet, but who knew? Maybe college-Vivi would be up to the challenge.

"All right, then. Welcome to Westerly!"

Vivi took a deep breath, calling on her last reserve of strength to haul her suitcases up three stone steps and through the wooden door that had been propped open. She started up the narrow stairs, dragging her suitcases awkwardly behind her. She hoped to make it to the second floor before taking a break, but after a few steps, her arms gave out.

"Shit," she said under her breath as her bags slid back down the stairs and landed with two heavy thuds.

"Need a hand?"

Vivi turned to see a white boy with dark curly hair standing at the base of the stairs, looking up at her with an amused grin.

She wanted to tell him she had it under control, but then she realized how ridiculous that would sound, given that he was currently looking at the suitcases she had just dropped. "Thanks, if you don't mind."

"I don't mind. And even if I did, I'd do it anyway." He had a faint Southern accent that elongated his syllables. He lifted both suitcases at the same time and bounded up the stairs, brushing past Vivi.

"I guess the Southern-manners thing is real," Vivi said, then cringed, immediately regretting her cheesy, awkward words.

"Oh, this isn't about manners," the boy replied, slightly breathless. "It's a public-safety issue. You could've killed someone back there."

Vivi felt her cheeks turn red. "Here, let me take one of those," she said as she ran to catch up.

They reached the second floor, but the boy didn't set the suitcases down. "No can do," he said cheerfully. "My love of chivalry and public safety makes it physically impossible for me to set these bags down until they're out of the danger zone. What's your room number?"

"Three-oh-five. But you really don't have to do this. I'll be fine the rest of the way."

"Don't give it a second thought," the boy called back. Vivi followed him as her stomach fluttered with a mixture of guilt and excitement. No boy had ever carried her stuff for her before.

When they reached the third floor, the boy turned right and, with a groan, set her suitcases down in front of a door. "Here you go. Room three-oh-five."

"Thank you," Vivi said, feeling even more awkward. Was she supposed to ask him his name? His major? How did normal people make friends?

"My pleasure." He grinned, and for a moment, Vivi couldn't focus on anything except the dimple that had just appeared in his left cheek. But before she could think of anything else to say, he turned and started back down the hall. "Try not to kill anyone!" he said over his shoulder, and then disappeared down the stairs.

"I make no guarantees." She tried to sound playful and sexy, but there was no point. He was already gone.

Vivi opened the door to the room, steeling herself to meet her roommate, but the room was empty. Just two extra-long twin beds, two nicked-up wooden desks, and a full-length mirror on the back of a closet. As far as dorm rooms went, it was nice—spacious, light, and airy. The exact opposite of the cramped, stifling apartment in Reno.

She dragged one of her suitcases to a bed and unzipped it, wondering when her roommate would arrive and what the protocol was for claiming a side of the room. Before she had the chance to take anything out of her bag, a window blew open and a gust of warm, fragrant air filled the space, sending the papers in her orientation folder flying. The window had been latched closed when she walked into the room.

Vivi gathered up the papers with a sigh, reminding herself that a significant temperature difference between the air in the room and the air outside could create enough pressure to push the window open. That phenomenon was just one of many Vivi had memorized over the years to explain the strange things that always seemed to happen around her.

That was when she noticed the single tarot card positioned neatly at the head of her bare mattress, as if placed there by a careful hand.

It was the Death card her mother had given her.

The skeleton leered up at her with a gruesome smile, and for a moment, it almost looked like its eyes glowed red. Vivi shivered, despite knowing that it was a trick of the light. *I told you. Westerly isn't a safe place, not for people like you,* Daphne's voice whispered in Vivi's ear.

A door slammed down the hall and the sound of laughter from the quad floated up through the window. Vivi shook her head, coming back to herself. Here she was, free of her mother for one day, and she was already looking for signs from the universe. Daphne would have almost been proud.

With a dismissive snort, she shoved the Death card into her desk drawer and shut it tight. Vivi didn't need signs. She didn't need magic. She didn't need her mother's voice in her ear. She just needed to make a normal life here.

Starting with that rush party.

CHAPTER FOUR

Scarlett

Kappa House had transformed. The modern metallic gray wallpaper had faded into the pale pink that had once graced the walls, and the low-slung velvet couch had become a gilded chaise. The room was almost unrecognizable. Only the music blaring from a Bluetooth speaker revealed that they were still in the twenty-first century. The recruitment party was in two hours, and every sister was hard at work—the sophomores were in charge of décor, the juniors were dealing with food and drinks, and the seniors were scurrying around making sure any trace of magic was safely out of sight.

After they finished giving instructions to the catering team, Scarlett and Tiffany went upstairs to change into their dresses. Tiffany's room was two doors past Scarlett's and she peeked inside as she passed.

"Oh my God, I can't believe you still have this," Tiffany said, coming in and grabbing a decrepit three-legged elephant from Scarlett's dresser.

Scarlett laughed. "I should probably put that away before the rush party."

"First impressions are everything," Tiffany agreed.

The first time Scarlett met Tiffany, it was at their own recruitment soiree two years ago. Even though she'd been born and bred for Kappa, Scarlett had been fearful all the same—afraid she'd be found lacking, afraid she'd disappoint her family. But then Tiffany stood next to her and gestured at Dahlia's perfect slope of a nose and whispered, "I'd bet you my whole trust fund that nose is a glamour." Scarlett didn't laugh, but she'd wanted to. Suddenly their membership chairwoman didn't seem so imposing and Scarlett's nerves melted away. It turned out Tiffany didn't have a trust fund, far from it, but she was rich in magic, spontaneity, and irreverence. Scarlett hadn't known just how much she'd needed those last two until she met Tiffany.

That year, the theme had been a black-and-white ball, and they'd danced the night away in their floor-length gowns, barely caring that, come dawn, the white hems were smudged with dirt. Later that morning, Scarlett had taken Tiffany to her favorite antiques store downtown, the one that the tourists and other witches hadn't discovered yet. They walked through rows and rows of dusty furniture and lamps, tiny figurines, and old coffee-table books, and Tiffany stopped at the kids' aisle with the excitement of a preschooler. "Stuffed animals and dolls are the best—so much pure energy. So much pure love," she gushed.

Scarlett picked up an elephant whose leg was missing. "So much pure *something,*" she said with a laugh, and Tiffany joined in. But Scarlett knew what she meant.

"Thanks for sharing your spot with me," Tiffany said softly, pulling a well-loved Elmo to her chest for a hug.

They'd gone home with dozens of objects perfect for spells—and they had been inseparable ever since. Tiffany was the kind of sister Scarlett had always wished she had. They balanced each other well. Scarlett was bound to the norms of magic, while Tiffany liked having fun with her gift. The Kappa motto translated to "Sisterhood. Leadership. Fidelity. Philanthropy," which Scarlett always took to mean that they were supposed to rule and save the world. But Tiffany didn't think of witches as superheroes only. "What's the fun of being a witch if you can't use magic to make the Starbucks line move faster?" she always said. Scarlett saw her point; what good was helping the world if you couldn't help yourself, too?

Tiffany's blue eyes glittered whenever she had one of her brilliant ideas or used the lightest touches of magic to even the scales of small, daily injustices, like magically spilling the drink of a frat boy who stared a little too long and hard at a sister or giving a truth serum to a sexist professor who gave only boys As. She was smart and funny and just the right amount of mischievous. Tiffany was the one person who got Scarlett out of her own head and reminded her of the joy, not just the duty, of being a witch. And usually when they were together, Scarlett felt at once at ease and excited for whatever they would do next.

The tarot might have explained their connection—Cups and Swords were always fast friends—but Scarlett liked to think that she and Tiffany would have been connected with or without magic. Right that moment, though, she felt suddenly apart from her.

Scarlett took a deep breath, remembering what Dahlia had said earlier. "Tiff, do you ever think about Harper?"

Tiffany stiffened. "We agreed to never talk about that."

"I know, but what if it ever got out—"

"How could it ever get out? We're the only people who know," Tiffany said.

That wasn't entirely true, though. Gwen, another girl from their pledge class, also knew the truth about what really happened. But Gwen was long gone, and they'd made sure she could never, ever tell.

"Everything is fine, Scarlett. Trust me, we're golden," Tiffany said firmly, shoving the elephant into Scarlett's closet and smoothing down her dress.

"Knock-knock," a deep voice said.

Scarlett whirled around. "Oh my God, Mason! I thought you weren't back until tomorrow."

"I got home early," he said with a smile.

If he hadn't been her boyfriend, he would have been irritatingly good-looking. His mouth quirked up on one side, as if he were always on the brink of laughter. His skin was a deep, golden tan. His hair was longer than it usually was, twisting in curls at his temples, and his T-shirt couldn't hide his well-defined muscles.

Tiffany cleared her throat. "I will leave you two to it . . . See you downstairs, Scar," she said, waggling her brows.

As soon as Tiffany left, Mason closed the distance between them, wrapped his arms around her, and pulled her into a deep, long kiss. The moment their lips met, her eyes fluttered shut, and she sank into him. Even after two months, he still tasted the same, like warm summer days.

Scarlett's mother had said once that there was no such thing as love at first sight, but there was such a thing as love at first joke. Her father had swept her mother off her feet with his dry sense of humor, and even now, thirty years into the marriage, Marjorie Winter could look at her husband and remember in an instant why she loved him—even if she hated him at the moment.

For his part, Mason Gregory had hit Scarlett double: it had been love at first sight *and* first joke.

They had met at a Kappa/Pi Kappa Rho mixer, the Pikiki, where every Kappa girl wore a hula skirt over her bikini, and PiKas wore just the hula skirts. PiKas lei'ed any Kappa they fancied as they circulated through PiKa House, which was decorated like an island, complete with live palm trees and an inflatable water slide that extended from the roof to the pool. With a silly but charming joke about not getting laid that easily, Mason had refused to give Scarlett his lei; instead, he gave her a single plumeria from it. She'd lightly demanded the rest, but he told her about an island tradition. "A girl places a flower behind her right ear if she's available and interested, behind her left if there's no chance in hell." She laughed and put the flower behind her right ear. They had been together ever since.

Scarlett had her own theory about love; to her, there was something more than humor, something more than looks. There was a rhythm to love, like there was a rhythm to a spell. And Mason and Scarlett had had that from the first second they met. There was nothing Scarlett felt more sure of in life than her place by Mason's side. Or, rather, his place by hers.

He broke the kiss and stepped back to sweep his eyes over her, lingering where the buttons met the white lace of her bra and where her skirt grazed her thighs. "You look incredible, as always. How do you do it? Seriously, I've never seen you have so much as a bad hair day."

"Magic, of course." She winked.

He didn't know she wasn't joking. Ravens were sworn to secrecy. Only members and alumnae like Scarlett's mother and sister knew they were really a sorority full of witches. Mason had a fondness for history, and in another life he would have relished the rich witch lore that surrounded her people. His room at the frat was filled with biographies, most of which weren't listed on any syllabus. He would have loved knowing how magic had shaped the world and who in history had been a witch, subtly guiding civilization forward. But the rules were clear; he could never, ever know. There were times when the secret sat between them like a steel wedge, but as much as Scarlett loved Mason, as much as she wished he could know all of her, she would never betray her sisters.

"You don't look half bad yourself. You're so tan. Let me guess, you got stuck on Jotham's yacht again?" she said. Jotham was a fellow PiKa and Mason's best friend. And he was the reason that Mason had gotten stuck across the pond. Jotham had taken Mason along to his brother's wedding and the rest was summer-vacation history. She reminded herself to cast a spell on Jotham later as punishment.

Mason shook his head. "No, I skipped the yacht. It turns out Portugal has a killer surf scene."

"I didn't realize you were an aspiring beach bum." Scarlett kept her voice light, but she was irked. She hadn't known Mason was interested in surfing. Why hadn't he texted her about it? The past few weeks had been so chaotic that they'd barely had a chance to talk. But Scarlett being swamped at her internship was different from him being busy *surfing.*

Mason grinned. "Jotham took the yacht on to Ibiza with some girl he met at the wedding. I didn't want to third-wheel it. I don't know what came over me, but I hopped on the Eurail. I even stayed in a hostel a few nights."

Her eyebrows shot skyward. "You stayed in a *hostel?* Over a *yacht?*" Jotham's family's yacht was practically a cruise ship.

"It really wasn't that bad."

"Are you sure you didn't bring home bedbugs?" She eyed him suspiciously, which made him burst into laughter.

"I wish you'd been there. You would have liked it."

Scarlett wrinkled her nose. "A hostel? Yeah, I don't think so."

"Honestly, Scar, it felt like being in one of those subtitled movies that you like," Mason said.

"You hate those movies," she protested lightly. He always said that if he wanted to read, he'd pick up a book.

His voice turned serious. "It was different from all those family vacations or friend vacations we have to go on. There were no walking tours, no galas, no yachts, no expectations . . . none of it. I made my own map. I set my own schedule. I decided who I wanted to see, where I wanted to go. I felt . . . free." He was speaking faster, like he always did when he got excited about something.

Only usually he was really excited about Kant, or *The Iliad,* or the Dow. If she hadn't known better, she would have thought he was spelled.

"You almost sound like you wish you'd stayed out there," she blurted.

Mason's expression was thoughtful. "A part of me wishes I could have. But only if you were with me, of course," he added hurriedly. "Everything here just feels so . . . predetermined. Do you know what I mean?"

Scarlett raised an eyebrow. "No. What are you talking about?"

Mason groaned. "All the internships and clerkships and extra degrees. My dad takes for granted that I want to follow in his footsteps and be a lawyer."

"I thought you wanted those things." *I thought* we *wanted those things.* Part of what she loved about Mason was his ambition. It almost rivaled hers. They'd had it all planned out since their one-month anniversary: they'd go to the same law school, preferably Harvard, then come back for their internships at their parents' firms, and when they had enough experience, they'd break away and start their own firm.

"I know . . . I thought I did too. But maybe . . ." He paused and sighed, as if searching for the right words. "I don't know. There are, like, a million other careers and startups out there that only require you to have a computer and Wi-Fi connection. Have you ever thought of just saying 'fuck it' to our parents and Westerly and leaving this all behind?"

Scarlett narrowed her eyes. A startup? Was he Mark Zuckerberg now? "Everything I've ever wanted is right here. Kappa. You. Our families. Bumming around the world is for people who don't know where they're going in life. That's not us."

Mason shrugged and fiddled with a frayed rope bracelet around his wrist that Scarlett had never seen before.

"Mason, is everything okay?" She was quiet as she stared at him. Sometimes being quiet was more powerful than talking. Some people couldn't bear silence, and Mason was one of them. He had to fill it like a candle had to fill the dark.

Finally, he looked up and smiled at her. "Of course I'm okay. I'm with you." He leaned over and gave her another light kiss, then shook his head slightly. "I'm sorry I'm being weird. I'm just jet-lagged and my head is still back in the waves." He slipped his fingers through hers and pulled her close.

She felt the rush of comfort that his touch always gave her. She closed her eyes for a second and tried to believe what he said about jet lag. She had felt pretty drained after some of the long days at her mom's firm. She knew better than anyone about parental expectation. He just needed to get acclimated to Westerly again. And after they spent some time together, he would be back to himself. He had to be.

"I did miss you, Scar," he said. "Can you get out of here so we can make up for lost time?"

For a moment, all Scarlett wanted was to follow him out the door to PiKa House. But then she remembered the timing and cursed under her breath. "Mason, I can't. Rush is tonight," she reminded him.

"I know, but it looks like everything is under control." He ran a finger down her arm. "So you leave for an hour, what's the big deal?"

She put a palm on his chest. "It *is* a big deal. I can't just abandon my sisters right before rush. How would that look?"

He frowned. "Who cares how it looks? We haven't seen each other in months—"

"And whose choice was that?" Scarlett said.

"You could have come, you know," Mason pointed out. "It would have been so fun. Two months together, no plans, no one to be accountable to except each other . . ."

"Well, unlike you, I didn't want to disappoint my family," Scarlett said, suddenly feeling exasperated. "I'm just not the kind of person who can pack up and leave my life for two months at a moment's notice." *And I thought you were the same way,* she felt like adding.

A line appeared between Mason's eyebrows and once again Scarlett couldn't help but worry that something was wrong. This wasn't exactly the homecoming she'd pictured. A few seconds ago she had felt close to him again and then, just as suddenly, she felt space opening up between them. First Tiffany and now Mason. This was supposed to be *her* year. Why didn't it feel like that? What was going on with him?

From the moment she'd met Mason, Scarlett knew that he was going to be hers—that she would do whatever it took to make him hers. But she had been sparing in using her gifts with him. She had done what any Raven would do: she made her skin more luminous, her hair shinier, her teeth whiter, her laugh more musical. But she hadn't reached out once. Not into his head or his heart. It was a rule, of course, not to *change* the heart under any circumstances, but there was no rule against looking.

Tiffany always looked; it was somewhere between science and poetry for her. "How lucky are we to glimpse the human heart?" she once said. Scarlett had shaken her head then, but now, for the first time, she felt tempted. What harm would it do, just this once, to understand what Mason was thinking and feeling?

Scarlett reached up and ran a hand through his hair. As she summoned her magic, she felt a familiar flutter—this time, though, it wasn't of love or excitement but of fear. Fear of what she would see. What if she looked and found less love than there should be?

No, Scarlett couldn't risk it. And she couldn't invade Mason's privacy that way. That wasn't who she was. But she could remind him just how good they were together. She moved her hand lower, ran it down his neck, then his back, then along his thigh. "I don't have an hour, but I do have five minutes," she murmured.

Mason's eyes widened. "Here?" They never hooked up at Kappa; partners weren't allowed in the house at night.

She flashed a single lingering backwards glance at him as she crossed her room and pulled the door shut.

"Scar—" Mason started.

But she was way ahead of him. She reached up, wrapped her arms around his neck, and pulled his face toward hers. Any hesitation she'd sensed in him earlier melted at her touch, and his kiss turned hot, hard. He pinned her against the wall, one arm around her waist and the other buried in her hair.

She smiled against his mouth, her hands snaking down his muscular chest. Now *this* was the Mason she knew. This was the way things were between them. Soon he'd forget about leaving everything behind and traveling the world. He'd remember that they were exactly where they were meant to be. That they belonged here together.

"Time's up," she said after a few minutes, breaking away. His breath was ragged as she led him to the door.

"Scar, you're killing me," he said with a groan.

"Meet me tomorrow morning after our selection ceremony. We can finish what we started." She hid a smile as he gave her one last kiss and then reluctantly turned to go down the stairs.

See? No magic required. He was already under her spell.

CHAPTER FIVE

Vivi

It took Vivi only fifteen seconds to realize that coming to the party had been a terrible mistake.

When she first stepped through the doors of Kappa, she'd been momentarily dazzled by the splendor of her surroundings. The rush party was speakeasy-themed, which was a natural fit for the house's pale pink wallpaper and velvet-cushioned mahogany chairs. Everyone wore tuxes or flapper dresses; even the wait-staff, serving drinks in delicate porcelain teacups, were in 1920s outfits.

Everyone fit the theme—except Vivi. She wore a navy dress with sunflowers on it, the only dress she'd brought with her. Her empty social calendar back in Reno hadn't exactly called for formalwear. She tugged at the hem, which she realized now had a stain on it, and eyed the laughing, dancing partygoers with a combination of awe and envy. Orientation week had begun just twelve hours ago. How had so many people made friends already? And how had every girl known to pack a flapper outfit? Across the crowded foyer, she spotted two girls she recognized from her dorm, but they were smiling and whispering confidentially, and years of being the new kid had taught Vivi what happened when you tried to sidle up to people midconversation.

Things at Westerly hadn't exactly been going according to plan so far. Her roommate, Zoe, had finally arrived and promptly put a duct-tape line down the center of their room to delineate her space from Vivi's. She'd also brought nearly a dozen candles, each of which had its own strong scent and none of which complemented the others, meaning that their room smelled like a mix of patchouli and sickly sweet vanilla. And when Vivi had finally mustered the courage to ask Zoe if she wanted to check out the dining hall with her, Zoe had barely looked up from her phone before mumbling, "Sorry, I have plans."

The longer Vivi stood in the foyer of the bustling Kappa House, the warmer her cheeks grew. She'd spent so much time fantasizing about college, convinced that it'd be her chance for a brand-new start, and it turned out she was just as much of an outsider as ever. Maybe her chronic loneliness had nothing to do with always being the new girl. Maybe she was just too awkward, too weird to make friends.

She turned, about to retreat out the door, but someone barred her path. Vivi's stomach flipped over like it used to during their stint living in LA when she'd spot a celebrity at the upscale mall in Calabasas. It was the girl with the mint-green dress she'd seen crossing the quad with two other Ravens.

She'd changed into a stunning white beaded dress, and her dark brown eyes seemed to glow with amusement beneath her long lashes, like she knew something that no one else did and enjoyed keeping the secret. "Hello," the girl said, raising her eyebrows slightly as she gave Vivi's outfit the once-over.

"Hi," Vivi managed. It was the first word she'd said since her exchange with Zoe hours earlier.

The girl held something out—a sparkler, Vivi realized. "Thank you so much for coming tonight," she said. "And I hope you don't feel uncomfortable in your cute little outfit. Don't worry about ignoring the theme. After all, not everyone can pull off a 1920s silhouette."

Vivi's cheeks flushed. "I didn't think to pack for a cocktail party," she said, reaching out for the sparkler.

The girl's fake smile grew even stiffer. "A potential Kappa should be prepared for anything."

"Oh, no, I'm not a—I mean, I wasn't planning to rush." It was a lie, of course. She would have loved to rush. But after having been here for all of five minutes, Vivi realized how delusional this whole endeavor was. The best she could hope for was to make sure this girl knew that Vivi recognized she was out of her league here.

"I see," the Kappa said, pursing her lips.

"No offense to you all, of course. Kappa seems great. I'm just not . . ." *Good enough,* Vivi thought, cringing as she trailed off awkwardly.

"Usually when people say 'no offense,' they've just said something offensive." The girl's smile returned but her eyes hardened. "A word of advice? If you don't plan to pledge Kappa, don't waste anybody's time. But if you *are* considering it, I wouldn't leave this party just yet." She spun on her heel, the white fringe of her dress swishing a wordless goodbye as she moved toward the back patio. Vivi stared after her, wondering how the girl knew Vivi had been about to bail and why she cared. Regardless, she decided to stay another few minutes, just to save face, and she trailed after the Kappa through the crowded front hall and out into the garden.

It was like stepping into a fairy realm. The yard was enclosed by a tall wrought-iron fence covered in ivy, and strings of tea lights swayed in the moss of the live oaks, suspended on wires Vivi couldn't quite see. Hurricane candles stood on the small round tables scattered across the grass, casting a flattering glow on the faces of the unusually attractive guests. A line had formed at the bar, where a bartender was serving some kind of punch from a crystal bowl.

Her eyes fell on two impossibly beautiful girls dancing, laughing as they moved with the music.

"Kind of intimidating, aren't they?" Vivi turned to see another striking girl next to her. With her wavy black hair, flawless brown skin, and enormous doe-like eyes, she was just as pretty as the Kappa who'd snubbed Vivi earlier, but the genuine smile on her face made her infinitely more approachable.

"Yeah, kind of," Vivi said, surprised and relieved that even a girl who looked like Kappa material was nervous. "How did everyone know to pack for this?" she asked, looking around the garden.

"Rush is a big deal here. Serious pledges come prepared for anything. Some people even hire consultants to help them get through rush. My mom went to Westerly, so I kind of knew what to expect," she said, gesturing to her own fringed dress.

"Do you want to pledge?" Vivi asked.

"Yes, if I get a bid," she said wistfully, sounding like someone who was longing for the last slice of cake but was too polite to take it. "I'm not going to get my hopes up, though. Kappa's the most selective sorority on campus, and the smallest."

Even for a Greek novice like Vivi, it was clear that the sorority occupied a special place at Westerly. She hadn't officially met any of the Kappas—the girl in the white dress hadn't introduced herself—but they were easy to spot in the crowd. Unlike the would-be pledges, whose nervous shifting belied their wide smiles, the Kappas moved with grace and assurance. Vivi watched with unabashed awe as an Asian girl in a red beaded flapper dress stopped to take a dainty sip of her drink. Her shiny black hair was cut in a smooth chin-length bob, and her deep crimson lips looked like they belonged to a classic Hollywood starlet. She was easily the most glamorous person Vivi had ever seen in real life, but it was her composure that captivated Vivi. She observed the party with detached amusement, in no apparent hurry to find someone to talk to. As the perennial new girl, Vivi was accustomed to standing on her own, but it never got easier. She was always aware that people were watching her, wondering why she was all alone.

"I'm Vivi," Vivi said, returning her attention to her new acquaintance. She extended the hand that wasn't holding her sparkler.

"Ariana," the girl said as she gave Vivi one of the two teacups she'd just accepted from a passing waiter. "Apparently Kappa is the only sorority that can get away with serving alcohol at recruitment events, so I'd take full advantage."

Vivi took a casual sip, praying that she wouldn't do anything to reveal that this was her very first drink. It was difficult to be a rebellious, hard-partying high-schooler when you had no friends and were never invited to parties. She braced for a burning sensation, but the pink cocktail was delightfully sweet. "Why does Kappa get to break the rules?"

Ariana shrugged. "I heard they get all sorts of special treatment."

"Hi." Vivi turned to see a black girl in a sophisticated, slinky blue dress smiling at them. "I'm Jess. Are you girls having fun?"

Vivi froze, unsure how to respond after her last encounter with a Kappa. Was she supposed to gush that this was the best party she'd ever been to? Or was it better to play it cool and act unimpressed?

"Absolutely," said Ariana, who thankfully was able to talk to strangers without having a complete meltdown. "Y'all really went all out for this. Are the waiters wearing vintage suits?"

Jess nodded. "There's a certain pleasure in forcing slovenly college boys to dress up," she said, surveying the crowd. "Though I require only three things in a man: he must be handsome, ruthless, and stupid."

"Pardon me?" Ariana said while Vivi laughed.

"Dorothy Parker, right?" Vivi asked.

"Sorry, it's impossible not to quote Parker when you're drinking cocktails out of teacups." She gave Vivi a wink and excused herself.

"That was a little strange," Ariana whispered after Jess walked away.

"But kind of great," Vivi said with a smile. In seventh grade, she'd stumbled across a collection of Dorothy Parker's poems and essays in the library, and for Vivi, it'd been almost like making a friend. She'd never heard anyone her own age mention Parker, and she certainly hadn't expected her to come up at a sorority party, but the exchange turned out to be the first of many surprising conversations with Kappas throughout the evening. A white biochemistry major named Juliet told Vivi all about her research on love hormones, and then Vivi found herself in a fascinating discussion about Chinese politics with a history major named Etta and some of her classmates. It was a subject she knew little about, so she mostly listened, but she never felt awkward or out of place. Despite the fact that none of the older students knew her, they seemed perfectly happy to let Vivi join their conversation. By the time she found Ariana again, Vivi felt nearly giddy. An unfamiliar combination of relief and happiness filled her with warmth. Her first college party was a success.

Ariana was talking to the girl in the red beaded dress she'd spotted earlier. As Vivi approached, the girl smiled warmly, revealing teeth as white as the pearls strung around her neck. She took a long sip of her drink, and when she lowered her cup, her lipstick was still perfect. There wasn't even a trace of crimson on the white cup.

"I'm Mei," she said, extending her hand. "It's nice to—" Her voice was drowned out as jazz suddenly swept through the garden. Vivi turned to see five smartly dressed musicians in black suits playing a familiar-sounding song. "Ooh, the Charleston!" Mei shouted. Without letting go of her teacup, she began to swivel on the balls of her feet while moving her arms in perfect rhythm. "Come on!" She grinned and grabbed Vivi's hand.

"No, I can't," Vivi said, stepping back. She'd never danced in public before. She couldn't actually remember dancing in private, either. She was so bad, she embarrassed herself even when she was alone.

Mei mercifully dropped her hand, and less than a second later, she was swept up by a member of the band in a black suit. Vivi watched in awe as they danced in such perfect unison that she wondered if they'd choreographed the whole thing. "I wish I could do that," Vivi whispered to Ariana, who was also staring, mesmerized.

"Your turn," Mei called cheerfully. She pulled away from the boy and gestured toward Vivi.

"No, I'm serious. I can't." Vivi stepped back as her heart pounded a frantic alarm. But the boy, still under Mei's spell, would not be put off. Vivi just had time to give Ariana her teacup and sparkler before the boy took her hand and began to push and pull her in time to the music. For a moment, all she could do was stare in horror and sway awkwardly. She didn't know what to do with her feet or her free hand. Her face started to burn. How many people were staring at her right now?

But just when she thought the panic would overwhelm her, her feet began to move seemingly of their own accord. Her hips swayed from side to side as she shifted her weight from one foot to the other. The boy grinned at her, and without thinking, she grinned back. No matter which way he moved, she followed seamlessly, as if connected to him by a string.

"I knew you could do it," Mei said with a mixture of amusement and satisfaction. Vivi was having so much fun, she barely stopped to wonder how she could hear Mei's low murmur over the music. Or why it sounded like the girl's voice was inside her head. Because when Vivi glanced over her shoulder, Mei was gone.

The song ended and a slower one began. The boy cocked his head to the side with a smile, wordlessly inviting Vivi to join him for another, but she didn't want to push her luck. "I should find my friend," she said. "But thank you. That was . . ." She blushed and cut herself off. "Thank you."

"That was amazing," Ariana squealed as Vivi approached. "I wish they'd taught the Charleston at *my* ballroom-dancing school." She looked around the garden, sighed, and handed back Vivi's drink and sparkler. "It's hard not to be a little hopeful about getting a bid, isn't it?"

Vivi nodded, feeling the same way. She'd never imagined herself as part of a sorority, but then again, she'd never known that there were sororities like Kappa. These girls were smart, curious, and passionate—just like the people Vivi had always dreamed of befriending in college. But wasn't it arrogant to assume that they'd be interested in *her?* Just because she'd managed to go a few hours without mortifying herself didn't mean she belonged in the most glamorous, exclusive sorority at Westerly.

A murmur went through the crowd and a moment later, a current of electricity buzzed through Vivi's fingertips. The sparkler crackled to life in her hands, sending bluish-gray sparks streaming into the air.

Vivi gasped. Ariana looked at her in astonishment as her own sparkler erupted to life, red sparks raining down at her feet. All over the garden, sparklers lit up one by one.

But not all of them caught fire.

"I think I got a dud," a girl to Vivi's left complained, shaking the sparkler and then trying to light it with a nearby candle. Another girl in a silver gown hit her sparkler against her palm as if willing it to catch fire.

"But we didn't even light them," Ariana whispered to Vivi, waving her sparkler in a figure eight.

"Must be a party trick or something," Vivi said, even though that didn't explain the electricity still buzzing in her fingertips.

"God, I hope I get a bid," Ariana said longingly.

Vivi felt a prickle on the back of her neck and glanced over her shoulder. The beautiful girl who'd handed Vivi her sparkler was staring at her. There was a strange, almost challenging look on her face. But instead of looking away, Vivi met the girl's gaze. "Me too," she finally said, and she realized that she meant it.

CHAPTER SIX

Scarlett

Scarlett stood on the roof of Kappa House, gazing out over the quiet campus. The recruitment party had ended hours ago and the rest of the girls were sleeping. The night was dark and starless, the only light coming from the antique gas lamps flickering along the path to the house. Somewhere overhead, ravens circled, and an owl hooted in the distance. A light breeze rustled the trees of the forest that edged up against their backyard.

Scarlett didn't know why she was up here. She didn't even remember coming to the roof. A cooing sound came from the aviary behind her. When she turned, she could see all the birds lined up, rustling in their sleep. The ravens were their familiars and they were once kept in the girls' rooms to watch over the sisters. But as time went on, it was thought to be cruel to keep them in the confines of the sorority. They could serve their purpose and still be free to roam. Now they resided here and were able to come and go as they liked. But they always returned.

One raven's eyes popped open and looked at her. Yellow eyes glowed in the dark. Scarlett was sure it was her favorite, Harlow.

Suddenly, she heard shuffling behind her. "Hello?" she called. "Is someone there?"

All that met her was silence.

She spun once more and noticed a pentacle etched into the roof at her feet, the circle rimmed with coarse salt. A long white tapered candle dotted each point of the star. The ritual layout looked familiar, but Scarlett had never used it herself. White was for banishments or bindings — for getting rid of negative things in your life or preventing your enemies from harming you. Had one of her sisters been performing a spell up here and forgotten to clean up after herself? It seemed unlikely. Scarlett's unease intensified.

That was when the chanting began. She didn't recognize the words. It sounded like ancient Greek, but not any of the blessing chants she'd memorized. This was something else, something darker. The words sounded guttural. Whoever was speaking them practically snarled each syllable. "What's the matter, Scarlett?" a husky voice rasped in her ear. "Did you forget the words?"

Scarlett spun around in horror. A cloaked figure had appeared on the roof, blocking the doorway down to the house. It approached her slowly, leaving bloody, smeared footprints in its wake. Scarlett opened her mouth to ask what was wrong, but she choked on her own tongue. She made to run, but her muscles were frozen in place, magically bound so she was nothing more than a terrified statue.

"Or is it something else?" the voice rasped.

The chant had become a growl. The wind picked up, out of nowhere, and flung Scarlett's dark curls into her face, obscuring her vision.

The figure leaned in, so close that Scarlett could feel its hot breath on her cheek. Then it tore the hood from its head and Scarlett gasped.

Harper.

Her hair was tangled around her pale white skin. Her eyes were dark fathomless pools, wild and wide. A tear dripped down her cheek, leaving a blood-red trail. Around her neck was the silver heart-shaped locket she always wore. "Guilt will be the death of you, sister," she whispered.

Without warning, she shoved Scarlett. Hard. Scarlett stumbled backwards and tripped over the railing. With a scream, she felt herself freefall toward the ground four stories below, her stomach in her throat, and—

"Scarlett!" Tiffany yelled. "Wake up."

Scarlett startled upright in her bed, drenched in sweat. Tiffany stood over her, looking worried. "You were shouting in your sleep."

Scarlett drank in her bedroom with a gasp of relief. It took a minute for her heart to return to its usual rhythm. She pressed her palm to her chest, shutting her eyes against the light streaming in through the sheer curtains. *It was just a nightmare,* she told herself. "Thanks for getting me. I hope I didn't wake the whole house."

"Sounded like a bad dream," Tiffany said, perching on the side of the bed.

"That's an understatement." Scarlett shook her head.

"Well, it's over now. You're okay," Tiffany said, rubbing her hands together in anticipation. "And everyone's already up and getting ready for the selection ceremony."

Tiffany's eyes landed on Scarlett's bedside table, where she'd laid out Minnie's tarot cards the night before; she'd tucked the set her mother had given her in her desk drawer.

"I've always loved these cards," Tiffany said, flipping through the deck and admiring the simple yet distinctive etchings. The cards were old but well preserved, and one of a kind. "That Minnie had excellent taste."

"She did," Scarlett said. "I'm just glad Eugenie didn't get them."

"Seriously. I guess I'm lucky I'm an only child. No one to fight me for my mom's cards when she passes." Tiffany's eyes welled up.

"Tiff . . ." Scarlett said softly, putting a hand on her friend's arm.

"I'm fine!" Tiffany said in an artificially bright tone, blinking away her tears as she set the cards back down reverently. "Now, up and at 'em—it's time to pick our latest round of victims."

After Tiffany bustled from the room, Scarlett groaned and forced herself out of bed. *Note to self: be a better sister,* she thought as she pushed aside her curtains and opened the windows to let in fresh air, hoping it would wake her up a little. From her balcony, she could see the red brick of the campus buildings that formed a rough square around the quad, a bell tower at its heart. In the other direction were the old, thick trees that marked the start of the woods on campus. One of the ravens from the aviary swooped toward the trees and disappeared from view.

It was all reassuringly normal, everything exactly as it should be. Except for one thing. There was a slight metallic glint in the ivy along the wrought-iron latticework of the balcony. Scarlett moved closer, brushed some of the leaves aside, and dug her fingers into the groove to free the object. Last year this room had belonged to a senior named Lyric; she'd since moved to New York City to work at a social-justice nonprofit. Perhaps she'd accidentally left something behind. Scarlett yanked away more of the ivy to get a better angle. She tugged at the object again, and it came loose and landed in her palm. Scarlett stared at it for a long moment, her pulse picking up. It was a silver necklace. The chain was kinked and tangled, and the small silver heart was tarnished.

It had been two years, but Scarlett would have recognized it anywhere. It looked exactly like the one Harper used to wear.

The sisters sat in a circle on the south lawn. Dahlia picked up a bottle of bubbles, the kind they'd all played with as kids, and blew them up into the air. A distraction spell, to keep the rest of campus from noticing what they were doing. Each girl held a Kappa Book in her lap. From far away, they looked like an ordinary study group. But from up close, they were deciding the fates of the next class of Ravens.

"In front of you, you'll find a full profile on each girl whose ability was strong enough to ignite a sparkler last night," Dahlia said. "Let's start reviewing our potential sisters."

Scarlett sat between Mei and Tiffany, only half paying attention as the book spread across her lap shimmered, its blank pages shifting to display images of the freshmen who'd attended their recruitment party the night before.

"The first girl is named Starla. She's the oldest of three girls . . ."

Scarlett stared at the face of a white girl with wavy brown hair, and for a moment, it was almost like Harper was looking up at her. Her breath caught in her throat. But when she blinked, the picture rearranged itself. The girl's hair was two shades lighter than Harper's, her nose longer and her lips wider.

Scarlett shook her head slightly. She was just spooked because of her dream. But that was *all* it was. A dream.

Or was it?

A dream didn't explain the necklace. Then again, there were a million necklaces like that out there. Even Scarlett had something similar in her jewelry box back home, a sweet-sixteen gift from her parents. There was no proof that the necklace had ever belonged to Harper. It had probably been wedged there for ages. It was just a coincidence that Scarlett happened to find it that morning.

Right?

Earth to Scarlett. Tiffany's voice sounded in Scarlett's head, and she felt a gentle nudge to her thigh.

Scarlett looked up, startled to find the entire circle's gaze on her. One of Dahlia's perfectly plucked eyebrows was raised as if she was waiting. "Um, yes. I agree," Scarlett said uncertainly, hoping they were asking if she was on board with the first potential.

Dahlia nodded, seemingly pleased. "Cast your votes." She opened a box of snow-white ravens' feathers and passed them out, one for each of the twenty sisters. People often thought ravens were a sign of bad luck or ill intent, but, like witchcraft itself, their history was so much more complicated than that. As early as ancient Greece, they were associated with prophecy, singled out to keep the deity's secrets and share its wisdom. Witches, like ravens, understood the secrets of the universe, and both got a bad rap for it.

It was why, hundreds of years ago, the founders of the coven had named themselves the Ravens. They'd continued to call themselves that even after they'd incorporated as a sorority, cloaking themselves in the protection of the Greek system. What better way to hide in plain sight while recruiting and initiating new members into their coven?

To vote a Raven in, one simply changed the color of the feather from white to black, a blank canvas transformed by knowledge and ability. By *power.* When Scarlett was a little girl, she'd dreamed of the day the feathers would transform for her.

Now Scarlett forced herself to focus on the task. One by one, starting with Dahlia's, the feathers ruffled, as if disturbed by an unseen hand, the white slowly filling with an inky, iridescent black.

Technically the feather ceremony was a mere formality—this was just the first step; the real choosing would happen during the first test night, when the sisters saw what kind of crop they were working with this year. If they were lucky, they'd find at least one girl per suit, which would keep the house well rounded. Wands witches like Dahlia worked fire spells. They tended to be healers and athletes. Swords witches like Tiffany specialized in air—literal air, like the wind, and things to do with memory, mental control, and influence. Pentacles witches like Mei worked with earth magic, such as glamours that altered the appearance of things in the physical realm. They usually had serious green thumbs too.

A Cups, Scarlett was best around water spells—scrying,

manipulating minor bodies of water, altering the chemistry of liquids (including beverages). Cups witches were also rumored to have the advantage when it came to casting love spells, though Scarlett herself had never needed to.

Every suit had both minor arcana—easy everyday spells—and major arcana. The latter were things witches could do only in extreme circumstances or by expending a ton of energy. A Cups could create a rainstorm like the one Scarlett had conjured when Minnie died; a Swords could summon a tornado or hurricane; a Wands could burn a forest to a crisp if she desired; and, in theory, a Pentacles could set off an earthquake, though to Scarlett's knowledge, no one ever had.

But the reason it mattered so much who they picked to join Kappa was that the Ravens had discovered how to bind their magic to one another's. Each full moon, they performed a house-wide union ritual that gave each Raven the ability to use the minor arcana of every suit, not just her own. It was what made them the most powerful coven in the world.

And these weren't the only decisions happening today. This was also the meeting when Dahlia would pick jobs for the top contenders for president. Scarlett was keeping her fingers crossed for membership chair. Everyone knew it was the most important job—the lucky sister was tasked with ushering the new members through the pledging process, essentially mentoring the newest class of witches. If the membership chair did a good job, she almost always ended up president.

And if Scarlett got the job she wanted, she had the perfect way to celebrate. She was meeting up with Mason after this for a proper hello . . . assuming she could get herself in the right mindset for it after everything that had happened this morning.

Dahlia finished the vote for a girl named Kelsey; only a handful of feathers changed colors. Next up was a gorgeous South Asian girl with a chin-length bob and piercing brown eyes.

"Sonali's mother, Aditi Mani, was a Raven," Dahlia said. "And although we don't show special favoritism toward legacies, it is something to take into consideration, since we know magical ability tends to run in families, and her mother was a fairly powerful Cups witch. Yes, Etta?"

Next to Dahlia, Etta was sprawled barefoot on the grass, dressed as usual like she was about to audition for the part of a fairy in *A Midsummer Night's Dream,* her skin milky-white in the sunlight. "You said she wants to go into politics. Are we talking Reese Witherspoon in *Election* . . . or Elizabeth Warren in 2020?" The other girls around the circle leaned in with interest. Etta's concern was valid. Witches with political ambitions were always viewed with more scrutiny. Ravens who mixed power with politics had to be beyond moral reproach.

"Hazel, you spoke to her more than I did," Dahlia said. "What was your read?"

Across the circle, Hazel, a Korean-American sophomore from Florida and a Wands witch like Dahlia, looked up from her hymnal. She wore leggings and a running shirt, though judging by her perfectly sleek bun and the lack of sweat on her face, Scarlett guessed it was because she planned to go for a run after this meeting, not that she'd just come from one. Then again, with Hazel, it was hard to tell. She was Westerly's resident track star, and she had a sprint time that made Scarlett feel terrifyingly out of shape. She also somehow made athleisure look elegant even at a mixer, while Scarlett always felt underdressed in gym clothes, even at the gym. "She's whip-smart, ambitious, but still scrupulous. More of an idealist than a charmer."

"I'm all for a Raven in the White House." Etta nodded and relaxed.

"And her name will be Scarlett Winter," Tiffany teased with a smile to Scarlett.

Scarlett returned the smile, loving that Tiffany always had her back.

"But Etta's right, we should stay vigilant on this one," Jess, the lead reporter for the *Gazette,* added in what Scarlett had come to recognize as her "I'll get to the bottom of this myself" tone. Jess's suspicion made Scarlett want to root for the new political witch. She knew now what color her feather would be.

"Do your worst, Lois Lane," Dahlia quipped. "All those in favor of extending a bid to Sonali?"

Each girl around the circle picked up her feather. Scarlett snatched hers up from where it had fallen beside her. Again the feathers ruffled and deepened to the shade of midnight. At a whispered command from her, Scarlett's changed color too, making for a unanimous vote. She gazed around the circle at all the other Ravens, her sisters, with pride. These were girls who, once upon a time, had faced this same process. Whatever faults they might have, they were bound by more than just magic. The Ravens were a sisterhood. A beautiful, diverse sisterhood built on love and power. The girls they voted in now would become their Littles, the next generation. Girls who would one day carry on their legacy.

"Next up is Reagan Ostrov, who has a very interesting background." The image of a girl with fiery red hair filled the page, and as Dahlia spoke, words appeared showing Reagan's history and potential futures. There was a murmur among the Ravens.

"She's a witch, although her family descends from a different coven in New Orleans. She's fully aware of her powers, but it's unclear what level of control she has. There was a fire at her old school. It was discovered quickly, and luckily no one was hurt." Dahlia's smile was grim. "It started in the theater, where, *coincidentally,* Reagan had just been passed over for the lead in the school play. It took four fire trucks to put it out."

"Looks like we have a Fire sign on our hands," Mei said.

"Obviously, she is powerful, but she poses a risk. This kind of magic cannot be done publicly."

"You can't be suggesting we don't invite her?" Scarlett asked, surprised. Scarlett had always subscribed to the notion that Kappa was as much about sisterhood as it was about magic, but Dahlia looked at it a little differently. She wanted Kappa to be the *best*—the best sorority *and* the best coven. And to her, that had always meant initiating the most powerful witches.

Dahlia shook her head. "Just that we have to be careful with her."

Even before Dahlia had finished talking, all the feathers transformed. Reagan Ostrov was in, and Scarlett couldn't help thinking that the Ravens would deserve what they got.

"Very well," Dahlia said.

Something soured a little in Scarlett's stomach when they all turned to the next page of the book, and she saw the annoyingly naïve, brown-haired white girl she'd handed a sparkler to staring up at her. *Vivian Devereaux,* the page said.

"She told me she didn't even want to pledge," Scarlett said before anyone else could speak up. "Why would we consider someone who doesn't like us?"

"Did she actually *say* she didn't like us?" Mei arched a perfectly sculpted eyebrow. Her hair, which she'd done in a sharp bob for the rush party, was waist-length and tipped in lavender today.

Scarlett waved a dismissive hand. "She said she's not the sorority type—which she's right about, by the way. So why waste a bid?"

Dahlia watched her through narrowed eyes. "Normally you're all for inviting as many people as possible. What did you argue last year? 'We'll never know how strong someone is until we test them'?"

Dahlia was right. It was something Minnie had always told her.

Tiffany leaned forward. "I'm with Scarlett." Scarlett flashed her best friend a grateful smile. "Besides, is this really all we know about this girl?" She gestured to the nearly blank page in the Kappa Book.

Mother: Unknown.

Father: Unknown.

History: Unknown.

"She moved around a lot," Dahlia said. "We found records from her most recent school in Nevada, but she only attended classes there for four months. Before that, she was homeschooled in a town near the Northern California border—"

"I think she has potential," Mei said. "She doesn't even know she's a witch yet. I for one would like to see what she can do."

"Scarlett." Dahlia looked at her. "It's up to you."

Scarlett blinked in surprise. Normally decisions like this were the president's to make. But she understood Dahlia's underlying meaning: *If you're going to lead Kappa next year, you need to be able to make decisions for the group, not just yourself.* After a slow, deep breath, Scarlett nodded. "You're right, Mei. We should give her a chance." Mei flashed her a smile. Etta grinned too. But Scarlett remained poker-faced as she held up her feather to darken once more. Just because she'd chosen to be magnanimous didn't mean she had to *like* it.

They finished voting for the remainder of the potentials: a girl named Ariana Ruiz and one named Bailey Kaplan, who also didn't know they were witches; a set of twins; and a legacy whose sparkler hadn't ignited so much as sparked feebly. Scarlett doubted that one would pass the first rite.

When they finished, Dahlia cleared her throat. "Before you go, ladies, I have one more order of business."

Scarlett sat up straighter, giving Tiffany an excited grin.

"Tiffany. Scarlett. Mei." Dahlia eyed each of them in turn. "You three are my strongest junior witches."

We're your only *junior witches thanks to the disaster freshman year,* Scarlett thought, then pushed the thought away.

"To ensure that we have an incredible class of new sisters this year, I'm assigning each of you a special role. How you perform in these roles will help us decide on our next class of officers."

Help you decide who's stepping into your shoes, you mean. Scarlett fixed her eyes on Dahlia. Whatever it took, she needed to make sure it would be her.

"Tiffany, you'll be taking on the position of social chair. Organizing all our events and functions falls to you."

Beside Dahlia, Tiffany nodded eagerly. "I'll do my best."

"Mei, you'll be our representative on the Panhellenic council. You'll liaise with the other Greek organizations on campus and manage our alumnae relationships."

Scarlett didn't envy her friend that. It meant dealing with powerful women like Scarlett's mother, who had strong opinions about how Westerly in general and Kappa in particular should run. She shot Mei a commiserating wince, and Mei plastered on a brave smile in return.

"Scarlett."

She straightened.

"You'll be the membership chair. You'll design the group Hell

Week trials, vet our new inductees, and train them in basic spells —not just during Hell Week but all year, once we select our new sisters."

Yes. Scarlett bowed her head to hide the sudden, huge grin on her face. Out of the corner of her eye, she saw Mei's smile falter. This was the most important job, and everyone knew it. "I won't let you down."

"I know you won't." Dahlia nodded. "Remember, sisters, Hell Week, and the whole pledge process, is not about torturing anybody. It's about finding rare and unusual talent among the sea of average at this school. We need to find girls who will uphold our legacy. Who, like us, are ambitious, talented, driven, smart, and powerful. True Ravens." She closed her hymnal with a definitive snap and then, with a wave of her hand, burst the distraction spell. Scarlett and Tiffany got to their feet, the sounds of the main green rushing back into their circle.

"Ready for a little competition, sis?" Tiffany asked.

"Bring it on," Scarlett said, locking arms with her best friend.

Tiffany grinned as her voice sounded in Scarlett's head. *May the best witch win.*

CHAPTER SEVEN

Vivi

For the first time in years, Vivi woke up smiling. Golden sunlight filtered through the gap in the curtains she'd forgotten to close, but she didn't mind. The sweet gum tree by the window filled the room with the scent of dew, and in the distance, the bell in the clock tower tolled.

The first orientation activity today wasn't for another hour, so Vivi rolled onto her side and snuggled deeper into her pillow. She replayed the events of last night. The music. The dancing. The sparklers. Her very first party hadn't been merely a success—it'd been like something out of a dream. Vivi's lids grew heavy, and she was just about to drift back to sleep when something caught her eye, a lavender envelope on her otherwise empty dresser top. Blinking drowsily, she reached out and picked it up, then settled back into bed. It was surprisingly heavy and unmarked except for her name in cursive and a strangely shaped wax seal on the back—an inverted five-pointed star.

She recognized the symbol and frowned. It was on her mother's tarot cards, though usually with the point upright.

"Someone left that for you," said a curt voice that made Vivi flinch under the sheets.

Right. Zoe. In her post-party daze, she'd managed to forget about the existence of her roommate for a few hours. Now she squinted at the girl on the far side of the room, who was already up and, apparently, painting her nails, judging by the astringent scent emanating from her desk area.

"Who?" Vivi yawned as she forced herself into a seated position and then stood up.

"I don't know. It was just there this morning when I got back from the shower. Whoever it was, tell them not to come into our room without permission again."

Vivi made a noncommittal noise as she slid her finger under the seal and removed the cream-colored card inside. There was a handwritten message:

Vivian,

It was a pleasure meeting you last night. We would love to get to know you better and cordially invite you to pledge Kappa Rho Nu. We look forward to seeing you at Kappa House on Tuesday evening at eight.

Yours,

Dahlia Everly, President

Vivi stared at the card in confusion. "It's from Kappa. They've invited me to pledge."

Even Zoe seemed surprised and fixed Vivi with an appraising look, as though searching for something about Vivi she'd missed in her first assessment.

Vivi didn't blame her. She was having similar doubts. "I have no idea what I could've done to make a good impression."

"Don't look a gift horse in the mouth," Zoe said, sounding both impressed and irritated. "Besides, if you're accepted, you know you get to move out of here and into Kappa House, right?"

Suddenly, Vivi had another burning reason to want to join the sorority.

Her stomach rumbled, a reminder that it was finally time to brave the dining hall. She'd had chips from the vending machine for lunch yesterday, and last night there'd been a "pizza welcome mixer" in the dorm's common room, but she wouldn't be able to put off a trip there for much longer. She'd always hated going to the cafeteria for the first time at a new school. It was never clear how much you were allowed to take and what you were meant to do with your tray afterward. She couldn't afford to let her awkwardness win out this time; she refused to become the star of the viral video "Girl Spends Seven Full Minutes Befuddled by Milk Dispenser."

She showered quickly in the communal bathroom, then returned to her room to grab her phone and ID card. At the last minute, she plucked the Kappas' invitation off her bed. Perhaps if she read it again after coffee had kicked in, it'd make a little more sense. As Vivi pulled on a pair of sweatpants, she could almost *feel* the look of derision Zoe was shooting her way, but she didn't care. Vivi didn't own an outfit that would impress her stylish roommate and it was pointless to waste time pretending otherwise.

As she stepped out of her dorm, an elegant brick building

covered with ivy, Vivi felt some of her anxiety melt away. She actually *lived* here, on one of the most beautiful campuses in the country. It was going to feel like home soon, she just knew it.

"So you're the Kappas' next victim, I see?" Startled, Vivi turned to see a girl in tight black jeans and a shredded black shirt sitting cross-legged in the grass. She raised an eyebrow meaningfully at the lavender envelope in Vivi's hand.

Instinctively, Vivi tucked the envelope into her purse. She wasn't sure how this worked. Was she allowed to tell people she'd been invited? Or was it a secret? She went for noncommittal. "I don't really know much about it yet."

The girl gave Vivi a penetrating look that made Zoe's stares seem friendly by comparison, then smirked and rose to her feet. "Be careful with them," she said, almost more to herself than to Vivi, then sauntered away.

That was weird, Vivi thought as she continued toward the dining hall. Maybe the girl was jealous? Kappas were selective, and lots of people had been at that party vying for bids, which made Vivi wonder all the more why they'd chosen her. She hadn't been dressed properly and didn't know how to dance well. The Kappas she'd met had been nice to her, but they'd been welcoming to everybody. What about Vivi had caught their eye?

Zoe's right, she thought for the first and possibly last time ever. *Don't ask why. Just be glad something good is finally happening to you.*

Before she had time to grow nervous about entering the dining hall alone, Vivi saw Ariana waving at her from a few yards away. "Are you going to breakfast?" Ariana asked. "Thank God. I was afraid I was going to have to sit by myself." She bit her lip. "Sorry, I mean, it's fine if you're meeting people. I don't want to force you to eat with me."

"That'd be great," Vivi said with a smile, relieved to learn that even girls like Ariana had the same concerns she did.

"How are you holding up after last night?" Ariana asked as they climbed the stone stairs. "I think I had one too many of those teacup cocktails; my head is *pounding*."

"Nothing a little coffee won't solve," Vivi said. Then she hesitated for a moment, thinking back to the envelope she'd tucked into her purse. "So I found something on my dresser this morning . . ." For a split second, she regretted saying anything, in case Ariana hadn't received a bid herself.

But to her relief, Ariana gave her a broad smile. "You got a bid? Me too. Exciting, right?" Ariana's face fell again almost immediately. "Oh God, what am I going to wear? They didn't give any guidelines. Do you think it'll be dressy, like the cocktail party? Or more, like, business-casual, maybe . . ."

Vivi felt her own panic growing as Ariana rattled off possibilities until the jingling of a phone stopped her midstream. "Shoot." Ariana paused on the dining-hall steps and frowned at the screen. "My roommate locked herself out. Can I get a rain check on breakfast? I'm sorry to ditch you like this. Will you be okay?"

"I'll be fine," Vivi said. She prayed it'd be true.

"You're the best. Oh, let me grab your number—I can text you later."

Vivi recited her phone number, then watched Ariana bound off, curls coming loose from her bun and bouncing back and forth atop her head. A few seconds later, Vivi's phone buzzed with a new text. ARIANA RUIZ'S NUMBER! Vivi smiled as she slipped her phone into her pocket. She might have to face eating alone, but at least one friend prospect was looking up.

She took a deep breath and continued up the wide steps. The large stone building looked more like a church than a cafeteria, and when Vivi pushed open the heavy door, she found herself in an enormous space unlike any she'd seen before. Exposed wooden rafters soared across the ceiling, and twelve-foot-high windows filled the room with sunlight that glinted off the glass vase in the center of every round table. It was as if Martha Stewart had redecorated Hogwarts.

There was no line at the breakfast buffet, where Vivi gleefully filled her plate with scrambled eggs and pancakes. But when she started walking toward one of the many empty tables, she realized she'd made a terrible mistake. There was a waffle bar. What was she doing wasting her time with pancakes when there was a *waffle* bar? She carefully set her tray down at the bar and began to ladle waffle batter into the iron. There was a loud hiss and she jumped back in surprise as sizzling batter dripped down the sides and spilled onto the table. "Shit," she said under her breath, unsure what do to. Was it possible to set a building on fire with batter?

"You really are a menace to public safety, aren't you?"

Vivi's breath caught as she turned to see the boy who'd carried her bags yesterday grinning at her. "I'm just joking," he said. "I can tell you have everything under control, though you might want to flip that at some point. Here, allow me." He reached out and turned the waffle iron over.

"Is this some weird hobby of yours?" Vivi managed to say, regaining some of her composure. "You sneak around campus waiting for girls to embarrass themselves so you can swoop in and be the hero?"

"The hero?" he repeated thoughtfully. "You know what? I like that. Mason Gregory, breakfast hero." He stuck out his hand. "Saving innocent girls from the indignity of eating slightly misshapen waffles. Excuse me. Duty calls." He reached past Vivi, opened the iron, carefully removed the golden-brown waffle, and tipped it onto her plate. *"Voilà, mademoiselle."*

"Vous êtes trop gentil, monsieur."

He raised an eyebrow. "Oh, so you're fancy, huh? In that case, allow me to prepare the specialty of the house, waffles à la Mason." He began to scoop toppings onto Vivi's waffle, first strawberries, then chocolate chips, then a swirl of whipped cream.

"Okay, that's enough," Vivi said with a laugh as she reached for her plate.

"Non, non, mademoiselle," he said with a terrible French accent as he held the plate in the air. "It is not finished yet." He carried it over to the cereal bar and sprinkled cornflakes on top.

"What? No!" Vivi said as she tried to grab the plate.

Mason pivoted and managed to add a serving of Lucky Charms before she yanked her breakfast from his grasp. "This is disgusting," she said, eyeing the concoction.

He looked hurt. "Are you doubting my culinary skills? Just take a bite. It'll blow your mind."

"I'll be sure to report back. Unless . . . are you sitting with anyone?" She paused as her heart began to race, just as it always did when she did something that could potentially end badly. "Do you want to sit together?" The moment the words left her mouth, she immediately regretted saying anything. They'd had a fun exchange, and now she'd ruined everything by being a weirdo.

"I'd be honored," he said with a smile. "I'm Mason, in case you didn't catch it earlier."

"Vivi," she said.

"Vivi," Mason repeated. "I like it."

She followed him to one of the round tables and lowered her tray gingerly, careful not to let her coffee or orange juice slosh over the sides of the cups.

"Ah, freshmen," Mason said. "So innocent, so lacking in tray-holding muscle memory." He placed the tray on the table with an exaggerated flourish.

"Are you a sophomore?" Vivi asked.

"Senior."

"Then how come you haven't learned how to make an edible waffle by now?"

Mason faked an offended gasp. "How can you say that? You haven't even tried it yet." Without asking, he reached across to cut himself a piece. For a moment, Mason's arm brushed Vivi's and she felt a spark at the touch.

She ignored the heat in her cheeks at the intimacy of the gesture and was about to cut herself a square when he swallowed his own bite and grimaced.

"Ha! See?" she said. She lowered her knife and fork and picked up a strip of bacon instead.

He smirked. "So, besides attacking people with suitcases and burning waffles, what do you enjoy doing? Are you one of those freshmen with their whole four years planned out already or the kind who changes their major three times?"

"The latter, probably. I've spent my whole life barely able to plan my next week, let alone years, plural."

"Really?" he asked, surveying her with new interest. "Why's that?"

She took a sip of coffee to stall for time. The last thing she wanted to talk to a cute guy about was her exasperating mother. "My childhood was a little . . . unconventional. We moved around a lot, sometimes without much notice."

She braced for a look of confusion—or, worse, pity—and was surprised to see a trace of wistfulness in his face. "It sounds nice, getting to start over now and then."

"Trust me, being the new kid gets old pretty fast."

"Yeah, but if things didn't go well at one school, you could try something completely different at the next one. You could write angsty poetry with the goth kids, or join the fencing team, or decide to wear a top hat and monocle every day."

Vivi cocked her head and furrowed her brow. "Maybe . . . if you were the new kid at school in 1894."

Mason laughed. "Fair enough. But I do think there's something to be said for making friends who haven't known you your whole life and who think they know you better than you know yourself."

Vivi considered this. On the one hand, she'd give anything for a group of friends who knew her that well. But on the other, it was freeing to make a radical change, like rushing a sorority, and not have anyone judge her for it. "So what would you do if none of that mattered?"

"I'm not sure," he said as he placed his silverware on the table and ran his hands through his curly hair. "I guess that's the problem." He smiled and shook his head. "Sorry, that's too much deep talk for breakfast."

"Does this count as deep?" Vivi asked. "Feels like advanced small talk to me."

"You've got a lot to learn about the South, sweetheart," he said, exaggerating his drawl. Even though she knew he was teasing her, the word *sweetheart* made her chest tingle. "The only things you're allowed to talk about at breakfast are the heat and sports scores."

"Well, it's not that hot out and I don't know anything about sports, so I guess we'll have to sit here in silence." She paused. "Or else see if it's not too late for me to transfer to Oberlin."

He laughed. "So what about you, New Girl? Who are you going to be at Westerly?"

"That's . . . a big question." In any other situation, she would've steered the conversation toward less personal ground, but Mason was looking at her with such interest and sincerity, it felt almost rude not to answer truthfully. "I guess I want to find something I'm passionate about. Something real."

"What does *real* mean?"

"Something that'll help me understand the world, like environmental science or history or psychology." She paused, waiting for him to call her out on her pretension, but he merely nodded, encouraging her to continue. "I've spent too much time surrounded by people who refuse to accept reality. I don't want to be afraid of the truth. Does that make sense?"

"Yes," he said, nodding slowly, though his expression had turned serious. Maybe she'd gone too far and he was figuring out how to extract himself from the conversation. She was considering faking a text from Ariana just to give Mason a way out when she was saved by the arrival of someone else joining them at the table. At least, so Vivi thought, until that person stopped to rest a hand on Mason's shoulder. "There you are," she drawled. "I thought we were meeting on the quad."

It was the girl from the rush party who'd handed her a sparkler. She bent to kiss Mason on the cheek, and Vivi's stomach flipped like she'd just missed a step on the stairs. *Uh-oh.*

"Shoot, sorry. I lost track of time." Mason's chair scraped against the floor as he rose abruptly and picked up his tray. "I'll just return this. Be right back."

"That's all right," the girl said sweetly as Mason hurried off. She turned to Vivi. "I'm Scarlett. Vivian, was it?"

"Yes. Vivi."

"So, Vivi, I see you've met my boyfriend."

The word landed hard, sending ripples of embarrassment and disappointment through her. *Boyfriend.* Of course Mason was taken. And by a Kappa, naturally. "Yeah, he showed me how to use the waffle maker," Vivi said quickly. "Cooking's not really my thing."

"Always the gentleman," Scarlett said, the sweetness draining from her voice. "You're so brave, coming to breakfast dressed like that." She nodded at Vivi's sweatpants. "I wish I could be so . . . uninhibited."

Vivi blushed and, to her annoyance, she was still searching for a retort when Mason returned and took Scarlett's hand. "Stay out of trouble, Vivi," he said before following Scarlett out of the cafeteria.

Too late. She was already knee-deep in it.

CHAPTER EIGHT

Scarlett

As Mason walked Scarlett to class, clouds gathered, dark and low, on the horizon. She wasn't 100 percent sure if it was her or Mother Nature brewing the storm.

"I am so sorry I missed our breakfast, Scar," he said again. He'd been brimming over with apologies since they'd left the cafeteria. "Let me make it up to you. Why don't we skip? We can go down to Miss Deenie's and get some real food."

"I would, but one of us is clearly already full," Scarlett said icily.

"Scar, it was just breakfast."

But it wasn't *just* anything. *Some of us don't skip. Some of us care. Some of us show up where we are supposed to be instead of making waffles for wide-eyed freshmen.* It wasn't just that she'd found him playing waffle sous-chef for that unfortunate freshman charity-baby witch. She could usually set her watch by Mason.

"*I* can't skip," she said firmly.

"Scar . . ." he pleaded. But when he realized that she was standing her ground, he sighed, gave her a quick peck on the lips, and moved on, his shoulders slightly slumped.

After he disappeared into the fog that had suddenly descended like a curtain, Scarlett couldn't bring herself to go into the lecture hall. Instead, she strode back across campus toward Kappa House, clenching her fists so hard, her nails left crescents in her palms.

Just who the hell does this Vivi girl think she is?

How could Mason stand her up for the same irritating girl whom Scarlett hadn't even wanted to vote into Kappa? She was beneath them, this girl with her ratty clothes and childlike innocence. Was this what Mason was talking about when he'd asked her if she ever thought about just saying screw it all and traveling the world? Screw *that*. Thunder rumbled in the distance, and she forced herself to take slow, calming breaths. She could *not* use major arcana right now. Not with so many witnesses. But she felt the magic itching in her veins, begging to be let loose.

It wouldn't take much. Not at this point with her nerves as frayed as they were.

"You might want to get inside soon," a surly voice said.

Great. Jackson had just jogged up beside her on the quad.

"Why's that?" she replied coldly.

"Don't witches melt in the rain?"

Scarlett nearly tripped over her sandals. She forced her expression to stay calm, removed. Forced herself not to study him too hard out of the corner of her eye. "Someone's been reading a little too much urban fantasy."

He kept pace with her. "Just calling it like I see it."

"Jackson, I'm not in the mood."

"Come on, Scarlett. Take a joke."

She whirled on him finally, her hair whipping as the storm kicked up more power. *"Leave me alone,"* she growled. If not for the burgeoning thunderstorm soaking up all her power, she would have already cast a distraction charm to send him away. But her control would be tenuous right now. Irritating as he was, she didn't want to make a mistake and hurt him. She couldn't go through something like that again.

Jackson set his jaw. For a moment, she thought he'd refuse. But with a deafening clap of thunder, the rain began, and he scowled, flung up the hood of his sweatshirt, and stalked away.

She watched him leave, every muscle in her body taut. She crossed her arms over her chest, cut off the quad, and headed into the forest that ran alongside campus. It was a slightly longer walk to Kappa this way, but the trees provided cover from the worst of the storm.

Normally at this hour, the path would be crowded with students who lived in other parts of campus. Right now, thanks to the rain, it was abandoned. With the dark clouds above, it looked like nighttime almost. Scarlett picked her way through the gloom, scowling.

At least the weather matched her mood.

Vivi. What the hell was she going to do with her? She'd known she wasn't Kappa material from the moment she'd set eyes on her. She was rude and unstylish, and she had flirted with Scarlett's boyfriend right in front of her.

Sure, Mason had apologized for flaking on her. But she couldn't help noticing the way his eyes had tracked that Vivi girl as they left the dining hall. Or the way he'd been smiling and laughing before Scarlett approached their breakfast table . . .

And the way he'd stopped smiling and laughing when Scarlett took Vivi's place.

It's just all the distance. The summer apart had been a mistake. She'd have to remember that going forward. Because they *would* go forward. They had their life plan all set. This? This was nothing more than a blip. Hardly worth worrying about, really.

Tell that to this thunderstorm, she thought wryly, cutting through a small wooded park that led to Greek Row. Another rumble of thunder sounded, followed by a crack. Like someone stepping on a branch.

She whirled around, but the path remained empty. Gloomy. Too dark to see more than a few feet in front of her. Her breath started to come just a little faster.

Snap.

Behind her again. She turned, slower this time, eyes fixed on the trees. *There.* A faint shadow in the distance. Skinny, tall. She began to whisper under her breath, a low, humming protection charm. But most of her magic had already been poured into the storm, and what remained would barely be enough to light a candle, much less protect her against . . .

What?

She was at Westerly. A few steps from her sorority house. What did she honestly think was out here, stalking her through the forest?

But she knew better than anyone that bad things could happen at Westerly. She could never forget the night with Harper. It would haunt her forever. But Harper was gone. And Gwen was gone too. And while witches were real, ghosts were not . . .

Still, she looked behind her once more and then—

"Boo!"

Scarlett screamed and whirled back around to find Tiffany beside her. Her heart still racing in her chest, she glared. "Not funny."

Tiffany grinned. "Wasn't it?" One glimpse of Scarlett's expression, though, and she sobered. "Sorry. I couldn't resist. You just looked so tense."

"I thought I heard . . ." Scarlett glanced back through the trees. No one was there. "Never mind." She shook her head, willing her pulse to stop pounding. "What are you doing out in this?"

"Coming to find you, of course." Tiffany pointed at the sky. "I figured something must be wrong. What happened?"

Scarlett crunched on through the woods, toward Kappa House, grateful to have her best friend at her side. At least it would stop her from jumping at every shadow. "Just . . . Mason." Scarlett sighed.

"Am I gonna need to hurt our resident campus pretty boy for messing with my girl?" Tiffany arched a brow.

She almost smiled. Almost. "Not yet. But I need you to help me dissect what's going on."

"Well, then." Tiffany looped her arm through Scarlett's. "You've got me. But I'm also available for actual dissection if need be."

Scarlett laughed and felt a surge of gratitude for her friend.

"I'm serious, Scar. Dahlia had me help her dissect owl pellets last night for some spell she's working on." Tiffany wrinkled her nose. "I think she was annoyed that I wasn't more grossed out, but she forgot that I was a biology major for a hot second in freshman year."

“Did it not occur to you to pawn that task off on your Little?” Scarlett teased as they looped up the path and turned the corner toward Kappa House.

“You know how it is. Dahlia says jump . . .” Tiffany nudged Scarlett. “For real, though, are you okay? Because if Mason needs a reminder that he somehow managed to score the smartest, funniest, hottest woman on this entire campus, I’m your girl. You deserve the best and I don’t want anyone treating you—”

Tiffany stopped short the moment their house came into view.

“Oh my God,” Scarlett gasped.

Tacked to the front door, there for everyone to see, were four tarot cards: The Queen of Swords. The Queen of Wands. The Queen of Cups. And the Queen of Pentacles.

And slashed through each one was a blood-red *X*.

CHAPTER NINE

Vivi

As she made her way up the narrow brick path to Kappa House on Tuesday, Vivi realized she'd never actually accepted the offer to pledge. There'd been no RSVP card. No email address or phone number. A flare of rebellion rose up within her, bringing her to a stop. She'd never even heard of this sorority until a few days ago—why would they automatically assume she'd want to join? Yet as she stared at the elegant sorority house, she knew she wouldn't turn back around.

Although the past few days had been a whirlwind of orientation activities, classes, parties, and appointments with various advisers, she hadn't been able to stop thinking about the invitation. It hovered at the edge of her thoughts during her first neuroscience class, which she'd gotten special permission to take as a freshman. She felt a shivery thrill of excitement down her spine in the museum-like rare-books library where, to Vivi's amazement, anyone was allowed to study. The only thing threatening to dampen her enthusiasm was the memory of how foolish she'd been in the dining hall with Mason the other morning. A cute boy had been nice to her for five minutes and Vivi had somehow managed to convince herself that he was interested. Her stomach clenched as she recalled the look on Scarlett's face when she'd approached their table, her cloyingly sweet, condescending smile. She hadn't liked Vivi from the start, and this clearly wouldn't help. The question was how much it would hurt her chances in the sorority.

The Kappas' four-story gray house was set far back from the street, nestled among the live oaks that cast long shadows in the twilight. The tea lights she'd thought had been strung up for the rush party still hung in the trees, though they created a different effect without the buzz of music and laughter.

Vines curled up the wrought-iron balconies that adorned each floor, and Vivi couldn't keep herself from imagining what it'd be like to sit out on the wraparound porch with a mint julep. Whatever that turned out to be.

As she waited for Ariana, whom she'd promised to meet outside, Vivi looked at the neighboring houses. Although they were all enormous, they couldn't have been more different from the sterile McMansions that constituted luxury in Reno. There were sprawling Victorians, a few stately Georgians, and one Greek revival complete with marble columns, all of them with the wrought-iron balconies that Vivi had come to associate with Savannah. Most had ivy covering at least one of the walls, and a few had flaking paint, but while these details might seem shabby in other neighborhoods, here they only added to the feeling of decadence. The houses reminded Vivi of the eccentric British aristocrats she'd read about, the ones who wore designer clothes with muddy boots and let their priceless oil paintings fade in stuffy attics.

"Sorry to keep you waiting," a breathless voice said. Vivi turned to see Ariana hurrying up the walk looking harried but gorgeous in the black cocktail dress Vivi had seen that morning. The night before, when Vivi admitted that she didn't have any formalwear, Ariana had insisted she come to her room the next day to borrow an outfit—she had half a dozen party dresses left over from her cousins' recent quinceañeras.

"I wasn't in any rush to go inside, trust me," Vivi said. "So should we knock?"

"I guess so." Ariana eyed the door warily.

"This doesn't really strike me as the walk-right-in kind of place," Vivi said. All the shutters were closed, and there were no sounds of activity coming from inside.

As she and Ariana stared at the door, it suddenly opened, revealing an empty vestibule. "Who did that?" Ariana asked.

"Maybe it was the wind," Vivi said, wondering why the wind always insisted on behaving strangely whenever she was around. She and Ariana exchanged a look of wordless agreement, then stepped inside.

The recruitment party had been mostly in the garden, and Vivi realized she hadn't gotten a good look around the interior. Paintings lined the walls; some featured women in old-fashioned clothes while others depicted beautiful but slightly melancholy settings: a forest shrouded in mist, a raven perched on a barren tree in a lonely field. Yet the house itself conveyed elegance and warmth, from the candles flickering on random surfaces to the overflowing vases of flowers scattered about.

"Whoa," Ariana said under her breath. "Look at this." She was pointing down a hall that led to an enclosed greenhouse. Moonlight filtered through the glass, illuminating a tangle of plants, potted trees, and vines climbing up the walls.

"I guess the Kappas are into gardening?" Vivi said.

Faint conversation drifted from another room. Vivi gestured for Ariana to join her and followed the sound to the living room, where two girls sat on a pair of couches facing each other. Jess, the Kappa who'd quoted Dorothy Parker at the party, was leaning forward, listening intently. She wore thick-framed glasses that accentuated her delicate cheekbones and an elegant white silk blouse that Vivi would never have been able to keep clean. This evening, her twisted braids were pulled back from her face with a clip.

The white girl talking to her, clearly a new member, twirled a piece of her long black hair nervously as she chattered. "I was obviously really relieved when my boyfriend and I were both accepted to Westerly. But then, at the very last minute, I mean, like, four hours before the deadline, he decided to go to Vanderbilt instead. I had already sent in my deposit and there was nothing I could do. We're going to try to do the long-distance thing, but I'm really worried because he posted this photo on Instagram of him and this *really* pretty girl and the caption said 'The benefits of new friends,' which could be read a bunch of different ways, but still . . ."

Vivi wanted to motion for the girl to stop talking. She couldn't believe how much she was sharing with a virtual stranger, especially one evaluating her for the sorority. Jess turned to Vivi and Ariana. "Nice to see both of you again. Come have a seat." Ariana shot Vivi a nervous smile, then hurried to sit next to the other pledge, leaving Vivi to sit on the couch next to Jess. "You're Ariana and Vivian, right?"

"Vivi," Vivi said, trying to remember when she'd told Jess her name at the party.

"Vivi. Of course. How do you like Westerly so far?"

"I like it. My classes have been great, and everyone I met has been really nice." *That's how you do it,* Vivi thought. Polite, cheerful, but not blabbing every thought.

"Where are you from?"

"Oh, lots of places. It's a little complicated," Vivi said with a wave of her hand, planning to stop the conversation there.

Jess nodded. "I can imagine." She was looking at Vivi with a mixture of curiosity and understanding that filled Vivi's chest with a strange warmth.

"I never stayed anywhere for more than two years," Vivi continued. The longer Jess looked at her, the harder it became to stay quiet; it was as if the words were being pulled out of her by a mysterious force. Yet she didn't mind. It felt good to talk to this sympathetic girl with the kind eyes who seemed genuinely interested in getting to know her. Vivi was just about to start telling her about her mother when four more girls entered the room.

"Welcome to Kappa," one of them said crisply. She was tall and blond and pretty in a striking, angular way. "I'm Dahlia, president of Kappa Rho Nu. This is Scarlett Winter, our pledge master."

Vivi's stomach dropped. Scarlett was the pledge master. Great. "And this is Mei, our alumnae liaison." It took Vivi a moment to recognize Mei from the other night. Instead of a blunt bob, her hair was now waist-length with purple tips. But how was that possible? Vivi was 99.9 percent sure that Mei hadn't been wearing a wig the other night, and she clearly wasn't wearing extensions now. "And this is Tiffany, our social chair." A friendly-looking girl with white-blond hair held up a hand and smiled.

Over the next few minutes, about a dozen more girls filed into the living room, including a tall redhead Vivi had seen dancing on a table at the recruitment party and a white, round-faced brunette in hipster glasses who seemed so nervous, Vivi worried she might actually vomit. "It looks like we're ready to get started," Dahlia said. "Y'all can sit wherever there's space." Vivi scooched closer to Jess to make room on the couch while some of the Kappas drew up velvet-covered armchairs and footstools to form a circle.

"I hope this doesn't go on forever," Jess whispered to the Kappa on the other side of her. "I have to file my article for the *Gazette* by midnight." Vivi wasn't surprised to learn that Jess wrote for the Westerly school paper. She seemed to have a gift for getting people to spill their secrets.

Someone turned off the lights. The candles and the full moon gleaming through the large window provided plenty of illumination. Dahlia leaned toward the low coffee table in the center of the circle and lit the remaining candle. At least, a flame appeared, but Vivi didn't see a lighter or a match in Dahlia's hand.

"Welcome, sisters and new members," Dahlia said. Her voice

had grown quieter, though Vivi had no trouble hearing her in the silent, still room. "Those of you joining us for the first time will notice that Kappa is very small—we are the most selective sorority at Westerly, and we may even be the most selective in the entire country. That's because we look for something rare and special in our pledges, qualities that set us apart. We recognized some of those qualities in all of you, which is why you're here this evening."

Vivi felt a prickle of unease. She honestly couldn't think of a single one of her "qualities" that would be attractive to the Kappas—unless they wanted pledges who'd gotten a five on the AP Bio exam and had a severe shellfish allergy. She looked around the room, wondering who else felt the same mixture of doubt and confusion. Ariana seemed similarly nervous, as did the majority of the dozen or so hopefuls. But a handful of pledges—including the redheaded girl—exchanged excited, knowing smiles.

"Kappa doesn't have a typical recruitment process," Dahlia continued. "If you impress us tonight, you're in. But don't get comfortable." She pinned each of them with a stare. Vivi couldn't suppress a shiver when Dahlia's eyes met hers. "We only initiate those who bring their all to this sisterhood. Historically, at least one potential new member fails to make the final cut. Sometimes, no one makes it."

The whole room seemed to hold its breath until Dahlia smiled again. "But tonight's test is a simple one."

"What kind of test?" Ariana asked. Her eyes widened in surprise after she spoke, as if the words had flown out of her mouth of their own accord. Vivi was glad Ariana had asked the question, though —she was wondering the same thing.

"You'll see in a moment. But don't worry—there was nothing you could've done to prepare, and nothing you can do to screw up. You're either a Kappa or you're not." Dahlia nodded at Mei, who placed a stack of cards on the coffee table next to the candle Dahlia had just lit, a long one in an ornate silver candleholder. Vivi and Ariana exchanged a look. Did the Kappas make their decisions based on a card game?

Dahlia spread the cards out in a fan face-down on the table. "Let's see . . . who's first? Bailey, please take a card." She paused. "Bailey?"

The girl with the thick glasses was looking uneasily from Dahlia to the cards. "Sorry, I'm a little confused. What are we doing, exactly?"

Dahlia smiled. "Just relax and trust us. Take a card, please."

Bailey leaned forward, let her fingers hover momentarily in the air, then plucked one of the cards out of the fan. The moment her hand closed around the card, the room grew darker. The flames of the other candles shrank to wispy flickers, yet the light from the candle on the coffee table grew stronger and brighter, casting a strange glow on her face. "Oh my God," she whispered, and almost released the card.

"Hold it," Dahlia said calmly, looking amused.

The flame grew and danced until it was taller than the silver candlestick. Then the flame divided into two streams, as if the wick had split in half. A moment later, those two flames split again and began to curl in the air, looking like strands of hair made of fire. Ariana murmured something under her breath, but Vivi didn't look at her. She couldn't tear her eyes away from the dancing flames, which, to her growing shock and confusion, seemed to be forming an image. A glowing red-orange bird hovered in the darkness above the candle, which had gone out. A phoenix, Vivi realized. It flapped its fiery wings and began to rise toward the ceiling, then it vanished in a cloud of sparks that rained down on the circle.

It's a hologram, Vivi thought, trying to convince herself. *Or a projection. Just a trick to make all this more fun.* Yet even in her own brain, the words sounded hollow.

"Please place your card face-up on the table," Dahlia said.

With trembling hands, Bailey did as she was told, revealing an image of a beautiful woman with long dark hair and a mysterious grin. A large orange-red bird perched on her shoulder, and in one hand she held a long, slender wooden object.

These weren't playing cards, Vivi realized as icy prickles ran down her spine. They were tarot cards. Except they looked nothing like the garish, brightly colored pack her mother used with her clients. The image on the card reminded Vivi of a faded oil painting in the back of a shadowy church—a forgotten masterpiece lost to the world.

"The Queen of Wands, the Fire sign," Dahlia said with a smile. "Welcome to Kappa Rho Nu, Bailey."

What just happened? Had Bailey been accepted because her card bore an uncanny resemblance to the image in the candle flame? But how was that possible? And how could such an extraordinary thing happen more than once?

"Sonali, your turn," Dahlia said. An elegantly dressed South Asian girl who'd been fiddling nervously with her gold bracelets ever since she sat down nodded with surprising assurance. The moment she chose her card from the deck, the candle's flame reappeared and started to grow, just as it had before. But this time, instead of a phoenix, the flames formed a glowing cloud that drifted through the darkness toward the ceiling.

That's impossible, Vivi thought, blinking rapidly. But no matter how many times she refocused her eyes, the glowing image remained the same. After a few seconds, a lightning bolt made of flames shot through the cloud, and it turned to a shower of sparks.

"Place your card on the table, Sonali," Dahlia said calmly. The girl turned her card over and Vivi suppressed a gasp. The card featured another beautiful woman, although this one was dressed all in white and held a glowing blue sword. In the tarot, each suit was connected to one of the elements. Swords were associated with air, hence the thundercloud. But how on earth could someone have arranged that? Even if the candle was some sort of hologram, how could the Kappas have known which cards the girls would choose?

"The Queen of Swords, the Air sign. Welcome to Kappa Rho Nu, Sonali."

Vivi's heart had begun to race, and she braced herself for a rush of fear. But to her surprise, tingling excitement filled her chest instead. Her fingers practically itched to pick a card.

The chatty, dark-haired girl who'd been talking to Jess was next. Hesitantly, she reached for a card, and Vivi leaned forward so she could see better. But the flame didn't appear when the girl touched her card. Nothing happened.

After a long, tense moment, Dahlia broke the silence. "Well, that's a shame." She stood, practically snatched the card out of the girl's hands, and shoved it at Mei. "Come with me, honey."

In a daze, the girl rose shakily to her feet and allowed Dahlia to lead her out of the room. Vivi looked from Mei to the other Kappas, but none of them appeared particularly concerned. A minute later, Dahlia returned and sat back down. "Who's next?"

"What happened to her?" asked Bailey.

"Don't worry about her," Dahlia said airily. "Once she stepped through the door, she lost all memory of tonight. She'll be none the wiser. Now, let's continue . . . go ahead, Ariana."

Ariana seemed paralyzed by fear until Vivi nudged her and whispered, "You can do it." Although she had no idea in hell what "it" meant.

Ariana chose a card, her fingers trembling. A few seconds passed, then the candle flame grew into a cresting wave.

"The Queen of Cups, the Water sign," Dahlia said after Ariana turned over her card. "Welcome to Kappa Rho Nu, Ariana."

The process was repeated three more times for girls who also failed to create a flame. With each exit, Vivi felt her excitement and dread grow in equal measure.

"You're up, Vivi," Dahlia said, nodding at her.

Vivi stared at the cards on the table, arms at her sides. She didn't want to be shunted into the night and leave all this behind. She didn't want to forget what she'd seen. *But that's impossible,* she told herself. *A sorority president can't wipe someone's memory.* She inhaled deeply, then extended her hand toward the table and let her fingers hover over the cards.

She hesitated, unsure how to decide. But then she felt something tug on her wrist with such force that she thought someone had grabbed her. Vivi looked up, but all the other girls were in their seats. No one had moved.

Vivi relaxed, letting the force pull her like a magnet until her fingers brushed against a card. The moment she touched it, the tugging sensation disappeared. Her hand trembling, Vivi grabbed the corner of the card and pulled it from the fan.

A second later, a flame shot up from the candle's wick, nearly reaching the ceiling. Vivi gasped as her skin began to buzz. It felt like a current of energy was rushing up her arm, almost as if she were being electrocuted. But there was no pain. Just the opposite, in fact. She felt powerful, alive.

Except that the energy wasn't running up her arm. It was the other way around, she realized. The energy was flowing *from her.* Vivi gasped again as the flame split into five streams that danced and curled through the air before forming a five-pointed star.

This time, the exceptional sight didn't cause a surge of confusion. Vivi felt a wave of calm pass over her, sweeping away knots of anxiety and uncertainty she hadn't even been aware of.

"Place your card on the table," Dahlia said. A note of smug satisfaction had crept into her voice.

Vivi turned her card over and found herself staring at an image of another woman. She wouldn't describe this one as beautiful, exactly. Her pale face was slightly too long, her expression much too fierce. But Vivi hardly gave it a passing thought, for what was beauty compared to this woman's power? In one hand, she clasped a large golden disk carved with a five-pointed star. Thick vines and flowers curled around her other arm, and it was clear that the woman was causing them to grow. She was surrounded by creatures of all sorts—birds, snakes, deer—magnificent creatures drawn to her energy.

"The Queen of Pentacles, the Earth sign. Welcome to Kappa Rho Nu, Vivi."

Vivi felt Ariana squeeze her hand, but she was too numb to do more than shoot her a vague smile before turning her attention back to the proceedings. Another girl was rejected, and the redhead named Reagan, a Fire sign, was the last pledge to be accepted.

Once every pledge had been tested and the failures had all been escorted out, Dahlia swept the cards up and placed them back in a neat stack. "Welcome, pledges, to the oldest, most prestigious, and most powerful sorority in the country. We've been waiting for you. Whether you realize it or not, your destiny has led you to Westerly and to Kappa Rho Nu."

"What are you?" Ariana asked hoarsely.

Dahlia grinned. "*We* are witches."

Witches. The word seeped through Vivi, as slow and sweet as Dahlia's honey-thick drawl. *Witches.* For a moment, it felt more comforting than strange, as if a part of her had always known it.

But then Vivi forced herself to return to reality. This had to be an elaborate prank, part of the hazing process or, worse, some sort of stunt to put on YouTube. Yet Vivi had spent most of her life observing charlatans like her mother, and even she was hard-pressed to imagine how the Kappas could've pulled off a trick like this.

"You were born witches," Dahlia continued. "But tonight you've taken your first step toward becoming something even more important—a sister. Kappa Rho Nu is much more than a sorority; it's the oldest, most powerful coven of witches in the country. It was founded in the seventeenth century to help women escape persecution, and over the years, it's become one of the most influential organizations in the world." She looked around the circle with a meaningful expression. "Witches are powerful on their own, but together, we're unstoppable. Over the next four years, we'll teach you how to harness and control your magic, how to unlock abilities beyond your wildest dreams. But you have to work for it." She looked at each new member, one after the next. "To become a full Kappa, you'll need to survive Hell Week. Then you must continue to impress your sisters over the weeks that follow. It's not enough to have magic; you have to become one of us."

Vivi shivered at the word *magic*. Less than an hour ago, she would've scoffed at the notion. But she couldn't think of a better term to describe what she'd just witnessed, the power she'd felt unfurling inside her.

Could she really be a *witch?* The thought was at once so intoxicating and so alarming, she couldn't keep herself from blurting out a question. "Does anyone outside of Kappa know what you . . . I mean, what *we* are?" she asked, thinking about her mother. Her heart thudded loudly. Did this mean Daphne was also a witch?

"Definitely not," Mei said with a shake of her head. "Not unless they were Ravens too."

"But during the rush party, you had lots of non-Kappas here . . . Isn't that sort of risky?" Vivi asked. She could almost *feel* magic crackling in the air, a hint of electricity like in the moments before a thunderstorm. She wondered why she'd never felt anything like it before. "What if someone notices something strange?"

Dahlia spoke up again. "Witches have been hiding in plain sight for centuries—the Ravens are just one of many covens around the country. But most people are incapable of opening their eyes to the truth. The more we act like a regular sorority with nothing to hide, the more likely we are to be left alone. That's why we became a sorority in the first place—it was the perfect cover for a coven." She looked around at the new members. "Performing magic isn't easy, and if you're not extremely careful, it can be quite dangerous. That's why each of you will be assigned a Big Sister, just like at other sororities. Except that your Big's responsibilities extend beyond ensuring that you wear the right shade of teal to spirit week. She'll tutor you in magic and make sure that you don't blow yourself—or Westerly—up." Dahlia paused while the girls snickered. "Sonali." The girl looked up and nodded. "Your Big is Mei."

Mei stood and smiled warmly, motioning for Sonali to stand next to her.

Dahlia continued with the pairings until she reached Vivi. "Vivi, your Big is Scarlett."

Vivi's heart sank. Of *course* Scarlett, the only girl who didn't seem to like her, was her Big. For the first time since she'd walked into the room, Scarlett met Vivi's gaze. The other girl's tight smile didn't reach her eyes.

But before either of them could say a word, a loud bang sounded at the front door.

CHAPTER TEN

Scarlett

All chatter ceased and everyone turned toward the front door. Dahlia, a frown marring her pretty face, caught Scarlett's eye. "Send whoever it is away. Closed ranks tonight."

Scarlett nodded once, annoyed at missing her chance to savor Vivi's visible terror at being named Scarlett's Little. Just like the magic chose the sisters, it also chose the Big-Little pairings. The cards had their own sense of poetic justice; it would now be Scarlett's sanctioned right to torture Vivi as her Little.

She flashed an ashen Vivi a smile and headed for the main entrance. They'd dimmed the hall lights and lit hurricane candles to add a certain mystique to the house for the pledges' first night here. Scarlett trailed her fingertips along one wall while her eyes adjusted to the gloom, the sounds from the living room falling away to a muted hush. The candles cast flickering shadows against the walls, the shapes reminding her of a metal candle carousel Minnie had given her for her eighth birthday. It had delicate gold stars and moons that rotated slowly around a lit tea candle, a little bit of magic before Scarlett could fully wield her own.

Bang.

The knocker sounded again, louder this time. Before Scarlett could call out that she was coming, the knob began to twist. Then the door swung open and slammed against the wall. A wild, unnatural wind whipped into the hallway, extinguishing all but two of the candles.

Scarlett gasped.

A girl stood in the entryway. Her eyes were hard and black. Her hair hung loose and flowing to her waist, but it was snarled and tangled. She wore ratty black jeans and a baggy black hoodie that looked like it hadn't been washed in weeks. On her left hand, she had five silver rings, one on each finger: A skull. A serpent. A pentacle. A rose. And a sword. Her other hand was raised in a fist, as if she'd just punched the door open. Her mouth was twisted in an angry grimace.

It was someone Scarlett had never expected to see again. But it wasn't Harper, the girl who'd been haunting her dreams. It was Harper's best friend.

Gwen.

For a second Scarlett wondered if this was a nightmare. Scarlett hadn't seen Gwen since that long-ago night. Gwen had been hooked up to life support, her body battered and bruised, machines breathing for her and keeping her alive. When she was finally released from the hospital, she'd dropped out of school and gone home to Nashville. No one had heard from her since. She was never supposed to come back.

Scarlett forced herself to inhale. Then exhale. *Breathe.*

"Holy shit, Gwen," Scarlett managed to say when she found her voice again. "What are you doing here?"

Gwen just stared at her, the fire from the remaining candles flickering in her dark eyes.

"Answer me," Scarlett said.

Gwen stayed silent, breathing heavily, as if it cost her something just to stand there.

"You can't be here. You need to leave," Scarlett said. Scarlett took a step back. Then another. She heard voices. Then a gasp, then footsteps. She turned to see Tiffany flying up the hall toward her. Behind her, a handful of the older Ravens—Etta, Hazel, and Jess—had gathered, all peering at the front door curiously.

Tiffany stepped up next to Scarlett and said, her voice steely, "What are you doing here?"

"Say something, Gwen," Scarlett said, emboldened by her sisters' presence.

Gwen opened her mouth as if to speak . . . and began to choke. It was a horrible guttural gagging sound deep in her throat. She clutched at her neck, then fell to her knees, gasping for breath.

Shit.

"Oh my God!" Jess cried.

"We need to call 911. Sh-she's choking," Scarlett stammered, rushing forward to help Gwen. The girl's face was turning red; spittle was flying from her open mouth, and her hands clawed at the ground.

"She's not," came a cool voice. Dahlia pushed through the crowd. "It's the magic."

"What?" Scarlett asked.

"Girls, join hands," Dahlia commanded, gesturing for everyone to join her on the front steps of the house.

Scarlett joined hands with Tiffany and Jess, completing the circle with her sisters. Usually being hand in hand with the coven was when she felt most powerful, most whole. But now, as she watched Gwen writhe and gasp, her face contorting painfully, Scarlett didn't feel powerful. She felt . . . scared. Scared of the ugly side of their power. Scared of what it had wrought.

"Scar, focus," Dahlia ordered as if she could sense Scarlett's hesitance. As Scarlett exhaled her panic, Dahlia began to whisper a spell. Scarlett let her magic flow into her sisters, their powers merging as the spell found its target.

Gwen's rasping stopped, like a TV switching off. The angry light in her eyes was snuffed out. Her shoulders slumped, like a marionette with her strings cut. The anger was gone, but it was as if Gwen had disappeared with it. The fire had drained from her eyes, leaving in its place a dull, vacant stare.

"Good night, Gwen," Dahlia pronounced.

Without another sound, Gwen stood up and began to march down the front walk, away from the house.

As soon as she was out of sight, Scarlett rounded on Dahlia. "What the hell was that?"

"The binding spell," Dahlia said. "The magic is very specific for this exact reason."

"What do you mean?" Scarlett asked, her stomach sinking even further.

"We didn't just strip her powers; we forbade her to talk about magic ever again. This is the consequence if she tries."

"Why is she back? More important, *how* is she back? We banished her," Mei said, glancing around at her sisters.

"We banished her from the coven, not the house," Scarlett said quietly.

"But what does she want from us?" Mei asked.

Scarlett gazed down, careful not to look at Tiffany. She concentrated on catching her breath. The way Gwen had looked at her . . . it was like she'd wanted to kill her.

"Full moon tonight," said Vivi softly. Scarlett jumped. She hadn't heard the younger girl approach. She realized with a sinking feeling that her new Little had witnessed the tail end of this mess. "My mom always said that made people do strange things."

Scarlett knew better than anyone that Gwen didn't need a full moon to act out. She had reason enough on her own. Not that that was any of Vivi's business. She felt a new wave of annoyance at her Little's intrusion into her house, into her life. "Being my Little doesn't mean you have to be my shadow, Vivi," Scarlett snapped. "Who said you could leave the party?"

"Go back inside, Vivi, and bond with your new sisters. We'll be right in," Dahlia said. Her voice was gentler than Scarlett's, but there was steel behind her words.

Vivi looked from one girl to the other, a frown tugging her mouth downward, looking like she wanted to say more. But after a moment, she heeded Dahlia's words, stepped inside, and made her way back to the living room.

"We should all go in. This is an important night for welcoming the new girls into the fold. Not another word about this until the pledges leave," Dahlia ordered with a clap. The older sisters nodded curtly, then slipped back inside, whispering among themselves. Scarlett grabbed Dahlia before the older girl could step back into the foyer.

"Dahlia," she said quietly. "The tarot cards on the door . . . it was Gwen, wasn't it?"

Before the bid ceremony, Scarlett had shown Dahlia the tarot cards she and Tiffany had found nailed to the front door. Scarlett had wanted to cast a spell to figure out who had left them—and why. Scarlett thought they were a message—a threat—but Dahlia had waved it off as a stupid prank and insisted that Scarlett get rid of the cards before the pledges arrived. "We don't want to scare them off before they've even pledged," she said. "Don't make this into something bigger than it is." After all, Dahlia pointed out, they had done a tarot-themed recruitment party last year; someone was probably still pissed that she hadn't gotten a bid. People were always jealous of the Ravens. Dahlia had promised her that their secret was safe.

Now Scarlett wasn't so sure.

Dahlia didn't look worried, though. Just irritated. She always hated when sisters challenged her authority. "We'll cast a protection seal on the house once the pledges leave. Let everyone know. We'll need all hands for the rite."

Scarlett nodded, not trusting her voice quite yet. She let go of Dahlia's arm and swung the large front door shut.

She had just gotten to the living room when she heard another heavy *thud.* Steeling herself, Scarlett stalked down the hall and wrenched the door open again. "Gwen, we told you, you can't—"

She froze. There was no one there. Rap music floated from Psi Delta Lambda House down the street. Cicadas chirped, unseen, in the grass. But the street was completely empty. Just a few parked cars and a tattered red communal campus bike propped up against an oak tree.

Then she saw it. Something small and silver glimmering in the walkway. It was one of Gwen's rings, the silver skull. It must have fallen off while she scrabbled at the ground. Scarlett moved forward to pick it up and her foot hit something soft. She glanced down and let out a shriek. At her feet was an enormous jet-black raven, its neck twisted at an unnatural angle. She recognized it from the aviary on the roof. Scarlett's heart beat wildly. This was an unequivocal sign. It meant only one thing.

Death.

CHAPTER ELEVEN

Vivi

It'd been nearly twenty-four hours since the ceremony, but Vivi's heart hadn't stopped racing. She felt almost hypnotized by a combination of power and vertigo, as if she'd launched herself off a diving board and was now falling through the air, unsure what would happen when she hit the water. Or if she'd hit it at all. Everything she thought she'd known about the world had been wrong. Magic was real. She was a witch. And she wasn't the only one.

On the short walk from her dorm to Kappa House, Vivi pulled out her phone and called her mom for the third time that day. Once again, it went straight to voicemail. She'd never minded when her mother went off the grid in the past, but this was an emergency. She had to find out how much Daphne knew about this. Was she also a witch? Were her tarot readings actually legitimate? Or was she as naïve as Vivi, unaware that magic was very, very real?

Magic. She kept remembering the pentacle blooming out of her candle flame. The buzz in her fingertips. She wanted to feel it again. To understand it. To know what she'd been missing all these years. To discover how it was going to change the rest of her life.

She used her newly issued key to let herself into Kappa House, then paused on the threshold, marveling at the fact that the interior looked completely different than it had during her previous two visits. Today, it was filled with modern, light wood furniture and cozy, blush-colored cushions that made the rooms look airy and inviting.

Vivi began walking toward the living room to wait for the others, but she'd barely made it two steps before a hand pressed against her shoulder, holding her in place. "Watch out."

It was Mei. She was standing in front of Vivi, pointing at a straight line of pinkish-gray salt on the floor that Vivi had almost walked into. In Mei's hand was a jar of what looked like crushed-up herbs floating in oil. It reminded Vivi of the rosemary olive oil her mother liked to cook with.

"Sorry, I didn't see that," Vivi said, glancing at the salt before turning her attention back to Mei. Instead of the purple tips she'd sported last night, her hair was now jet-black and cut in an angular bob that emphasized her high cheekbones. "I like your hair. Did you . . . I mean, is it . . ." She trailed off, realizing that she didn't even have the vocabulary to ask the question.

Mei smiled and tucked her hair behind her ears. "It's called a glamour. It's a spell that comes pretty easily to Pentacles like us."

The words *like us* made Vivi shiver with anticipation. "So what does that mean, exactly?" She knew the tarot suits, of course. It was impossible to grow up with Daphne Devereaux and not have a working knowledge of the major and minor arcana, but she wanted to know exactly what that meant for her—for her magic.

"Our powers fall under the Earth sign. That means it's a bit easier for us to influence or manipulate nature, whether that's trees, animals, or"—she shook her hair and struck an exaggerated modeling pose—"our natural beauty." Mei pulled her phone out of her pocket and tilted her head as if preparing to take a selfie, but as she pursed her lips, her straight bob turned into beachy waves, and her nude lipstick deepened into maroon.

"Can you teach me to do that?" Vivi asked, awestruck.

"Sure," Mei said, staring at her phone as she uploaded the photo to a verified Instagram account. Vivi had Googled all the Ravens she could remember that morning and knew that Mei was an incredibly popular beauty blogger originally from the Bay Area with nearly a million followers. "Though you should probably start out by focusing on whatever Scarlett wants to teach you."

Vivi suppressed a grimace as she imagined Scarlett's fake, condescending smile. "Shouldn't you be my Big, since we're the same suit?"

"What makes Ravens special is how our magic plays off one another. It's not what we have in common but the ways that we're different—each of our unique strengths—that make us powerful. It sounds cheesy but it's true. You have more to learn from someone different from you. Does that make sense?"

"Got it. So what's the jar for?" Vivi asked.

Mei gestured to the front door. "I'm anointing the entry points of the house. A little extra protection against those who wish us ill."

Vivi nodded, her mind flashing back to last night. She'd been on such a high after the ceremony that she'd barely processed the commotion with the dark-haired girl. But the more she thought about it, the more disturbing the incident seemed. Vivi thought she might've been the girl who'd stopped her on the quad to warn her about the Ravens, but her features had been so twisted by pain and anger, it was hard to know for sure. "Who was that girl?"

Mei pressed her lips together and glanced over her shoulder, though Vivi couldn't tell if she was looking for backup or checking to see who was in earshot. "She used to be a Raven. We removed her a couple years ago after she broke our most important rule."

"Which one?" Vivi asked, suddenly worried about what unnamed rules she might've broken already.

But Mei just smiled vaguely. "Don't worry. Scarlett's your pledge master; she'll explain everything you need to know at your lesson. She's waiting for you out in the greenhouse."

"Okay, thanks." Vivi could tell Mei didn't want to discuss the incident further, but Vivi couldn't quite banish it from her mind, couldn't shake the image of the girl's frantic expression or the image of her writhing on the front steps, trying to claw her way into the house.

All she knew was that she didn't want to end up like her, on the outside looking in.

Vivi hadn't spent much time in greenhouses, but even she could tell that this one was extraordinary. Despite the glass walls, it was surprisingly dark; everywhere she looked, enormous plants stretched out of large clay pots, their ample leaves casting myriad shadows.

She inhaled, noting the unusual combination of scents: lavender, pepper, mint, ripe fruit, sage, and a hint of rot.

Four other pledges were already seated at a round table in the center of the greenhouse—Ariana, Bailey, Sonali, and Reagan. It took Vivi a minute to reach them since there was no clear path through the plants; she had to duck under a number of climbing vines, their dew-covered leaves brushing against the back of her neck.

She slid into the open seat between Sonali and Bailey just as Scarlett appeared carrying a woven basket covered with a gauzy purple scarf. "Welcome, ladies," Scarlett said briskly as she reached into the basket and began setting items on the table. A few squat red candles. An engraved silver dish. A midnight-black feather. Across from Vivi, Ariana shuddered as Scarlett placed a final item on the table—a human skull—but Vivi nearly lurched forward with anticipation. This was it. After a lifetime on the periphery, she was going to learn the most powerful, closely guarded secret in the world—how to do real magic.

"The five of you have been invited to pledge Kappa because we sense promise in you." Scarlett's gaze drifted to each of them, lingering on Vivi the longest. For some reason, Vivi didn't find this comforting. "But natural ability isn't the only thing that matters when it comes to witchcraft. Magic requires discipline. Magic can be your best friend. It can open doors for you—literally. Or it can make you a danger to yourself and everyone around you." As if to illustrate her point, all the plants in the greenhouse began to sway and whisper, moving in an invisible wind. Vivi gasped as something brushed the top of her foot. She glanced down and then leaped to the side as something long and dark green slithered past her.

"It's just a vine," Bailey whispered, watching it with wide eyes.

Scarlett snapped her fingers and all the plants froze. "But before we go further, it's essential that you understand and commit to our laws. The first is no infringing on anyone else's free will . . . too much."

"What does that mean, exactly?" Bailey asked, blinking behind her black glasses.

"That means distraction spells and influencing spells are okay, within reason. But we don't use mind-control spells or spell people to make them behave in ways that could change the course of their lives or bring harm to them in any way," Scarlett said. "The next law is that we don't physically harm anyone unless it's in self-defense. And of course, the third and most important law—"

"Never betray your fellow Ravens," Sonali said quickly.

Scarlett nodded. "That rule isn't just about magic. We have each other's backs, no matter what. These girls are your sisters. When they need you, you help them. You walk in pairs at night, and you check in at parties. Never let a sister wander off alone at night after they've been drinking, and never, under any circumstances, go to a private room during a frat party. Remember that alcohol clouds judgment *and* magical abilities, and your safety is paramount."

Scarlett paused as if to let her words sink in, then continued. "Most of the magic we perform is spell-based. You'll start by learning your own minor arcana spells—those are the simple, everyday spells. We'll save your major arcana—big, complex spells—for later in your training. The first thing you need is your own tarot deck." Scarlett reached into the basket and placed eight different decks on the table. "Pick the one that calls to you."

A few of the decks were familiar to Vivi from her mother's readings, with bright, lurid art and figures in exaggerated poses. She reached out to run her fingers along a deck with lavender backs and delicate, black-and-white line art. But before she could pick up the cards to examine them further, something glinted in the corner of her vision. It was a stack of rich brown cards with gold-leaf drawings that shimmered like jewels, although there was barely any light for them to reflect. She brushed her fingertips against the top card and exhaled as a strange, soothing sensation spread through her, like sinking into an unexpectedly soft bed.

"Shuffle the cards and then place the top two figures face-down on the table," Scarlett ordered. The pledges did as they were told. "Now turn them over."

With slightly trembling hands, Vivi flipped her cards over to reveal the Fool and the Empress.

"Holy shit," Bailey whispered next to her. Vivi glanced over to see the same two figures in front of her. The pledges exchanged excited, nervous looks as they realized what had happened. They'd all drawn the exact same cards.

"The Fool represents an innocent, naïve being at the start of a journey. That's you all," Scarlett said, clearly unsurprised by what had just transpired. "The Empress is the goddess incarnate. These are the two major arcana forces you'll need to channel to cast your first spells, though I'm going to give each of you a different challenge, depending on your respective suits."

"Will we always need the cards with us to perform a spell?" Bailey asked, still transfixed by her new deck.

"No," Scarlett said. "The most powerful Ravens can summon the magic of any suit. And, with practice, all of you will be able to perform your own suit's spells without the cards. At least, those of you who become full-fledged Ravens." She caught Vivi's eye. "Because some of you probably won't make it that far." She turned to Sonali. "Okay, Sonali, you're up first. Please turn over a third card."

Sonali did as she was told, revealing the Queen of Swords, the same card she'd drawn last night. "Ready to conjure the magic of a Swords witch?" Scarlett asked. "Repeat after me: 'I call to the Queen of Swords, wise and fair. Lend me your power to summon the air.'"

Her voice quavering slightly, Sonali repeated the words. Nothing happened.

"It's okay," Scarlett said, sounding unusually kind. "Right now, they're just words. In order to turn them into a spell, you have to speak with more than your lips and breath. You need to feel the words come out of your heart." It was something Vivi could picture Daphne saying while trying to con one of her clients, but here in Kappa House, it was enough to make Vivi's skin tingle.

Sonali took a deep breath, and when she spoke again, her voice was steady and sonorous. "I call to the Queen of Swords, wise and fair. Lend me your power to summon the air." The temperature in the greenhouse seemed to drop, and the air became heavy, like it did right before a thunderstorm. Vivi could've sworn she felt a breeze on the back of her neck, but that was impossible; all the greenhouse windows were shut tight.

Yet to Vivi's amazement, the plants around her began to sway as a soft but unmistakable wind blew through the greenhouse, building slowly until Sonali's hair flew out behind her.

No one spoke. No one even breathed until Scarlett smiled and said, "Well done, Sonali," as if she'd just returned a tricky tennis serve instead of bending the rules of nature. "Bailey? Please turn over your third card."

It was the Queen of Wands, the Fire sign Bailey had drawn during the first test. "For centuries, new Wands witches have started their magical training with a simple fire-summoning spell," Scarlett explained. "Now focus your energy on one of the candles and repeat after me: 'I call to the Queen of Wands. Show me your might by giving us light.'"

Bailey took a deep breath and said, "I call to the Queen of Wands. Show me your might by giving us light." The final word had barely left her mouth when smoke began to curl up from the wick in front of her, and a moment later, the candle sparked to life. Bailey stared at it in disbelief, then her face broke into a huge smile. "I still believe that worked. How the hell am I supposed to go back to physics class after this?"

As Scarlett made her way around the circle of pledges, Vivi's heart began to beat so quickly, it was hard to catch her breath. She was desperate to try her first spell and utterly terrified that it wouldn't work, that'd she be revealed as a fraud, forcing the Ravens to wipe her memory. She couldn't go back to her normal life after getting a taste of something so extraordinary.

When it was finally Vivi's turn, she flipped over her third card to reveal the Queen of Pentacles. Even though she'd expected it by this point, the power of the cards still made her shiver.

Scarlett reached into her basket and produced a small pot filled with dirt. "You're a Pentacles, so your magic is rooted in nature," Scarlett said, handing Vivi the pot. "I planted a seed in here. I want you to make it grow by repeating after me: 'I call to the Queen of Earth. Show us your power over death and rebirth.'"

"Okay," Vivi said, trying to steady her nerves. "I call to the Queen of Earth. Show us your power over death and rebirth."

Nothing happened.

"Try again," Scarlett said. "And take your time. You're casting a spell, not ordering at McDonald's."

Vivi took as deep a breath as her nerves would allow and repeated the words more slowly. The dirt remained resolutely still.

Scarlett crossed her arms and looked exasperated. "Do you know what it feels like to tap into your magic?"

Vivi thought back to the moment the sparkler crackled to life, to the energy that flowed through her veins. Another memory sprang to mind on its heels, unbidden. Mason touching her arm. That same spark. Throat tight, worried Scarlett might be able to peer inside her head and see her traitorous thoughts, Vivi forced herself to nod.

"Summon that feeling again."

Vivi shut her eyes, trying not to care if she looked ridiculous. She reached for the memory of the sparkler once more. She thought about the way her fingertips had tingled. The same way they had when she'd touched the tarot card last night.

It felt like a static shock or that time she'd accidentally touched the low-level electrified fence around the pond by their house in Oregon. It made her scalp tickle. The itch crawled down the back of her neck, ran along her arms and down her spine, like millions of goose bumps all at once.

"Now focus it," Scarlett said. It sounded as though her voice came from somewhere far, far away. "Think about what you want to see happen. *Believe* that it will happen."

Vivi felt something vibrate in her chest, and when she began to speak, her voice sounded rich and powerful. "I call to the Queen of Earth. Show us your power over death and rebirth." The pot trembled slightly and Vivi gripped it tighter. She could almost sense a faint pulse, like a heartbeat, and an image flashed through her mind—a quivering seed with delicate roots unfurling.

Vivi opened her eyes. Her hands felt shaky, her energy drained, as if she'd just run a long, hard sprint. But in front of her was a tiny sapling, no taller than her pinkie finger, with a single green leaf on top. A plant she'd grown through magic.

Vivi was on such a high after their lesson that it took her hours to stop beaming. Even Scarlett's chilly attitude toward her couldn't dampen her spirits. It was one thing to be told you were a witch. It was quite another to perform real magic. Her already goofy grin widened as she tried to imagine what else she could do with her powers. Could she create gourmet dishes without ever learning how to cook? Transform her dorm room into the height of luxury? Turn her roommate invisible?

But now, as she sat with the other girls in the science library at three a.m., she felt her buzz beginning to fade. For the second part of their training session, Scarlett had sent them off to study spell books that had been enchanted to look like dull, dog-eared organic chemistry textbooks to non-witches. "You have twenty-four hours to memorize every spell in this grimoire," Scarlett had said. "Tomorrow night, same time, meet me back here for your next test."

Unlike the rest of the historic campus, the science library was a modern, soulless, fourteen-story rectangle. Each floor was painted according to the pH scale. They were at a table on the first floor, the only students in sight. No one else had to pull an all-nighter during the first week of school. Even the librarian had gone home.

"It's humanly impossible to memorize this in one night," Reagan said as she shut her book with frustration.

"It's much more fun than real organic chemistry, trust me," Bailey said, staring at her grimoire in awe. She pointed at a spell printed in gold ink above a trio of gem-toned tarot cards that reminded Vivi of an illuminated medieval manuscript. "This is a spell to silence the voice of your enemy. Can you imagine?"

"I wonder if I can use it on my roommate," Reagan said as she leaned over for a better look. "She calls her boyfriend in Texas every night and spends hours recounting the banal details of her pointless life."

"That's a little mean, isn't it?" Sonali said.

Reagan fixed her with a glare. "She tells him everything she ate that day. Literally *everything,* like 'I went to the dining hall and had cereal with half a banana, and then for lunch I went to that bagel place but they were out of cinnamon raisin, so I—'"

"Oh God, make it stop," Sonali cut in as she rubbed her temples. "You're right. That's insufferable."

"I don't even know what language this is," Ariana said groggily as she frowned at her grimoire. "Is it ancient Greek?"

"I think so," Sonali said, leaning in for a closer look. Unlike the others, she'd seemed to grow more wired as the night went on, muttering to herself as she pored over the spells. "My mom was a Raven but she never said anything about memorizing an entire spell book overnight. Maybe she blocked it from her memory?"

"Or maybe she didn't want to scare you away from pledging?" Bailey said as she closed her eyes and rolled her shoulders back a few times.

Sonali let out a snort. "Hardly. It was, like, the number-one topic of conversation. She made it pretty clear that if I didn't get a bid, she'd disown me."

"This is a waste of time, trust me," Reagan said, then yawned. She stretched her arms over her head, causing her crop top to rise up even higher. "My mom and aunts are all brilliant witches, and I don't think they ever memorized any spells. Once you learn how to harness your magic, you don't ever have to look at a book again."

"What was it like, growing up with witches?" Bailey asked, suddenly alert again.

Reagan shrugged. "I never knew anything else."

Just then, Vivi's phone buzzed, startling her. No one called her, ever. Especially not in the middle of the night. But when she saw the name on the screen, she snatched her phone and hurried toward a bank of chairs on the other side of the room.

"Mom?" she whispered as she rushed away from the table and turned into the dark hallway. "Is everything okay?"

"Honey, I just got your voicemails." There was a crackling sound on the other end of the line that sounded like waves. "Sorry I couldn't call sooner. I've been trying this new immersive meditation technique that—"

"Mom," Vivi cut in. "Why didn't you tell me I'm a witch?"

There was a long pause.

"Mom, are you still there?" She stepped closer to a window, hoping for a better cell signal. This side of the library faced a thick cluster of trees and a small quad edged with administrative buildings.

"I did tell you, Vivi. You just weren't ready to hear it."

You're special, Vivi. You're full of magic. Daphne had spent Vivi's whole childhood repeating phrases like that. Vivi just hadn't known it was *real*. "Does that mean you're also a witch?"

"I have some . . . heightened abilities, but my powers are nothing like yours, darling."

"Why would you keep all this a secret from me?" Vivi snapped, suddenly shaking with frustration. "There's an entire sorority here full of witches and I might not make the cut because I don't know what the hell I'm doing."

Daphne was silent for so long that Vivi wondered if she'd hung up. "Mom? Are you there?"

"Vivian, listen to me: There are many ways to be a witch. Don't fall into the trap of thinking there is only one path forward."

"Their path is looking a whole lot better than your path." Vivi knew that would hurt her but right now, she was too angry to care. "These girls are incredible. They're going to run the world one day. I think some of them already are."

There was another long pause. "You need to be really careful, Vivi. You don't know what power does to people. I've seen it. You can't trust any of those so-called sorority witches."

Vivi felt a surge of anger burn its way through her foggy exhaustion. "At least they took the time to tell me I *was* a witch. Right now, it seems like they're the ones looking out for me." Furious, she ended the call.

The Ravens weren't the problem. Daphne was, just like she'd always been.

Vivi was about to rejoin the other pledges when something screeched outside the window. Startled, she wheeled around and craned her head for a closer look but saw nothing except for the shadowy outline of tree branches.

A few seconds later, the screeching noise came again, but there was still no sign of movement among the branches. "What the hell?" Vivi muttered. She was starting to inch forward when something slammed against the glass with a gruesome *thwack*. Vivi leaped back, heart pounding. She realized with a start that it was a moth, the largest she'd ever seen. It was banging furiously against the glass, so hard the pane rattled. Its wings were light brown, and there was a white shape in the middle.

A shape that looked exactly like a grinning skull.

Vivi gasped and dropped her phone, which skidded across the smooth floor. Before she could reach for it, the dim ceiling lights flickered and went out, shrouding the hallway in darkness.

"Shit." With a groan, Vivi crouched down and began to feel her way along the floor, praying that the next thing her fingers brushed against would be her phone. "Sonali?" she called. "Ariana? Are you guys in there?" Perhaps the other girls had been still for too long and the sensors had turned the lights off. Except that the large windows were also dark; the lights on the quad had been extinguished, and the lights illuminating the bell tower were out too. An eerie feeling settled over Vivi as she waited for her eyes to adjust. But the dark was too heavy, too complete; it was like she was locked in an underground vault. "Ariana!" she cried.

A chair scraped in the distance. "Vivi?" Ariana called. "Where are you?"

"In the hallway. I . . . I don't think we're alone," Vivi called back, her voice quivering. She remembered the girl who'd arrived at Kappa House the night before, the madness in her wide eyes. "I dropped my phone and can't see anything."

"Stay there. We're coming!"

But before the pledges could reach her, the front door to the library banged open.

"Who's there?" Vivi shouted, pressing her back against the wall. "What do you want?" She groped around wildly, trying to get her bearings. Then hands grabbed her shoulders roughly, and Vivi screamed at the top of her lungs.

"Happy Hell Week, witches!" a chorus of voices shouted in her ear.

All at once, the lights snapped back on. Scarlett, Tiffany, Mei, and Dahlia stood before her, along with the rest of the sorority's upperclassmen. The older girls were all grinning while Vivi and the other pledges, who'd just burst into the hallway, stood dumbly, blinking in the bright lights.

"This week, you'll be asked to do impossible things," Scarlett said. This time, her smile was bright and genuine. Contagious.

In spite of her still-racing pulse, Vivi started to smile too.

"If you can't hack it, you'll never be able to so much as mention magic again." Scarlett's gaze settled on Vivi. "But if you survive this week? Maybe we'll make a witch of you yet."

CHAPTER TWELVE

Scarlett

"You want me to do *what?*" Vivi gaped at her.

Scarlett eyed her calmly and explained. "Dean Sanderson reprimanded Hazel for protesting the male-only lineup of speakers on Class Day."

"That's terrible, but that doesn't sound like cause for . . . I mean, couldn't we just paint the admin building pink? Boycott Class Day?" Vivi asked.

Scarlett paused dramatically, then went in for the kill. "We protect our sisters above all. Which is why I want you to bring me the dean's heart."

"I thought we weren't supposed to harm anyone," Vivi said carefully, watching Scarlett with wide eyes, like someone afraid of upsetting a deranged killer.

Scarlett couldn't help it. The corners of her mouth twitched into a faint smirk.

Vivi sighed as her cheeks flushed bright red. "Oh. That was a joke."

Scarlett burst into laughter. "You should've seen your face." She doubted there had ever been such a naïve witch. And for what felt like the thousandth time, she wondered how someone so freaking simple could have made Mason forget their date. Part of Scarlett knew she was being unfair, but something about the girl rubbed her the wrong way, and it was more than seeing her talking to Mason. She was too eager, somehow. Too innocent, too . . . free. She'd lived a lifetime without the weight of expectation. This was all new and exciting to her. Scarlett couldn't tell if she envied her or hated her for that. All she knew was that she was going to enjoy every second of Hell Week.

Scarlett pointed to the staircase. "Second floor, third door on the left. Do be thorough."

"What?"

"Our bathroom. That's your task."

The embarrassment on Vivi's face faded away, replaced by a glare. "Let me guess: I have to do it with nothing but a toothbrush?"

Scarlett stared at the girl, deadpan and unamused. "No, Vivian, you're supposed to use magic."

Vivi stood there an extra beat, hesitant.

"Don't worry, Moaning Myrtle isn't in there," Scarlett said. She saw a flash of concern cross Vivi's face, as if she was seriously expecting the ghost that lived in the Hogwarts bathroom to have taken up residence in their sorority house.

She waited until Vivi had tromped up the main staircase before she traded grins with Tiffany, who was sprawled across the sofa next to her. Tiffany slow-clapped for her.

"You're wicked," Tiffany said.

"Why do you think we're friends?"

Tiffany swatted her arm. "What's in store for Little House on the Prairie, anyway? Did you go with blood or bugs?" Tiffany asked, looking up the stairs.

"Mold," Scarlett said, feeling a little embarrassed now for giving her a softball. If Gwen hadn't shown up on Tuesday night, Scarlett would have probably created a scary spell instead of a tedious one, like spell something Vivi was afraid of to climb out of the toilet. But given everything that had happened the other night, she just . . . couldn't.

Tiffany crinkled up her nose in judgment. "Don't tell me you're going soft, Winter."

"Never. I just want to lull her into a sense of security before I pounce," Scarlett said. Tiffany nodded, not looking entirely convinced. "Where's your Little?" Scarlett hadn't seen Ariana all day. The other pledges had been busy running errands for their individual Bigs—all of them except Bailey, who'd really lucked out to score Etta as her Big. The two had spent all day together in the kitchen, giggling and mixing up some new hair-relaxing potion Etta had been eager to try.

"Sent her to hex the boys over at Alpha Tau Pi."

"That'll piss off Dahlia," Scarlett pointed out. Dahlia was the type of president who wanted to know—and control—everything that was going on in the house. If you were planning to go off script, it was understood that you would tell her first. "Unless they did something to you that you're retaliating for . . ."

"Relax. The spell I gave her is a dud." Tiffany smirked. "All it'll actually do is make her hallucinate blood all over her hands for the next hour."

Scarlett snickered. "*You* are the wicked one."

Her best friend donned an innocent expression. "I'm just trying to teach my Little early on about the importance of magical law. If you curse someone else, there's almost always an unintended rebound on yourself."

Scarlett sighed. "When you touch evil, it touches you." She could still hear Minnie's voice in her head after all this time.

Tiffany darted a glance around the living room. But they were alone. "Scar," she murmured. "You need to stop fixating on that. It's in the past."

"But it's not, Tiff. The present is right here, on this campus. Gwen is *back*. I can't stop thinking about her face the other night. She looked so out of control, so desperate." Scarlett frowned. She thought of all the strange things that had happened since she'd arrived back on campus. The necklace on her balcony. The footsteps following her in the forest. The tarot cards on the door. Was it possible that it was all Gwen?

"After her . . . *fit,* there is no way she will dare come near us again," Tiffany said firmly. She tightened her ponytail. "I'll never understand why she was admitted to Kappa in the first place. Anyone could see that she was a serious bitch."

But Tiffany's words only made Scarlett's frown deepen. Scarlett had actually liked Gwen at first. She didn't have the years of polish that Scarlett had. And her style was more earthy than Southern belle, but she was smart and powerful and she had a caustic tongue that always made Scarlett laugh—until she turned it on Scarlett's best friend. Gwen was also a Swords and she and Tiffany were always in some unspoken competition to be the strongest Swords in the house. It had gotten really ugly by the end.

"I can't stop picturing her; it was like she was being strangled." Scarlett winced. "Our magic did that."

"You do remember what she did to me, right?" Tiffany grumbled.

"I know, Tiff."

"If we hadn't stopped her, who knows what else she would have done, who else she would have hurt?" Tiffany grabbed Scarlett's hands. "Scar. What happened to Harper was awful, but thank God no one else got hurt."

Scarlett's memory raced back to their freshman year, to an ordinary party at Psi Delt. To the day she tried never to think about. To the day that Harper died. It had started like any other. Gwen had been standing on the balcony overlooking the frat's backyard and Harper had joined her.

It all happened so fast. There had been so much magic. So much terror. And then . . .

All she remembered was Harper's face. Her terrible scream. The fear in her eyes as the balcony plunged to the earth.

A minute later, she was dead.

And it was all Scarlett and Tiffany's fault.

"It was an accident, Scarlett," Tiffany whispered. "Nothing would've brought Harper back. And we made sure Gwen could never hurt anyone again."

And that she could never tell what we did.

Scarlett sighed. "I just . . . sometimes I can't help wondering—"

When you touch death, it touches back. "Maybe we should have kept her here," she finished.

Tiffany gave her an incredulous look. "Where? Locked up in the basement? You really are wicked, sister."

"No, I mean we could have cast another spell, banished her from campus. Or—"

"If we'd heaped any more magic on her, I don't think she could have survived it," Tiffany cut in.

"But what if what we created is worse than what she was before?" Scarlett asked, giving voice to her fear.

"Not possible," Tiffany said firmly. "You worry too much, Scar. Maybe you're the one we should cast a spell on."

"What?" Scarlett looked up sharply.

"You're having nightmares," Tiffany said in a gentler tone. "Maybe a little forgetting spell would take the edge off."

Scarlett shook her head. As much as she wanted to forget, she didn't want to be caught unaware. If Gwen showed up again, Scarlett needed to see her coming.

"All done," Vivi announced loudly from the top of the staircase.

Scarlett startled—she'd forgotten all about her Little—and rose to her feet. "Let's see it."

She flashed a backwards glance at Tiffany, who was already getting to her feet. Most likely to wash some magical blood off her Little.

"Hey, Scarlett. Just try and chill, okay? Nothing's going to touch us."

Scarlett gave Tiffany a small nod before heading upstairs to join Vivi. To her surprise, her Little wasn't kidding. The whole bathroom was spotless from top to bottom. The clawfoot tub sparkled, its brass fixtures shiny as gold. The sink was missing its usual collection of smudged beauty products around the circumference, and even the mirror had been polished so brightly that Scarlett's reflection in it seemed to glow.

"Well?" Vivi bounced nervously at her elbow, clearly looking for a pat on the head and a reward.

She wasn't going to get one from Scarlett. "You missed a spot," Scarlett said.

"Where—" Vivi started.

But Scarlett was already concentrating her strength, tapping into her sisters' Pentacles magic. With a whisper, she brushed her hand along the tiled wall next to the bathtub, and mossy green mold sprang up beneath her palm. It followed the trail of her hand all the way along the wall to the doorway.

"When you're finished, get ready for the PiKa mixer tonight," Scarlett called over her shoulder. "And do me a favor: do not show up looking like JoJo Siwa. There's a point where someone is so adorable, you just want to kill them, you know? Think magical glow-up, okay?"

Technically it was Scarlett's job to make over Vivi for the mixer, which was James Bond–themed, which meant tuxes for the boys and glam for the girls. Some Bigs dressed their Littles up like they were their own personal Barbies, and Scarlett knew it was her responsibility to make sure that Vivi looked a lot less, well, like Vivi for the party. But truthfully, all she wanted to do was make Vivi disappear. A voice in the back of her head—Minnie's voice—knew it wasn't right. Knew that it wasn't how Scarlett herself had been treated back when she was a pledge. Knew it wasn't what a real leader did.

When Scarlett was a freshman, Dahlia had taken her upstairs to her room to make her over for her first mixer. Dahlia had raised her hand, then lowered it at once. "Don't tell anyone I said this, but I wouldn't change a thing. Winters are as advertised. Perfection." After a beat, she added, "Time will tell if you are as powerful as you are pretty."

If only she really knew. Scarlett left Vivi in the bathroom, went to her bedroom, and crossed to the small altar she had set up beneath her window box. Whatever Tiffany might say, there was something more to Gwen's return. She must have tried to come back to Kappa House for a reason. And Scarlett couldn't stop thinking about the horrible choking sounds Gwen made.

What was she trying to say? Was she trying to . . . tell?

She plucked the pure black onyx scrying bowl from her altar. Next to it, she kept a jug of water collected from the stream that ran behind the house and charged under the full moon. She filled the bowl and sat cross-legged before her altar, eyes closed, breathing in through her nose, out through her mouth, as she visualized golden light cleansing the space.

After a few more deep breaths, she opened her eyes and gazed into the bowl that she cradled between her palms. The onyx bowl slowly warmed beneath her touch, and the surface of the water rippled from her breath.

"I call to the Queen of Swords and to the Star," she whispered to the magic in her veins, the crackle in the air. "Reveal my enemy's thoughts from afar."

For a breath, nothing happened.

And then, all at once, the lights in the room were extinguished. There was just enough light seeping in through the windows for Scarlett to see, all too terribly, what was happening.

Something crept up her hands where she gripped the bowl.

With a shout, she dropped it, and oozing liquid splashed from it, staining her carpet. It looked dark and bloody, like viscera. As she watched, it spread, leeching into the carpet, staining the walls, her hands, her arms.

With it came a horrible, icy feeling. It gripped her wrists, burrowed deep in her veins. As much as it scared her, Scarlett recognized this feeling. She'd brushed up against it before, though never this fiercely. It went deeper than anger, deeper than hatred.

This was *loathing*. Pure and simple.

"What is that?" Vivi asked, her voice a mixture of wonder and fear.

Scarlett gasped and pushed back against the magic, breaking its hold. The illusion shattered. At once, the lights flickered on overhead. The cold sensation melted away, and Scarlett trembled in its wake. The bloody stains on her carpet and hands vanished too, leaving only clear spring water soaking her floor. And there was Vivi in the doorway, apparently having seen it all.

"Are you all right?" Vivi took a step closer, brow furrowing with concern. "Do you need me to get help?"

"I'm fine," Scarlett rasped, her voice low in her throat, almost a growl. She coughed, shook her head as if to clear it. She shouldn't have been so impatient. She should have waited for Vivi to be out of the house before she tried the spell. This was the second time Vivi had seen something she shouldn't have. And this time it could have been avoided. She wouldn't make that mistake again. She turned away. "Go. Get ready," Scarlett commanded.

"Scarlett—"

When she turned around, she found Vivi still lingering, a worried look on her face. For some reason, that infuriated Scarlett more than anything else. Maybe because Vivi's expression edged just a little too close to *pity*. "I said *go!*"

CHAPTER THIRTEEN

Vivi

PiKa House looked exactly how Vivi had always imagined a frat house would look. The exterior was a stately red brick with thick white columns and Greek letters stamped prominently above the portico. There was a green, spray-painted bench on the lawn, a half-crushed Ping-Pong ball in the grass, and what looked like a pair of boxers tangled in the bushes that lined the front of the house. The air wafting through the open door smelled faintly of stale beer and boy, and music pulsed through the windows.

Vivi took a deep breath and steeled herself. She had now officially been to one party, but this was the first one with actual college boys. The mixer was for four of the most prominent frats and sororities: Psi Delta Lambda, Kappa Rho Nu, Theta Omega Xi, and PiKa, which Vivi had learned was Mason's fraternity. The thought of seeing him again made her stomach twist with a combination of excitement and lingering shame. Had he been able to tell that she'd been doing her pathetic best to flirt with him? Was that why he'd acted so strange and hurried off once Scarlett arrived? For a moment, the thought of crossing the threshold of PiKa House felt more daunting than performing magic for the first time—if she couldn't manage a conversation with one boy without embarrassing herself, what would she do with a whole houseful of them?

Yet, while this was her first coed party, it was also her first time walking into a room with all of Kappa at her back. The second Vivi stepped inside with her new sisters, she understood what real power felt like. The whole party went quiet and every pair of eyes in the room swiveled to them. But it wasn't the angry, mistrustful stares Vivi was used to receiving as the perpetual new girl. People looked at them with desire. Like they'd give anything to *be* them.

Scarlett had gone MIA during the party prep, so before leaving Kappa House, Mei had pulled Vivi into her room and surveyed her critically. "Is it hopeless?" Vivi asked nervously, glancing down at the outfit she'd chosen after consulting with Ariana. "Work your magic—give me whatever I need."

Mei smiled. "It's not that dire. Trust me."

Vivi gave her a skeptical look. "Sure, as long as I don't stand next to you at any point tonight."

Mei closed her eyes and her elaborate makeup and hairstyle melted away, leaving her still beautiful but barefaced and unglamoured. "This is the skin I was born in," she said, then reached out to touch Vivi's arm. "This is the skin *you* were born in. Embrace it. Wield it. Change it at will. It is your instrument, but you are not defined by it—you define it, you can choose. That's what it means to be a Raven."

In the end, Mei had given her a quick "polish," as she called it, using simple glamours to lengthen Vivi's lashes, add extra shine to her hair, and alter her jeans so they clung more closely to her hips and legs. It was nothing that Vivi couldn't have conceivably achieved on her own through expensive trips to the salon and the tailor, but she'd never had the money or inclination to do anything like that. To say nothing of anyone to go with. But these simple changes were enough to make Vivi feel like a completely different person. Instead of shuffling with her eyes down, trying to avoid attention, Vivi entered the party with her head held high.

Two Theta pledges Vivi recognized from her biology class smiled and waved, bright-eyed with hope. When Vivi smiled and raised a hand to them, they giggled and whispered to each other, like they'd just been greeted by a celebrity. Next to her, Reagan was pretending to ignore the PiKa brothers ogling her from the couch as she made a show of tossing her long red curls over her shoulder.

Bailey's eyes were bright behind her glasses, and even the normally reserved Sonali seemed to relax as the girls moved through the front room. "I could get used to this," she whispered to Vivi as she began to move her hips in time to the thrumming music.

"Me too," Vivi said, trying to ignore a prickle of uncertainty. "If I flunk out of Kappa, I hope I still remember how cool I felt for this one week."

"Oh, come on," Reagan said with an exasperated smile. "You're *not* going to flunk out."

"I don't know. Scarlett is on a one-woman mission to get me to de-pledge."

"It's not personal. It's just Hell Week. Tiffany made me hallucinate blood," Ariana said, shivering slightly.

"I wonder how she did that," Bailey said curiously. The reveal that magic was real had short-circuited her scientist brain and she seemed to be treating the whole rush process like one big experiment.

"How are things going for you, Reagan?" Vivi asked. Of her four fellow pledges, Reagan was the hardest for Vivi to get a read on. She was from a prominent family of Southern witches who hadn't attended Westerly but who wielded substantial power.

"Fine," she said with a shrug as she surveyed the room, clearly more interested in the frat boys than in talking about her training. "I've been doing these sorts of spells since I could walk."

"Lucky. Scarlett sicced her bathroom mold on me." Vivi hesitated as she recalled what had happened in Scarlett's room. She hadn't been able to banish the image of Scarlett's terrified face as the strange stain spread up her arms. Just thinking about it made the back of her neck prickle like it used to when Daphne left her alone in the rambling Victorian house they once rented in Baton Rouge, and Vivi heard strange noises coming from the attic. "I saw something a little . . . weird. Scarlett was working on this spell and I think it backfired or something. It almost looked like blood was creeping up her arms?"

Sonali's eyes widened. "Are you sure? That sounds like wicked magic."

Wicked magic. The words perfectly described what Vivi had felt in Scarlett's room, the strange combination of menace and power, as if the air were full of thousands of invisible snakes waiting to strike.

"I don't know. Would Scarlett really perform wicked magic?" Vivi asked. Her Big certainly had a mean-girl streak, but the fact that she was a bully who put more effort into her hair than training her Little didn't mean she was evil.

"Only if it got me a discount at Lilly Pulitzer," a falsely cheery voice said.

Scarlett. *Shit.*

As usual, she looked absolutely flawless. Her golden-brown skin glowed. Her hair fell in waves around her face. Her blush-colored lace dress cinched perfectly at her waist. She held an actual cocktail glass in her hand, unlike the red Solo cups everyone else was sipping from.

"No, you're right, I'm sorry," Vivi said, backpedaling immediately. "I just wasn't sure what I saw."

"Hmm." Scarlett cocked her head to the side. "Well, it's best to keep matters of the sisterhood *in* the sisterhood unless you cast a distraction spell first. Which, of course, you don't know how to do yet."

Vivi's cheeks began to burn. "Right, yes, I understand. It won't happen again."

"Good." With that, she brushed past the pledges and went to join Dahlia and Tiffany, who were talking to a group of admiring guys.

Including Mason.

Vivi looked away before he had time to catch her eye. "Ugh," she groaned as she turned back to the others. "I can't believe I did that."

"It wasn't that bad," Ariana said reassuringly.

Reagan laughed. "I'm sorry, but she just accused her Big of performing wicked magic. It was bad."

Vivi put her face in her hands.

"Come on. You need a drink," Bailey said, hooking her arm through Vivi's. "And I need to talk to the Drake look-alike near the Ping-Pong table."

Vivi let Bailey steer her toward the drinks area. She'd been expecting a battered wood card table with bottles of cheap vodka, but PiKa had an actual wet bar made of gleaming oak that wrapped around a corner of the room. It was fully stocked with taps, dozens of bottles of hard liquor, and colorful spirits that Vivi had never heard of before. The only indication that they were at a frat party and not at a bar in downtown Savannah were the red Solo cups. Three pledges manned the bar and, Vivi noticed, gave more generous pours to Hazel and Etta than they gave to two pretty girls from Theta.

"What can I get you?" A cute brown-skinned boy with hazel eyes leaned over the counter and smiled at Vivi.

Vivi had no idea. She'd never actually ordered a drink before.

"Five shots of tequila," Reagan said with a wicked grin.

"Reagan, no," Ariana groaned.

"We have to. It's our first mixer. It's basically a rite of passage."

"What, getting drunk and puking?" Sonali said.

"Good thing I've already mastered the art of bathroom cleaning," Vivi said grimly.

"We'll have five mint juleps," Ariana said, ignoring Reagan's eye roll as she handed each girl a red Solo cup while the bartender mixed the drinks.

When she got hers, Vivi took a tentative sip and grimaced. "Okay, I'm sorry, but this tastes like paint thinner."

"Hold on a sec," Ariana said, and ushered them to the corner where a series of paddles lined the wall, each etched with a year, dating back to the early 1900s. "Boys cannot be trusted with flavor profiles. I'm going to try something Etta taught me." She placed one hand over Vivi's cup and whispered, "I call to the Queen of Wands and Ace of Cups. Show that your powers are true by perfecting this brew."

"There's no way that's a real spell," Bailey said.

Ariana raised an eyebrow as the cup began to tremble slightly, then nodded at Vivi. "Try it."

Vivi braced for another burning swallow, but this time, the frothy concoction tasted refreshing and sweet. "Whoa," she said, feeling her eyes widen as she looked from the cup to Ariana, who was smiling smugly.

"Just be careful," Ariana said airily. "I'm pretty sure it still has the same alcohol content as the paint thinner."

"Mine next!" Reagan said, holding out her drink. Ariana went to work on everyone's cup.

"Do all the spells rhyme?" Bailey asked Sonali. She shrugged and took a big gulp of her drink.

New and improved drinks in hand, the pledges navigated through the party, drifting between clusters of other Ravens. They were easy to find—always surrounded by a gaggle of fans or being admired from a distance.

They wound up at the edges of the party beside Jess and her girlfriend, Juliet.

"Come on." Jess tugged on Juliet's hand. "Dance with me."

"Someone needs to keep an eye out," Juliet said, looking around the room warily.

"Oh, relax. We don't need a bodyguard tonight. But *I* need someone to dance with me before I'm forced to go waste my evening with a PiKa guy with wandering hands."

Juliet reluctantly followed Jess to the middle of the room, though by the time she placed her arms around Jess and began to sway, the stiffness in her shoulders had melted away. It didn't take long before the crowd parted and re-formed around them, creating a makeshift dance floor as other couples joined in. Despite the boost Mei's glamours had given her, Vivi couldn't imagine feeling confident enough to be the first person to dance at a party. Juliet's serious expression morphed into a smile as she swayed in perfect rhythm with Jess, and Vivi's admiration turned to envy as she felt a pang of longing she'd never felt before. What would it be like to have someone look at *her* like she was the only person in the world? She turned away, not wanting to intrude on what was starting to feel like a private moment, and suddenly found herself looking at Mason.

He was talking to a couple of guys who appeared to be two of his frat brothers, a handsome, confident-looking guy with warm brown skin and a lanky white kid with the telltale straw-gray hair of a competitive swimmer. Instead of the tuxes that all the other guys were wearing, Mason had on jeans and a perfectly fitted white button-down that was open at the neck, revealing a hint of summer-tanned chest.

As if feeling her gaze on him, Mason looked over. He caught her eye and smiled, sending an electric thrill through her body, not dissimilar to the sensation she'd felt when she was working magic.

Before Vivi could decide whether to smile, wave, or pretend she hadn't seen him, Scarlett materialized at Mason's side. Heart pounding, Vivi spun around and took a few chugs of her drink, then winced. Ariana might have improved the flavor, but the alcohol was strong enough to burn her throat. As she stood with the other pledges, half listening to Reagan tell a story about a witch she knew who'd been a finalist on *The Bachelor,* the crowded room began to go fuzzy around the edges, and a comforting sense of warmth settled in her chest. Suddenly, the dance floor looked far less frightening—almost inviting.

Vivi gazed around until her eyes landed on the cute bartender. She waited a moment to see if he'd look up, but he was focused on drink-mixing, and even tipsy Vivi wasn't bold enough to cross a room and strike up a conversation with a stranger. Then she remembered a spell she'd read in the grimoire about catching the attention of someone who was otherwise engaged. It'd been one of the many non-English spells, but Vivi's French was just good enough to get the gist. *"J'en appelle à la Reine d'Épées et invoque la Force. Que ma volonté soit exaucée,"* she whispered under her breath. She felt pressure building as the warmth in her chest began to spread through her whole body, pressing against her skin as if trying to escape. A second later, the boy looked up and locked eyes with her across the crowd.

Vivi inclined her head toward the dance floor and raised one eyebrow quizzically, a gesture she hadn't even known she could perform, then felt a thrill as he grinned and nodded. They met in the middle of the room, and he wordlessly wrapped his arms around her waist and pulled her close. It was the most physical contact she'd had with a boy since middle school, when she'd had a boyfriend for exactly one week, during which time they spoke three times and kissed once. Yet while the sensation of the boy's touch was unfamiliar, it certainly wasn't unwelcome.

The weight of his hands made her skin tingle as he guided her side to side in time to the music. But although he was, hands down, the hottest guy who'd ever shown any interest in her, she couldn't help imagining he was someone else. Someone she absolutely, positively could not want.

Someone she wanted anyway.

An hour later, Ariana grabbed Vivi's hand and pulled her off the dance floor, where she'd been dancing with a second boy—one who'd approached her without the influence of a spell. The party had thinned out a little but the couples and groups of friends on the dance floor were still going strong, singing along to the Lizzo song blaring from the speakers.

"What's up?" Vivi asked, slightly out of breath. She was sweaty from dancing, and although she hadn't had anything else to drink, the world was spinning slightly at the edges of her vision.

"Nico wants to show us the pool room," Ariana said with a giggle, leading her toward a staircase at the back of the house, where Reagan, Bailey, and Sonali were standing.

"Who's Nico?" Vivi asked.

"The guy I was just dancing with. Didn't you see him? They don't make 'em like that where I come from. These Savannah boys can really rock a tux. Now come on." Ariana tugged on Vivi's arm. "He and his friends are waiting for us downstairs."

Vivi was buzzed, but not so buzzed that she didn't hear the alarm bells sounding in her mind. "I don't think we should. Scarlett told us not to leave the main party under any circumstances."

"Oh, come on," Reagan said, sounding both amused and slightly irritated. "It's not like they're strangers. This is our brother frat."

"She's not saying it's dangerous." Sonali looked nervously from Vivi to the others. "She's saying we shouldn't disobey Scarlett."

"Trust me, you do not want to make her angry," Vivi said with a shudder.

"Whatever. I saw Dahlia, Tiffany, and Mei disappear upstairs thirty minutes ago," Ariana said. "They're not even following their own rules."

"Are you girls coming?" a cute boy with messy blond hair asked. He brushed past them and disappeared down the steps.

"Yes!" Ariana said firmly; she grabbed Sonali's hand and pulled her after Reagan, who'd already started down the stairs.

"What do you think?" Vivi whispered to Bailey.

"I don't know," she said uneasily. "I don't like letting Scarlett tell me what to do, and playing a few minutes of pool doesn't sound like a big deal. But then again, I've never pissed off a witch before."

The stairs led down to a windowless room with a dingy tiled floor where a handful of PiKa boys were playing beer pong. Vivi's stomach lurched when she realized that one of them was Mason.

He caught her eye for a moment and smirked, then returned his focus to the game.

Vivi frowned. Something about his expression felt off. The smirk didn't seem to belong to the sweet, playful boy who'd carried her bags and helped her make waffles. His eyes seemed harder, and the laugh she heard from across the room had an almost cruel edge to it. Then his mouth opened wider and twisted into a strange, unnatural shape, as if his jaw had become unhinged. Vivi watched in horror as his skin began to droop like melting wax—just like the faces of the other boys.

"What the hell?" Bailey muttered, her words drowned out by Ariana's scream.

The boys' faces and bodies continued to melt and re-form until, a few moments later, Tiffany, Scarlett, Dahlia, and Mei stood in their place. Dahlia was looking at them sternly, her arms crossed, while Mei had a mischievous smile on her face as she pretended to inspect her nails. The whole thing must have been one of Mei's glamours, Vivi realized, although she hadn't known Pentacles magic was strong enough to change elegant Ravens into frat boys.

"As you've probably realized by now," Scarlett said, "this was a test. And you failed it."

"I *told* you," Sonali muttered under her breath.

"You're witches," Scarlett continued. "You're more powerful than most of you realize. With that power comes a responsibility to protect yourselves and your sisters. If we tell you to stick together, to stay with the group, then that's what you do. It doesn't matter who's trying to persuade you—a group of charming frat boys or an ancient demon you accidentally summoned through sloppy spellwork."

"Wait. Demons are real too?" Bailey asked.

"You'll find out soon enough," Tiffany said with a bordering-on-evil grin. "Y'all have earned yourselves cemetery duty."

"What does that mean?" Ariana asked, still trembling from the sight of the gruesome transformation.

The four older girls exchanged knowing looks. "Oh, you'll see," Mei singsonged.

Scarlett wiggled her fingers at the pledges, then headed upstairs with the older girls. "I just hope you're not scared of the dark," she called. "Or the dead."

CHAPTER FOURTEEN

Scarlett

The morning after the mixer, Scarlett lay sprawled on the main green with her head pillowed on Mason's chest. Students wove all around them, rushing off to classes or to meet friends. A clump of boys tossed a Frisbee back and forth. A group of women were hanging a banner for an upcoming student-gallery opening. Scarlett took comfort in the bright normalness of it all. Lying here with the steady, soothing thud of Mason's heartbeat pulsing in her ear was exactly what she needed right now.

She'd barely slept last night. She hadn't been able to stop thinking about the spell that had exploded in her room before the mixer. She'd never seen magic react that way before. Magic had an energy to it, an effervescence. It might exhaust you, but you didn't feel like it was devouring you from the inside out. When her spell had exploded, it was like a hungry, angry force was trying to invade her body. She'd spent all night worrying about what the spell meant, but here, in the bright light of day with the sun shining and Mason's fingers threaded through hers, it was hard to believe anything ominous was afoot at Westerly College.

And last night hadn't been all bad. She'd managed to enjoy shocking the pledges when she and the others had glamoured into the PiKa boys. The horrified look on Vivi's face was enough to make Scarlett smile even now.

"What's so funny?" Mason asked, his chest rumbling beneath her head.

"Just thinking about the mixer last night. It was fun, right?"

"I guess," he said. She felt him shrug.

"Not entertaining enough for you, Mr. Gregory?"

"I mean, it's a mixer. It's the same shit as always. Jotham spent half the night trying to win Molly back and then the rest of the night making out with one of her best friends. Benjamin threw up in the pool after everyone left. And the pledges, I swear, are clones of our class. Same bros, different color polo shirts. It's boring."

"Nice way to talk about your house's party." Scarlett frowned. She'd made a point to pull Mason onto the dance floor so that they would have some time together. He had looked like he was having fun, but had she misread it? Had she misread him? Sure, he hadn't worn a tux like he was supposed to, but he'd told her he'd forgotten to pack it after his vacation, and she'd taken him at his word. Now, though, she saw something else. Maybe he'd just *chosen* not to wear it. And, yes, maybe there were a few too many PiKas ordering their Solo cups "shaken, not stirred." But that was just part of Greek life, laughing at dumb expected jokes with your friends. With Gwen back, Scarlett wished the worst problem the Kappas faced was getting bored.

"Honestly, I don't know if they're going to be my house that much longer," Mason said.

Scarlett furrowed her brow. "What are you talking about?"

"When was the last time you read a book for fun?"

Scarlett tensed. This felt like a test. And she and Mason were supposed to be long past the stage of "Are we right for each other?" questions. "Why?"

He sighed, his look faraway. "Jotham ragged on me for half an hour for reading something that wasn't on the syllabus."

"That's just Jotham being Jotham."

"That's PiKa being PiKa," he corrected.

"I don't think you're being fair to your brothers."

"That's the thing—they aren't my brothers. They're not even necessarily my friends. I asked myself if I would choose them if they weren't already in PiKa, and honestly, I'm not so sure."

Scarlett squinted against the sun. "Where is this coming from? You adore Jotham."

"And he'll be my friend with or without PiKa."

"Without PiKa?" she asked, on red alert now.

She felt his chest rise and fall in a sigh. "I'm thinking about quitting PiKa."

"What?" Scarlett sat bolt upright and spun to stare down at her boyfriend. He stretched and sat up too, running a hand through his messy dark curls.

"What? It's not *that* big a deal."

"Mason, what about your brothers? What about your dad? Every male Gregory has been a PiKa for the past three generations."

Mason laughed and reached over to take her hand. "Scar, I admire your loyalty, but you take all this Greek stuff way more seriously than I ever have. I know Kappa is really special for you, and I respect that. But . . . 'brothers,' 'pledging.'" He shrugged. "PiKa is just a social club. It's a nice way to network, I guess, get to know people. But I only joined in the first place because my dad wanted me to, and last night, as we stood there talking to the same old people about the same old shit, I just felt . . . bored. Like, is this how I want to spend my nights for the rest of college?"

"You mean with your best friends and your girlfriend?" Scarlett said pointedly. She flashed back to the first time she met him. The Pikiki party. The plumeria. PiKa was part of their story. And now he was shitting on it.

"Scar, our relationship doesn't depend on my membership in a fraternity." His expression sobered. "Or at least, it shouldn't."

"Of course it doesn't. I just don't understand. Did something happen—did you get into it with another PiKa?"

Mason shook his head. "No, nothing like that."

"So what's the problem, then?"

"I just . . ." He sighed again, clearly frustrated. "Don't you ever just want to try something new? Throw out all the rules and plans and find out what life *could* be if you stopped telling it how it *should* be?"

Scarlett stared at her boyfriend. Where was this coming from? Why was he changing so much, so suddenly? An image of Vivi and Mason laughing in the cafeteria, the easy way he'd rested his hand on her shoulder, rose in her mind. They hadn't talked at the mixer last night—Scarlett made sure of that—but there was one moment, so brief she almost wondered if she'd imagined it, where she thought she saw something pass between them across the room.

Mason held his arms wide. "The world is bigger than PiKa. It's bigger than Kappa. We're bigger than both of them. I wish you could see that."

"I do see that." But was he judging her for staying with her sisters? And if he wasn't now, would he in the future? Was this the first step before he asked her to choose him over them?

A swell of unwanted emotion washed over Scarlett, and she stood up before Mason could see the hurt in her eyes. "Don't forget, we're having dinner with my parents tonight," she said, avoiding his gaze. "Unless those are the kind of plans you want to throw out the window."

Mason shot her a pained look. "Scarlett . . . don't be like that. Stay."

"Don't you have your sociology study group now? You should really go. You have an exam coming up," she said.

Mason hesitated. Scarlett knew he wanted to talk more, but she could feel a tightness in her throat and a burning behind her eyes. She refused to lose it here on the main green, where everyone could see. Ravens did not cry in public. So she summoned her magic, the burning behind her eyes replaced by a burning in her fingertips. *Leave,* she urged him. *Go now.*

"I have to get to study group now, Scar," Mason said suddenly, responding to her subliminal magical command. He kissed her on the cheek and turned to leave. And even though she'd been the one to issue the command, it still broke her heart to watch him walk away.

CHAPTER FIFTEEN

Vivi

Is that what you're wearing tonight?" Vivi asked, eyeing Reagan's hot pants as the two of them lounged in the shade of one of the dozen enormous live oaks that bordered Westerly's main quad. She and Reagan were in the same astronomy class and tonight was their first trip to the off-campus observatory, a brand-new building funded by a wealthy Kappa alum. Vivi wasn't sure how long the assignment would take, so she was trying to get as much reading done as possible that afternoon. Classes had just started, yet she was somehow already behind. It'd been much easier to keep up with schoolwork back when she didn't have any friends.

"Are you worried about me scandalizing the telescopes?" Reagan asked, rolling onto her stomach and closing her eyes, clearly not planning to use the free afternoon to catch up on reading. From what Vivi had been able to piece together, Reagan was highly intelligent but completely uninterested in academics—Ariana told her that Reagan had been kicked out of three different prestigious boarding schools. Vivi had a feeling that the Ravens must have pulled some strings to get her into Westerly despite her lackluster grades, possibly as a way to gain favor with her powerful witch mother and aunts. It was still a little mind-boggling to think of witches living all over the country—and all over the world. Women whose ancestors had used their magic to shape history . . . and who had sometimes paid the ultimate price.

"I'm more worried about you getting bug bites on your butt cheeks," Vivi said, more flippantly than she felt. "Apparently, the observatory is next to a big swamp."

"You make an excellent point, Devereaux." Reagan rolled over, then stood up. "I guess I'll change before dinner. See you tonight."

Reagan sauntered off, and Vivi opened her math textbook, but she hadn't gotten very far before a shadow fell over the page. "Indulging in a little light reading, I see."

She looked up to see Mason standing over her with a warm smile. Vivi raised the book and looked at the cover quizzically. "It's only calculus. I'd call that pretty light reading."

"Compared to what? Advanced neurosurgery?"

"Compared to the nonlinear algebra class I'm auditing. Freshmen aren't allowed to take it officially."

"Well, aren't we the little overachiever?" Mason's smile widened, revealing the dimple that made Vivi's heart flutter.

Pull it together, she told herself. *He's your sorority sister's boyfriend. Don't be a creep.* "Don't try to act all too cool for school," Vivi said, attempting to sound playful without being flirty, though she'd be the first to admit that she was ill-equipped to make that distinction. She pointed at a paperback sticking out of his leather messenger bag, a worn copy of *Love in the Time of Cholera* festooned with colored Post-its. "Is that for class?"

"For fun," Mason said, slightly sheepishly.

"So you're as much of a nerd as I am."

"Oh, I'm a *much* bigger nerd, trust me. Come with me. There's something I want to show you." He extended his hand to help her up, but Vivi hesitated. She wanted to go with him, but she wasn't sure how Scarlett would feel about Vivi spending one-on-one time with her boyfriend.

"Sorry," Mason said as he let his arm fall awkwardly to his side. "I realize you're perfectly capable of standing up by yourself. My mother's etiquette lessons were a little outdated."

"No, it's fine," Vivi said as she scrambled quickly to her feet. "I was just thinking about my schedule, but I have time. What did you want to show me?"

His expression brightened. Vivi wasn't sure she'd ever met someone whose emotions showed so clearly on his face. "It's right over here. You'll see in a second."

Mason led her across the quad and down the tree-lined path to Westerly's most famous library, the Hewitt, which, according to the guide on the tour Vivi had taken during orientation, housed the school's collection of rare artifacts.

"Are we allowed inside?" Vivi asked. "My tour guide said that it was only for grad students and visiting scholars."

"The archives require special permission, but the museum is free and open to the public."

"There's a museum on campus?"

"Tsk-tsk." Mason shook his head. "Either you had a delinquent tour guide or you weren't paying attention. I'm not sure which of those scenarios breaks my heart more."

As they climbed the white marble stairs toward the columned façade, Vivi surveyed Mason with a smile. "If your heart breaks *that* easily, life is going to be hard for you."

He placed his hand on his chest. "You have no idea, Ms. Devereaux."

"How do you know my last name?"

"You nearly assassinated me your first day on campus. I told you, I need to keep tabs on you for public-safety reasons."

Vivi raised an eyebrow. At least, she hoped that was what she was doing. It wasn't a gesture she was particularly adept at, and there was a good chance she'd merely contorted her features strangely. He opened the door for her, and although Vivi was sure he did this for every woman, the courtly gesture still sent a tingle through her chest.

"The archives are that way," Mason said, pointing at a set of wooden double doors. Next to it was an ornate desk occupied by an imperious-looking woman with gray hair and steel-rimmed glasses. "That's where they store most of the collection. There's only room to display about ten percent of it in the museum, which is right over here." He approached the desk and smiled. "How are you, Miss Irma? Do you need to see our IDs?"

"It's fine, Mason," the woman said, her stern expression softening. "Go on in."

He led Vivi into a long, narrow room lined with display cases.

"What kind of museum is this, exactly?" Vivi asked as her eyes traveled from a bejeweled tortoiseshell to an antique tobacco pipe to what appeared to be a musical instrument made from an elephant tusk.

"I think its official name is the Hewitt Collection of Oddities and Curiosities, but basically, it's just a hodgepodge of strange and valuable stuff people have donated over the years."

Vivi took a few steps toward a diorama of taxidermied mice dressed up for a tea party. "I can't believe anyone would want to part with this."

"There's some good stuff in here, trust me. Come on—I'll show you my favorite piece." He led her quickly down the center aisle to a case in the back corner where a small, green clothbound book rested on a red cushion.

Vivi leaned in and squinted, trying to decipher the gold-leaf type on the front cover. "It's a collection of Emily Dickinson poems."

Mason nodded. "This was found in the pocket of a soldier who died in France a few weeks before the end of World War One."

"That's so sad," she said softly, feeling an ache in her chest for the boy who'd never made it home. "Why's it your favorite?"

"I love that he brought a book of *poetry* into battle with him. After all the death and destruction he must've witnessed, he was still able to find beauty and meaning in language. I think that's pretty inspiring." From the wistful look in his eyes, it was clear he meant it.

"They should have *you* give tours," Vivi said, afraid of what she might say if she didn't revert to banter.

"Oh, they do. I'm one of the most popular guides on campus."

"Why am I not surprised?" Vivi asked as they made their way outside. She glanced down at the clock on her phone and let out a small yelp. "Shoot, I have to go, I'm sorry. They gave us cemetery duty tomorrow night and it's thrown my whole schedule off."

"Ah yes, cemetery duty. That's what all the girls say when they want to get rid of me."

"I'm serious. It's a Kappa thing—I have to run. See you later?"

"I certainly hope so," he said with an expression she couldn't read.

Her heart began to race and she spun around quickly so he couldn't see the expression on *her* face—one she was sure he'd have no trouble reading.

A large cloud passed overhead, casting long shadows on the grass. The quad had emptied—no one was sitting on the benches or lounging under the oak trees. Vivi skipped down the steps, buoyed by the fizzy excitement that had formed during her conversation with Mason.

As she hurried along the path that would take her through the main gates, she caught sight of a solitary figure on the far side of the quad. Someone standing perfectly still, eyes locked on Vivi.

It was Gwen.

In the fast fading light, she looked almost unearthly with her dark hair and startlingly pale face, and she was staring at Vivi with a look Vivi had never seen directed at her before.

Pure hatred.

CHAPTER SIXTEEN

Scarlett

Scarlett sat in the Kappa library, her psychology book open and unread in front of her. The room was her favorite in the house. All four walls were covered from floor to ceiling with old leather-bound books, some dating as far back as the 1500s, well before the Ravens became a formalized coven. Interspersed with the books were apothecary-style drawers containing crystals, herbs, and yellowed remnants of half-written spells from sisters past. The ceiling was painted a lapis lazuli blue with the stars of the night sky etched in gold leaf. In the center of it all was a circular compass, the cardinal directions delineated not with letters but the elemental signs for fire, air, water, and earth. Sitting in here was like stepping back in time, a reminder of all those who had come before her—a reminder that her problems were small and passing in the face of history, in the face of the universe as a whole. A reminder she sorely needed in this moment.

She'd gotten home an hour ago from a typical Winter dinner: Her mom had fawned over Mason. Her father had grilled him about his postgraduation plans and LSAT scores. Eugenie had bragged about her mountain of casework while asking pointed questions about Scarlett's bid for president. And Mason had charmed them all, like he always did. He'd also apologized to Scarlett for their fight earlier and brought her a plumeria, like the one he'd given her from his lei the night they'd met.

It all should have felt fine, good even. But things still seemed . . . off. Even in a houseful of people who were supposed to love her the most in the world, she felt alone. Like she was the only one who noticed that the ground was shifting subtly beneath their feet. Then again, she always felt Minnie's absence more deeply at home, where all the spaces she used to occupy were so conspicuously empty.

Just like Kappa House was tonight, which wasn't helping her mood. Everyone was either off studying or out at the bars.

She sighed and opened her psychology notebook, then let out a sudden, sputtering laugh. Someone had drawn a stick figure in the margins and charmed it to dance. It almost looked like it was flossing. Scarlett smiled as she remembered all the nights she and Tiffany had spent choreographing ridiculous dance routines, routines Tiffany would sometimes bust out in in public just to cheer Scarlett up when she was having a bad day. Tiffany must have doodled this in her notebook earlier; she always seemed to know when Scarlett needed a boost. Scarlett would have given anything to have her best friend with her right then instead of sitting in this quiet house alone.

She looked out the window and saw one of the ravens from the aviary perched on a tree limb, still as a statue. The moon through the skylight was a waning gibbous, the best time for casting spells to change and improve yourself, Minnie always said. A moon for new beginnings.

Perhaps whether you wanted one or not.

Scarlett took the plumeria from behind her ear and placed it on the table in front of her. Later she would put it in her Kappa Book alongside the original one she had pressed two years ago. But this flower didn't have the same effect as the first. The first was a promise of what was to come. Now she felt herself and Mason straining to remember that promise.

Voices and laughter sounded on the stairs, and a moment later, Dahlia, Mei, and Tiffany came into the library.

"Hey, girls," Scarlett said, pasting a smile on her face. "Where have you been?"

"Ugh, Homecoming budget meeting," Tiffany said with a roll of her eyes. Kappa was responsible for hosting the annual campus-wide event for current students and alumni. Every year the committee was amazed at how Kappa managed to come in under budget for décor. It was always a delicate dance of what they reported to the Greek council and what they hand-waved with magic.

"You should have heard Maria. She was trying to convince the council that Theta should take over Homecoming and Kappa should do the winter formal instead," Mei said.

"Typical," Scarlett said. Maria was the president of Theta, and Theta had been trying for years to compete with Kappa for top sorority. Like it even stood a chance. "Who even goes to the winter formal?"

"That's exactly what I said," Tiffany said, flopping down in the leather armchair next to Scarlett. *You okay?* Tiffany's voice sounded in her head. *You look upset.*

Leave it to her best friend to see right through her. Scarlett tapped into her sister's Swords magic to answer her: *I'll tell you about it later.*

Tiffany nodded, giving Scarlett's arm a light squeeze. "Can you even imagine what our moms would say if we lost Homecoming?" Tiffany said.

"They would die," Dahlia said with a shake of her head.

Mei laughed, but Tiffany went silent, her eyes suddenly glassy. "Yeah, literally, in my mom's case," she said.

Dahlia went ashen. "Oh God, Tiffany. I'm sorry, I didn't mean . . . I didn't think—"

But before she could finish her thought, a crack rang out, almost like a pistol shot. It was followed by a loud popping sound and another crack.

"What the hell is that?" Tiffany said.

The girls looked at one another, confused. "Do you smell smoke?" Mei asked, wrinkling her nose.

"Ugh, if Sig Tau is setting off firecrackers again . . ." Scarlett pushed aside her textbook, stood up, and crossed over to the window, which looked out over the front yard and Greek Row. But it wasn't fireworks at all.

Down on the lawn, someone had hammered four wooden stakes into the grass. Tied to each was a scarecrow wearing robes and a pointy witch's hat.

And they were on fire.

For a second, all Scarlett could do was stare. Then she let out a shout and they all flew into action. She thundered down the stairs to the first floor and burst out into the muggy night, her sisters at her heels.

The scarecrows blazed, the flames leaping and dancing as they consumed the straw, the fabric of the robes melting and twisting. Up close, Scarlett had just enough time to see that the scarecrows had leering, overwide smiles drawn on in red marker. A moment later, their faces caved in, devoured by fire.

Scarlett flung her arms up and instinctively reached for her magic, summoning water to douse the flames.

"Scarlett, no!" Dahlia hissed.

That was when Scarlett realized that a small crowd had gathered. A couple of drunk brothers from Sigma Zeta Tau stood off to the side, mouths agape, beers in hand. A few girls from Beta Beta Beta in pajama shorts and flip-flops stood in a clump, whispering to one another. Two Thetas ran out of their house hand in hand, stricken looks on their faces.

"Bonfire!" one of the Sig Tau guys cheered, pumping his fist in the air.

"Are you okay?" a boy asked, hopping off his bike and rushing to their sides.

"Are those supposed to be . . . *witches?*" said a girl whom Scarlett recognized as the president of Gamma Theta Rho.

"Looks like someone's taking Hell Week too far this year," Scarlett said quickly as more students approached with concerned and curious expressions. Someone pulled out a phone as if to take a video.

"If another house did this to you, we should take it to the

Panhellenic council. Hell, we should call 911," one of the Tri Betas said, the orange flames reflecting in her dark eyes. She reached for her cell.

"We don't want to get another house in trouble, even if they deserve it," Scarlett said, trying to defuse the situation. She threw Dahlia a panicked look. Dahlia whispered something under her breath and Scarlett felt the telltale hum of magic. Immediately, the Tri Beta's eyes glazed over, and the entire crowd became subdued. The Tri Beta turned on her heel and walked back to her house; the rest of the students scattered as well, returning to the bikes they'd let fall on the grass or wandering back into their houses.

"Holy shit," Scarlett breathed shakily as soon as everyone had dispersed. Then, without a moment's hesitation, she summoned her magic. Electricity crackled in her veins; her fingertips burned. She reached out, pushing wider and wider until it felt like every drop of water in the atmosphere was singing to her, caught in her expanding web. She knit the molecules together tighter and tighter and then, with a final burst, released them. Immediately a soaking rain began to fall. The flames hissed and sputtered before finally going out. Scarlett fell to her knees, spent.

The charred husks leered at them until Mei cast a spell that caused them to crumble to dust, then she glamoured away the scorch marks in the grass. "That could have been really bad," Mei said, breathing hard from her efforts.

"Understatement." Scarlett shook her head as she got back to her feet. "Dahlia, something is really wrong here," she said, putting words to the mounting feeling of unease that had gripped her body ever since she'd seen the first lick of flame. "First the tarot cards, now this. I don't think they're coincidences or harmless pranks. Someone is gunning for us, and they're getting more daring."

Scarlett expected Dahlia to argue with her, but the older girl just nodded. "This doesn't feel like a random coincidence. Someone wants to hurt us—or expose us."

"Then we have to protect ourselves," Tiffany said firmly. "We're witches. We're powerful. It's our duty to keep our sisters—and our secret—safe."

"What about the Hell Week task tomorrow night at the graveyard?" Scarlett asked Dahlia. "Maybe we do something else? We could have the sophomores whip up a graveyard in the backyard *tout de suite*."

Dahlia thought about it for a moment, tapping her magically flawless manicured nails against her palm. "No, it stays on. It's tradition. And we are not going to be scared off by some maniac. Tiffany, Mei, and I will come with you to help monitor." When Scarlett nodded, Dahlia went on. "Mei, come back into the house with me. I want to check our protective spells. Tiff, Scarlett, please tell the others to be on alert."

As Mei and Dahlia walked back toward Kappa House, Scarlett turned to Tiffany. "I can send a house-wide text to stay on alert—" She broke off. She'd just seen a flash of black hair beneath a streetlamp at the end of the road.

Gwen.

The girl's eyes were narrowed, her mouth an angry red slash.

As soon as Scarlett caught her eye, she stepped away from the light and disappeared into the darkness.

"Tiff." Scarlett grabbed Tiffany's arm.

"I know, I saw her too," Tiffany said grimly.

A chill traveled down Scarlett's spine. "You have to admit it's weird timing. Gwen shows up, back on campus after all these months, right when strange stuff starts happening."

Tiffany raised her eyebrows. "What are you implying? You think she's behind it all?"

"Is it really so hard to believe?" Scarlett asked.

"But we cast a protection spell on the house; she can't step foot on the property without feeling like she's walking on coals or whatever torture Dahlia added to that spell . . ."

Scarlett knew what Tiffany was doing—she was trying to deny the only explanation that made sense. The only explanation that made this their fault. But Scarlett knew in her heart that somehow Gwen had gotten around the spell and done this.

"I did a spell last night looking for bad intentions on campus."

Tiffany inhaled sharply and a shadow fell over her face. "What did it tell you?"

"Well, nothing specific," Scarlett admitted. "The spell kind of exploded, but I know what I felt. It was really . . . *dark*."

There was another type of magic, one that was darker and more dangerous than what the Ravens practiced. The kind of magic that involved death and pain.

The kind of magic that could get people killed.

But instead of reflecting Scarlett's own mounting terror, Tiffany's expression cleared. "That sounds super-scary, but you said it yourself—the spell didn't work. And Gwen isn't even a witch anymore. We made sure of that."

"I'm serious. Gwen is back for a reason," Scarlett argued. "What if she's behind all this? What if she's trying to get some sick version of revenge for losing her powers? Because if that's what's going on, that's on us."

Tiffany took Scarlett's hand. It was clear from her expression that she thought Scarlett had totally lost it. "I love you, you know I do, but even if it *is* Gwen, what exactly do you think she can do to us? She's just a pissed-off wannabe witch who lost her chance to be part of a kick-ass coven. She'll back off eventually if we stop letting her get a rise out of us."

Scarlett shook her head. "I don't know. I just have this horrible feeling. What if Gwen figured out how to get her powers back? If she's trying to hurt the people who hurt her, then we're all in danger. We need to stop her."

Tiffany narrowed her eyes. "What exactly are you proposing?"

Scarlett bit her lip. "I think we need to tell Dahlia what happened—what really happened."

"You know we can't do that," Tiffany said, her voice hard. "If we told Dahlia, who knows what she'd do? At best, we'd be sanctioned; at worst, she'd kick us out and bind our powers. We can't take that risk. We are witches, and *no one,* not Dahlia, not Gwen, is taking that away from us. We were young and stupid and we made a horrible mistake. I'm the first person to admit that. But think about what you're saying."

Scarlett rubbed her arms, trying to dispel her goose bumps.

"Hey." Tiffany put her hands on Scarlett's shoulders and looked directly in her eyes. "What happened was an accident. It'll be all right, Scar. I promise. You and I are the baddest witches around. Nothing is going to happen to us or our sisters. We won't let it. If it comes to it, you and I will deal with Gwen ourselves. But you saw it with your own eyes: She doesn't have her powers back. The binding spell worked. Gwen can't even *say* the word *magic,* let alone use it to kill anyone. Don't let her be the reason you lose your powers too."

Scarlett looked at her friend, her sister. Tiffany's eyes were wide and earnest. And she had to admit the truth of her words. Losing her magic wasn't a risk she could take. Without that, she had no idea who she even was.

"You're right." Scarlett let out a slow sigh. "I'm being ridiculous." But try as she might, she couldn't shake the nagging feeling that she was missing something. Something painfully obvious.

Something that could get another one of her sisters killed.

CHAPTER SEVENTEEN

Vivi

Vivi rubbed her arms, less for warmth than to banish the chills she felt from the unsettling events of the past few days. Both her startling encounter with Gwen and the story of the burning scarecrows had left her with a cold, sinking feeling that the Savannah sunshine hadn't been able to dissipate, and it had only grown worse since she'd entered Bonaventure Cemetery that evening.

The trees in this section of the famed burial ground grew so close together that their branches formed a canopy that blocked most of the moon. The dripping Spanish moss made the oaks appear to be wearing veils, as if they were in perpetual mourning for the bodies buried beneath their shadows. Even the scraggly plants that poked up between the headstones seemed diminished by grief, their drooping leaves and pale petals a far cry from the lush flora Vivi had come to associate with Savannah.

The pledges walked in silence as they threaded their way through the graves. They were supposed to meet the older girls at something called "the Tomb of the Horned God." Whatever that meant. Internet searches hadn't turned up anything helpful.

"Look at that one," Ariana whispered. Vivi followed her gaze to a statue of a little girl standing in a grassy plot bordered by a wrought-iron fence. Everything about her had been rendered in exquisite detail, from the hair ribbons in her curls to the buckles on her shoes. Everything except her large, blank eyes, which seemed to follow Vivi and Ariana as they hurried to catch up with the other pledges.

"Could that be it?" Bailey asked, pointing at a massive mausoleum just past a copse of oak trees. Sure enough, there was a flicker of a torch next to the entrance and a cluster of figures around it.

"Good find," Vivi said, though she wasn't particularly eager to discover what awaited them. She hadn't done much to impress Scarlett during Hell Week, and she was growing increasingly worried about not making the cut.

When they reached the mausoleum, they found Dahlia, Scarlett, Tiffany, and Mei holding candles and dressed in black robes, hoods drawn low over their faces. They were standing underneath the portico of the mausoleum, which had been carved with the twisted, grimacing face of a man with two horns protruding from his temples.

"Welcome, pledges," Scarlett said, stepping forward. "We brought you here tonight to explain how important sisterhood is and tell you what happens when you don't take those vows seriously." She gestured to a simple, knee-height marble tomb with the name WATERS etched into it. "This is Evelyn Waters. Or, rather, the empty tomb dedicated to her memory." She paused dramatically.

"Why is it empty?" Bailey asked finally, taking the bait.

"Because Evelyn went missing her senior year, and her body was never found." Scarlett rested a perfectly manicured hand on top of the grave. "Evelyn was a Kappa president. She led the sorority for a year before her disappearance. In her time, the coven was even more powerful, even more important, than it is now. Have any of you ever heard of the Henosis talisman?"

Vivi shook her head, as did Ariana, Reagan, and Bailey. Only Sonali's eyes widened in recognition.

"*Henosis* translates roughly to 'unity' or 'oneness.' The talisman was forged in ancient Greece and discovered during an excavation in the late 1800s. Westerly acquired it for the history department, and a Kappa witch deciphered the tablet that had been buried with the talisman. It was a spell. It explained not only how to share power between witches but also how to permanently *take* another witch's power."

Vivi winced at the idea of someone taking her magic. Although she'd been aware of her powers for only a short time, it was frightening to imagine the feeling of emptiness and loss if they were taken. Because that was what had made the discovery so extraordinary; it wasn't as if the Kappas had waved a wand and given Vivi magic—they'd simply helped her harness the forces that had always been inside her.

"How can that happen?" Bailey asked. "Don't—"

"I thought you had to be born with magic," Reagan cut in. "I was always told a witch could only ever have as much magic as she started out with."

"True," Scarlett said. "Naturally. But if we're speaking

*un*naturally . . ." She let the word hang in the air. Tiffany went rigid, standing as still as the statues around them, while Mei shifted her weight from side to side. The only older girl who didn't seem uneasy was Dahlia. Her eyes reflected the dancing flame of her candle, which made them look almost red.

"The spell isn't easy," Scarlett continued. "It's not permanent, either—not without the Henosis talisman. That's the only object on earth that allows you to store stolen magic.

"With the talisman, you can take another witch's power for life. Without it, you're living on borrowed time. Plus, the theft comes at great cost." Scarlett met Vivi's gaze. In the moonlight, Vivi could have sworn Scarlett's eyes looked different. Darker, almost black. "To take another witch's power, you have to kill her."

Vivi shuddered as the wind whispered through the trees, making the hair on the back of her neck stand on end.

There was a distant crack in the woods, like a branch snapping. She whipped her head around to follow the sound. Dahlia and Mei didn't move, but Vivi thought she saw a flash of fear on Scarlett's and Tiffany's faces.

"So . . . you think someone killed Evelyn Waters? Stole her powers?" Reagan asked impatiently, clearly unbothered by the noise.

"All we know is that in the spring of Evelyn's senior year, she disappeared from Kappa House," Scarlett said, tracing the top of the gravestone with her fingertips. "The talisman vanished along with her."

"So when we say that sisters need to protect each other . . ." Mei said, speaking for the first time.

"We mean sometimes they must do so with their very lives," Scarlett finished.

Her words hung in the air as everyone else fell silent. But then a moment later, there was a loud crackling sound as the torch by the mausoleum entrance exploded in flames. The pledges all gasped and stepped back.

"Tonight, you'll have your first opportunity to work as a team and prove how far you'll go to protect one another," Scarlett said. She raised her hands and more torches burst into life, illuminating a stairwell that led down into the bowels of the massive mausoleum behind them. "This is part of a tunnel system connecting much of old Savannah to Westerly's campus. Once you enter, we'll seal you inside."

"We've left clues in each anteroom for you," Mei said. "You'll have to work together if you want to find your way back to Kappa House."

"That, or risk being trapped under the city forever," Tiffany chimed in, her voice full of morbid delight.

"Phones, please." Dahlia extended her hand to collect everyone's device. Vivi relinquished hers with trepidation. She could barely navigate *with* her phone.

Scarlett handed Vivi a worn silver pendant with strange symbols etched into it. "This will help you find your way. Good luck."

"You're going to need it," Tiffany said, then exchanged a knowing smile with Scarlett.

Reagan and Bailey started into the tombs first. Sonali hesitated briefly, then marched after them.

Vivi followed Ariana into the gloom of the mausoleum entrance and barely made it down the first two steps when she heard a loud grinding sound. She turned around to see the heavy door closing behind her. For a split second, she locked eyes with Scarlett. The older girl looked almost *worried,* Vivi thought, but before she could examine her Big's face further, the door was shut tight and they were plunged into complete darkness.

As she waited for her eyes to adjust, Vivi reached out to feel the wall for guidance. She grimaced as her hand touched something wet and slimy. The path sloped down, and although the logical part of Vivi's brain knew that there was plenty of oxygen down here, her natural response was to take shallow, panicked breaths. She couldn't help thinking about the rusted bells they'd seen next to some of the graves, a relic from the days before heart monitors and brain-activity sensors, when people occasionally awoke from a coma to find themselves buried alive.

"This is fucked up," Reagan said.

"Agreed," said Ariana. "They're going to have a few more empty graves if we get lost down here."

"I don't know," Bailey said, her voice echoing off the walls. "It's probably just some story they made up to scare us. I bet Evelyn Waters wasn't even a Raven."

"She was," said Sonali, so quietly Vivi almost didn't hear it. "My mother knew her. She really did go missing."

No one responded to that. The only sounds were their uneven breathing and a steady *drip-drip* somewhere in the distance.

"Are we going to try and find our way out, or are we going to stand here all night?" Ariana asked finally.

"It'd be helpful to see where we're going," Vivi said. "I suppose no one has a candle we can try to light."

"No, sorry, I left my candle collection in my other purse," Reagan said.

"I might not need a candle," Bailey said softly. "I've been practicing. Hold on." There was a slight rustling and then she said, "I call to the Queen of Wands. Show me your might by giving us light."

The last word had barely left her mouth when two glowing orange flames emerged in the darkness, hovering just above Bailey's upturned palms.

"Nicely done," Ariana said. "Do you have your cards on you?"

Bailey shook her head carefully, as if she were afraid of jostling the flames. "I guess the practice is paying off."

"Does it hurt?" Sonali asked.

"No, not at all," Bailey said, a note of surprise in her voice.

"It takes more than that to burn a witch," Reagan said with a grin, conjuring a flame in each of her palms too.

The light from the four flames was just enough to form a small wavering circle around the pledges as they continued down the narrow staircase, brushing against the clammy stones that seemed to be closing in on them.

After what felt like ages, they reached the bottom of the stairs and found themselves facing a stone pillar carved with etching that looked like hieroglyphics. Beyond it, three paths branched out in different directions.

"I think it's a glamour," Sonali said, running her hand over the carvings. "Look, the symbols aren't actually carved into the stone. It's an illusion. These must be the clues Mei mentioned."

Bailey stepped forward and raised her hands until the light from the flames reached the pillar. "They're alchemical symbols." She nodded at an upward-pointing arrow with a line through it. "That's air. The downward-pointing arrow with the line through it to the left is earth. This bottom arrow is water, and the right-hand one is fire. We learned them in my History of Science class last year."

"So what does it mean?" Ariana asked. "Are they directions?"

Sonali shook her head. "If this were a compass, then earth should be at the top, pointing north."

Vivi held up the pendant Scarlett had given her. "Bailey, what's this symbol?" she asked, pointing at a glyph that looked similar to the symbol for woman but with a crescent moon on top.

"I think that's Mercury, but I have no idea what it means in this context."

"What about something to do with Greek mythology?" Reagan suggested. "Maybe—" She stopped talking as a faint hiss filled the air, like distant rain falling. "What the hell is that?"

Vivi spun around to search for the source of the noise and felt her stomach plunge. One of the passageways had suddenly filled with churning water, and it was headed straight toward them. "Oh, shit," she said, spinning on her heel and shoving her pledge mates forward. "Come on! We have to run. Now!"

The hissing sound grew into a roar as the water drew closer.

"Mercury was the winged messenger god," Sonali said, panting. "The god of speed. The symbol was . . . telling . . . us . . . to . . . move."

Bailey's and Reagan's flames went out as they sprinted, returning the tunnel to pitch-darkness. Vivi stumbled on the uneven ground and her ankle rolled painfully. But then she felt the spray from the rushing water on the back of her neck, and a jolt of adrenaline surged through her. She kept running, trailing just behind the others, until Ariana's cry rang out: "It's blocked. There's a wall."

The five of them skidded to a halt. Vivi squeezed her eyes shut and braced for the slam of surging water, but just like that, the roaring noise went quiet, and the water began to recede like hunting dogs called to heel. The damp still hung in the air, but now the tunnels stood silent.

Vivi took slow breaths through her nose, trying to calm her racing heart. There had to be some way back to Kappa that didn't involve swimming across an underground river. "Does anyone know a locator spell?"

"There's a spell to find the owner of an object," Sonali said, also breathing heavily. "We could use it on that necklace to find Scarlett, but it's a major arcana spell. We're not supposed to attempt those until we're full Ravens and have the power of all four suits."

"I'm for trying it," Reagan said. "Anything beats standing around in the dark waiting for another sneak attack."

"We're doing it," Ariana said firmly. "Sonali, tell us what we need to do."

"First we need to join hands." There was some shuffling as they all stumbled to find one another in the dark. Finally, they linked up. Vivi held Ariana's and Bailey's hands. "Vivi, do you have the necklace?"

"I'm wearing it."

"Okay, everyone, repeat after me: 'I call to the Hierophant and to the Star. We seek your wisdom to track from afar.'"

Vivi shut her eyes. "I call to the Hierophant and to the Star. We seek your wisdom to track from afar." Her voice came out shaky, hesitant. But as the other girls took up the chant, she grew louder, surer. Before long, their voices echoed through the tunnels, the sound so rich and resonant, it seemed like the sleeping dead had joined the chorus.

"I call to the Hierophant and to the Star. We seek your wisdom to track from afar."

At first, all Vivi felt was the tingling in her fingertips, the now-familiar sign of her own magic stirring. But a few seconds later, the pleasant buzz began to swell into something else. Painful jolts of electricity shot through her chest, and her blood pulsed so thick and fast, she thought her veins would explode. The ground began to rumble beneath their feet, shaking loose dust and debris from overhead.

"Vivi," Ariana shouted. "Pull back. You're giving the spell too much power."

Vivi gritted her teeth and tried to imagine her magic receding, but it felt like attempting to restrain a tornado. "I can't." She gasped, struggling for air. The rumbling grew more violent, and larger rocks began to fall. Vivi tried to raise her hands to protect herself, but she couldn't move her arms, not even as something cold and jagged scraped against the side of her face.

"You have to!" Sonali cried as the entire tunnel shook. "We're going to be buried alive. Everyone else, keep chanting!"

Vivi clutched her friends' hands tighter and pulled in as hard as she could, straining like she was trying to dead-lift a tanker truck. Just when she thought she was going to burst, the pressure in her limbs began to subside and the rumbling grew fainter.

"I call to the Hierophant and to the Star. We seek your wisdom to track from afar." The words echoed off the tunnel.

After a moment, the chain around Vivi's neck tugged.

"I call to the Hierophant and to the Star. We seek your wisdom to track from afar."

The pendant lifted off Vivi's chest and hovered in front of her. Then, with a sharp jerk, it whipped around and dragged her backwards, up the leftmost tunnel. She gasped as the chain around her neck bit into her skin.

"Vivi? What's wrong?" Ariana called through the darkness as Vivi dropped her hand.

She tried to answer, but when she opened her mouth, no sound came out. Desperate, Vivi yanked at the chain as stars started to appear at the edge of her vision. Using her last ounce of strength, she managed to pull the chain over her head. She took a huge gulp of air, grasping the pendant in her hands.

Flames flicked up in Bailey's palms once more, revealing the pledges' worried faces.

"You okay?" Sonali asked, her eyes wide.

Vivi nodded and took a deep breath, wincing with the effort. "This way."

She led them in a stumbling parade, the pendant straining before her as if dragged by an invisible cord. Finally, she heard a *thunk* as the pendant collided with something solid. Ariana stepped next to Vivi and began to feel along the wall. "It's a door." She found the knob and wrenched it open, flooding the tunnel with light.

Vivi winced and shielded her eyes as Ariana grabbed her arm and laughed with relief. "We made it," she said hoarsely.

"Made it where?" Vivi asked as she staggered out of the tunnel into what looked like a basement lined with dusty bottles. Some had strange labels: ADAM AND EVE, ATTRACTION, BETTER BUSINESS, DOUBLE-CROSS. Others, like wine bottles, were more recognizable.

The pendant gave a sharp tug and pointed at the nearby steps just as someone opened the door to the basement.

"You're here already?" Tiffany appeared at the top of the staircase with Scarlett, who was staring suspiciously at the pledges.

Vivi released the pendant's chain, and it went flying across the basement.

Scarlett caught it just before it collided with her. She turned the pendant over. "Did you use a locator spell on this?"

"What else were we supposed to do?" Vivi asked, glancing at her fellow pledges.

"The symbols on here were clues to the directions we painted in the tunnel. We wouldn't expect first-years to do a locator spell."

"Well, it was Vivi's idea and it worked," Ariana said, a note of defiance in her voice as she took Vivi's hand.

Sonali told them how the tunnels had rumbled and almost caved in. "I've never seen power quite like that before."

"Wow," Tiffany said, looking impressed. But Vivi was focused on Scarlett, who was staring at her, stonefaced.

Vivi braced herself for a reprimand, but to her surprise and relief, Scarlett just smiled.

"Nicely done, Little Sis. Now let's celebrate."

CHAPTER EIGHTEEN

Scarlett

A tiny witch's mark hidden in the flourishes of the calligraphy on the sign was the only indication from the outside that the little shop in old Savannah was anything more than a plant store. The sidewalk was an explosion of succulents and orchids, herbs and mini–fruit trees. But inside, if you knew which mirrored, unmarked door to open . . .

"Whoa."

Scarlett could barely suppress a grin at the new girl's dazed expression as she walked into Cauldron and Candlesticks for the first time. Dried herbs dangled from the ceiling. Crystals lined one wall, and candles in every color and carving populated another. The last two walls were taken up by bookshelves crammed with everything from ancient tomes to modern-day pop-witch books.

"It's like a magical speakeasy," Vivi gushed.

In the center of the room were shelves for the larger ritual equipment: brooms, altars, god and goddess statues from just about every pantheon you could think of. And, of course, the cauldrons and candlesticks from which the store took its name.

"What are all these for?" Vivi gestured to a row of crystals.

"Rose quartz for opening the heart, obsidian for grounding,

lapis for opening the third eye. People carry them to enhance their moods or as protection charms." Scarlett pointed to the herbs dangling from the ceiling. "Everything has energy within it. Certain herbs and crystals lend their particular energy to spells you're performing, making them stronger." She gestured toward the cauldrons. "Ritual items help focus your intent. They make you a stronger witch."

This was a mandatory Big-Little activity. It had been a few days since someone had burned the witch scarecrows on their front lawn, and they needed more supplies to fortify their protection spells, but Scarlett had to admit that shopping with Vivi was kind of fun. She was completely without shame. She gaped at every new thing like a baby tasting sugar for the first time. It was sort of amusing.

She also had to admit that her Little was a lot more powerful than she'd realized. According to Sonali, Vivi had nearly caused an earthquake in the tunnels. That kind of power was rare—and, in the wrong hands, dangerous. But Vivi was working hard at control. Just that morning, during a lesson, she had managed to glamour the entire greenhouse to look like a rainforest.

"So is this what we're low on?" Vivi held up a bundle of juniper.

"Yup. Grab at least five. We go through it like nobody's business." Scarlett held out the basket. "It's kind of a catchall cleansing or smudging herb. Anytime a spell calls for bay leaves or cedar, you can substitute juniper."

"How do you know all this?" Vivi asked as she piled the dried branches into the basket.

"My mother taught me."

"You're lucky," Vivi said wistfully. "My mom never even told me I was a witch."

"I'm not sure *lucky* is the right word. I mean . . . don't get me wrong, I'm glad I'm a witch. But it comes with a lot of expectations . . ." She paused, unsure how much to reveal. "My mother puts a lot of pressure on me."

"I think I would've preferred that." Vivi ran her hands over a row of crystals. "My mom never explained any of this to me. We used to just move on a whim. Like when we were living in Vegas, I came home one day to find all my things packed in the car. She said we were heading to San Diego that very moment because she saw 'a wickedness' in her tea leaves."

"And you *didn't* wonder if you might be a witch?" Scarlett said pointedly.

"Touché." Vivi laughed a little. "I mean, I guess the signs were all there. But I spent most of my childhood assuming my mom was a fraud. And maybe she is? I'm still not quite sure whether she knows any real magic or if she's just really good at telling desperate women that their deadbeat husbands are about to have a lucky turn."

Scarlett's eyebrows rose. She hadn't expected that. For some reason, she'd been imagining Vivi's childhood as . . . well, *normal*. Free from all the pressure of the magical world. Free from the constant need to be the best, the smartest, the strongest. "She's probably a real witch. Magic like yours doesn't skip a generation."

Vivi tilted her head, considering. "So she hid it in plain sight my whole life? Somehow that seems worse."

"You think that's bad? In the middle of my high-school graduation party, my mom gave a speech about how proud she was . . . of my sister."

"Whenever I fell behind in class, my mom always turned it around on the teachers. She claimed she knew things about them from the cards. Once, she even took on the principal and announced that he was part of a pay-to-play for college admissions. And she decided to do that while I was onstage for the talent show."

Scarlett laughed. "I'm sure you were super-popular after that."

"Positively drowning in friend requests. Of course, I guess Mom was probably right about every single thing. I just didn't believe her," Vivi said. "And hey, look at me now—about to join the most powerful sorority on campus. *If* you let me in," she amended quickly.

"Stranger things have happened," Scarlett said, selecting a few more crystals for the house's general supply. "I'll be honest, I didn't have much confidence in you at first."

"This is a really rousing pep talk, Big Sis."

Scarlett shot her a look. "Let me finish. I was lucky. I didn't have just my mom growing up. I also had Minnie, my nanny."

"Of course you had a nanny."

"She was much more than that. She was with my family through two generations. She was a witch, though she never belonged to a formal coven. She preferred to practice on her own and keep her own rules. There have always been independent witches, some who shunned covens completely, others who chose to guide and teach, like Minnie taught me. Outsider witches are essential. They are impartial and have no stake in individual covens; their concern is for all witchkind. And the independent witch is an additional defense if a whole coven ever goes bad."

"Do you think my mom is an independent witch?"

Scarlett shrugged. "Maybe. Have you tried asking her?"

"Getting my mom to give me a straight answer would require Swords magic." Vivi sighed. "Minnie sounds amazing, though."

"She was. She wasn't blood and she wasn't a Kappa, but she was a far kinder teacher than my mother. She filled in the gaps. And not just the magical ones." Scarlett's throat tightened. "She passed on last year."

"I'm sorry, Scarlett," Vivi said softly.

"Even though Minnie practiced alone, she used to say, 'A single witch is powerful. A coven is unstoppable.' You're powerful, Vivi. Probably the most powerful Pentacles we've had in years. If I can see that, so will Dahlia."

Vivi gave a small smile but then her expression became troubled. "Scarlett, everything that's going on . . . the burning witches on the front lawn . . . The Ravens are going to be okay, right?"

"Of course," Scarlett said quickly. "The Ravens have been around for centuries. We're the most powerful coven in the country. Nothing is going to stop us."

If only she could believe her own words.

She pointed toward the bookshelves on the far side of the store. "If you want to get ahead, I'd check out *The Herb Compendium*. I'm assigning that in our next session."

Vivi practically leaped at the shelf in response.

Which gave Scarlett time to collect what she'd really come here for. Yes, the house-protection spells needed to be renewed. But she also needed something very specific for herself.

She checked over her shoulder to make sure Vivi's nose was buried deep in the herb book. Then she walked to the back of the store.

To a maroon-shrouded shelf that held a grinning skull.

Scarlett pulled her jacket tighter around her. Her phone buzzed in her purse.

Mason: Study break?

Scarlett: Can't. Official Kappa business.

Mason: C'mon. I miss you, Scar.

Scarlett: I miss you too. Txt u later.

She put her phone back in her bag, feeling a pang. That was the third time she'd put Mason off in as many days, but being pledge master was a total time-suck. She'd given the pledges hours of lessons on the phases of the moon, had them practice doing tarot readings for one another, and gone through their wardrobes to select items that were not suitable for Ravens, which frankly had been half of Vivi's clothes. But she wasn't working on pledge tasks right now . . . She double-checked to make sure the ring was in her jacket pocket. The silver ring Gwen dropped when she'd come to Kappa House.

Vivi's locator spell had given Scarlett an idea. She'd modified the spell a little, set it to find the place the ring belonged, not Gwen herself. She'd hoped it would lead her to wherever Gwen was staying, because after charming the registrar, Scarlett had learned Gwen didn't live in any of the dorms or Greek houses.

Scarlett had had enough speculation and worry. If Gwen had her powers back, if her return was related to all the strange things happening on campus, Scarlett needed to know.

But now, as Scarlett turned onto a dilapidated block lined with neglected houses on the outskirts of Savannah proper, she wondered if this had been such a good idea after all.

The ring pulled her toward a squat, rundown hardware store. It had an aggressive red CLOSED sign hanging beside a narrow screen door, the hinges bent so far they'd nearly broken off. Next to the screen door, an overflowing ashtray held a pile of cigarette butts, one still smoking.

Taking a deep breath, Scarlett knocked on the edges of the screen door. Through the screen, she could see a hallway, then a staircase. "Hello?" she called after a moment. "Anyone home?" From the registrar, she knew Gwen was supposed to be in a medieval history seminar, but she wouldn't put skipping the class past a girl who liked dabbling in wicked magic. She knocked again.

No one answered.

Heart hammering, she checked over her shoulder. Nobody else in sight. She tried the screen door. Open.

She stepped into the hallway, then hesitated. The ring tugged her up the stairs to a door marked with a crooked *3*. She knocked once more, louder this time, counted to twenty, then muttered an incantation under her breath. "I call to the Priestess and Strength to guide me true. Please allow me to pass through."

She'd learned this spell her freshman year when Dahlia, her Big at the time, gave her a Hell Week assignment to break into the president of Westerly's office and rearrange her furniture.

That door had proven a lot harder to open than this one. The lock barely protested at all. It screeched inward, the rust just about the only thing keeping it shut. Scarlett swallowed hard, took one last look around the dingy, poorly lit hallway, and stepped into the apartment. She wasn't sure what she'd expected. Skinned animals, a sacrificial altar still wet with blood, maybe some bones or heaps of grave dirt. A lock of hair. Instead, she found . . . a normal living room.

There was a couch with some pieces of stuffing falling out. A boxy TV that looked like it'd been salvaged from the year 1998. A threadbare rug and a shelf with nothing on it but a few Philip Pullman books.

She headed farther into the apartment on tiptoe. She found a small bathroom with a tight shower and dollar-store shampoo. A bedroom with a twin bed, unmade, and an Ikea dresser with half the drawers open, black clothes hanging out of them.

Nothing. Not only were there no signs of wicked magic; there were no signs of magic, period. No candles, herbs, incense. Not even any protective crystals.

Scarlett spotted a book on the nightstand, the spine cracked from overreading: *How to Combat Loneliness*. Beside it stood a single photograph in a cheap frame: Gwen dressed in a graduation gown standing with an older couple, presumably her parents but possibly her grandparents. They had their arms around her, and all three were smiling for the camera.

Scarlett hadn't seen Gwen smile like that since before the incident.

Feeling a pang of guilt, Scarlett turned and was about to leave the bedroom when her gaze fell on another photo. This one wasn't in a frame, just tucked into the edge of a mirror, creased and wrinkled with time. But the faces were instantly recognizable. Gwen, laughing. And beside her, with an arm wrapped around her neck in a hug . . .

Harper.

Scarlett tore her gaze away and headed back into the living room. She dumped her purse on the floor and dug through it until she found the ingredients she needed. Her onyx bowl went in the center of Gwen's shredded rug. Then, with a grimace, she took out the small zip-lock bag that held the item she'd acquired at Cauldron and Candlesticks. "I'm sorry, Minnie, I have to," she whispered in the near dark.

Bile surged in the back of her throat when she opened the bag. The smell of formaldehyde mixed with blood filled her nostrils. The smell alone made her eyes water and burn. But in magic, like called to like. To detect wicked magic, you needed to dabble in it yourself. Scarlett held her breath and upended the contents of the bag into her scrying bowl. It landed with a horrible squelch.

She lowered her hands over the bowl, as close as she dared. Then she shut her eyes. Concentrated. Magic gathered and sparked in the air. The lights flickered on and off, over and over. Wind rattled the windows.

"Heart of wickedness, heed my command," Scarlett whispered, hardly daring to say the words any louder. She'd never done anything like this before. Her mother would flay her alive if she found out. She forced the anxious thoughts from her mind. She needed to concentrate. To focus on the spell. "Blood to blood, like to like, let any wicked magic be revealed to my sight."

Silence. A beat. And then, just as she started to wonder if she'd said the words wrong . . . *thud. Thud, thud.*

She cracked open an eye, her own heart racing. In the scrying bowl, the preserved rabbit's heart she'd purchased had begun to beat. *Thud, thud. Thud, thud.* She watched, horrified, as viscous blood leaked from it, filling her scrying bowl.

Quickly, she extended her hand and let Gwen's silver ring drop into the bowl. It landed on top of the thick liquid, then slowly sank beneath the surface, like it was being swallowed up. Her stomach roiling with nausea, Scarlett closed her eyes again, repeating the chant. "Let any wicked magic be revealed to my sight." Her voice grew stronger with every repetition, steadier. The pulse of the heart in the bowl kept up, getting faster, faster. *Thud-thud. Thud-thud-thud.*

Finally, when she felt the energy crackling, aching for release, her eyes snapped open once more. "Show me," she commanded in a voice deeper and huskier than her own.

The blood that now filled the bowl shimmered and shifted. While Scarlett watched, an image resolved in the muck. Gwen's face—not as she'd looked in those smiling photos in her bedroom, but as she'd appeared when Scarlett last saw her. Thin and wan, her hair and skin a mess.

The spell should reveal any ill intent, any proof Gwen had dabbled in the kind of wicked magic she'd shown an interest in as a freshman. But her face in the bowl remained unchanged. After a moment, a faint yellow glow suffused her image. It spread until the whole scrying bowl glowed with golden light, so bright Scarlett couldn't even see the heart at its center anymore.

She glanced around the room. Nothing. No smoky clouds, no apparitions lurking in the corners. No signs of any magic at all. Just that steady yellow shine.

Gwen hadn't used wicked magic. She hadn't cursed anybody. If the contents of her apartment were any indication, she didn't have any powers whatsoever.

Scarlett sat back on her heels, unsure whether to be relieved or upset. That was when she heard the distant *bang* of the screen door out front. "Shit." Scarlett scrambled to her feet and grabbed the plastic bag she'd brought the heart in. She dumped the entire scrying bowl straight into it, nose wrinkled. She'd have to dispose of the contents somewhere along the walk home. No time to do it now.

Holding the bag of spent magic and her purse, Scarlett hurried to the apartment door and paused, one ear pressed to the wood, listening. No footsteps or sounds from the other side. It must have been a neighbor. Taking a deep breath, she eased the door open, turned the lock, and pulled the door shut behind her. She stepped lightly down the stairs and slipped out the screen door, careful to slow down the door so it wouldn't bang shut.

Someone right behind her said, "What are you doing here?"

Scarlett nearly leaped out of her skin. She whirled to find Jackson leaning against the brick wall beside the entryway. *Shit.* Why was he *everywhere* all of a sudden? It took her speeding pulse a moment to settle. When it did, she narrowed her eyes. "Me? What are *you* doing here? Following me?"

"Don't flatter yourself. I know this may come as a shock, but not everything is about you, Scarlett."

"Do you live here?" Scarlett forced as much derision into her voice as possible.

He grinned. "Why, were you looking for me?"

She made a point of eyeing him up and down, maintaining her best poker face all the while. He wore ripped jeans and a faded blue T-shirt. She paused a second too long on the rich brown skin that peeked through the purposeful tear above his knee. When she looked up, Jackson ran a hand over his close-cropped fade, and she found herself staring into his brown eyes, which popped with mischief above his enviable cheekbones. She had to admit he wasn't bad-looking—not that she was remotely interested. She had Mason. "Hardly," she said, head held high. "I was trying to find Gwen."

"She's not home right now."

"You seeing her or something?" Scarlett lifted her eyebrows.

Jackson tilted his head, that infuriating smirk growing wider. "Jealous?" Her glare must have been answer enough. Jackson's smile faded a little. "Gwen and I have someone we care about in common. Maybe you'd remember." Jackson moved closer, and Scarlett caught the faint scent of his cologne. Something woodsy and sharp.

She took a step backwards. "Who, some other jilted lover?"

Jackson's eyes narrowed; any trace of amusement was gone from his expression now. "My stepsister, actually. Harper Wilson."

Scarlett's breath caught in her throat. *Oh, shit.*

Jackson must have read the thought on her face. "Yeah. That's right." He crossed his arms, jaw set hard. "She was a Kappa. And two years ago, you and your sisters killed her."

CHAPTER NINETEEN

Vivi

Vivi was enjoying all her classes so far, but to her surprise, her favorite was art history. Growing up, she hadn't felt a particular affinity for art. It had been years since she'd lived in a city with major museums or galleries, and people gushing over the hidden symbols in wobbly blobs of smeared paint reminded her of Daphne's clients grasping for meaning amid the cruelty and randomness of the world.

But sitting in the art history hall on the ground floor of a converted nineteenth-century church, Vivi couldn't help but feel a sense of wonder as she watched Professor Barnum flip through slides that demonstrated Caravaggio's use of chiaroscuro. Studying magic had changed the way she thought about pretty much everything. The world *was* much less random than she'd believed; there were invisible forces at work and hidden meanings everywhere if you looked, and art was a reflection of that.

Yet despite Vivi's newfound appreciation, her assignments for Kappa took priority over her reading for class, and she knew she was woefully unprepared for today's art history lecture, which was an especially big problem, given Professor Barnum's slightly sadistic tendency to call on freshmen. Tiffany had asked for her help with a glamour for the Homecoming Ball that weekend, and last night she'd stayed up until almost four a.m. to finish an assignment from Scarlett: writing out spells to make a heavy object light as a feather, to summon a rainstorm, and one to make someone's toenails fall out. She fantasized about using that one on Zoe the next time her roommate invited friends over for a nightcap at two in the morning.

It was all wonderfully weird and fascinating, of course, but part of Vivi wished the sisters could spend a little less time on toenails and a little more time on the strange things that'd been happening at Kappa House lately. Vivi was only a freshman, but even she could tell that something wasn't right. Her encounter with Gwen on the quad the other day had left her almost as shaken as when she heard about the burning scarecrows, but Scarlett seemed unwilling to discuss any of it.

"Vivian, would you care to answer?"

Startled, she sat up in her seat to find Professor Barnum standing in front of her, looking characteristically antagonistic. He was a brilliant lecturer but not known for being sympathetic. Rumor had it that he'd once failed a student who'd missed a midterm because of emergency surgery.

Next to her, Sonali stared at Vivi wide-eyed, as if trying to communicate something.

"I'm sorry." Vivi looked at the slide on the screen. It was a dramatic oil painting of a boy wearing only a sheet and holding out a glass of wine. "Can you repeat the question?" she asked, stalling for time.

"I asked why Bacchus was such a popular figure among

sixteenth-century patrons. Perhaps, though, the question shouldn't be relegated to such a historical context, given your own wan appearance and lack of interest in my lecture. I might recommend laying off the late-night Greek life activities and focusing on the real reason you're here: academics."

Vivi felt her face turn bright red. A few people in the back of the class snickered until the professor turned a narrowed glare on them, too.

Then, like a lifeline, Sonali's voice sounded in her mind. *Patrons often commissioned portraits of Bacchus to reflect their own wealth and success.*

Without stopping to wonder what spell Sonali had just used, Vivi shot her a grateful look, then turned back to Professor Barnum. "I'm sorry, I didn't hear you at first," she said, then repeated Sonali's answer. She was about to sit back in her seat when Sonali sent her another thought, so she continued speaking. "This particular portrait, which was commissioned by Cardinal del Monte, also alluded to both Caravaggio's and the patron's surmised sexuality. It contains pagan undertones recast in Christian symbolism."

The professor stared at Vivi for a moment, then nodded. "Very good. Now, as a counterpoint, let's talk about Titian's *Bacchus and Ariadne* . . ." He moved on.

Thanks, Vivi mouthed to Sonali with a grin, making a mental note to ask her to teach her that spell.

Anytime.

Warmth flooded Vivi's chest, but for once, the heat had nothing to do with embarrassment. Sonali hadn't hesitated a second before coming to Vivi's rescue. For most of her life, Vivi had been hard-pressed to find people she thought of as real friends, and now she had a whole house of them. Better than friends, in fact. Sisters.

He needs a bacchanalia of his own, Sonali thought at her. *Maybe then he'd relax a little.*

A mischievous, un-Vivi-like idea took shape in her head. She opened a new Word document on her laptop and typed: *Maybe we should help him with that,* then tilted her screen toward Sonali.

Sonali's lips curled into a smirk. *Hell yes.*

Vivi glanced at the other people in their row to make sure no one was looking, then closed her eyes and whispered the illusion spell she'd been practicing, keeping her words hidden beneath Professor Barnum's booming voice.

A moment later, the slide on the wall glamoured into a nude portrait of none other than Professor Barnum himself, sipping wine on the edge of a hot tub with a strategically placed towel over his lap. A couple of people gasped. Barnum whirled around to look at the screen and turned a fiery red. He cursed and grabbed his laptop, frantically clicking through slides, but the glamoured photograph stayed stubbornly on the screen.

Vivi and Sonali traded delighted grins as muffled, shocked laughter filled the room.

"We're clearly having some technical difficulties. Class is dismissed for today," Barnum said, then muttered about IT tampering with his computer and about filing a complaint with the administration.

Vivi managed to contain herself until they'd fled the classroom, then she and Sonali fell into each other, laughing so hard, they both began to cry.

"That was amazing," Sonali said, wiping her eyes.

"*You* were amazing," Vivi told her. Her phone buzzed in her bag. She pulled it out, and her giddiness evaporated at the sight of the text on her screen. I need to talk to you immediately. Meet me in the woods in back of Kappa House. Leave now.

Vivi felt her stomach drop into the rich brown ankle boots she'd glamoured that morning to mask her Converse. Whatever this was about, it didn't sound good. She glanced over to see Sonali staring perplexedly at her own phone. "Did you get one too?" Vivi showed her the message.

Sonali nodded. "Just now, from Mei." Her forehead pinched with worry. "You don't think they know about . . ." She glanced pointedly over her shoulder at the classroom.

"I don't know . . ." Vivi trailed off as a new wave of panic rose up within her. Using their magic out in the open like that had been risky, especially since they weren't full-fledged sisters yet. Maybe their Bigs had some way to monitor them to ensure they didn't use their magic inappropriately.

Vivi wasn't actually sure how the process of failing a pledge worked. Was there an official ceremony where everyone gathered? Or could Scarlett summon Vivi at any time to tell her she hadn't made the cut? What else could *I need to talk to you immediately* mean besides "I have bad news for you"? And then what would happen? Would Scarlett wipe her memory so that the best weeks of Vivi's life became nothing more than a strange twinge in the back of her mind? For the first time, she had friends; she had purpose. Was she about to lose it all?

"We'd better go," Vivi said with a sigh. "Whatever they want, we'll only make it worse if we're late."

The sun was setting by the time Vivi and Sonali reached Kappa House. Instead of going inside, they walked around and headed for the thick glade of trees that grew beyond the back garden. The temperature had dropped suddenly, and Vivi rubbed her arms, wishing she could grab a sweater before stepping into the shadowy gloom.

"Do you think we should wait here?" Sonali asked. They'd spent most of the walk from campus in silence, too preoccupied by their own worries to speak.

"They told us to meet them *in* the woods, so I guess we should keep walking?"

Wordlessly, they stepped into the forest. It was like entering another world—the tangle of thick tree branches blocked most of the setting sun, though every now and then, they'd pass a pool of light on the mossy ground.

"I think we should go that way," Sonali said, pointing to the right.

"How do you know?"

Sonali laughed and nodded at a flowering vine with pink blossoms growing in a peculiar pattern that formed the words *Initiates, this way*. The end of the vine had been transformed into an arrow. Despite her nerves, Vivi laughed too. The Ravens could be infuriatingly cryptic, but they certainly did everything with style.

She and Sonali walked on until the trees began to thin out, revealing patches of indigo sky above them. Up ahead, they could hear the murmur of quiet voices; they followed the sound until they stepped into a small clearing. The entire sorority was there, all of them dressed in black robes except for Dahlia, who was in blood red. They were standing in a large circle, and as Vivi and Sonali approached, the circle opened to let them inside, where the other pledges were waiting. Ariana was looking around with wide eyes, while Bailey had gone still and rigid, though her darting eyes betrayed her anxiety. Even Reagan, who usually maintained an air of ironic detachment, was fidgeting nervously.

Without saying a word, the pledges' Bigs stepped forward and approached their Littles. Scarlett's face was unreadable as she came up to Vivi and draped a black robe around her shoulders, then placed a garland of white flowers on her head. The other Bigs did the same, although with different colored garlands, then returned to their spots in the circle.

Dahlia, who'd been standing next to a large pile of wood, stepped into the center of the gathering. "It's time, witches. Welcome, Vivi, Bailey, Reagan, Ariana, and Sonali. You've entered the woods as pledges, but you'll leave it as sisters. This is your initiation to Kappa. Now, please, take your rightful places in the circle."

Despite the solemnity of the setting, Vivi couldn't keep an enormous grin from spreading across her face. Next to her, Sonali let out a long sigh and muttered, "Thank God," while Ariana squealed and clapped her hands.

"So, just to confirm," Bailey said slowly. "This means . . ."

Dahlia laughed. "Yes, you made it. All of you did. You're here to become full sisters."

It took all of Vivi's self-control not to skip as she joined the circle, which had widened to make room for the new sisters. She'd done it. For the first time in her life, something she'd dreamed about had actually come true. Nothing would ever be the same again. She was a witch with magical powers, and, even better, she was a Raven.

"We've gathered here to cement the bonds of sisterhood and welcome our newest initiates into our family. But first I want to thank Scarlett, our pledge master." Dahlia turned to face Scarlett. "This is the first time in several years that all of our pledges have been accepted to full sisterhood, and we have her training to thank for it."

Scarlett grinned, her eyes shining with pride.

"And now we begin." Dahlia picked up a branch from the mossy ground, and an instant later, one end exploded in flames. "Join hands, and let us cleanse this space." Vivi smiled as she clasped hands with Mei and Scarlett, then watched as Dahlia dropped the branch onto the pile of wood, setting it alight. The flames leaped around them, beating back the encroaching dark. Vivi could have sworn she saw images of soaring birds and dancing girls.

The sisters began to hum, producing a sound that made her

scalp prickle. A shiver passed through the circle where their hands were joined, and for a moment, it felt to Vivi as if they were one creature, breathing together, vibrating in sync. In the firelight, the coven looked spectral, like spirits who'd appeared in these woods, hair loose and wild in the wind.

"By my will," Dahlia intoned, "I cast this circle. By my word, it is conjured."

Mei and Scarlett released Vivi's hands. Together, the sisters turned in one direction, arms raised. Vivi did the same, following the others.

"We call upon the Queen of Swords, spirit of the East," Dahlia cried. "Hail and well met."

They pivoted south. Vivi caught Ariana's eye for a second and smiled.

"We call upon the Queen of Wands, spirit of the South," Dahlia continued. "Hail and well met." The wind picked up. Vivi's hair swirled around her face like a miniature tornado.

They turned again.

"We call upon the Queen of Cups, spirit of the West. Hail and well met."

As one, the sisters in the circle turned north. Vivi turned with them, hands raised in the air.

"We call upon the Queen of Pentacles, spirit of the North. Hail and well met."

A crackle of energy ran through Vivi's whole body, starting at her feet and extending all the way to her palms.

"I invoke the Empress and the High Priestess, spirits of magic, witchcraft, and the divine feminine," Dahlia called. Her voice had turned deeper, as if the ritual had loaned her some of its power. "We bid thee join us tonight as we initiate these new sisters into our fold. Look upon them and bless them with your strength, your knowledge . . . *your power.*"

Vivi shuddered as the buzz of energy grew stronger, making the hairs on her arms stand on end. Although most of the wood had turned to ash, the flames were burning even higher and brighter than before.

"Who ushers Initiate Sonali into our sisterhood?" Dahlia asked.

Mei stepped forward. Tonight, she had her hair in a gray pixie cut shot through with streaks of black. It made her look witchier than ever. Especially because, even without makeup, her eyes still looked unnaturally big, her lips a perfect bow. "I do."

"Who ushers Initiate Vivi into our sisterhood?"

Scarlett stepped forward. "I do," she said seriously.

One by one, Dahlia called the initiates and their Bigs until they all stood slightly inside the circle.

"Kneel, initiates," Dahlia said. "From this moment on, this ritual is binding. Once you rise, you will be full members of this sisterhood, with all the rights and responsibilities thereof. Do you accept the laws of Kappa and agree to abide by them from this day forth?"

"I do," Vivi said at the same time as Bailey, Ariana, Sonali, and Reagan.

"Prepare to accept your sisters' power." Dahlia looked around the circle. "We will now raise our magic and direct it at all our initiates. If the magic becomes too strong or too much, Scarlett, you will step in to assist the initiates in grounding the excess energy. Do you consent?"

"I do," replied Scarlett.

Vivi shivered at the words *If the magic becomes too strong,* remembering what had happened back in the cemetery when she'd nearly caused the tunnel to cave in. Could something like that happen tonight? Magic wasn't all charms and glamours—it was a system connected to the most powerful forces in the universe and it had the potential to go very, very wrong, just as it had for Evelyn Waters.

Dahlia nodded and all the sisters in the circle raised their hands, facing their palms at the initiates. "Empress and High Priestess, grant them our power," Dahlia chanted. "Empress and High Priestess, grant them our power." The others joined in, their voices growing louder with each repetition.

Vivi felt a tingling in her fingertips, which then began to spread, trickling down her arms like water droplets, seeping slowly through her body. The chanting grew even louder until Vivi could feel the voices vibrating in her chest. "Empress and High Priestess, grant them our power."

It came in a rush, a wild flood through her body. It felt like a first kiss, like standing outside during a lightning storm. Dangerous and thrilling all at once.

Vivi spread her arms out, accepting the magic from her sisters. Her hair rose, drifting around her forehead as if she were submerged in water. Her whole body rose, her feet floating inches off the ground. Out of the corner of her eye, she saw the others rising as well, but she didn't need to see them to feel them. A single thread bound them all now, and she experienced it with every beat of her heart. She could feel Sonali's pride, Ariana's giddy excitement, Bailey's mix of trepidation and delight, and, most surprising of all, Reagan's desperate relief.

"Empress and High Priestess, grant them our power." The Ravens' voices swelled into a crashing chorus. "Empress and High Priestess, grant them our power."

Just when Vivi thought she couldn't take any more, that she'd explode from the surge of energy coursing through her, Dahlia shouted, louder than any of them, "As above, so below. So mote it be!"

The wind died down. The flames stopped leaping toward the stars, and Vivi dropped back like a rag doll, falling helplessly until a number of Ravens caught her just before she hit the earth.

One of them was Scarlett, who gave Vivi the most genuine smile she'd seen since they'd met. "Welcome to Kappa, sister."

CHAPTER TWENTY

Scarlett

Tiffany had outdone herself.

Every year, Kappa organized the Homecoming Ball. As the social chair, Tiffany had planned this year's dance, and from the moment Mason opened the door of the limo they'd rented with a few other PiKa-Kappa couples, Scarlett couldn't stop staring.

After Dahlia's big thank-you at initiation night for the pledges, Scarlett thought she had the presidency nomination in the bag. But she had to admit this was impressive.

"What do you think?" Her best friend swept up to greet Scarlett and Mason with cheek kisses. She wore a slinky golden sheath dress, which stood in contrast to Scarlett's midnight-black gown. Scarlett looked like the sky on a moonless night next to Tiffany's bright, glimmering sun.

Tiffany's gown matched the glittering shrubbery behind her. She'd decided to throw the ball at the Coastal Georgia Botanical Gardens. It was a perfect choice. The Ravens were glamorous creatures but they never forgot where their power came from: the earth. And coming to the gardens in their ball gowns felt like coming home.

Scarlett had been to the gardens during the day but it was different at night. Lit up by the moon and delicate strings of lights, it was the kind of woodland you found only in fairy tales.

Too bad she wasn't sure how this fairy tale would end. Was she the fair maiden or the evil witch? Depended on who you asked, maybe. She glanced around looking for Jackson, though guys like him didn't usually come to these events.

She hadn't seen him since she left Gwen's apartment. She'd denied his accusation, of course, and stalked off. But she hadn't felt totally like herself since then. What did he know? What did he *think* he knew?

The only consolation was that Gwen didn't have her magic back. That, and the fact that there hadn't been a single strange incident since the scarecrows in the yard. Tiffany was right; despite Gwen's beef with the Ravens, at least she didn't have any magic to back up her threats. Let her try to come at them. A single mortal girl was no match for an entire coven.

Well? Tiffany's voice sounded in Scarlett's head. She blinked at Scarlett, clearly waiting for praise. Scarlett realized she hadn't actually given it.

"Bestie, I'm jealous I didn't do it myself," she said. Tiffany beamed at her.

"It's amazing, Tiff," Hazel said, coming up behind them.

Overhead, the string lights that had been spelled through the branches of the Spanish oaks shimmered as they moved like bright golden serpents. Flickering candles lined the central path, and

Tiffany had created, in place of the usual dirt track, a solid sheet of ice, clear as glass, that reflected the lights above—an impressive feat given the eighty-degree heat.

"Too bad I forgot my skates," Mason said with a smile.

"Not to worry." Tiffany took a big step back onto the ice on her sky-high stilettos and gestured around her. "It's a special design."

Magic, obviously. And that was the least of it.

The leaves overhead kept shifting, turning brilliant fall colors—yellow and red and bright orange—then falling from the trees in a shower of what looked like snow, after which buds grew and re-sprouted into spring. It was as if the whole forest were fast-forwarding through the seasons every few minutes.

"These projectors must have cost a fortune," Mason said when they stepped onto the ice, which felt as steady underfoot as pavement.

"How *did* you pull all this off?" Scarlett asked Tiffany quietly.

Tiffany shrugged. "Mei helped a lot. And Dahlia and Etta, of course. I even convinced Juliet and a few sophomores to pitch in. Your Little came up big, actually. She's powerful, that one."

"You didn't need me?" Scarlett arched an eyebrow. Between Hell Week and Gwen's reappearance, she hadn't had much time to talk to Tiffany. Still, knowing that Tiffany had asked everyone but her for help stung.

"You had your hands full with the new members."

Scarlett didn't miss the implication: *You've already had enough chances to show off.*

Mason took it all in, his gaze distant, unreadable.

She squeezed his hand. "Everything okay?" He'd been a little quiet in the limo. She hadn't thought much about it, but he did seem distracted.

"Sure," he said, pushing ahead.

A jazz band played in front of a wooden dance floor. Tables dotted the perimeter, and tux-clad waiters circulated with hors d'oeuvres. Westerly students in dresses and suits mingled with alumni and top college brass. Lights twinkled in the tree overhead, these branches also dripping with Spanish moss.

Just to the left, Scarlett saw her mother, draped in a gorgeous jewel-blue satin sheath dress. She was standing with Scarlett's father and Tiffany's mother, Veronica. Marjorie and Veronica had overlapped for one year in Kappa. They weren't close at the time, but they had become friends through their daughters.

Marjorie waved Scarlett over, a strained smile on her face—the one she wore when she had to mingle with attorneys from rival firms. Scarlett was surprised to see it now; Homecoming was her mother's favorite social event of the year.

"Mother. Mrs. Beckett." Scarlett hugged Tiffany's mom. "Tiffany didn't tell me you'd be here."

Scarlett couldn't help but notice how thin Mrs. Beckett was. She wore a scarf bound tightly around her head, and she had deep bags beneath her eyes and hollow cheeks. Scarlett could feel every vertebra in the woman's back when they embraced. Her heart sank and filled with guilt. How had Scarlett been worried about being left out of Tiffany's decorating efforts when she should have been asking about Tiffany's mom?

She turned to her friend. *Oh, Tiffany . . . why didn't you tell me?* she asked silently.

There's nothing to tell. She's stronger than you think, Tiffany responded.

Scarlett nodded, playing along, but they both knew better.

"Veronica and I were just reminiscing," Marjorie broke in, speaking in a false, overly bright voice.

"Yes, we were discussing the importance of sisterhood. As you near the end of your life, it becomes incredibly clear what—and who—matters." Mrs. Beckett's words were warm, but her tone was icy. Scarlett looked at the two women, wondering at the tension between them.

"I'm sure Tiffany's glad you could be here to see this. She did a wonderful job," Scarlett said, trying to shift the mood.

"She certainly did," a familiar voice said behind her.

Scarlett spun slowly, forcing a smile as her sister, Eugenie, leaned in to kiss her cheek. Hooked on her arm was a new man, but that was hardly surprising. Eugenie went through dates the way debutantes went through ball gowns.

"I figured this was your doing," Eugenie said to Tiffany. "Scar would never have the imagination for it."

Scarlett stiffened. Her best friend rested a placating hand on her arm.

"Actually, Scarlett's had her hands full this term initiating five new Ravens. That's more than either of the years you were in charge, isn't it, Eugenie?" Tiffany's smile could cut diamonds.

Scarlett resisted the urge to kiss her friend. Even in her darkest hour, Tiffany was still protecting her.

"You should have heard Dahlia at the ceremony," Tiffany went on. "She couldn't stop talking about what a great job Scarlett did with the pledges. She's a shoo-in for president."

"That's my daughter," Marjorie said with an approving smile.

Scarlett shot Tiffany a look of gratitude.

"Well, good luck locking it down, sis," Eugenie said quietly as Marjorie excused herself to talk to the provost of the college. "My money's still on Tiffany."

Before Scarlett could respond, Mason gestured at her. It was subtle, just a tilt of his head and a one-shouldered shrug. They'd developed that deceptively simple signal long ago at a mixer at Epsilon Omega Tau, the broey-est frat on campus, when Scarlett had gotten stuck talking to a pledge about beer pong for an entire hour. It meant: *Get me out, now.*

"Don't fret, Eugenie," Scarlett said just before she left. "One of these days, you'll manage to lock down a man for more than three dates." And with that, she ducked away to snag Mason, Tiffany's soft snicker ringing in her ears.

She steered him toward the bar, letting out a sigh only once her sister was safely out of earshot. But a part of her was still with Tiffany. She felt like a total asshole for being bothered about Tiffany not including her in the party decorating when Tiffany clearly had bigger concerns.

"Thanks for the rescue," she murmured. "I needed that."

"Actually, I was asking for me." Mason's mouth flattened at the edges. "I hate the way they talk to you. Family or not, no one gets to talk to you that way."

"Tell that to generations of Winters. Passive-aggressiveness runs in our blood," Scarlett said sarcastically, expecting a laugh, but Mason looked serious.

"You get to choose what kind of Winter you're going to be," he said gently.

Before she could ask him what he meant, the crowd of people waiting to get to the bar suddenly parted, the way crowds always did when Ravens arrived, thanks to their subtle mental suggestions.

Mason, however, waved for the nearest couple to go ahead of them.

"Why do you always do that?" Scarlett asked, feeling more annoyed. She needed a drink stat after her chat with Eugenie.

"I just don't like skipping ahead in lines all the time." He nodded to where the line had slowly re-formed. "We should wait our turn like everyone else."

Scarlett laughed. When he didn't join in, though, she stopped. "What's with you tonight?"

"Nothing."

"I'm not an idiot, Mason. I've known you for two years. I know when something is off. You've been weird all night," she replied. She took a step toward him, but he mirrored her, backing away.

"Scarlett, we're at a party. Let's just try to have fun and we'll talk about it later," he said, looking at the bar, at a couple dancing, at anything but her. "I don't want to do this right now."

Her heart skipped a beat, fear flooding her veins. Dimly, in the back of her mind, she was aware of a few Thetas side-eyeing them, watching the show. *Fuck off,* she thought viciously, and almost instantly, every single person within a ten-foot radius turned away from them.

"Look, I know things haven't been completely normal between us lately," she said, trying to stay calm, trying to reason with him. She could save this. She was Scarlett Winter, after all. "You were gone all summer, and I've been distracted with the new members' education. But we'll get back on track. We're great together. You *know* that."

Mason took a deep breath and ran a hand through his hair. His nervous tic. His poker tell. One she'd always found adorable until right this very second. Because when he did that, she knew.

Such a tiny gesture to snap her heart in two.

He moved closer, and despite her throat squeezing shut with panic, she held his gaze, like a drowning woman who wanted one last gasp of air before she went under. He put his hands on her shoulders, his touch ever so careful. Like she was something fragile, breakable. Like she was a stranger.

"I care about you, Scar. I always will. That hasn't changed. But I have."

This was really happening. He was using all the words and phrases of a bad romantic comedy. He was a breath away from saying, *It's not you, it's me . . .*

He shook his head. "I don't think our futures are as compatible as our pasts. And deep down, I think you know that too."

No, Mason. I don't know. Explain it to me, she wanted to shout. She wanted to shake him until he said something that made sense. But she could already tell his mind was made up. Maybe it had been for a long time, and she'd just been too busy, too oblivious to notice. "You don't mean that, Mason. You love me and I love you. We are supposed to be together."

His face fell. She knew what he was thinking—he didn't believe in "supposed to" anymore. But it really didn't matter which words she used. She could see that from his resolute face and his squared shoulders. This wasn't a spell, where if you said the right things and held the right cards, someone would love you the way you wanted him to. There were love spells, yes, and it would be possible to woo him back magically, to force him to act like someone in love. But that was all it would be: an act. You could bend a heart to your will, but underneath, it still beat to its own rhythm. There was no changing that.

"I've given this a lot of thought," he was saying. "And I'm sorry, I didn't mean to do this here, tonight. I love you, Scar, but I think we'd be better off as friends."

Her throat was thick with unshed tears. *Friends*. Screw that. She took a stumbling step back.

"Scarlett, wait." He started after her.

She raised a hand to ward him off, stopping him with her magic. "Please. I . . ." *Shit*. She was going to start crying, right here. "Later," she managed, practically flinging herself into the party.

She needed to get out of here. *Now*. Before she really lost it, before she brought this party crashing down around them.

She pushed her way through the crowd on the dance floor, shoving people aside with her elbows and her mind. The party throbbed around her, everyone shrieking with laughter, dancing, kissing, staring up at the décor in wonder. For everyone else, everyone but Scarlett, this was just another amazing night at Westerly.

The exit was finally in view when her mother and Eugenie stepped into her line of sight. *Shit.* She could not handle them right now. Not at her most vulnerable. She couldn't stomach her mom's disappointment, her sister's ill-disguised glee. She couldn't even begin to imagine how she'd break the news to her mother. She was stumbling back through the party, looking for another exit, when someone grabbed her arm.

Jackson. Oh God. She just couldn't. "Jackson, can you please yell at me another time?" she said, angrily brushing away a tear that had escaped down her cheek.

Jackson's expression shifted instantly, losing its usual sharp edges. He looked at her with something bordering on understanding, like he knew what it was like to lose your shit in the worst possible place. Of course, given that Harper was his stepsister, he probably did. Scarlett's heart gave a painful squeeze that had nothing to do with Mason.

Until a few days ago, she'd had no idea that Jackson was Harper's stepbrother. She'd always liked Harper, but they'd never been that close. After she died, Scarlett never let herself think about Harper's family or all the people she left behind. The collateral damage of what happened reached so much further than she'd ever imagined.

Now Jackson took her by the elbow and steered her through the crowds toward a side exit she hadn't noticed before. It led to a path that wove through darkened woods, running parallel to the front walk.

"It dead-ends half a block from the main entrance," he said. "Last I checked, there was a whole row of cabs waiting; I'm sure one will take you wherever you want to go."

For a moment, she just stared. "Why are you helping me?"

He shrugged, looking as uncomfortable as she felt. "Like you said, I can yell at you another time. Go home and get some sleep."

Scarlett took a few steps down the path and then turned to thank him. But he was already gone.

CHAPTER TWENTY-ONE

Vivi

Having now attended a grand total of three parties, Vivi could confidently say that Homecoming was the best one of her life. It wasn't just the lively, romantic music of the jazz band, the festive mood of the glamorous crowd, or the way the warm, late September air caressed her skin as she twirled on the dance floor with Ariana. It was the feeling of knowing that she could go anywhere and find someone who'd be happy to talk to her, from her new sisters to their countless admirers.

It felt like the entire school had shown up tonight. A few kids from her art history class were gossiping at the bar. A pretty redhead she'd chatted with once in the cafeteria was dancing by herself under a lemon tree. Etta swayed with an androgynous-looking person with razor-sharp cheekbones and a heart-melting smile. Juliet and Jess were kissing under the twinkling lights, and Tiffany was swaying with a handsome guy Vivi recognized from the PiKa mixer. Even Professor Barnum was there, sucking down a whiskey by himself in the corner. The only person she hadn't seen was Scarlett, but no doubt she was somewhere in the throng of people, judging the partygoers with the imperious gaze that scared Vivi a little less now that she'd seen the softer side of her Big.

"I'll be back in a minute," Vivi shouted to Ariana in the middle of the sweaty crowd moving to the beat of the band. "I still haven't learned the spell that keeps you from needing to pee every thirty minutes when you're drinking."

She pushed through to the edge of the crowd and made her way to the bathroom. The line was long, but Vivi struck up a conversation with an anthropology major who'd recently returned from a year abroad in Peru. Just a few weeks ago, Vivi would've been far too intimidated to make small talk with upperclassmen, let alone a poised older girl who'd just received a grant from *National Geographic,* but becoming a full-fledged Raven had tempered her fear of embarrassment and rejection. What did it matter if someone didn't like her? She had a whole houseful of friends waiting for her.

Vivi had finally made it to the front of the line when Tiffany sauntered toward her holding a drink in each hand. She looked just a tad unbalanced but somehow still impossibly elegant in her golden cocktail dress. "Do you want one of these?" she asked Vivi. "The bartender insisted on giving me an extra one 'for good luck,' whatever that means."

"I'm fine," Vivi said with a smile. "If I have one more sip, I might not make it."

"We wouldn't want that." Tiffany giggled. "Can't have our new superstar peeing her pants."

"Superstar?" Vivi repeated. "Hardly."

"No, listen to me, Vivi." Tiffany stepped forward until her face was right next to Vivi's. "I felt your power during the ceremony. And I know what happened in the tomb. I want you to know that it's okay. It's okay to be powerful. Do you understand me?"

"Um, yeah. I understand you," Vivi said, pulling back slightly.

Tiffany's expression turned serious. "You should never apologize for being powerful."

"I won't . . . I promise."

"Okay, good. Because we need witches like you. Everyone will want you to learn to control your power, but don't ever lose that feeling you had the other night. That's *real* magic."

With that, Tiffany spun on her heel, tilted to the side as her shoe sank into the grass, righted herself, and sauntered off.

"Go drink some water!" Vivi called after her.

By the time Vivi left the bathroom, her feet were smarting from the hours she'd spent standing in high heels. She scanned the grounds and spotted a few wood benches scattered at the far perimeter of the festivities, near a large pond. Vivi eased off her shoes and, enjoying the feel of the cool grass underfoot, made her way to one of the benches. The music thrummed in the distance, the lights twinkling like fireflies. She didn't know how anyone could look at all this and *not* see magic.

She still couldn't believe this was her life. Just that morning, she'd moved into a sweet little bedroom on the fourth floor of Kappa House. It had cheerful rose wallpaper and gilded furniture, including a desk that looked like it belonged in a palace in France and a twin bed with golden posts, a little black crystal ball topping each one. Dahlia had said she could redecorate the room however she liked, but Vivi thought it was already perfect. For once, *everything* in her life was perfect. She had friends. She had sisters. And she had power. *If my mom could only see me now . . .*

Someone coughed and a dark shadow shifted on the bench several feet over. Vivi started, surprised to realize she wasn't alone. "Hello?" she called, her voice wavering slightly. *You're a witch,* she reminded herself. *The things that go bump in the night should be afraid of* you *now.*

"Vivi?" The shadow stood and stepped into the wan light of the clearing.

"Oh, Mason," Vivi said with relief while her heart continued beating quickly for a different reason. His hair was tousled and his bow tie hung undone around his neck. He smelled faintly of smoke. A tumbler was in his hand, nothing left in it but melting ice.

"What are you doing out here all alone?" he said. It was a question that would've mortified Old Vivi, an acknowledgment of her awkwardness or friendlessness, but it didn't bother New Vivi at all. She'd become the type of girl who could sit alone on a bench by the forest and look thoughtful and mysterious instead of lonely.

"Just taking a breather. What about you?" Somewhere nearby, an owl hooted. There was a soft rustle of an animal moving in the underbrush; the sounds of the party were a low murmur in the distance. "Where's Scarlett?"

Mason gave her a pained smile. "We just broke up."

"What? Like, *tonight?*" Mason nodded. "Shit. I mean, I'm sorry. Are you okay?"

"Yeah, I'm okay." He gestured to the spot on the bench next to Vivi. "May I?" When Vivi nodded, Mason sat down heavily beside her, the heavy fabric of his tux pants brushing against her leg. Vivi shivered despite the warm night air. "I love Scarlett and I'll always care about her, but to be honest, we weren't meant to be together."

"From the outside, you looked like the perfect couple," Vivi said. Of course, she of all people should know that things weren't always as they seemed.

"I used to think that too," he said, shifting to look at Vivi. The moonlight illuminated half his face, casting his cheekbones in high relief. "But things just . . . changed for me this year."

Vivi took a sharp, shallow breath as she met his gaze. His hazel eyes shone in the moonlight as they searched hers. The air between them felt charged, and for one fleeting, desperate moment she wanted to ask if the breakup had had something to do with her. But she knew that was silly. She and Mason had barely even talked. Whatever connection she felt with him was just on her side. A crush, that was it.

As if eager to change the subject, Mason smiled and said, "So I hear you're a Kappa now."

"The rumors are true," she said, trying to keep her tone playful and light despite her racing heart. It was beating so loudly, she was almost tempted to cast a silencing spell lest Mason realize what his presence was doing to her.

He shifted again, his knee grazing hers. She'd never been this close to him before, so close that she could reach out to touch him if she dared.

"That's a shame," he said.

"Why?"

Mason turned to her with a wistful smile. "Because that means I can't offer to be your waffle-making tutor. It's purely altruistic, of course, but I don't think the . . . optics would be great."

Vivi froze on the bench as the meaning of his words filtered through her defenses. *Oh my God . . . he* does *like me.* She wanted to stand up and squeal, spin in a circle, text Ariana. Anything to release the fizzy joy bubbling up in her stomach. Or go full New Vivi and lean in for a kiss. For the first time in her entire life, a boy she had a crush on liked her back. Yet—the realization sank through her, heavy and sobering—there was nothing she could do about it.

Things had changed for her this year too. Magic had blown her entire life open. It gave her the power to alter her appearance, to reroute wind, to summon the most ancient and mysterious forces on earth. It had the power to welcome her, an only child, into a family of amazing women. But it couldn't change the fact that Mason was the ex of one of her new sisters.

Mason was right. Vivi was a Kappa now. And if she had to choose, the answer was clear . . . "Yeah, it probably wouldn't be a good idea."

Mason leaned back against the bench and sighed heavily before turning to her with a sad smile. "The Kappa bond is pretty strong, huh."

"It is . . . and I'm really lucky to be a part of it."

Mason nodded, then fell silent. "Take care of her for me, will you?" he said finally.

"I will." Vivi took a deep breath and forced herself to stand up. "Bye, Mason," she said, and turned back toward the party, wishing she knew a spell to heal an aching heart.

CHAPTER TWENTY-TWO

Scarlett

"Not again," Scarlett whispered. She crossed her arms over her chest and hugged herself as she shivered in her thin nightgown. She was in the second-floor hallway of Kappa House. All the doors to her sisters' rooms were closed. But she could hear the rumble of thunder and see the storm booming outside the window at the end of the hall.

The sconces on the walls flickered. She heard laughter, deep and throaty, behind her. But when she whipped around, there was no one else there.

The pictures, she realized. The photographs on the walls were all laughing at her. Row upon row of portraits, Raven sisters of old, pointing their fingers at Scarlett and cackling with glee. Even though she was horrified, her eyes went to the faces she knew best to see if they were laughing too. Her mother. Her sister. Dahlia. Mei. Gwen. And, finally, Harper.

She staggered on her feet. Started to run. The laughter got louder. Harsher.

She reached the end of the hallway and crashed into solid wood. No door. It was a dead end. She spun around, then froze in terror. There was someone else in the house. Someone coming toward her. Dressed in a cloak—a long flowing garment with shredded sleeves, one hand extended toward her, fingernails like bloody claws. She had long dark hair, glowing eyes. Beneath her hood, a red, red mouth filled with teeth opened wide. Harper. Always Harper.

Scarlett startled awake to the sound of her own gasp. *Just a nightmare. Just another nightmare.* She gripped her sheets, bathed in sweat, even though for once, the temperature had finally dipped below seventy for the night. Outside, lightning crashed and storm clouds gathered. Her heart continued to slam against her rib cage, an incessant beat, refusing to let her go back to sleep. She wondered if the storm was her doing or if it was just the perfect backdrop for a shitty night.

She reached with trembling hands for the water she always kept on her bedside table, but the nightstand was empty. Belatedly, she remembered why. It came in flashes: The cab ride alone after Homecoming. Stumbling into the empty house. Sobbing her eyes out in the bathroom, then finally collapsing face-first onto her bed, not even bothering to clean off her makeup.

She probably looked like a nightmare now. Judging by the black streaks on her pillow, she figured her mascara was in runnels.

She levered herself out of bed, shivering in the cool evening air. In the bathroom, she ignored the mirror and splashed water on her face. She scrubbed until her skin stung, then buried her head in a towel. When she finally peeked at her reflection, her eyes were puffy and swollen, red veins creeping across the whites.

Another crash of thunder outside. Louder. The storm was getting closer.

She went back into the bedroom, checked her phone. It was just past three in the morning. With a groan, she collapsed back onto her bed, one arm across her forehead.

Didn't matter. Sleep wasn't going to happen, not for the rest of the night. Her fingers itched to check more on her phone. Recent messages. Social media. Maybe Mason had texted. Or called. Or posted something.

He hadn't.

Scarlett hauled herself out of bed and threw on a robe. Then she shuffled down the long hallway in the general direction of the kitchen. Maybe she'd make some tea. Brew a little sleeping draft. As she passed Tiffany's bedroom, she heard a heavy *thunk* inside, like a footstep. Scarlett hesitated. The house was silent, heavy with sleep.

She pressed her ear to the wood. "Tiffany?" she whispered. No response, although she thought she heard *something* within: *tap-tap, tap-tap,* followed by a shuffling sound, like furniture being dragged. She knocked softly, then reached for the doorknob.

It turned easily in her hand. She pushed open the door. "Tiff?"

The bed was rumpled, unmade . . . and empty. Frowning, Scarlett flicked on the light. Then she screamed at the top of her lungs.

Blood. Everywhere.

On the crumpled sheets. Splattered across the walls like paint. Pooled on the carpet. Smeared across the shattered glass of the mirror. The balcony doors were flung open, shuddering on their hinges, creaking and tapping out a rhythm against the wall as they blew in the storm's wind. And right by the windowsill, on the cream-colored wallpaper, she spotted a single bloody handprint.

Scarlett screamed again.

This time, footsteps thundered from all sides. Doors opened, people called out, asking what had happened. But Scarlett could barely hear them over the rapid pounding of her heart; she hardly noticed the faces filling up the doorway behind her, the added shouts and screams that echoed her own.

That was when she noticed it. Placed delicately on the pillow like an invitation, a single red envelope. *To the Ravens,* it read in neat cursive writing. Writing she didn't recognize.

She grabbed it off the pillow and opened it just as Dahlia's voice rang out behind her.

"Everybody, get back. Scarlett, come on." Dahlia's hand came to rest on her shoulder, warm and strong. "Let's get you out of here."

But Scarlett was frozen to the spot, reading the note:

> *If you want to see your sister again, find the Henosis talisman. No outside help. No police. I will come for it the night of the new moon. Fail, and your sister dies. Fail, and I will take another and another —until I have what I want.*

"What is that?" Dahlia said, plucking the note from Scarlett's hands. The sisters in the hall grew quiet as Dahlia read the letter aloud, her voice steady, her shoulders square. Only her trembling hands gave away her nerves.

The house fell silent, but it was a far cry from the heavy silence of undisturbed sleep. The air felt thin, as if their screams had used up all the oxygen, making it difficult to breathe.

Jess was the first to speak. "Only a witch could have done this. No one else could have gotten through our protective spells."

Hazel nodded, her eyes wide and frightened. "The new moon is in two days," she said hoarsely. Juliet and Etta traded long looks.

"We have to do something," Mei said from the hallway. "Call the police, or—"

"No," Dahlia interrupted, her eyes narrowed at the letter. "None of us are going to the police."

"We have to, Dahlia," Scarlett countered automatically. Tiffany had been kidnapped and the struggle had clearly been violent. There was no time to worry about magical protocol, not when her best friend could be bleeding to death.

"And what do we say, Scarlett? 'A witch kidnapped our witch sister using witchcraft'?"

"We can leave the magic out of it. We just have to find her." Scarlett tried to push aside the image of Tiffany's tear-streaked face as she cried out in pain. Or worse, her face still and silent as the life drained from her body.

"There is no leaving magic out of it. Magic is the motive and the weapon and the victim. And hopefully magic is what saves her," Dahlia insisted. "If we call the police, we'll spend the next twenty-four hours answering pointless questions instead of looking for Tiffany."

"Dahlia's right. The police are out of their depth—and we can't risk that kind of exposure. Not yet, anyway," Juliet said.

Scarlett hesitated, then let out a long sigh and released the phone that she'd been gripping in her pocket. "So what do we do?"

Everyone fell silent again; the only sound was the beating of the rain against the windows.

Dahlia looked around Tiffany's room, taking in the chaotic scene. Her eyes landed on the pool of blood on the floor, and for a moment, her steely resolve seemed to crack. Her face crumpled and she let out a sob. Scarlett had seen her president cry only once, when her grandmother died. Somehow, on this already horrible night, it made things feel even more hopeless. But the moment was over as quickly as it came; Dahlia regained control once more and set her jaw determinedly. She took a deep breath and gazed out over the coven: Juliet and Jess clutching each other. Vivi, pale as a sheet, standing next to Ariana, who had tears streaming down her face. Scarlett knew Dahlia must have felt the weight of every sister's anxiety on her shoulders.

"We'll find the Henosis talisman, like it says." Dahlia refolded the letter carefully. "We don't have any other choice."

"But the talisman's a myth," Mei said, looking from Dahlia to the frightened faces of her sisters.

"So were witches. And then we came along," Dahlia said.

"But we have only two days." Scarlett pressed her fingers against her temples. "And if we don't find it . . ." She couldn't even manage to translate her terrifying thoughts into words.

"The Ravens have done the impossible before. We've been outsmarting our enemies for hundreds of years. Even the blackest magic can't stand up to our combined powers. Tiffany is our sister. We will find her together." Dahlia lifted her chin and gazed at each of the sisters. Hazel pressed her lips together and nodded. Vivi's face was ashen but determined. Sonali had a hard look in her eyes.

"Together," Mei repeated, reaching out to grab Scarlett's hand.

"Together." The word echoed like a chant in the hallway.

Together.

Scarlett forced a smile for her sisters, then turned to Dahlia. "I want to scry for Tiffany. Make sure she's okay. The letter says no outside help, but it doesn't say we can't use our magic."

"Maybe we can try to find the writer of the letter, too," Vivi suggested. "There's got to be a spell for that."

"I'll prep the kitchen," Etta said. She nodded at Hazel and Juliet to follow her.

"I'll check my grimoire," Mei said, spinning on her heel.

"Meet in the greenhouse in fifteen." Dahlia held on to Scarlett's hand as the rest of the sisters dashed off to prepare. "Scar, are you with me?"

"Dahlia, I can't feel her," Scarlett whispered.

Dahlia tightened her grip on Scarlett's hand. "She's Tiffany. No one messes with her. Remember the time she got locked in the coffin during Hell Week? When she couldn't spell her way out, she managed to claw her way out without an ounce of magic. She's a survivor."

Scarlett shook her head. "You saw all that blood. We'll be lucky if she's even conscious, let alone strong enough to fight back. We tell every pledge, 'Just because you're made of magic doesn't mean you can't be hurt.'"

"Tiffany has grit, Scarlett," Dahlia countered. "And she needs your strength right now."

"We need to save her, Dahlia."

"And we *will.* But if this person's looking for the Henosis . . . well. We all remember what happened to Evelyn Waters. We need to be careful, Scar. If anything goes wrong . . ."

"Then together we'll be strong enough to beat it," Scarlett replied, sounding far more confident than she felt. They would have to be strong if they were going to find her best friend.

CHAPTER TWENTY-THREE

Vivi

The rain landing on the greenhouse's roof sounded like thousands of sharp-beaked birds trying to smash through the glass. It was still hours before dawn and pitch-black outside, with heavy storm clouds shrouding the stars. But although most of the Ravens had just been roused from sleep, there was nothing drowsy about their expressions as they stood holding hands in a circle ringed with white taper candles. Some of the girls looked frightened, some angry, but most of the older girls looked stony and fierce, gathering the strength and focus they'd need for the task at hand—finding Tiffany.

Vivi stood next to Ariana, who was gripping Vivi's hand so tightly, it made her bones ache.

"Just a few hours ago we were in this room and she was teaching me how to perfect minor arcana skills. And now she's . . . gone," Ariana said, holding back tears.

"She's not gone—she just needs to be found," Vivi said firmly.

Tiffany was Ariana's Big and the two had grown close during the rush process. But Ariana's distress couldn't compare to that of

Vivi's own Big, who was standing across the circle, trembling visibly as she watched Juliet light the candles.

Vivi wished someone would enchant the candles to provide more light, as the flames did little to illuminate the darkness beyond the walls of the greenhouse. Although she was surrounded by a coven of powerful witches, she still felt exposed and vulnerable standing next to the glass wall. Someone had managed to gain entry to Kappa House despite its myriad magical protections. And that meant whoever it was could do it again. Was this what her mother had foreseen weeks ago? Or was there still more—something worse—yet to come?

The decision not to go to the police worried her. She understood Dahlia's reasoning for following the instructions in the note. Plus, whoever had taken Tiffany had done so by employing wicked magic, rendering the police pretty much useless. But a girl was missing and her kidnapper was still out there. Someone who'd promised to come back for more Ravens.

Dahlia moved into the center of the circle and knelt to examine a cauldron Etta had filled with a brew of red wine made from grapes that grew wild in a graveyard in Burgundy, mugwort, and cedar to enhance visions.

"Sisters," Dahlia said as she stood back up. "Join me."

The girls moved in until they'd packed themselves as tight and close to Dahlia as they could. Overhead, the storm battered the windows with frenzied abandon.

"Tonight, we seek she who has been stolen from us." Dahlia

raised her hand, revealing something clutched in her fist. Vivi's stomach lurched. It was a torn shred of Tiffany's bedspread, parts of the white satin stained almost black with dried blood. "We seek news of our sister—of who did this to her and whether she is still in danger."

Dahlia opened her fist and let the fabric flutter down into the cauldron; the unstained portions of the material turned dark red as the wine seeped into the satin.

The other girls began to hum, and Vivi felt the telltale throb of energy in her chest. For the first time, she was afraid to let it spread through her body. She'd seen the ugly side of magic tonight, and she wasn't eager to open herself up to something that could be so dangerous. But as she clutched Ariana's hand, Vivi reminded herself that finding Tiffany was worth every risk.

"I call to all the Queens, ancient as the dawn," Dahlia whispered. "Show us the sister who is missing and gone."

The rain picked up and the humming was nearly drowned out by the shriek of the wind rattling the glass panes of the greenhouse. Then the cauldron began to glow from within as the liquid started to bubble and boil; the dark red-wine mixture turned thick and black as tar. An image appeared on the uneven surface, and although the face was distorted by the rippling liquid, there was no doubt who it was.

Scarlett let out an anguished cry at the sight of her best friend. Bright red scratches raked down both sides of Tiffany's face, bloody streaks from her temples to her chin. Her mouth was gagged, her eyes wide with fear as she struggled against some kind of invisible bond.

"Oh my God," Ariana whispered as tears began to stream down her face. "We have to help her. *Now.*"

"Show us who did this," Dahlia commanded, an edge of desperation in her deep, sonorous voice.

A plume of smoke rose out of the cauldron, and a pungent, rotten stench hit Vivi with the force of a wave. She covered her face and stumbled back while a few of the other girls gagged.

The smoke grew thicker until, with a sound like eardrums popping, the cauldron exploded, showering a portion of the circle with scalding liquid. Dahlia yelped and winced as she muttered a healing spell; next to her, Mei did the same for Jess, who was clutching her wrist, her face contorted in pain. Vivi turned around to help Hazel and Reagan extinguish the candles that had tipped over and now threatened to set some of the drier plants alight. "What was that?" Vivi asked once the candles had been snuffed out.

"That," Dahlia replied, her hoarse voice sounding in the darkness, "was wicked magic."

CHAPTER TWENTY-FOUR

Scarlett

Tiffany, wherever you are . . . we're coming for you . . ."

Scarlett stared at the bright morning light filtering through her balcony doors. She'd locked them tight when she returned to her room after they'd cast the spell. Or tried to cast it, rather. Dahlia was right—wicked magic had interfered with the spellcasting, just as it had when Scarlett had tried to divine Gwen's intentions.

In her arms she held the stuffed elephant from the antiques shop. It was missing a leg. She could have fixed it with a simple glamour, but both she and Tiffany liked it just as it was, loved so much it was practically disintegrating. She wished there were a spell she could cast on it that would lead her to Tiffany. But because the spell last night hadn't worked, Scarlett didn't know what would. Whoever had taken Tiffany had erected a strong, protective wall of magic around both of them—one that even the Ravens couldn't penetrate.

Mei was asleep in Scarlett's bed; neither girl had wanted to sleep alone. Not after what happened to Tiffany. Every time Scarlett closed her eyes, she saw it. Bright red spray across the wallpaper.

Blood everywhere. There had been so much that it was hard to believe that Tiffany was still alive, even after the spell had said she was.

And now they had to find some mystical talisman that might not even exist. Scarlett had no idea where to begin to look. All she knew was that witches were in danger.

And it was all her fault.

Whatever you put out in the world came back to you threefold. And what she and Tiffany had done in their freshman year—what they'd hidden for so long—had finally caught up with them. And now Tiffany might pay for it with her life.

Scarlett quietly slipped out of bed. Mei stirred, and Scarlett put the stuffed animal back into her closet. She padded down to the kitchen. The house was silent. She wondered how many girls had spelled themselves to sleep and how many had spelled themselves awake to be sure they were ready for whatever came in the night. For once, Scarlett didn't want to use her magic at all; she was saving it up for what was to come. She and her sisters needed to be at full strength to get Tiffany back.

In the kitchen she grabbed a mug and started the espresso maker. As it hissed and sputtered, she stared out the window. The campus was just beginning to rouse. Students rode past on bicycles or walked leisurely with earbuds in, their backpacks slung over their shoulders. It was almost surreal that the world was just proceeding as normal while Tiffany was being held somewhere, in pain, waiting for Scarlett and her sisters to save her.

"Hey," a voice said, cutting through her thoughts. Vivi stood in the doorway, her hair sticking up slightly, her eyes puffy and red. "How are you doing?"

"How do you think?" Scarlett said, pouring the coffee into the mug. A little splashed over the sides, scalding her thumb, but she welcomed the pain. She deserved it and so much more.

Vivi blinked. "I'm sorry. That was a dumb question. I can leave if you want to be alone . . ."

Scarlett shook her head. "No, I'm sorry. I'm just really on edge."

"Of course you are." Vivi hesitated, then completely surprised Scarlett by wrapping her in a hug. "I'm so sorry this happened. I know how much Tiffany meant to you. *Means* to you," she quickly amended as Scarlett's heart gave a painful squeeze. "And I'm sure this pales in comparison to what you're going through with Tiffany, but I was also sorry to hear about you and Mason."

Oh God, Mason. Scarlett hadn't thought about him since she'd found Tiffany's bloodied room. She sat down at the table clutching her mug, staring into its depths as if she could scry for answers there. In one night, Scarlett had lost the two people she cared about most in the world.

"He was right to break up with me," Scarlett admitted. She didn't deserve to be happy, to move on with her life with an incredible guy at her side. Harper would never have that chance. And now Tiffany might not either. "He'll find someone better than me."

Vivi looked surprised. "Scarlett, he'll never do better than you. You're . . . perfect," she said finally.

"You don't have to do that."

"Do what?"

"Flatter me. You're a Raven now," Scarlett said.

"Trust me, it's not flattery."

Scarlett huffed out a faint laugh. "Well, Mason can do better. And he will. And I have to accept that." Scarlett curled both hands around her mug. "I'm not a good person, Vivi. I was awful to you, perhaps a little more than was required."

Vivi sat down at the table and shook her head. "You helped me. You trained me even though you don't *like* me. And you want to find your friend, whatever it takes. Even if it means putting yourself in danger."

"Of course I have to find her," Scarlett said. She'd never even considered the alternative. "It's my fault this happened to her."

"Scarlett, there's no way this is your fault." Vivi leaned forward and reached for her again, but Scarlett pulled away.

"It is," Scarlett insisted, growing angry. Not at Vivi, but at herself. "It *is* my fault."

"How in the world is it your fault?" Vivi argued. "You didn't—"

"We killed someone, Vivi," Scarlett burst out.

Vivi sat back in her chair, her face ashen. "What?"

Scarlett buried her face in her hands, pressing her palms into her eyes, finally letting herself admit the truth after so long. Finally letting herself remember that night in full relief.

It was March of freshman year and the weather was starting to turn warm. They'd all been at a Psi Delta Lambda mixer and the party was wilder than usual. Everyone was drunk and the crowd had spilled into the backyard, where the brothers had set up the kegs. Dahlia, who was already membership chair as a sophomore, was dancing with Sadie Lane, their president, and some of the other upperclassmen girls while a cluster of Psi Delt guys cheered someone doing a keg stand. Gwen was on a second-floor balcony looking down at them with a vaguely disgusted expression on her face.

"Look at her. That witch thinks she's above us all," Tiffany said to Scarlett. "She's literally standing above the fray. I say we bring her down a little."

"I don't know, Tiff," Scarlett said. Gwen and Tiffany had just had yet another fight—Scarlett didn't even know what about—and Tiffany was still seething.

"Come on, it'll be fun," Tiffany said, her eyes shining as she grabbed Scarlett's hand.

Scarlett hesitated. She didn't like Gwen either, now that she'd seen with her own eyes how cruel she could be to Tiffany, but doing anything out in the open like this, with all the sisters and Psi Delt guys there, was risky.

"Do I need to remind you that just last week she called us frivolous bitches who couldn't even control their magic enough to do a summoning spell?" Tiffany asked. Scarlett felt a flash of anger; *no one* insulted her spell technique.

"Ugh. She really is the worst. Our spells are flawless," Scarlett said. Maybe it was the alcohol, maybe it was the way Gwen was sneering at them just then, but against her better judgment, Scarlett finally agreed. Tiffany's grin was infectious, and Scarlett had to admit she was sick of Gwen's sanctimonious shit. "So what are you thinking?"

Tiffany just kept smiling and made a crawling motion with her fingers. Scarlett laughed. Of course. The only chink in Gwen's armor was her paralyzing fear of spiders. They'd discovered this during their Hell Week graveyard task when they'd had to collect spider webs for spellwork. Gwen had screamed and cried like a three-year-old.

"You wicked little witch," Scarlett said, but she couldn't help laughing as they joined hands and whispered the incantation.

For a moment, nothing happened. Then Gwen let out a bloodcurdling scream and started hopping around the balcony, swatting at the air. No one else could see anything, but to Gwen, spiders were everywhere, climbing all over her, skittering across every surface. The entire party turned to watch her. "Get them off me!" she shouted.

"What the hell?" Dahlia said as some of the boys burst out into laughter. One pulled out his phone and began filming as Gwen writhed and twisted.

Tiffany laughed long and loudly, cutting through the crowd. Gwen's gaze locked on her and Scarlett. Her eyes narrowed in understanding and she started moving her lips rapidly, fists clenched, beginning a spell of her own. But Scarlett and Tiffany were ready for her. As soon as they felt Gwen's magic rebound on them, Scarlett shoved back, hard, almost knocking Gwen off her feet.

Gwen fixed Scarlett with a look that stopped Scarlett in her tracks, a glare of pure loathing, then she clenched her fists harder, tapping into her power once more. Tiffany and Scarlett joined hands and sent another wave of power at Gwen to counteract her next spell. That was when Harper stepped out onto the balcony and touched Gwen's shoulder, no doubt to calm her. Harper cared about Gwen, and above all, she cared about her sisters' public image.

Scarlett didn't even know how to describe what happened next. Gwen must have lost concentration mid-spell and her magic flooded out of her in a tidal wave and collided head-on with Tiffany and Scarlett's new spell. The magic slammed together and exploded, blowing everyone and everything in the immediate orbit away.

Before anyone could move, before Scarlett even had the chance to take a breath, the sound of metal bowing rent the air, and the balcony cleaved right off the side of the house; it crashed to the ground with a thunderous clang. Gwen and Harper were thrown to the ground like rag dolls.

Harper died instantly, crushed on impact. Scarlett could still see the blood pooling around her on the concrete patio. Scarlett had raised a shaky hand to stanch the blood, but Tiffany pushed it down.

"Someone will see," Tiffany hissed, eyes wide and wild.

"We have to help them," Scarlett said, not caring about appearances, not caring about anything but her injured sisters. She raised her hand once more and began to chant a spell under her breath, but Tiffany pushed it away once more.

"They're gone," Tiffany whispered, hugging her friend.

At that moment, a boy checking Gwen's pulse let out a shout. "She's still breathing," he exclaimed.

Gwen was rushed to the hospital in critical condition.

Scarlett was stricken and frantic with guilt. She only kept it together for Tiffany; she'd never seen her friend look so shaken. Later that night, before the all-hands house meeting, Tiffany had made a confession of her own. "Scarlett, do you know what Gwen and I were fighting about?" she said. "I found a deer heart and a wicked grimoire in her bedroom. She didn't want me to tell Sadie, and as much as I don't like her, I didn't want to rat out a sister. But she was using evil magic. If Harper hadn't interrupted her, who knows what Gwen would have done?" Tiffany broke down in tears.

Scarlett felt sick to her stomach and she began to cry too. Her mind was swimming with if-onlys. If only Tiffany had told her about the heart. If only they hadn't pulled that stupid prank . . . but it was done. They were the most powerful witches in the country, but they couldn't bring Harper back.

"We screwed up, Scar. We didn't start this, but we have to stop it. We have to stop Gwen," Tiffany said.

"Gwen can't hurt anyone anymore," Scarlett said, thinking of the unconscious girl getting wheeled away by the paramedics.

"She's a witch. She's stronger than me. What do you think she'll do to *us?*" Tiffany said.

Scarlett opened her mouth to protest, but Tiffany was trembling, the air around them in the room picking up speed with her emotion. "We can't tell. And we can't let her hurt anyone else!"

The window of the room blew shut from the force of her feelings.

Scarlett relented. "We won't tell. We won't let her hurt anyone else," she repeated.

Immediately the wind died down and Tiffany collapsed on her bed, spent.

After the meeting, they'd told Sadie and Dahlia what Tiffany had seen in Gwen's room, and everything that happened after that went exactly according to plan. The sisters bound Gwen's powers that very night. The administration had blamed the balcony collapse on faulty construction and spent the summer reinforcing all the balconies on campus. And no one was any the wiser about *why* Gwen had freaked out and done that spell in the first place.

For two years Scarlett had told herself that it wasn't her fault. Not really. Gwen was the one who'd lost control. Gwen was the bad witch, the one going down a dangerous path. She and Tiffany had been right to stop her. But deep down, she'd always known what they'd done.

Now she recounted the incident to Vivi in a wooden tone. When she finished, she looked up at her Little. "Don't you see? We blamed it on Gwen, but it was us. We're the reason Harper is dead. If we hadn't played that stupid prank on her . . ."

"Oh, Scarlett." Vivi looked stricken. "That's awful. Really awful. But you didn't *kill* Harper. You said it yourself—it was supposed to be a harmless prank."

"But it *wasn't*. We told ourselves back then that we were protecting the Ravens from Gwen. But we created this," Scarlett argued. "If we hadn't done it, Harper would still be alive. And Gwen . . ."

"And Gwen would still have her powers," Vivi finished, realization dawning in her eyes. "Do you think she wants them back?"

"Wouldn't you?" Scarlett said.

"And now she's on campus again." Vivi sat back in her chair for a moment, as if to let the news settle.

"And now Tiffany's been kidnapped," Scarlett said. "By someone who wants a powerful magical talisman." She shot Vivi a pointed look. "The kind of item that could probably break an old binding spell . . ."

Vivi let out a low whistle. "Scarlett, I think you need to tell Dahlia the truth. All of it."

Scarlett shook her head vigorously. She'd thought of that, of the sweet relief of unburdening herself finally. But she couldn't yet. Not to protect herself, but to protect Tiffany. "She'd kick me out. Strip me of my powers—and I need them more than ever right now." Scarlett's breath came faster. "I have to find Tiffany. *I have to.* She's my best friend; I can't just walk away from witchcraft right when she needs me most. It's my fault. Don't you get it? Gwen did this to get revenge, and it's my fault for letting it happen. You have to promise me you won't tell, Vivi."

"Hey." Vivi put a hand on Scarlett's forearm. "Deep breaths." She waited for Scarlett to inhale a couple of slow breaths before she spoke again. "Nobody's taking your magic away, okay? I promise I won't tell a soul." She pursed her lips. "What about the Henosis talisman? If we find it, we'll get Tiffany back."

Scarlett let out a faint, humorless laugh, struck by the irony that someone to whom she had been so cruel was being so kind to her now. If she was the bad witch of this story, surely Vivi was the good one.

"What is it, Scarlett?"

"The talisman is hopeless. Nobody's seen it since it vanished from the house *decades* ago. If it ever existed in the first place."

"There are all kinds of spells to find lost objects," Vivi pointed out.

"Spells our foremothers tried, no doubt." It was at times like this that she longed for Minnie. Minnie knew every bit of witch history, forgotten spells and things that weren't forgotten but weren't written down in hopes that they *would* be forgotten. She wanted Minnie here for another more selfish reason, though. She wanted to talk to her. She wanted her hugs, her cups of mystery tea, and her words—the words that weren't spells yet did the trick of making her feel better all the same. But Minnie wasn't here; Vivi was. And they somehow had to figure this out on their own.

Vivi shrugged. "Maybe there's something they overlooked. We can check the archives, not to mention all the older tomes in the rare-books collection at the library. Didn't you say the talisman initially belonged to the school?" Vivi caught Scarlett's gaze and held it. "We'll find her, Scarlett. Whatever it takes. We'll find that talisman, and then we'll use it to bring Tiffany home."

Scarlett nodded. She appreciated Vivi's fire, but a new idea was blooming in her mind. Maybe they didn't need to find the talisman.

Maybe they just had to find the person who wanted it.

CHAPTER TWENTY-FIVE

Vivi

This is ridiculous," Ariana said as she, Vivi, and Sonali completed their third circuit around the oddities and curiosities museum on the first floor of the Hewitt Library. "Of course the talisman isn't here. Why would it be? Don't you think someone would've noticed if one of the most powerful magical objects in the world was being displayed on campus?"

"I doubt many Ravens spend much time here," Sonali said, wrinkling her nose at a shriveled, shrunken head in a glass case. "It's kind of creepy, isn't it?"

Vivi had to agree. While the collection had appeared mysterious and romantic when she saw it with Mason in the middle of a sunny afternoon, the macabre items seemed very different in the evening light as she, Sonali, and Ariana searched desperately for a clue that'd save their sorority sister's life.

"Have you not seen the dried frog's toes in the supply closet at Kappa House?" Ariana asked.

"That's different. Those have a practical purpose. They're not so-called curiosities."

"Whatever," Ariana said. "We're wasting our time here. Why would it be on campus at all?"

“Scarlett said it was rumored to have some connection with Westerly,” Vivi said. “Let’s check the archives. You’re right, if the talisman were in plain sight, Tiffany’s kidnapper wouldn’t have gone to so much trouble.” She was about to mention what Mason had said about how only 10 percent of the collection was on display for the public, but she wasn’t sure she wanted to explain how she’d ended up on a non-date with Scarlett’s boyfriend.

It’d been about twelve hours since the scrying ritual and it didn’t seem like they were any closer to finding Tiffany . . . and now they had two days to locate the talisman before her kidnapper made good on that grim threat. They’d tried three house-wide spells to locate the talisman and had come up empty each time. After that, Jess, Juliet, and Mei had spent all day examining the inventory records of libraries and museums around the world, while Dahlia, Hazel, and Etta had contacted trusted witch friends to put out feelers, although they had to be careful. If word got out that Kappa was trying to find the Henosis talisman, it could be interpreted as an act of aggression by others in the magical community. It was clear that freshmen had been assigned the least important task—searching for the talisman in person in the incredibly unlikely event that it was somewhere on campus.

Yet, although it was a long shot, it’d be foolish for them to leave without examining every inch of the building, including the archives. Vivi turned to cast a wary glance at the librarian behind the front desk who’d pretended to ignore them while watching them carefully the whole time. It was the same woman who’d been here when she visited with Mason, the one he’d called Miss Irma.

Vivi approached the desk with a warm smile, channeling her inner Mason. "Excuse me, ma'am," she said. Just a few weeks in Savannah had made it clear to her how much manners mattered here. "I'm sorry to bother you, but we're doing research for a class and we were wondering if it'd be possible to check out the archives."

The librarian raised an eyebrow as she looked pointedly at the brass clock on the wall. "We close in fifteen minutes. Last entry to the archives is an hour before closing."

Vivi opened her mouth to protest, but Sonali put a hand on her arm. She muttered something under her breath, and a moment later, the librarian's icy smile softened into something more genuine, and her eyes turned glassy.

"Will you please show us the archives?" Sonali said sweetly.

"Yes, of course," the librarian murmured. "Follow me, please."

"Shoot," Sonali whispered as she looked down at her phone. It was the first time Vivi had ever heard her curse. "Reagan needs help charming the archivist in the rare-manuscripts collection. I have to go. Meet you back at the house?"

Vivi nodded while Ariana grabbed her hand to pull her after the librarian, who'd picked up speed despite her dazed expression.

As useful as Swords magic was, Vivi didn't know how she felt about it. Now that she was a full sister, she could tap into that suit's power, but she hadn't tried it yet. There was a fine line between influence and mind control, but if it helped them find Tiffany's kidnapper, then it was worth venturing into an ethically gray area.

Vivi was still processing everything Scarlett had told her. What had happened to Gwen and Harper was horrible, and Vivi wasn't sure how she'd live with herself if she'd caused someone's death. At the same time, no one could've predicted how those spells would interact. Scarlett had never meant to hurt anyone; she wasn't a killer. But Vivi knew without a doubt that Gwen was.

They followed Miss Irma down a hallway and into an elevator. "So how are the archives divided?" Vivi asked.

"It's a bit of a hodgepodge, I'm afraid," Miss Irma said. "Which class is this for?"

There was a long pause. "Religion and Mysticism Through the Ages," Ariana said finally. "It's, um, it's a sort of independent study."

Vivi winced, but luckily, Miss Irma didn't seem bothered by the vagueness. "A fascinating subject. Prayers and spells provide a very interesting peek into the minds of the penitents. We can use them to deduce what people wanted, their major drives in life, the big disasters or societal changes they faced at the time."

The elevator dinged and the doors parted to reveal what was tantamount to a vault, windowless and sealed off from the world above. Dim lights cast shadows across the room, and in the center stood a series of metal shelving units with wheels on each end so they could be moved around. Along the walls were display cases filled with a wide variety of objects, including bronze statues, ceramic plates, and a number of dusty-looking books.

It would take hours to go through it all.

"Have you ever come across an item called the Henosis talisman?" Vivi asked.

Miss Irma's brow furrowed. "No, but you're not the first person to ask me about it. Someone came by a few weeks ago looking for the same object."

All the air seemed to rush out of the room as Ariana and Vivi exchanged glances. "What a funny coincidence," Vivi said, doing her best to keep her tone light. "Do you remember their name?"

"Or what they looked like?" Ariana asked quickly.

"I'm not sure . . . I think . . ." Miss Irma's head jerked to the side.

"Are you okay, Miss—" Vivi gasped as Miss Irma twisted around to face them. Her eyes had turned solid black.

"No one," she murmured. "I see no one."

"What the hell?" Vivi whispered, looking from Miss Irma to Ariana.

"I think whoever asked about the talisman tried to erase her memory," Ariana said, staring at Miss Irma with wide, frightened eyes. "We need to tell someone about this. I'll call Dahlia."

Vivi nodded. "Let's take her upstairs so we can keep an eye on her until Dahlia tells us what to do."

"I'll do it. You stay here and hunt for the talisman. We can't waste any more time." Ariana looked at Miss Irma uneasily, clearly not keen to be alone with the bewitched librarian with creepy dilated eyes. Gingerly, she touched Miss Irma's elbow and guided her back into the elevator. "Come with me," she said to her. "We're going to find you help."

As the elevator doors closed, Vivi turned and headed to the first row of shelves. She didn't even know what they were searching for. None of the Ravens had any idea what the talisman looked like.

Luckily, most of the items in the glass cases were labeled: BURIAL JAR (301 BCE); CURSE POPPET (75 BCE). The latter, a clay doll with metal nails driven through its neck and heart, made her shudder as an icy numbness spread through her limbs. It felt like the reverse of harnessing her power, a deadening instead of an awakening. She was reminded of what she'd felt when they'd cast the spell to look for Tiffany—the unmistakable sense of wicked magic. Vivi wondered how much further Gwen would be willing to go to get her hands on the talisman and how many Ravens she'd willingly harm in the process.

The fact that Tiffany's kidnapper had already come here looking made the idea of finding the Henosis talisman on campus seem slightly more probable, though Vivi still had no clue where to start. Scarlett had taught her a spell to reveal traces of magic, but that would help only if the talisman was in the building. Still, it was worth a try.

"I call to the Queen of Wands," she whispered. "Reveal the signs of magical bonds."

At first, it seemed like nothing was happening. But then Vivi spotted a faint gleam on the handle of a nearby dagger. She stepped to the case for a closer peek and saw what looked like glowing fingerprints, as if her magic had revealed the grip of the last person to wield it. "'Dagger, fifteenth century,'" Vivi read from the card. "'Believed to be a murder weapon.'" Did that mean a witch had used this to kill someone?

Vivi continued to scan the items but didn't see anything else until she turned into the next row and came face to face with a bowl that was glowing so brightly, it looked like someone had placed a light bulb inside. "'Ceremonial bowl, third century BCE. Discovered in the Temple of Apollo,'" Vivi read aloud.

Halfway down the row, something in another case was glowing. Inside was a red cushion like those used to display jewelry in museums, but there was nothing on it—only the faint outline of a necklace.

The outline was glowing.

Vivi turned to look at the information card next to the case. "'Decorative pendant. Origin uncertain. Also known as the Henosis talisman. Missing since 1997, presumed stolen.' Oh my God," Vivi whispered as her heart began to pound. The card included a photograph of a small blue glass oval with smaller ovals set into it. Like an evil eye, except the center wasn't a black circle. Instead, it was a small, red seven-pointed star. Vivi pulled out her phone to take a photo and was just about to text Ariana when the sound of distant laughter made her start. "Ariana, is that you?"

There was no answer save for another peal of laughter.

Then the overhead lights began to flicker.

On-off.

On-off.

On-off.

"Ariana?" Vivi called again. The cold, numb feeling she'd felt looking at the doll returned, but this time, it didn't seem to be emanating from a specific object—it felt like it was coming from the air itself, closing in on her, invading her every time she took a breath. She reached for the wall to find a light switch but instead of touching cool plaster like she'd expected, her fingers brushed against something hard, bumpy, and throbbing. The wall was *moving*. Vivi jerked her arm back with a gasp. "What the—"

She aimed her cell phone flashlight at the wall and shrieked.

The wall was swarming with enormous, dark brown cockroaches. They skittered over one another, spilling from the tops of cases. There were hundreds—no, thousands—of them, swelling in a wave toward Vivi, a dark mass dyeing the floor black.

Vivi's head swam with horror as she stepped back, her mind racing for an explanation. Another distant laugh echoed over the shuffling of the insects. *We made her hallucinate spiders,* Scarlett had said about Gwen. Maybe this was also magic.

Vivi took off running toward the sound of laughter, her stomach roiling as her feet skidded over the insects. *Not real. Not real. Not real,* she told herself, praying it was true.

She focused her energy on the overhead lights, repeating an incantation to turn them back on, and after a few tries, the lights blazed to life. She squinted into the glare and could just make out a dark-haired figure disappearing around a corner.

A figure who looked exactly like Gwen.

CHAPTER TWENTY-SIX

Scarlett

Scarlett could feel her classmates watching her as she hurried across the quad, though she wasn't sure if their curiosity had been piqued by her unladylike haste or her decidedly uncharacteristic outfit. Scarlett hadn't worn jeans on campus since she'd started at Westerly, and she hadn't worn flats since Tory Burch ballet slippers went out of style, but for the first time in her life, she was too busy and exhausted to worry about what she looked like.

Thirty-six hours had passed since Tiffany was taken, and the Ravens had found nothing. They'd scoured the archives, tried various summoning spells, called numerous alumnae from that time period—including Scarlett's mother—but come up empty-handed. For her part, Scarlett had been secretly trying to track Gwen, but the girl hadn't been back to her apartment in days. And when she'd tried scrying for her, Gwen hadn't shown up *anywhere,* which was incredibly concerning. It meant she either was dead . . . or had somehow magically covered her tracks. Scarlett felt each second ticking past with the beat of her own heart. Each wasted minute was another one Tiffany was spending alone, consumed by terror and pain.

Scarlett wasn't used to feeling so powerless and she didn't like it, but she was desperate enough to do something she liked even less—ask for help. That was why she was now walking across campus, taking long, purposeful strides. There were only a few minutes left before his class let out and she didn't want to miss him.

The moment the class doors swung open, she spotted him, squinting into the distance with the serious, intense gaze that always made him seem slightly out of place among the carefree Westerly students. "Come with me," she instructed; she grabbed Jackson by the arm and led him onto a secluded path that looped behind the academic buildings.

"Are you kidnapping me?" he asked with a mix of boredom and amusement, as if she were a puppy who refused to leave him alone.

Scarlett winced at his choice of words, and Jackson's face softened a tiny bit. "What's going on?"

The unexpected note of concern in his voice was almost enough to undo her, and to her dismay, she felt her eyes prickle. *Get it together,* she ordered herself. Crying in public wasn't an option, let alone crying in front of Jackson. "Look, I know you don't like me, and I don't particularly like you either. But I think we could help each other now."

"Hey, I never said I didn't like you." Jackson stopped and raised his hands. "I just don't trust Kappas. *Any* Kappa."

She didn't ask him why. She didn't need to. The guilt that had been her constant companion for two years fluttered once more in her chest, and her hastily erected defenses crumbled.

"I am so sorry, Jackson. About what happened to Harper. I'm

sorrier than I can ever tell you," she said, forcing herself to meet his gaze despite the pain flashing across his face. "And you're right . . . what happened was a horrible accident. If she hadn't joined Kappa, she'd still be here." That was as much as she could say.

Jackson was quiet for a long moment, his jaw clenched. When he finally spoke, his voice sounded stiff, as if it was taking all his self-control not to shout. "It's not just how she died, Scarlett. It's everything that came before it. Harper and I were really tight. She was my family; we never kept secrets. Then she joined your sorority, and suddenly . . ." His gaze went distant, unfocused. "It's like she became a different person. She had all this stuff she couldn't tell me about. Secret traditions, late-night meetings nobody else was allowed to attend. The way she talked about the sisterhood, I'll be honest, it sounded like she'd joined a cult or something."

The familiar knot of guilt expanded, pressing against her until it became uncomfortable to breathe. Immersing herself in the Ravens had made her own world so much larger and brighter; she'd never stopped to think about the people who'd been pushed into the shadows. "We can be a little tight-knit."

"It's more than that, and you know it. The way you closed ranks after she died . . . even Gwen, who was supposed to be her best friend, would barely talk to me." Jackson shook his head. "That's why I came here, you know. This may come as a shock to you," he said wryly, gesturing at his frayed jeans and Hendrix T-shirt, "but this preppy Southern campus wasn't exactly my first choice. I was all set to go to Columbia when Harper died. But I knew I needed to come here if I was ever going to make peace with what happened."

His usual sardonic expression faded, and for a moment, Scarlett got a glimpse of the scared, confused boy who gave up his dreams to cling to his sister's memory. To follow a ghost. But then a new stab of fear shot through her. "Did Gwen tell you anything?"

Jackson shook his head. "We had this one conversation. But she just kept . . . I don't know, choking up or something. I had never seen her like that. I know it's traumatic for her, too. I mean, she was *there.* She almost died too. But I know her, and I know she wanted to tell me something. But she was so terrified and so scared . . . What would make her scared like that?" he said.

Scarlett rifled through her brain for an excuse before she realized he wasn't actually looking at her for an answer; he was just lost in his own memory.

"After that she started avoiding me . . ."

"So you started following her," Scarlett said.

Jackson crossed his arms, defensive. "You're the one who broke into her apartment."

"Guilty." Scarlett held her palms up. "It's just that . . . well . . ." She hesitated, unsure if this was the right thing to do. Confiding in an outsider went against every tenet of Kappa. But he was the only person in the whole world who might know where Gwen would go, and finding Tiffany took precedent over every tradition and protocol. "Look, this is a secret—"

"Shocker," Jackson cut in.

"I know, but this is really serious." Scarlett inhaled and then in one long breath said, "One of my friends is in trouble. She went missing after Homecoming. We can't go to the police—there was a note. It was really specific, and I think Gwen might have had something to do with it. I know you've been watching her too, and if there's anything you've found out or anything weird you've seen, I need you to tell me."

"You think Gwen took your friend?" Jackson asked, his skepticism bordering on disdain. "Why would she do that? What did you do to her?"

Scarlett forced herself to maintain her composure. For all Jackson knew, Gwen was a scared, fragile girl who'd suffered a major trauma. He had no idea what she was really capable of. "It's . . . complicated. But I promise, I don't want to hurt Gwen. I just want to help my friend."

"You're going to have to give me a *lot* more than that. If she's hiding from you, she probably has a damn good reason."

Her fingers itched, prickling with the anticipation of magic. Out of respect for Harper, she was going to give Jackson one chance to work with her, but she was prepared to use magic if she needed to. Altering someone's free will was against the rules, but now was not the time to worry about coloring inside the lines. "She's not safe on her own. I think there's a chance she could hurt herself and anyone she has with her."

"Why would she do that?" Jackson's voice was still hard, but the defiant look on his face was fading.

"I'm not entirely sure, but I can't risk losing another sister."

Jackson closed his eyes, and for a moment, Scarlett panicked, thinking she'd gone too far. As close as the Ravens were, her losses were nothing compared to Jackson's. Finally, he sighed. "There's a cabin out on Skidaway Island," he said wearily. "I've followed her there before. She goes at least once every couple of weeks."

Scarlett dug inside her purse for her car keys. "Think you can find the place again?"

"It just occurred to me we are doing the absolute opposite of everything we learned from horror movies," Jackson said after a few minutes of scanning through her radio presets and giving crisp directions.

"This isn't a horror movie. And there are two of us and only one of her," Scarlett countered.

"Easy for you to say. You're the Final Girl and I'm that poor sap who called shotgun. If I remember right, it doesn't turn out well for my character."

"Depends on the movie. There are a few where the boy survives too."

"Name one."

"Cary Elwes in *Saw,* Bruce Campbell in *The Evil Dead,* Corey Feldman in—"

"Friday the Thirteenth: The Final Chapter." He gave a low whistle. "Scarlett Winter knows her horror movies. Are we in the Upside Down now?"

"You don't know me, Jackson. You just think you do."

"So educate me."

She sighed, not really wanting to get into it. But he'd agreed to help her and she owed him, even more than he knew. "The woman who helped raise me loved horror flicks. She liked screaming at the screen, telling the characters to be smarter when inevitably they did something not so smart to keep the plot moving, like splitting up or making out when they knew a killer was on the loose."

Jackson laughed. "I always sort of wanted to write a horror movie. I thought I'd be the next Stephen King or something, but then my real life kind of took a plot twist."

"You're a writer?" she asked. At first she was surprised, but when she thought about it, it made sense. He was smart—he was the only person in class whose answers were almost as elegantly constructed as her own, and he certainly was quick.

He shrugged. "Not anymore."

"I'm sure Harper wouldn't want you to stop doing what you loved."

Jackson's expression hardened. "What Harper would have wanted was to still be alive. But given that she's not, she would want me to track down whoever did this to her and make sure they were locked away for the rest of their lives. That's what she would want."

"You're right. I have no right to presume what Harper wanted," Scarlett admitted. She'd bristled every time someone had told her how to grieve after Minnie died.

"I always thought once I put this to rest, once I knew what really happened, I would get back to it. But what used to matter to me before matters a whole lot less now."

Scarlett took this in. Her plans. Mason. Being president of Kappa. That all did pale now in the shadow of what had happened to Tiffany. And what they'd done to Harper. "I'm so sorry, Jackson."

He shrugged again. "Not your fault. All you're doing is fighting for your sister. I shouldn't have taken the fact that I lost mine out on you."

Scarlett swallowed her guilt. Part of her—the good part of her, the part that came from Minnie—wished she could tell him the truth. At the same time, the worst part of her—the part that had let herself keep this horrible secret for two long years—was grateful that she couldn't. Grateful that she was bound by the secrecy of magic. By her vow to her sisters. She knew she was taking the easy way out, but how could she ever tell him without explaining who—*what*—she really was?

When she looked back at Jackson, he was staring out the window pensively. They didn't talk again for the rest of the drive.

"Maybe we should knock." Jackson's voice sounded thin, unsteady.

They stood deep in the forest of the island park near Savannah about five feet from the door of the most rundown, horror-movie-looking cabin she'd ever seen. This far into the woods, it looked like twilight already. The trees cast shadows over the gravel path and the sagging wooden porch up ahead.

The looming dusk only made the cabin look more forbidding. A bundle of thorns was nailed over the door. The windows were marred with dark streaks. Paint peeled from the wood siding in long furls. There was a stain on the porch that looked almost like blood. *Are you in there, Tiff?* The words were more like a prayer than a question. Scarlett closed her eyes, trying to pick up on a trace of magic, but the air felt dry and thin—the opposite of how it felt when Tiffany was nearby.

Scarlett realized just how far they were from help—or an escape route. They'd parked at a small turnoff about a ten-minute hike from the cabin. They hadn't passed a single house on the way here. The trees were scrubby and gnarled, the grass long and untended. The only signs of life were the shards of broken beer bottles and cigarette butts underfoot. There was one area where a perfect circle had been burned into the grass. It was blackened and charred and devoid of vegetation, almost like the earth itself had been cursed.

The cabin appeared just as lifeless. There were no cars parked in the gravel driveway, no lights on inside.

"And say what?" Scarlett said. "'Hello there, seen a strange girl around, possibly dragging a kidnapping victim?'" Nothing was going to stop her from finding Tiffany. She had to get inside. Now.

"Do you have a better plan?" Jackson asked. He cast another look at their surroundings. "Maybe we should just go. I have a bad feeling about this, Scarlett."

So did she, and she had a whole lot more magical senses at her disposal. "If you don't want to come with me, just wait here," Scarlett said, and then she took off, striding toward the front door before she could rethink this.

Her scalp itched. Her feet pricked as though from a thousand pins and needles. She'd felt this before. It was a protection spell trying to make her turn around, flee. Shadows danced at the edges of her vision, like spiders skittering along the eaves, as she stood on the porch.

It's not real, she told herself. Just a spell to drive away unwanted visitors. Nothing more. Nothing that could actually hurt her.

The floorboards of the cabin's porch creaked behind her, and Scarlett gasped, whipping around. But it was only Jackson, climbing the steps. "I can't let you face a haunted house alone," he said.

"Trust me, I can take care of myself," Scarlett replied as she scanned the front door. Simple key lock. Good.

"That's not in doubt," Jackson said, leaning against the wall of the cabin with his arms crossed. She pulled a pin from her hair and knelt before the door, careful to obstruct his view of what she was doing. She concentrated hard as she pretended to pick the lock. The lock made a soft *click;* she glanced up at him to catch the look of appreciation on his face, then tested the handle. It turned in her grasp. She hoped he assumed this was due to her lock-picking skills —skills she did *not* have. It was pure magic. And a little acting. She took a deep breath and pushed the door inward.

It took a moment for her eyes to adjust. All the windows had blackout curtains pulled tightly across them. The dim light filtering in through the door illuminated a rickety wood table with two chairs, the only furniture in the room. An unused, cobwebbed kitchen stood off to the side, a gap where presumably the stove used to be. She peeked into a tiny bedroom off the main room that had nothing in it but an overturned crate. There was a small den with a burnt-orange couch that looked like it'd lost some of its stuffing to mice.

Shoved in the corner, between the couch and the wall, was a cardboard box. It looked newer than the rest of the objects, less dusty and decrepit. Scarlett crossed the room quickly and peeked inside. Her heart sped up when she saw the contents: a cheap-looking black polyester robe and witch's hat, just like the ones the burning scarecrows had been wearing. Nestled below them was a garish set of tarot cards. Scarlett quickly flipped through it. The Queens of Swords, Wands, Pentacles, and Cups were missing. So, ominously, was the Death card.

A whisper of triumph ran through her. She was right. It'd been Gwen all along. But her satisfaction drained away a moment later, replaced by the grim realization that she still didn't know where Gwen was and that Tiffany was still in danger.

The house was silent. There was no one here.

She lifted a blackout curtain and looked outside. About a hundred yards away and barely visible through the trees was another small building, this one slightly larger than an outhouse.

"Jackson," she whispered, and he nodded grimly.

Together they walked quietly out of the house, cut through the overgrown grass, and, keeping to the shadows, made their way to the shed. The trees grew haphazardly back here; the ground was covered with a mix of dead leaves and sandy dirt. A squirrel skittered along a branch, and a bird let out a high-pitched cry. Scarlett's heart beat loudly in her chest as they drew closer to the shed.

It was weather-beaten, made of long, splintered wood planks

held together with rusted nails. The door stood crookedly on its hinges, and there was a grimy, half-shattered window set into the left side.

And that was when she heard the muffled *thump*.

She whirled around, grabbed Jackson's arm, and pressed her finger to her lips, then tiptoed to the window. Jackson's breath was hot on the back of her neck as he edged up behind her.

From this angle, she could see only a small slice of the room—but it was enough.

The shed was lit by flickering candlelight. There was a pentagram painted on the floorboards in a dried reddish-brown substance—something that looked an awful lot like blood. Taper candles surrounded the pentagram. And kneeling in the center, lifting something small and wriggling over her head . . .

Gwen. Scarlett would have recognized that dark flowing hair anywhere.

The object in Gwen's hands writhed again, and Scarlett's stomach lurched. She noticed the long whipping naked tail, caught a glimpse of frightened red eyes. *A rat*. Then, with a sound like twigs crunching, Gwen broke the animal's neck.

In that instant, a flood of energy exploded through the shed. It vibrated like a blown-out speaker, bringing with it a loud, angry ring, almost like the molecules in the air were screaming at her.

Magic.

But it was magic as she'd never felt it before, raging and violent and raw and *hungry*. It sent her stomach into free fall and constricted her lungs. It was so strong, it blew the remaining shards of glass through the window—and knocked Scarlett backwards. She fell into Jackson and they both landed hard against the side of the shed. "Who's there?" Gwen shouted. Maybe it was because Scarlett hadn't heard the girl speak since her return, but something about her voice sounded deeper, more ominous than before, almost like she was speaking in two registers at once—her own, and a lower, more gravelly one.

Scarlett didn't stop to think. She grabbed Jackson, hauled him upright, and sprinted as hard as she could for the road. To his credit, Jackson didn't waste any time asking questions. He ran right with her, eyes wild, as they raced down the gravel path and through the woods, brambles tearing at their faces and clothes.

Only when they reached the main road did he ask, through panting breaths, "What . . . the hell . . . was that?"

Scarlett couldn't answer him. She could barely admit the truth to herself.

Her worst nightmare had come true. Gwen had her magic back. Wicked magic.

CHAPTER TWENTY-SEVEN

Vivi

Vivi stared out the window of the West Tower, a campus snack bar that felt like the kind of exclusive country club her mother used to mock during their stint in New England. It stood at the highest point on campus, the top floor of the clock tower, and offered a view of the sprawling quad through massive bay windows. She'd been camped out in one of the leather armchairs for the better part of the afternoon, scrolling through page after page of the digital archives of the *Gazette* on her laptop, hoping for any mention of the talisman. It'd been nearly twenty-four hours since her discovery in the archives, and Jess, investigative journalist extraordinaire, had taken charge, assigning the younger Ravens a number of periodicals to review while the older sisters continued to work magical leads. They now had less than a day to find the talisman, and apart from discovering that it had been stolen from Westerly, they had learned nothing.

After reading about nearly every jewelry theft in Savannah this century, Vivi was staring out the window, a cup of coffee in her hand. She was starting to feel like she'd hit a wall, and she knew she wasn't the only one who felt like that. Dahlia had taken to muttering under her breath as she walked the halls of Kappa House, pausing for long moments in front of Tiffany's room. Mei, who hadn't glamoured herself in days, had bitten her nails to the quick, and Scarlett seemed on the verge of a nervous breakdown. Vivi had never seen her look so frayed before—she'd left the house that afternoon wearing just a tank top and jeans. Vivi hadn't even known Scarlett owned jeans.

Scarlett had been horrified when Vivi told her what happened at the library and agreed that it sounded like Gwen's doing. But she'd also raised a good point: If Gwen wanted them to find the talisman, why was she trying to scare off the people looking for it? Was it because she knew the archives were a dead end?

"Is there a UFO out there or something?" a deep voice said, startling Vivi enough that she spilled the gross cup of cold coffee she'd been absently sipping for hours.

Mason's face fell as she looked up at him. "I'm sorry. I didn't mean to frighten you."

Despite her fatigue and the coffee seeping into her sleeve, Vivi smiled. There was something quaint about his use of the word *frighten* when most people would've said *scare* or *surprise*. Every time she and Mason spoke, he revealed some charming, unexpected quirk at odds with his frat-boy exterior. "You're not exactly frightening," she said. *Especially compared to the shit I've seen lately.*

He ran his hand through his hair and looked uncharacteristically flustered. "I mean, I want to respect what you said—at least, what you kind of said—the other night about not wanting to make things weird with Scarlett. I don't want you to think I can't take no for an answer."

Vivi tried to ignore the pang in her heart. "It's fine. I still want to be friends. I mean it."

"Good." He smiled. "And in that case, show me that UFO you were looking at, because if I upload a photo to Reddit, they'll make me their god emperor."

"No UFO, unfortunately. I was just staring into space." She shot him a quizzical look. "You're a Redditor?"

"I like the history threads. I've been in a three-year fight with this adjunct professor in Alaska who believes the Confederacy won the Civil War."

"That sounds like an excellent use of your time."

He grinned and gestured to the empty chair next to her. "Mind if I join you?"

"I'd be honored. But why are you here instead of out partying?"

"You sound so suspicious!" Mason laughed as he sat down. "Do you think I came here to creep on unsuspecting students?"

"No! I don't think you're creepy." She bit her lip. "Sorry, that didn't come out right."

"No, that's okay," Mason said, nodding gravely. "'I don't think you're creepy' is probably the nicest thing anyone's ever said to me." He took a sip of his coffee and pulled a laptop out of his messenger bag. "To answer your question, my adviser's writing a book on women in colonial Savannah. I've been reading letters and diaries at different libraries across the city and I need to synthesize my findings for her. It's due Monday."

"You're a history major?"

"I am indeed. Why do you sound so surprised?"

Vivi considered this. She knew he liked history, but she had never imagined that he was majoring in it. Embarrassingly, the real reason was that, in her head, historians wore tweed jackets and muttered to themselves; Mason looked like an off-duty Ralph Lauren model in his snug white T-shirt and preppy green twill shorts. "You seem too outgoing for a history major," she said, though that hardly sounded convincing. "Shouldn't you be studying something like public relations or, I don't know, sports marketing?"

"*Sports marketing?* That's not even a major here!"

"Excuse me for not memorizing the course catalog," Vivi said, raising her hands in surrender.

"Sports marketing," Mason repeated as he shook his head with mock dismay. "Do you know that Westerly has one of the best history departments in the country? Do yourself a favor and sign up for History of Cemeteries. Every week, there's a field trip to a different graveyard. I know it sounds morbid, but it's really fascinating." He paused. "I'm creeping you out again, aren't I?"

"No, not at all," Vivi insisted, although she'd already spent more time than she cared to in a local cemetery. Vivi looked at Mason in a new light. She'd never heard an attractive guy speak so passionately about history. She'd never heard *anyone* speak so passionately about history. For a moment, she imagined herself in a white sundress, wandering arm in arm with Mason through a graveyard dripping with Spanish moss, then blushed and shook her head slightly to dispel the ridiculous notion. She'd already tried to go down this road and knew it had a bold DO NOT ENTER sign on it.

"Seriously, though, why are you holed up here instead of out with your sisters?" he asked. "We might be the only people on the entire campus working right now."

"I'm doing a little history project of my own," she said, turning her computer screen toward Mason. "I'm tracking former Kappa sisters through the ages." She figured a half-truth was safe enough.

"Ah, a favorite activity of mine."

"Now, that *does* sound creepy."

He laughed and leaned back in his chair. "Sorry, you're right. I'll just open my laptop here and we can spend the rest of the evening working in companionable silence. Unless you'd rather have some alone time?"

"No, I'd appreciate the company." After all the chaos and anguish, she thought it would be nice to be around someone who wasn't caught up in a magical kidnapping. She waited for him to continue the lighthearted banter, but his expression turned serious as he scrutinized her.

"Are you okay? You look a little . . ." He hesitated, clearly searching for the most diplomatic phrase. "Worn out."

"I'm fine," she said. "I just fell a little behind during rush and now I'm trying to catch up."

"Are you sure there's nothing else going on? You can talk to me, you know."

She tried to imagine what it'd be like to confide in him, to have him listen quietly and sympathetically as she told him all about the ongoing nightmare of Tiffany's disappearance and the hunt for the talisman. As a historian and a researcher, he might even be an asset. But talking to Mason about this wasn't an option. Nothing would put the Ravens in greater danger than spilling their secrets to the outside world. "It's nothing, I promise. I guess studying hard just doesn't suit my delicate constitution," Vivi said, forcing a smile.

"I didn't mean it in a bad way," Mason said quickly. "Sorry, I just thought you looked a little tired. But still beautiful."

The moment the word escaped his mouth, Vivi could tell he regretted it. He turned slightly red and shook his head. "Okay, I'm clearly not doing a very good job with this 'friend' thing. I'll leave you alone now."

He stood and began to stuff his laptop into his messenger bag. "Mason, wait," Vivi said, reaching for his arm. The word had landed on her skin like a butterfly she was afraid to touch lest it flutter away. No one except her mother had ever called her beautiful. "It's fine. You don't have to go."

He paused, then lowered himself back into the chair with a sigh. "You're sure I haven't made you uncomfortable?"

"Just the opposite." Without thinking, she placed her hand on his arm. "It was nice of you to say."

"I cannot tell a lie," he said in a mock-serious tone. Then he went quiet, his eyes locking with hers, and he leaned in slightly; she could see the flecks of gold in his eyes, his jet-black eyelashes, the tiny scar in his left eyebrow.

She should move. Lean away. But she stayed where she was, unable to breathe, unable to make her muscles shift so much as an inch. She shivered as he touched her cheek lightly with his hand and then leaned forward until his lips grazed hers.

A bolt of electricity shot through her, burning away all thoughts except how good his lips felt and how much she wanted to lean into his kiss.

But instead she pulled back. "Mason, we can't do this. I'm sorry." She couldn't kiss her Big Sister's ex-boyfriend, especially not when Scarlett was in such a bad place.

He sat back and let his head fall into his hands. "I know. You're right, Vivi, I just wish . . ." He trailed off, then sat up and looked at her with a sad smile. He took a deep breath and said with forced cheer, "Okay, then. Back to work." He glanced at her open laptop and frowned. "Hey, is it just me or does that girl look familiar?"

"What girl?" It took Vivi a second to find what he was looking at among all her open research tabs. In the corner of her screen was a color photo, faintly blurred. The caption read: *Members of Kappa at Homecoming.* It looked like it had been taken in the ballroom of the main administrative building. There were seven beautiful girls in the picture, all dressed in timeless little black dresses. One was Evelyn Waters; Vivi had seen a picture of her at the house and recognized her strawberry-blond hair and high cheekbones.

But it was the girl in the center of the photo who caught Vivi's attention. She was the only one looking at the camera. She had her arm around Evelyn's waist, and around her neck she wore a large oval pendant that looked almost like a geode. It was blue glass with a series of circles and what could only be described as an evil eye at its center. On the girl's face was a little half smile, as if she knew something the rest of them didn't. Vivi recognized the smile. She'd seen it nearly every day of her life.

"Did your mom go to Westerly too?" Mason asked.

Vivi didn't answer. She could only stare at young Daphne Devereaux, grinning up at her from the past.

Not only was her mother a witch—she'd also been a Raven.

And she was wearing the Henosis talisman.

CHAPTER TWENTY-EIGHT

Scarlett

It was dark by the time Scarlett pulled the car up in front of Kappa. She turned the engine off and stared forward, watching as the streetlights flickered on one by one.

"Scarlett, we have to talk about what happened," Jackson said.

Scarlett kept staring ahead. She hadn't been able to say a single word the entire ride home. She hadn't had the energy to concoct some elaborate cover story to explain what Gwen was doing. It'd taken all her remaining strength to keep the car on the road and keep the gaping emptiness inside her from filling with tears. Scarlett had failed, which meant Tiffany was going to spend another terrifying night wondering if every breath would be her last.

If she was even still alive. Scarlett's hands itched for her cards and for their library. She needed a spell, a proof-of-life spell, something that would tell her that Tiffany's heart was still beating. She needed proof that it wasn't too late, because not only had Gwen regained her powers, but her magic seemed even darker and more potent. She'd been willing to harm Tiffany before her accident—who knew what she was capable of now?

Part of her had wanted to storm into the shed, confront Gwen right then and there, and force her to take her to Tiffany. But how was Scarlett going to make that happen? Rain on her? A few drops of water couldn't counteract the evil she felt pouring off Gwen. She needed her sisters' powers to take her on.

"Have you ever seen anything like that? Do you know what Gwen was doing?" Jackson asked.

"No, of course not," Scarlett lied. "It was some kind of weird fucked-up serial-killer stuff."

"I don't think serial killers make a habit of using pentagrams and candles," Jackson said. "That looked like something ritual. It looked like . . ." He paused for a long moment, as if searching for the right word. "It looked like *witchcraft*."

Scarlett turned to him. His face was hollowed, his eyes slightly bloodshot. She'd seen him be angry and sanctimonious. She'd seen him be kind. But she'd never seen him be scared before. She put her hand on his. It was warm beneath her grip.

"There's no such thing as witchcraft." Her voice sounded thin, even to her. She'd never had to say those words aloud. Most people lived their small lives in an ignorant stupor—too dull or unimaginative to sense the magic lying just out of reach. She'd always pitied them, living in a black-and-white world when there was a dizzying array of colors just beyond the veil. But at this moment, she'd trade places with any of them in a heartbeat if it'd bring Tiffany back. What was the point of magic if you couldn't protect the people you loved?

"Come on, Scarlett." Jackson shook his head. "You know what

we saw. You know what we *felt*. That blast that knocked you back—how do you explain that?"

Scarlett shrugged and sat back. "There wasn't a blast. I just lost my footing when I saw her."

"Don't lie to me, Scarlett." He shifted in the passenger seat and took hold of her shoulder. Turned her body toward him. She set her jaw. But one peek at the expression on his face melted her resistance. She recognized it all too well. Desperation. The kind she was only just beginning to understand, with Tiffany missing.

"I have been watching your house for an entire year," Jackson said. "There's something different about you Kappas. Something strange. And I saw your expression tonight. It wasn't *surprised*. It was worried." He paused, his brow furrowing. "Gwen used to be one of you. My *sister* was her best friend. And I found things after she died—that pentagram on the floor? She drew that symbol in a lot of her notebooks. So . . . just tell me what she was involved in."

The desperation in his voice was almost enough to undo her. Jackson had suffered as much as any of them. More, in some ways, because he'd had no one to confide in. No one with whom he could share the disturbing thoughts forming from the fragments of his grief. But she couldn't tell him the truth without endangering the Ravens. "We're just a sorority," she said hoarsely.

"*Please*. Was she a . . . witch? Was it like *that?*" He sounded horrified. "I mean, did she kill things, eat babies, what the hell—"

"No! Of course not. Harper was nothing like that. That's wicked magic. We're not like that." The words were out of Scarlett's mouth before she could stop them.

Jackson let go of her and sat back heavily in his seat. "Holy shit. So she *was* a witch. You're all witches."

Scarlett stared at him, frozen with shock at what she'd just done. This went against every rule in the book, everything that her mother and Minnie had taught her, and everything she'd vowed when she was inducted into Kappa. They were forbidden to tell anyone without magical ability the truth about Kappa. About what they really were.

She'd protected her secret fiercely for years, even hiding the truth from Mason. And if there was ever anyone she was going to tell outside of Kappa, it was him. But here she was telling Jackson, a boy she couldn't stand a few weeks ago—hell, even a few hours ago. Maybe this *was* the Upside Down. Nothing was as it was supposed to be.

She wrapped her hands around the steering wheel and leaned her forehead against it. "You can't tell a soul, Jackson. It won't end well for either of us if this gets out."

He'd gone still and silent but she knew his brain was racing to process the information she'd just inadvertently revealed. Finally, he swallowed hard and asked, "Did Gwen . . . did Gwen kill Harper?"

A series of memories flashed through her mind: Gwen's expression of loathing as she turned to look at Tiffany and Scarlett from the balcony. The acrid smell of wicked magic singeing the air. The flash of terror on Harper's face as the building began to crumble beneath her. The blood on her pale skin. Scarlett shook her head slowly. "Not on purpose. But I'm convinced that Gwen kidnapped Tiffany. For all I know, she's killed her by now. She hated Tiffany. We're the ones who got her kicked out of Kappa . . ." She trailed off as a ragged sob tore its way out of her chest. "I don't know what I'll do if she hurts her, Jackson. I seriously don't. I wish she'd taken me instead."

When she leaned back in her seat again, she felt the soft brush of Jackson's fingers over her cheekbones.

"I won't let her hurt you." He laced his fingers through hers and held tight, and for a moment, the warm pressure was enough to keep the panic at bay. But what would Jackson say when he found out that Tiffany and Scarlett had been taunting Gwen—that they were the ones who'd caused her to lose control on the balcony?

She smiled through her tears. "No offense, but you're the last person who'd be able to stop her."

"What, are you doubting my normal-guy powers?" He gave a small smirk.

"I'm sure they will come in really handy when Gwen's using a mind-control spell on you."

Jackson's eyes widened. "Hold up. You all have *mind-control* spells?"

There was a sharp knock at the window of the car, so close and loud that Scarlett gasped and startled. The fear didn't fade when she spun in her seat to find Dahlia outside the car, arms crossed.

"Shit," Scarlett swore under her breath. *Does she know that I told?* She quickly wiped away her tears and rolled down her window. "Hey," she said, forcing her voice to sound normal.

Dahlia stared pointedly at Scarlett's right hand. Still wrapped around Jackson's, she realized belatedly. Scarlett jerked it free and plastered on an innocent smile.

"Where have you been?" The older girl's eyes narrowed. "I need you at home right now, Scarlett, for house business. Of all the times to run off with . . . someone." *Someone like* him, she knew Dahlia meant. Scarlett could hear the disdain dripping from her tone.

"Sorry. Something came up. Something important." Scarlett turned to Jackson. Forced her voice into a casual, dismissive tone as she said, "Thank you again for your help. Your information was very useful."

Jackson nodded, not missing a beat. "All right. Well, if you need anything else, here." He pulled out a piece of paper, scribbled down his number, shoved the paper into her hand, and climbed out of the car. He tossed a backwards wave at them and then walked quickly down the road and into the woods, disappearing into the night.

"What in the world was that about?" Dahlia asked, tucking a lock of blond hair behind her ear. "Are you seriously hooking up at our funeral, Scar?"

"No, of course not. I'll tell you inside the house," Scarlett said, getting out and slamming the car door closed. She cast a look up and down the street, fighting a shiver despite the warm evening air. "And we're not dead yet." Not if Scarlett could help it. All she could think about was Gwen, who had her powers back. Gwen, who could be anywhere. Doing anything. Gwen, who could be coming after all of them right now.

"But we need to talk inside the house," Scarlett said. She wanted the full force of the Ravens' protective spells between her sisters and the girl trying to destroy them.

CHAPTER TWENTY-NINE

Vivi

Vivi sprinted across campus, ignoring the amused or confused looks from the revelers she left in her wake. She passed groups of giggling girls teetering in heels, boisterous boys wearing too much aftershave, and cozy couples walking hand in hand or sitting under the romantic glow of a gas lamp.

Her shame over kissing Mason, so urgent and intense just moments ago, had been swept away by a supercharged mix of adrenaline and fury. She'd finally made a breakthrough with her talisman research and found a real clue. Except that the clue led directly to her mother and meant that she'd apparently been lying to Vivi her entire life.

As she ran, Vivi pulled out her phone and called her mother for the third time since she'd left the snack bar. This time, Daphne picked up. "Everything all right, sugar snap?" she asked. "I'm in the middle of a crystal ritual but I saw your missed calls and thought I'd better check."

Vivi slowed to a fast walk. Panting heavily, she asked, "Do you have the Henosis talisman?"

Daphne paused just a fraction of a second too long, then said, "What on earth are you talking about, sweetheart? What talisman?"

"I saw a photo of you wearing it. Why do you keep lying to me? I know you were a Raven and I know you have the talisman."

"I never *lied* to you, Vivi. Everything I did was to protect you."

"Well, you've done a pretty shitty job at it, because now some psycho is threatening to kill the Ravens one by one until we hand over the talisman."

"You have to get out of there," Daphne said urgently. "Right now. I'll find somewhere in Savannah you can stay, and then I'll come get you."

"What? Are you serious? I'm not abandoning my sisters. I just need the talisman. Do you have it with you? I won't tell anyone you were the one who stole it, I promise."

"I didn't *steal* anything." A chill had crept into Daphne's voice. "The situation is far more complicated than you understand—"

"That's not an excuse! Keeping information from me doesn't make me safer. Why can't you understand that? Where are you now? Let me come get the talisman and you can explain everything to me then."

There was a long pause. "I can't do that, Vivi, I'm sorry."

"Okay . . . then bring it to me. It's a matter of life and death. My friend Tiffany is going to *die* if we don't find the talisman."

"I'm sorry," Daphne said again softly. "But it's not in my power. Please take care of yourself, okay? I love you."

The line went dead.

Vivi cursed and threw her phone down on the grass, then crouched to pick it up again with a groan. Fine, if Daphne wanted to be cagey, then Vivi would just have to find her.

Even before she made it up the front path, Vivi could tell that the house was abuzz with activity. She stopped to catch her breath next to Mei, who was standing on the walkway waving a bundle of herbs in front of her face. Across the lawn, Etta was planting a shrub with white flowers. She wore thick gardening gloves and seemed to be taking care not to let the blossoms touch her skin.

"What's going on?" Vivi asked, still breathing heavily from her sprint across campus.

"It's Gwen," Mei said without looking away from her herbs. "Scarlett saw her perform wicked magic to undo the binding spell."

"So it's true?" Vivi said, shivering despite the warmth that lingered from her run.

"Yes, she apparently got her powers back somehow. And after what happened with Tiffany, we're not taking any more chances. Dahlia says we can't let Gwen get near any of us, so I'm increasing the protective charms while Etta plants hogweed in the lawn—it hides the presence of magic, which will make it more difficult for Gwen, or any intruder, to identify the spells we used."

"Got it. So where's Scarlett?" Vivi asked, wiping her sweaty forehead with the back of her hand. "I need to talk to her."

"I think she's with Dahlia in Dahlia's office."

With a hurried thanks, Vivi tore off toward the house, mind already racing through the list of things she needed to do. Tell Scarlett and Dahlia about her mother and the talisman. Then find Daphne.

And tell Scarlett that you just kissed her ex, a voice reminded Vivi. At the moment, the prospect seemed almost more terrifying than facing wicked magic.

She ran up the stairs to the fourth floor, jogged down the long hallway, and skidded to a stop when she heard raised voices spilling out of Dahlia's office.

"—irresponsible. Working with some outsider over your own sisters." Dahlia sounded *pissed.*

"I already told you; he's been following Gwen. He had useful information." Scarlett's voice was softer, almost contrite.

"But he didn't see anything, did he? You didn't tell him anything about us."

Scarlett hesitated for a fraction of a second. "Of course not," she said in a haughty tone that didn't quite conceal the note of worry.

To judge by the long pause that followed, Dahlia heard it too. To Vivi's surprise, though, after a moment, Dahlia just sighed. "Scarlett, you're not acting very presidential right now. I expect our future leader to put the needs of Kappa before anything else. Especially before her own hormones. And you can stop lurking out there, Vivian," Dahlia called in a louder voice. "Come in."

Vivi's face flushed with embarrassment that only increased when Scarlett opened the door. "What's wrong? Are you okay?" she asked, surveying Vivi with such genuine concern that her embarrassment quickly gave way to shame. *No, I'm not okay, because my mother has been lying to me my whole life but even that's not as shitty as what I just did to you.* "I think I may have a lead," Vivi said as she stepped into the office, a small but beautifully decorated room with an ornately carved wooden desk, wine-colored wallpaper, and shelves full of books, candles, and animal skeletons.

"Really? Great. What did you find?" Scarlett asked eagerly, her excitement a stark contrast to Dahlia, who was staring at Vivi with an inscrutable expression. "What's going on?" Scarlett said, turning from Dahlia to Vivi.

"Ask your Little," Dahlia said coolly. "Though I'm surprised you don't know already. Her thoughts are so loud, she's practically screaming."

"You know I'm not good at mind-reading. Can you please just tell me so we can keep things moving?" Scarlett crossed her arms and glowered.

Dahlia raised an eyebrow at Vivi. "I think it's better if Vivi explains."

She can't know, Vivi thought desperately. There were mind-reading spells but she didn't think even Dahlia was powerful enough to read Vivi's thoughts on the spot, without even touching her.

"Fine," Dahlia snapped. "Vivi is afraid you'll find out what just happened with Mason."

Scarlett staggered back as if Dahlia's words had been a physical blow. "What are you talking about?" she asked in a voice too fragile for her. Too close to breaking. "Vivi?" she said, studying her Little.

"I . . ." Her brain raced for an excuse, an explanation, or even a lie, but she couldn't do it. She wasn't sure whether it was guilt or magic, but the words came tumbling out. "I didn't mean to do it, I swear. And it'll never happen again. I'm so sorry."

"*What* won't happen again?" Scarlett asked, no longer sounding fragile.

"I . . . we weren't thinking . . . it was an accident. Just one stupid kiss—"

"You *accidentally* kissed my boyfriend?" Scarlett's voice was cold, but heat was radiating from her, charging the air with fury and magic.

"It was so stupid and I stopped it immediately. I'm really, really sorry."

"Oh, so *you* stopped it," Scarlett spat. "You're saying that Mason couldn't control himself around you?"

"No, of course not. I'm so sorry, Scarlett. I—"

"Cut the bullshit. You've had your eye on him since you got here. And you took advantage of him in a vulnerable moment, because, let's be honest, you know there's no way in hell he'd ever go for you otherwise." She sneered and let out a forced, mocking laugh. "Socially awkward freshmen aren't exactly Mason's type."

Although Vivi knew Scarlett was lashing out in anger—anger that was more than justified—it wasn't enough to take the sting out of her words. Vivi knew that she wasn't Mason's type. It made absolutely no sense for him to go from someone as glamorous, sophisticated, and talented as Scarlett to someone like her. He was probably still reeling from the breakup and looking for an easy distraction. And who was easier than a naïve freshman so desperate for attention that being called beautiful made her lose all reason and self-control?

"Okay, Scarlett, that's enough," Dahlia said with a smirk, as if she was enjoying the proceedings. It seemed odd and out of character for the normally stern yet empathetic president, but perhaps the pressure was making everyone act strangely. "We have more important things to discuss."

"I'm not discussing anything in front of *her.* It's like I've been saying all along—a little bit of magic can make up for only so many shortcomings." Scarlett gave Vivi a tight, cruel smile. "We both know that you don't belong here, so why don't you go back to telling fortunes at a strip mall in Reno?" Before Vivi could respond, Scarlett brushed past her and strode toward the door.

Vivi almost let her go. She couldn't bear to be in the same room as Scarlett for one more second. All she wanted to do was curl up in a ball on her bed and try to drown out the words she knew would keep echoing in her skull: That she didn't belong. That it was a huge mistake to make her a Raven. But she couldn't let Scarlett leave without telling her what she'd discovered. "Hold on. I have to tell you something. My mom was a Raven. I found a photo of her with Evelyn Waters and I think—"

"Why don't you tell Mason all about it instead?" Scarlett called over her shoulder. "Maybe he can help you. Or maybe you can just make out some more while my best friend is being held captive by a psychopath."

Vivi flinched as Scarlett slammed the door shut behind her. How could she possibly make this better? Even if they found the talisman and rescued Tiffany, things would never return to normal. Vivi had spent her whole life wanting to belong, and after finally finding a group of amazing girls who offered her not only friendship but *magic,* she'd ruined it through an act of supreme stupidity and selfishness.

Dahlia's hand landed on her shoulder. "She'll cool off in a bit. Now, tell me what you learned about your mom."

Vivi took a deep breath and tried to steel herself. She was only slightly less anxious about the fallout from this information than she'd been about kissing Mason. What would the Ravens say when they found out that Vivi's mother had *stolen* the Henosis talisman? That she'd been a Raven herself and never told Vivi anything about it? It was all majorly shady and definitely would reflect about as well on Vivi as her kiss with Scarlett's ex-boyfriend had.

"Holy shit," Dahlia said, her eyes growing wide when Vivi finished her story. "Have you spoken to her about it yet? Does she have any idea where it might be now?"

Vivi shook her head. "I talked to her but she wouldn't tell me anything about it. All she said was that I'm in danger and need to be careful."

"Yeah, well, we know we're in danger. Where does she live? Should we go pay her a little visit and search for the talisman?"

"I don't even know what state she's in right now. She refused to tell me." Vivi felt a prickle of shame. Not only had her mother stolen a priceless magical object, but now she was on the run. However, Dahlia looked unfazed.

"Try again. Tell her you're in over your head and you need help."

"I did that already. It didn't work."

"Then I guess it's time to up the ante," Dahlia said. "Channel your inner Jennifer Lawrence and give an Oscar-worthy performance."

"Okay . . ." Vivi said uneasily. Unlike her mother, Vivi had never been a very good actress, and Daphne could always tell when she was lying. "And what happens if I do manage to find the talisman? Are we actually going to hand it over to Tiffany's kidnapper?"

"Once we have the real talisman, I should be able to use a replicator charm to create a fake one. That way, the magic won't fall into the wrong hands." Dahlia paused. "The worst possible hands."

Vivi nodded, pulled out her phone, and called her mother. It rang a few times, and for a moment, Vivi worried that Daphne wouldn't pick up at all so as not to be forced to discuss the talisman again. But just when Vivi expected the call to go to voicemail, she heard a weary-sounding "Hello?"

"Mom, it's me. Listen, I know you don't want to talk about this, but it's really, really important. I need to come see you." She tried to inject as much urgency as she could into her voice, but she didn't think it was possible to sound more desperate than she already was—finding the talisman was literally a matter of life or death for Tiffany.

Daphne was silent for a moment. "There's an old inn a couple miles from campus called the Rose and Thorn," she said finally. "I'll meet you there in an hour."

Next to her, Dahlia began to mutter a spell. "I call to the Moon and to the Tower, source of the shadows that seek to devour."

"Mom, I can't stay in Savannah," Vivi said, taking a step away from the older girl. "You don't understand, it's not safe for—" She cut herself off with a gasp. She'd just caught sight of her reflection in the gold-framed mirror behind Dahlia's desk. But it wasn't her, not really. Her skin had grown paler and taken on a greenish tint while her face was bloated and misshapen, like a body decaying underwater. She made a noise that was half sob, half shriek as a worm twisted its way out of the reflection's ear.

"Vivi?" Daphne said sharply. "Are you all right?"

Vivi turned away from the mirror and took a deep breath.

"Vivi?" Daphne said again, more urgently this time. "Tell me what's wrong."

"You were right, I'm not safe here." When Vivi finally found her voice, it was trembling. "Please, please, Mom, I need to get out of here. Tell me where you are."

This time her mother didn't hesitate. "I'm on Jekyll Island, south of Savannah. Thirty-eight Wisteria Lane. You'll be safe here, I promise."

"See you soon," Vivi said faintly. She ended the call and turned around to see Dahlia smiling at her.

"Great job," she said.

"Was all that really necessary?" Vivi gestured toward the mirror, where, mercifully, her reflection had returned to normal. Despite taking a few deep breaths, she was shaking, and her heart was still racing from the image of her dead body.

Dahlia shrugged. "It worked, didn't it? Now, ready for a little road trip?"

CHAPTER THIRTY

Scarlett

"We're trying to stop Gwen, not make tea," Scarlett muttered as she stormed out the front door, startling Mei, who was scattering juniper, patchouli, and chamomile on the front steps, a protective measure against wicked magic. As the scents hit her, all Scarlett could think of was Gwen snapping the rat's neck in the shed. A few herbs were not enough to protect them.

"Where are you going? We're supposed to stay together," Mei called after her. Scarlett said nothing as she strode down the brick path. For the first time since arriving at Westerly, she felt like the outside world was safer and more welcoming than Kappa House.

As she marched down Greek Row, she passed PiKa House with its stately columns. Her heart wrenched and her mind helpfully provided plenty of mental images of what her ex—the guy who, until two days ago, Scarlett thought was the love of her life—could have done with her Little.

For the past two years, Scarlett had had a vision of her future. It had been laid before her so intricately and clearly in her mind, it was almost as if it were real, like that part of her life was already established and just waiting for her and Mason to step into it. With

Tiffany gone, Scarlett hadn't had a chance to grieve for the future she'd lost with Mason—at the moment, her future felt like a giant question mark—but now, as she hurried down the sidewalk, stepping over the gnarled tree roots sticking up through the cracked pavement, grief and anger washed over her in equal measure.

How could their meet-cute at the Pikiki be just an anecdote from a failed relationship? How could everything they'd built over the past two years, every inside joke, every conversation, every "I love you," just vanish, crumbling to the earth like it was no more meaningful than dust? How, when she saw him across the quad, was she supposed to walk by him like they were nothing more than strangers? How had they shared their last kiss without her even knowing it was the last?

And, she thought as she angrily brushed away a tear, how could he already have fallen for someone else? How could he do this to her—and with her Little? How could Vivi do this to her?

And Vivi wasn't the only Raven who'd betrayed her. Instead of chastising Vivi, Dahlia had practically laughed about it. That wasn't like her. Dahlia knew what Mason meant to Scarlett. Knew how long they'd been together. How devastating it was when one sister betrayed another.

There wasn't much Scarlett was sure of anymore, but she knew these two things were true: she was going to rescue Tiffany and she would do it without her so-called sisters.

Scarlett pulled out the slip of paper she'd folded up in her pocket. The one Jackson had given her. She dialed his number and held her breath.

It rang only once before he answered. "Scarlett?"

She raised her eyebrows. "How'd you know it was me?" she asked. She hadn't given Jackson her number.

"Just a lucky guess." He paused, then sighed. "That, and I was hoping you'd call. I haven't been sure what to do. It's pretty hard to just calmly head out to a party or something right after you find out witches are real and there's an evil one on the loose."

Just a few hours ago, his words would've released a wave of guilt and fear in Scarlett. For centuries, nothing posed a greater danger to witches than the threat of discovery. In the name of mortal fear, witches had been burned and drowned and institutionalized and incarcerated. The stories were true, and her mother and Minnie had made sure that Scarlett knew her witch history by heart.

But now, it was almost comforting to know that there was someone else to share her burden, someone she might actually be able to trust. Even if he was human. "In that case, how would you feel about helping me track down said witch?"

"Sounds dangerous."

"Extremely."

"What do your sisters think about it?"

"I don't know," Scarlett said, glancing over her shoulder despite the fact that Kappa House was already out of sight, concealed by the veil of moss that draped from live oaks that lined their street. Deep down, she knew Dahlia had a point. Leaders didn't do stuff like run off on a rogue mission. But then again, Ravens were supposed to put Kappa first. Tiffany was her best friend, a fellow sister in grave danger. Screw behaving like a well-groomed presidential candidate. First and foremost, Scarlett was a friend. She needed to act like one now. "There's one sister who can't afford to wait."

The line went quiet for a moment. Scarlett didn't blame Jackson for hesitating. In fact, she respected him for how quickly he was able to grasp the seriousness of the situation. "Can you come pick me up?" he said finally. "We can see if she went back to her apartment or if she's still at that freaky cabin."

"You sure you aren't a witch?" Scarlett asked as she fished her car keys out of her purse. "Because you just read my mind."

When she got to Jackson's place, she was surprised by the lack of furniture and the presence of a murder board. Also by the fact that he wasn't wearing a shirt.

"Just a sec," he called over his shoulder as he reached for a T-shirt and pulled it down over an impressively muscled and lean chest. He disappeared into a small bedroom in the back.

"Suspect number one, huh?" she said as she looked at her picture. It was pinned on a map of Savannah along with photos of her fellow Ravens, all of them connected by a tangled series of strings. Over Psi Delt House was a picture of Harper. Scarlett's breath caught in her chest at the sight of her wide smile. She looked so . . . alive. Next to that photo was Scarlett's own face, circled in red Sharpie.

"Sorry, I obviously need to update that," Jackson said, coming back into the room with a sweatshirt on.

"No problem," she said, but guilt flooded in once more. The

map, the near-empty apartment. This was the chaos she and Tiffany had left in their wake.

"Can I ask you something?" he said.

"I think you've more than earned the right," she said, expecting more questions about being a witch. But Jackson's question surprised her.

"When I ran into you at Homecoming . . . was that about Gwen? Had she done something then?"

Scarlett shook her head. "That was about my boyfriend dumping me."

He let out a low whistle. "At Homecoming?"

"Obviously, that's not important in the scheme of what's happening now," she said defensively, feeling hurt and embarrassed all at once.

"I think we really are in the Upside Down if someone dumped you."

"A few days ago you would have thought I deserved it," she countered.

"No one deserves to get dumped like that at a dance in front of her family and friends."

"Not even a sorority witch?" she said lightly.

"Well, maybe *some* sorority witches do. But you're different than I thought you were."

"Don't say that. It's insulting. I'm not like the other girls, right? Not like the rest of my sorority?" she said, getting her back up again at the thought of him putting other girls down in order to lift her up.

He raised an eyebrow. "Given that we just saw Gwen making a *Ratatouille* sacrifice, I'd say that it's a compliment. But that's not what I meant. When I first met you in class I didn't know you were a Kappa. I just knew that you were smart and untouchable. You kept people at a distance. It feels good to be on the inside."

"Even though the inside is filled with witches and witch killers?"

"Nobody's perfect," he said with a smile.

"You're different than I thought you were too," she admitted.

"Handsomer up close, wittier, more intelligent . . ." he quipped.

"Not a complete and total asshole," she said. But in her head she added, *Funnier, kinder, more forgiving.* "And sort of brave," she added aloud. She didn't know many other guys—*any* other guys—who would take finding out about the existence of witches in stride, let alone sign up to bring one down. "How come you aren't totally freaking out about all of this?"

Jackson thought for a moment. "For the record, I am kind of freaking out. But I also think a part of me always knew. I just didn't allow myself to realize it."

"What do you mean?" Scarlett asked.

"Believe it or not, when Harper and I were kids and she first came to live with us, I wasn't exactly the confident male specimen you see in front of you. I was a bit of a nerd."

Scarlett gasped for effect and found herself smiling for the first time in days.

"There were a couple of kids who made it their business to turn my life into a living hell, and one day Harper cornered them after school. A few minutes later, they emerged with black eyes. Harper swore she didn't touch them, but I remember how terrified they looked. When I asked how she'd managed to scare them so badly, she told me it was magic." He let out a low laugh. "Now I realize it was. And it wasn't just that. There were a lot of little things. Doors that opened and closed on their own. Sudden rainstorms. Other, smaller things, some that were more of a feeling than anything in particular. When I was younger, I half believed her. And now I know I should have believed her all along."

Scarlett took a deep breath. She'd already betrayed her coven, her sorority, when she'd shared their secret. It was wrong to go further down that path. But looking at him, seeing how much he loved Harper, how much he wanted to understand, and knowing she was the only person who could do that for him . . .

"She was a Cups like me. Her powers stemmed from water. But she could do other things, too. We all can. We are just stronger together. Or at least I thought we were . . ." She trailed off, thinking of what Dahlia had said, what Vivi had done.

"Gwen's on her own and she seems pretty damn strong," he countered.

"Yeah, because she's tapped into wicked magic. We Ravens never, ever do that. It's why we kicked her out and bound her powers in the first place."

"And now she has them back—and then some."

"Indeed," Scarlett said grimly.

Jackson paused to let it all sink in. "Thank you," he said. "Thank you for telling me."

"Not sure if you'll be thanking me after this is over," Scarlett said.

"On that note," he said, grabbing his keys and holding the door open for her, "witches first. I may be brave, but I'm not an idiot."

The front of Gwen's building looked dark when they pulled up. Blinds shut, lights off. Then again, the cabin had looked abandoned at first.

Scarlett cut the engine. "Do you see any signs of life?" she asked, unsure what kind of answer she was hoping for.

He shook his head. "Not even the upstairs neighbor or the yappy dog that lives in the shop next door. It's a complete dead zone here."

"Maybe she's still out at the cabin," Scarlett said uncertainly. The last thing she wanted was to return to that house of horror, but she'd go in a heartbeat if it'd lead her to Tiffany.

"Her car is here." He pointed to a beat-up old sedan parked by the curb.

Scarlett frowned. "I didn't see it by the cabin."

"Maybe she parked somewhere up the road, like we did."

Scarlett hunched lower in her seat, one eye on the building. "Something about this feels off. Doesn't it? I mean, she gets her powers back, which is *huge*. Then she just . . . comes home to go to bed?"

"Maybe all that wicked magic tired her out." Jackson held up his hands in response to Scarlett's withering glare. "Hey, I don't know how any of this works. That's your department. I'm just saying, it's been, what, three or four hours since we saw her out on Skidaway? Plenty of time for her to come back here, at least."

Or plenty of time to go off to wherever she's keeping Tiffany and torture her, Scarlett thought as a chilling mixture of horror and disgust seeped through her veins. It'd been more than two days already. How much more would Tiffany be able to endure? Scarlett winced as she imagined her best friend's face twisted in anguish, eyes wide with fear as she watched Gwen approach with a dagger in her hand or a cruel spell on her lips. There were spells that could make you feel like your spine was snapping. Charms that made every breath feel like inhaling fire. Chants that snapped joints and severed limbs. Was Gwen deranged enough to use one of these to get what she wanted from Tiff?

"Are you okay?" Jackson asked, watching her with concern.

She shifted in her seat. "Yes, fine. Maybe I should go inside and look around. Just to make sure."

"Because that went so well last time."

"Hey, last time I wasn't expecting an ambush. Now I'm ready."

He raised his hands in surrender. "Far be it from me to question your witchiness. I'm just spit-balling. Maybe we don't want the evil witch to find out we're here and fry us both where we stand."

"She won't fry you," Scarlett muttered. "I'm going in alone."

"I'm afraid I can't allow that," Jackson replied. "Wouldn't be very chivalrous."

"Didn't anybody ever tell you chivalry is just misogyny in a nicer outfit? Besides, only one of us is capable of cursing an attacker."

"All the more reason to let me tag along and clean up after you."

She rolled her eyes. "Is this your way of telling me you like to watch?"

His gaze flicked down and up as he gave her the once-over. She hadn't dressed up today, which wasn't like her. Just jeans and a tank top. The most casual thing she'd worn in public in years. Yet with him staring like that, she felt like she'd just stepped out in a skin-tight bodycon dress. "Only when it's someone worth watching."

She forced a series of inappropriate thoughts from her brain. Stupid adrenaline. It mixed up signals. Clouded judgment. "Look, just . . . be careful. If you see anything weird happen, the best thing you can do is get out of the way. Protecting you will only make my job harder."

He saluted, forcing a cocky grin for her sake. She looked at him a long beat. She'd misjudged him. He'd taken all of it in—learning that magic existed, bursting into an evil witch's lair—and he was still smiling, even if that smile was purely bravado for her benefit.

He straightened up and opened the car door, effectively ending the discussion. Scarlett felt a desire to reach for him, but she stopped herself. They got out of the car, crossed the empty street, and walked to Gwen's front door.

His gaze flicked past her, and his lips tightened. Her eyes followed his.

Scarlett watched tendrils of smoke creep out of Gwen's front door. Thick, vibrant red smoke, an impossibly bright color. Her eyes widened. As she watched, the smoke shaped itself into an enormous *X* across the door, like a giant magical DO NOT ENTER sign.

They traded sideways glances. "Last chance to turn around," Scarlett murmured.

To her surprise, Jackson caught her hand and twined his fingers through hers. "I'm not letting you face this alone, Scarlett."

For a second, their eyes locked. His hand was warm, and her heart beat against her rib cage, the adrenaline spiking. Her head buzzed from the explosion of unexpected electricity between them. But there was no time to think about it.

She shook her hand free of his and reached out toward the crimson smoke. It was some kind of wicked magic. She could tell from the way it made her fingers itch, made the back of her throat scratchy.

She pressed her palms flat against the door. Shut her eyes and drew on the well of power in her chest, the power her sisters shared with one another during their monthly rituals. She pictured it flowing from her, a golden light to drive back the evil.

Jackson exclaimed softly behind her. When she opened her eyes, the door had swung inward.

Scarlett stepped over the threshold carefully and walked up the stairs. The hall was dark, and she saw no light coming from beneath Gwen's apartment door. Still, Scarlett paused to press an ear against it, listening for any signs of movement within.

Nothing.

She tried the door. It was unlocked. She glanced over her shoulder at Jackson. His worried look mirrored her own.

She held her breath and gently inched the door open.

More smoke billowed out, gray and red tendrils all tangled

together. It didn't smell like a wood fire. It stank like rot, like death and decay and nightmares, like waking up unable to breathe in the middle of the night. She began to choke the second it struck her. Jackson started coughing uncontrollably.

"What is this?" he rasped, voice hoarse from the smoke.

She couldn't feel any heat. If this came from a fire, it wasn't a normal one. "No idea," Scarlett choked out.

Was this some kind of defense mechanism? Or a poison? Scarlett took a step forward and slipped. She caught herself just before she hit the floor, her palm landing in a pool of something sticky. Bile rose in her throat as she stared down at the puddle.

Blood. A spreading pool of it. Much like the one in Tiffany's bedroom, but larger, uglier.

Scarlett choked back a scream and lifted her gaze to follow the trail. A body lay face-down on the floor just an arm's length from her. Motionless. Scarlett's breath came out in a weak moan. *Not Tiffany, oh God, not Tiffany.*

Beside her, Jackson was cursing. He moved faster than she did. Reached around her to grip the girl's shoulder—it was a girl, Scarlett could tell that much from her yoga pants and tank top. But it was hard to see her face through the pouring smoke . . .

Smoke that, she now realized, looked like it was pouring *out* of the girl. Or at least, out of the area where her face lay pressed against the floorboards.

Jackson rolled the girl onto her back. Scarlett braced herself, fear flooding her entire body as she prepared to see her best friend's face.

But it was Gwen's empty eyes that stared up at them. Billows of smoky gray clouds poured out of her nose, her open mouth, even her ears.

"Gwen?" Jackson whispered, his voice filled with emotion.

Scarlett couldn't move. Couldn't speak. She watched Jackson feel for a pulse, then heard him swear again, longer and louder this time. He reached for his phone. Only then did Scarlett catch his wrist.

"We can't be here," she whispered. "When they find her, the cops . . ."

Jackson nodded sharply. He took Scarlett's hand and hauled her to her feet. "Come on." He led her from the apartment. She couldn't stop shaking as she stared at her palm, painted red in Gwen's blood.

And all the while, only one thought circled in her brain, over and over.

If Gwen's dead . . . who has Tiffany?

CHAPTER THIRTY-ONE

Vivi

As Vivi gripped the wheel of the car she'd borrowed from Dahlia, she wondered if there was a calming spell strong enough to temper the anxiety currently pulsing through her chest. At the moment, she didn't know if there was anyone she could ask. By now, word of her treacherous behavior with Mason would've spread from sister to sister, by conversation, text, and the soundless communication that came so easily to a number of Ravens.

Vivi groaned and hit the steering wheel. She'd spent her entire life wishing for friends, desperate for a way to belong, and then she'd thrown it all away in an instant. Just because a cute history major with an adorable accent had made her feel special. She was better than that, wasn't she?

If Vivi had been in the passenger seat, she might've been able to take some calming breaths of the fragrant sea air as she sped along the coastline. But she was driving—alone in a car for the third time in her life. Because she'd moved so often, it'd been impossible to build up enough driver's ed credits, and she'd gotten her license only a few months ago.

"You're okay . . . you're okay," Vivi muttered as a truck barreled past her on the left, as if she were soothing a frightened animal instead of talking to herself.

But surviving the drive was only half the battle. Once she arrived, she'd have to figure out a way to search her mother's house for the talisman. If it was even there. Daphne had had a few hours to hide it somewhere else.

Vivi had thought that Dahlia would come with her, but she ended up staying behind to prepare the complicated replicator spell they'd need to produce the fake talisman. Vivi wasn't sure what sounded more dangerous—handing the powerful magical item over to Tiffany's kidnapper or potentially risking the kidnapper's fury.

Vivi exhaled as the GPS voice told her to take the next exit for Jekyll Island, a spit of land about an hour south of Savannah. For all Daphne's talk about how much Vivi would hate Savannah and her fury over Vivi attending Westerly, it appeared she had settled nearby. It was just like her mother to forbid Vivi to do something that she thought was fine for herself.

Like joining Kappa.

A few minutes later, Vivi pulled up in front of a squat bungalow with a blue door and yellow shutters a few blocks from the beach. Thick fog was rolling in, and the wind chimes on the porch filled the air with a strange, atonal melody. She turned off the engine and got out of the car, looked in all directions, then walked up the short path lined with scraggly beach roses.

Before she reached the house, the door swung open, and Daphne appeared in the doorway. She had more gray streaks in her hair and deeper circles under her eyes than the last time Vivi had seen her, but otherwise, Daphne Devereaux looked the same as she had when Vivi said goodbye to her in Reno.

"Oh, Vivi, thank God." Daphne pulled her into a tight hug, then stepped back to examine her daughter. "The cards said you were fine, but I can't tell you how happy I am to see it with my own eyes."

Now that Vivi knew the real power of tarot, Daphne's instincts felt slightly less foolish to her. "Can I come in?"

Daphne hesitated, then glanced over her shoulder. "Now's not a good time, sweetheart. The place is still such a mess. Boxes everywhere. Why don't you and I walk into town? There's an adorable little café I think you'll like."

"Boxes everywhere, huh? Does one of them contain the Henosis talisman, by any chance?"

"Vivi, please, I—"

"One of my sisters was taken, and the kidnapper says if we don't deliver the talisman, she'll be killed."

Daphne's face went white and she brought one hand to her chest. "That's exactly why you can't go back to that place. Kappa is a lightning rod for danger." She moved aside just a few inches, as if still unsure what to do, then sighed and opened the door wide. "You'd better come in."

Vivi stepped inside and waited while Daphne locked the door behind her, using the regular deadbolt and all the extra locks Vivi knew she'd installed when she'd moved in, as was her custom. Her mother couldn't change a tire or install an AC unit, but her paranoia had resulted in her becoming a master locksmith. Though now her paranoia didn't feel quite as delusional as it had.

"So I guess Louisville didn't work out?" Vivi's sweet smile didn't match the edge in her voice.

In the kitchen, a teakettle whistled. "Kentucky has bad energy," Daphne said as she brushed past Vivi. "Tea? I'm working on a new strengthening brew. Chamomile and sweet basil—"

"Were you going to tell me that you'd moved an hour's drive away?" Vivi interrupted, following her into the kitchen. It was painted a sunny yellow with cheerful black-and-white floor tiles, but it was so narrow that their elbows bumped while Daphne poured her tea.

"I didn't want to interrupt your studies." She pressed the mug on Vivi, who accepted it in spite of her annoyance.

"So you ignore all my texts and calls, basically write me off for going to Westerly, but then you move to the same city yourself?"

"I wanted to be nearby. Just in case." Daphne shrugged in a forced gesture of nonchalance as she poured a second mug for herself.

"In case of what? In case I got in trouble?" Vivi let out a short, bitter laugh. "The reason the Ravens are in danger is that you stole a valuable object years ago and refuse to give it back. I know you've never cared about anyone but yourself, but a girl is going to *die* tomorrow unless you hand over the talisman."

Daphne closed her eyes for a second, looking pained. "I think we should sit down and talk about this," she said quietly, and led Vivi into the small living room, an unfamiliar space filled with many familiar things. Her mother's favorite knit blanket was draped over a blue velvet trunk Vivi had never seen before. The one shelf on the wall held the carefully selected books Mom lugged with her on every move. And in a glass bowl was the mixture of lavender and cedar Daphne always placed on their coffee table. For a moment, all Vivi wanted to do was inhale the comforting scent of the items that had surrounded her for her whole life, the only source of consistency she'd had growing up.

Daphne sat on the couch and motioned to the spot next to her, but Vivi ignored her and sat in a scratchy yellow armchair instead. "Why didn't you tell me about any of this?" Vivi asked. "It doesn't make sense."

"I never hid what I was," her mother replied, suddenly sounding exhausted. "But I couldn't *make* you believe in magic, Vivi. You needed to experience it for yourself."

"Then why did you try to stop me from going to Westerly?"

"You don't need to be a Kappa in order to be a witch. Those girls aren't what they seem. You don't know the lengths they'd go to for more power."

"Like stealing the Henosis talisman?"

"Who told you about that?"

"Nobody needed to tell me. I saw a photo of you wearing it in the *Gazette* archives. A photo of you and Evelyn Waters, the girl who went missing."

Daphne clutched her mug so tightly, her knuckles turned white.

"What happened to her?"

"She died, Vivi. Because she got involved in something she didn't understand. The same kind of thing you're poking around in now."

"Is that some kind of threat?" Vivi asked incredulously.

"Don't be ridiculous." Her mother set her mug on the coffee table with a clank. "Everything I've done, I've done to protect you."

"Protect me by keeping me in the dark? Sounds like a great plan."

"Yes, if that's what it takes!"

Vivi rose from her chair, trembling with anger and frustration. "We've spent our whole lives on the run, and from what? Nothing bad ever happened to us."

"Because nobody's ever found it," her mother snapped.

Vivi's frenetic childhood came back to her in vivid flashes. The sudden departures, the midnight packing sessions, the long drives through the night, her mother taking circuitous routes to unknown destinations. When she was young, it had felt like a game. They were spies, on the run from some big bad enemy, sneaking across the country in their own little world. When she was older, it had gotten painful. Always leaving friends, crushes, everyone behind. Dragged away every time Vivi started to feel like she'd found a home.

It was all because of this, she realized. All because of Westerly, because of what had happened at Kappa. "So it's true," Vivi said slowly. "You *do* have the talisman."

Daphne nodded. "It's my responsibility to keep it from falling into the wrong hands, a job I've taken very seriously over the years."

"So all this time, all the running, all the moves—was it because of what happened to Evelyn?"

"You don't understand—"

"Did you kill her?" The words sprang from Vivi's lips before her brain had time to process them.

Emotions flashed across Daphne's face. Shock. Hurt. Indignation. Then back to sorrow, the kind of bone-deep sorrow that aged her mother ten years in a blink. "How could you think that?" she asked.

"I don't know," Vivi said. "I don't know what to believe anymore. All I know is that I need the talisman to save my friend's life, but for some reason, you don't seem to care about that."

"Of course I care, but you're not looking at the big picture. Do you really want the kidnapper to have one of the most powerful magical objects in the world? You have no idea how many lives you'll be risking."

"So I'm just supposed to let my friend *die?*"

"This is the reality of magic, Vivi. It's not all charms and parties and magical facemasks with your sorority sisters. This is what I was trying to protect you from."

The anger that'd been simmering in Vivi's chest began to boil over. "Well, you might've been able to play games with my life, but I'm not going to let you do the same to Tiffany's." Her magic came rushing to her. She was a Pentacles, the suit connected to earth magic, health, and material value, so locating a highly coveted object required hardly any effort. *Find the talisman,* she thought.

Her magic responded eagerly, almost like it had been waiting for this. Her fingertips hummed; tingles raced along her palms and up her arms. Agitated as she was, the magic felt like a breath of fresh air to starving lungs. A relief. Finally, something she could control. *Find it,* she commanded, and the magic flowed easily to her fingertips.

"Stop, Vivian," her mother ordered, and Vivi felt the snap of competing magic in the air. Her mother was casting her own spell.

"Show me the Henosis talisman," Vivi commanded. A wind gusted—papers fluttered off the nearby table, photographs shivered on the walls, and the whole bungalow seemed to shudder.

"Stop," Daphne said again. The papers stilled; the photos slammed back into place so hard, the glass panes cracked. "You won't be able to find it this way—I've made sure of that."

Vivi racked her brain, trying to figure out what safeguards her mother would've used. She looked around the room, and her gaze settled on a pair of gardening gloves by the door, similar to the ones Etta had used to plant the hogweed. Without saying a word to Daphne, Vivi spun around, wrenched open the locks on the door, and ran outside. Sure enough, at the edge of the lawn was a shrub with white flowers. The soil underneath looked fresh, as if the bush had been recently planted. This was why Vivi's spell hadn't worked—the hogweed had blocked her magic from finding the talisman. But now that she knew where to focus her powers, the plant would no longer stand in her way, not when she had the earth magic of a Pentacles witch at her disposal.

As Vivi raised her arms, the dirt began to shift slightly.

"Vivi, stop it," Daphne snapped, hurrying toward her.

The dirt continued to churn, revealing roots and rocks and a few wriggling earthworms.

Daphne placed her hand on Vivi's shoulder, then withdrew it with a yelp. Her palm had turned red, Vivi saw, as if she'd been scalded by the energy coursing through her daughter.

Vivi felt a twinge of guilt and started to lower her arms, but then she thought of all the people counting on her: Dahlia, Scarlett, and, most of all, Tiffany. She clenched her jaw and lifted her arms higher, straining against an invisible pressure. The ground started to rumble and then a glass oval rose up out of the muck. The glass was bluer than in the photo, the evil eye starker.

"You're in danger at Westerly," Daphne whispered, clutching her hand. "I've seen it in your cards. I'm trying to protect you."

"Here's a suggestion, then." Vivi snatched the talisman out of the air and stuffed it into her pocket. "If you want to protect me? Stay out of my way."

CHAPTER THIRTY-TWO

Scarlett

Scarlett's phone buzzed in her pocket: Vivi. She hit Ignore. *Take a hint, Little Sis.* She was kind of busy here. Too busy to deal with Vivi's guilt about Mason. Not to mention that just seeing her name on the screen reopened the wound. Mason leaving her. Mason and Vivi together. Mason and Vivi kissing.

Scarlett closed her eyes, driving the pain of their betrayal from her mind with effort. She was a Winter. She was a witch. She was stronger than her broken heart. And she had more important matters to deal with. She stole a glance across the street at Jackson, who was hunched inside the pay-phone booth they'd finally found after half an hour of hunting for one.

A sense of unreality hung over the whole night, like this was just another of Scarlett's nightmares. She kept waiting to wake up . . . but this was real. The cars passing by, their wheels bumping over the potholed street, were real. The bar at the end of the block, with its flickering neon sign, was real. The goose bumps on her arms were real. The mounting dread in her gut was real. And it was real that Gwen was dead and Tiffany was . . .

Stop, Scarlett commanded herself, not letting herself go there.

The sky above was deathly dark. The night of the new moon,

when the earth, sun, and moon were aligned in such a way that left the moon completely invisible to the human eye. Minnie had told her that it used to be called the old moon. Whatever you called it, the symbolism was the same. It was a time for destructive magic, a time to cast powerful curses, a time to embrace your own wickedness.

It wasn't surprising that Tiffany's kidnapper had picked this night to perform a dangerous ritual. And now Scarlett had only a few hours left to stop it—only a few hours left to save her sister.

Movement caught her eye, and she tensed on instinct. But it was only Jackson hanging up the phone. He hurried across the empty street toward her, hands stuffed in his jean pockets.

"Did you do it?" Scarlett leaned against the roof of the car, watching him, worried.

"Used my best Batman voice, just in case."

She offered up a small smile. She knew what he was doing—trying to keep things just light enough to prevent her from sinking into despair over Tiffany.

They'd decided it wasn't safe to call the police from their cell phones. If they did, they'd have to explain what they were doing on the scene—and what could they possibly say? *We were breaking into this girl's apartment to find out if she's an evil witch who stole my sorority sister—sorry, Officers.*

Better to leave an anonymous tip. Jackson had just told them he'd smelled gas coming from Gwen's apartment. It'd be enough to get someone in the door. To let them find . . . what they needed to find. Scarlett had cleaned up all traces of magic and all traces of her and Jackson—anything that could lead the police to wonder, to ask too many questions. Then they'd turned on the oven and left.

Scarlett forced down the memory of Gwen's glazed eyes, her sagging mouth. All she could think about was Tiffany. *She can't be dead; she can't.* Scarlett couldn't imagine finding her best friend in that same state, lifeless and empty.

Jackson touched Scarlett's shoulder gently. She startled. She hadn't noticed him coming around to her side of the car. "Why don't I drive?" he asked, and she handed him the keys, too tired to argue. "You can stay at my place if you need to." She shot him a look as she circled to the passenger side and got in the car. He misunderstood it. "Not like that. I mean, you can have the bed. I'll take the couch," he said, looking a little embarrassed.

She looked at him a beat. She hadn't imagined it; he felt it too. In the middle of all this awfulness, something had shifted between them. Seeing Jackson Carter flustered by her was something Scarlett couldn't have imagined before tonight. And even though she felt completely scraped raw inside, his sheepish smile broke her despair for a split second before it descended around her again.

"Jackson, I appreciate the offer . . . but I need to be with my sisters tonight."

She needed to tell them what had happened. They needed to figure out a new plan. If Gwen was dead, then either she had been the kidnapper and she'd killed Tiffany before she . . . *Before she what, Scarlett? Cursed herself to death?*

There could be no mistaking the billowing clouds of smoke or the lack of marks anywhere on Gwen's body despite the sea of blood around her. Someone had done that to her. Somebody cursed her.

Which meant Gwen likely wasn't the kidnapper. Which left the Ravens back at square one.

Who is doing this?

Scarlett racked her brain for the answer. It was someone with power. Another witch. Maybe one of the girls they'd turned down for Kappa had somehow gotten her memories back. Maybe it was a witch who never even pledged. But why would anyone target the Ravens? Gwen had been the only person alive with a motive to hurt them, and now she was dead. Scarlett and Tiffany had joked about girls dying to get into Kappa, but she'd never imagined anyone killing for it. It just didn't make any sense.

Scarlett needed the full force of the Ravens to help her. Together, maybe they could try another scrying spell, like they'd done the morning after Tiffany went missing. Something, anything.

She looked at the sky. Searched for the moon that, just like Tiffany, she knew was there but couldn't see. She missed Tiffany so much, it physically hurt. She'd always felt so connected to her friend; sometimes they barely even needed words to communicate. But their connection had gone silent, as if severed by a magical wall. If only she could talk to her. If only Tiffany could tell her where she was.

She jolted straight up in her seat, an idea taking form in her mind. Maybe she *could* ask Tiffany . . .

"Are you sure you'll be safe there?" Jackson asked, interrupting her thoughts. "I mean . . . if whoever did this is targeting witches . . ."

She cut him a sharp glare. She felt a flash of impatience even though she knew he meant well. Jackson had an irritating way of always pointing out the truth. "So I'm just supposed to slink off to safety and let them hurt another of my sisters instead of me—is that your suggestion?"

"I didn't say that. Maybe you should *all* leave that house. Go somewhere safe, like your parents' or—"

"Not until I find Tiffany." Scarlett clenched her fists so hard her nails dug into her palms, although she didn't notice until Jackson reached over to touch the back of her knuckles. She forced herself to relax.

One look at his face told her he wanted to argue. But after a few beats of silence, he nodded and started the car.

"Trust me, Jackson. I can handle myself. Whoever is doing this messed with the wrong witch."

When they reached Kappa, the house had gone dark for the night. She felt a pang of guilt for leaving Jackson alone with the new knowledge of how big and strange the world was—not to mention what kinds of monsters it contained. But she had to be with her sisters right now.

And honestly? Jackson would be safer far away from her.

Scarlett unlocked the front door and held her breath as she

crossed the threshold. It sounded quiet. Too quiet for a house of girls in full-blown crisis mode. Her heart started to hammer in her chest, and in her mind's eye, she kept seeing Gwen again.

What if the killer had come here next?

Quietly, Scarlett eased the door shut behind her and started up the hallway, holding her breath. The creaky old floorboards sounded creakier than ever. Every step she took felt like she was announcing her presence, shouting, *Come and get me.*

She reached the main sitting room, which stood dark and silent, and squinted at the staircase. A single light burned at the top of the stairs.

"Scarlett?"

She nearly jumped out of her skin. She whipped around to find Mei behind her, frowning, arms crossed. "Where is everyone?" Scarlett asked, her voice overloud in the silence.

Mei's frown deepened, as if Scarlett were the one acting weird. "Sleeping. Or trying to, anyway. Though I think Sonali and a couple other sisters are still up on the top floor digging through the old files."

"What about Dahlia? I need to talk to her."

"She's preparing a new spell and had to run out to grab a final ingredient."

Scarlett fought the urge to curse. Dahlia truly believed that if they gathered enough magical objects and held hands and chanted, they would survive this. Then she thought about her phone and the missed call from Vivi. "What about Vivi?"

"She took off earlier. Something about her mother." Mei

hesitated and then reached out to touch Scarlett's forearm lightly. "Hey, for what it's worth, I think Vivi was way out of line with Mason."

"Thanks." Scarlett nodded. While she felt a rush of pain at the mention of Mason and Vivi together, this time it was coupled with a surge of gratitude toward Mei for being on her side, especially since she knew how much Mei liked Vivi, if for no other reason than being an incredible Before in her inevitable makeover. But it should have been Tiffany who was offering to hex Vivi into oblivion, not Mei.

"Are you okay?" Mei asked. "Maybe you should get some rest. You look beat."

"I can't." Scarlett took a deep breath and held it for a second, hoping it would steady her racing pulse. "Mei . . . Gwen is dead. I just found her body. It looked like she'd been cursed."

Mei's eyebrows shot so high they disappeared under her razor-straight bangs. Scarlett watched as her pretty face went through a strong cycle of emotions: Denial. Acceptance. What-the-effness. "Oh, man . . . she was evil, but still . . . that's awful. But then she couldn't have—"

"Kidnapped Tiffany? No. Doesn't look like it." Scarlett crossed her arms. "I have an idea for how we can find her. But I need everyone's help."

Mei hesitated, her gaze drifting past Scarlett toward the front door, but only for a moment. "Dahlia isn't here."

"If she were, though, I'm sure she'd agree with me. Wake the Kappas. Have every witch meet me in the greenhouse. Now."

"What's going on?" Juliet squinted blearily around the greenhouse, clutching Jess's hand. In the dark, with only half the taper candles lit, the trees threw gloomy shadows across the girls' sleep-deprived faces.

Scarlett had never led the sorority in a spell like this before. She felt the weight of it like a physical presence. *Help me, Minnie,* she thought, looking at her sisters. She hoped they were up to the task.

"Sisters, I need your help. Tiffany needs your help. But I can't command it. I am asking for it. Anyone who's not up to it can leave now."

Scarlett looked at her sisters, all in various states of undress. None of them budged.

"All right, then. This is higher-level magic. I need all your focus. We're casting a new spell to find Tiffany. Reagan, can you give us some light?" Scarlett gestured toward the candle in the center of the floor. Reagan stepped over to touch the wax base. A few heartbeats later, a flame flickered to life on the tip of the wick. Scarlett flashed the girl a grateful look and left her to light the remaining tapers.

"Should we wait for Dahlia and Vivi?" Jess asked, reaching for her cell as Scarlett stepped back into the circle of Ravens. "Do we need their power too?"

"We don't have time. Dahlia wants to find Tiffany just as much as we do." Scarlett crossed her arms and studied the girls ringed around her, one by one.

"In Kappa," Scarlett said, "we put our sisters first. And right now, one of our sisters is out there in grave danger. If we can help, we have a duty to try. Are you still with me?"

For a moment, her voice echoed in the greenhouse space. Then Mei stepped forward, eyes locked on Scarlett's. "I trust you," she said.

Etta bowed her head next. "Me too."

Around the circle it went, some people just nodding, others assuring her in words that they were on board. By the end, even Juliet, after flicking a glance at Jess, offered a gruff nod of her own. Jess twined her fingers through Juliet's and squeezed once.

"Earlier, I was looking at the sky," Scarlett said, "and I was thinking that even though we can't see the moon tonight, it doesn't mean it's not there. It still exists; it's just a shadow of itself." A few girls nodded. A slow smile spread over Etta's face; she clearly understood where Scarlett was going with this. "When something disappears, it doesn't just fall off the face of the earth. It has a history. It leaves a trace. A shadow."

When Scarlett was younger, Minnie had spoken often of old magic, of the ways things were before witchcraft was formalized into grimoires and covens and written spells. Spells helped focus the magic, but that narrowed focus meant you lost something—the *feeling* behind it, the desires that couldn't be put into words. Everything in this world had an energy, an essential essence, and people left behind a little bit of themselves in everything they touched. Whoever had taken Tiffany had blocked every one of the Ravens' commonly used spells to locate her physical body, but maybe the kidnapper hadn't thought to block spells searching for her energy, that metaphysical, unnameable thing that made Tiffany Tiffany. In fact, Scarlett was betting on it.

She opened the bag in her hand and spread the items out on the floor. A pair of leather ankle boots. A tweed skirt. A cream silk shirt. And an emerald-cut ruby pendant she'd taken from Tiffany's nightstand. It had been one of her favorite necklaces. *It* is *one of her favorite necklaces,* Scarlett corrected herself.

She arranged everything into the shape of a girl on the floor, the way Minnie used to lay out her outfits for her when she was a child, and then poured smoky black salt around the perimeter for protection and strength.

"Tonight, we seek our lost sister," she said, her voice lifting. She felt a chill along her arms, the whisper of wind, despite the enclosed greenhouse. "By Cups, we call her." The Cups witches echoed Scarlett's cry. "By Wands, we call her." The Wands witches followed, the freshmen looking to the older girls for guidance. "By Pentacles, we call her." And finally, Tiffany's suit. "By Swords, we call her." Scarlett felt the rush of magic around her as her sisters called upon their power.

"Ravens, lend me your strength," Scarlett commanded. It hit her with the force of a lightning bolt, power from all sides, of every suit, flowing through her. She had to grit her teeth just to stay grounded enough to speak again. "Reveal the shadow, show the path," Scarlett recited. "Show us what is missing at last."

The others joined in. At least, she thought they did. With the magic rushing through her veins, Scarlett could hardly focus on anything except the feel of Juliet's and Etta's hands in her own. She *willed* the magic to show her. Willed it to lead her to Tiffany.

"Reveal the shadow, show the path. Show us what is missing at last."

The clothes on the floor rustled, moving as if in that same eerie wind. They started to sway back and forth, then expand, almost as if they were making room for a body. What looked like black smoke began pouring into the room, tendrils filtering in from the cracks in the floor, seeping in through the windows, whispering through the plants. It swirled around the sisters, licking at their ankles, curling up their legs.

"Reveal the shadow, show the path," Scarlett whispered. "Show us what is missing at last." The necklace shuddered on the floor. The smoke started whipping, suddenly becoming so dense that Scarlett couldn't see the clothes on the ground, couldn't see the faces of her sisters across the circle. It turned acrid, choking her, just like it had at Gwen's apartment. That was when the magic started to burn in her veins. Scarlett could feel another will underneath hers, something vying against her. Something—or some*one*—did not want them to complete this spell.

Too bad. It was one individual's willpower against the combined force of all of Kappa. Scarlett narrowed her eyes and pushed back.

Show me my sister, she commanded, and the smoke roiled, swirling together, spinning like cotton candy into a funnel in the center of the room. Suddenly, it shot to the ceiling like a geyser and then careened down toward the floor.

Hazel let out a shout. Scarlett braced for impact. But just before it hit the ground, the smoke stopped, hovering an inch off the tiles like morning burn-off. Then it gently dropped down and seeped into the clothes, filling them, a filmy body sculpted in the shape of a person. And that was when Scarlett realized it wasn't smoke at all: it was a shadow.

The shadow-girl sat up, a wisp of a thing, a shaky afterimage of the sister who'd left them two nights ago.

Scarlett gasped. Juliet squeezed her hand so hard, she thought she felt something pop. Reagan's eyes gleamed in awe.

"Tiffany?" Scarlett whispered.

The shadow-girl raised her hand. Then she pointed straight at the doors of the greenhouse, toward the back patio of Kappa House.

Toward the forest beyond. Scarlett glanced up, met Mei's and Etta's confused gazes. Trembling, she realized what this meant.

Tiffany was *here*. Somewhere right outside those doors.

CHAPTER THIRTY-THREE

Vivi

For the first time in her life, Vivi broke her rule about not using her phone while driving. Because, for the first time in her life, there literally wasn't a moment to waste. Taking care to keep her eyes on the road, she called Scarlett. They might not be on good terms, but she was still Vivi's Big and Tiffany's best friend. The phone rang a few times and then went to voicemail. "Shit."

Vivi hung up and banged her head on the seat back, then flicked on her turn signal and took the exit toward Savannah.

Of course Scarlett wasn't answering. Vivi hadn't just hurt her —she'd betrayed her. After all this talk about how much she valued the Ravens and sisterhood, Vivi had gone right ahead and stabbed her Big in the back. She would have to figure out the best way to apologize and make things right later. At this moment, all that mattered was returning the talisman and rescuing Tiffany.

Vivi tapped her phone again, one eye on the road, and hit a different number.

Unlike Scarlett, Dahlia answered on the first ring. "How did it go?"

"I got the talisman," she said, getting straight to the point.

On the other end of the line, the normally unflappable Dahlia inhaled sharply. "So your mother had it?"

"Apparently she's the one who stole it from Kappa in the first place," Vivi said, wincing with shame. "I can explain more when I get to the house."

"There's no time for that."

"No time for explanations?" Vivi risked a confused glance at the phone screen.

"No, I don't have time to go back to the house. I'm collecting the ingredients we need for the replicator spell. I'm about to call the rest of the sisters now."

Something about the way she said it made Vivi's heart beat a little faster, and her mother's words echoed in her ears: *You have no idea how many lives you'll be risking.* "We're not going to actually *give* it to the person who stole Tiffany, are we?"

"Of course not." Dahlia sounded insulted at the very suggestion. "With the talisman, we'll have more than enough power to find Tiffany on our own. Trust me."

Vivi did trust her; she trusted all the Ravens. They'd given her the thing she'd craved her entire life, the thing she'd always been missing: a home, a place to belong, and a real family, one that hadn't spent years lying to her. "Where do you need me to go?"

"I'll text you the location now. Just please, hurry. We're running out of time."

This time, Vivi had no trouble navigating the highway. The magic she'd conjured to find the talisman still flowed through her veins, making her feel powerful and confident as she zoomed toward the location Dahlia had given her. Vivi checked and double-checked the pin on the map Dahlia had dropped for her. But no matter how many times she reloaded the page, it still looked the same. Right in the middle of a forest, which seemed strange. But maybe the spell needed to be done in a place like this?

She took the specified exit and turned onto a narrow, two-lane road bordered by tall trees. It looked like Dahlia was sending her the back way to Kappa House, except that the pin seemed to be in the middle of the woods behind the house. She kept going for another few miles, until the pavement turned to a gravel road and the trees grew so thick, they blocked the light of the faintly glowing stars.

The road dead-ended at a tiny dirt parking lot. There were no other cars, and for a moment, Vivi considered waiting there for Dahlia. But the pin she'd dropped for her was about a half a mile from the lot. For all Vivi knew, Dahlia could've parked somewhere else and was already waiting for Vivi in the woods. She looked down at her phone to see if Dahlia had texted, but there was no signal. And there was no time to waste.

Vivi headed up a steep slope, stepping carefully around the rocks and roots as she made her way toward the place marked by the little dot on her phone screen. Night had settled around her; at first, she could glimpse tiny patches of the star-strewn sky through the thick tree branches, but as she traveled deeper into the forest, the sky seemed to vanish.

The Henosis talisman weighed heavily in Vivi's pocket. Every step she took, she felt it tap against her thigh. A constant reminder of what she'd come here to do.

Westerly isn't a safe place, not for people like you.

You don't know what power does to people. You can't trust any of those so-called sorority witches.

Her brain felt like it was playing a constant loop of Daphne Devereaux's greatest hits, all the things she said to drag Vivi down, to make her doubt herself, her sisters, her friends.

Yet the whole time, it was Daphne who'd let everyone down, who'd betrayed her sisters and stolen from Kappa all those years ago.

No more. Vivi would right the wrongs of her mother.

The little blue dot was almost right on top of the red pin Dahlia had dropped for her.

"Hello?" Vivi called, feeling slightly foolish as her voice echoed through the woods. "Dahlia? Are you here?"

Now that she'd stopped moving, she realized how strangely quiet it was. There were no birds singing, no wind rustling the leaves.

Vivi spun in a slow circle, peering through the trees. Her cell's weak flashlight illuminated only so much. "Dahlia?" she called again, trying to keep the growing fear out of her voice. Her phone was going to run out of battery soon.

On her second rotation, she glimpsed a large clearing in the distance. The ground was littered with red and brown leaves. Autumn had only just begun, but the leaves here looked dead already, like it was late winter. Vivi put her dying phone away and whispered, "I call to the Queen of Wands. Show me your might by giving us light." A moment later, a small, quivering flame appeared above her palm. Keeping her arm outstretched, she made her way toward the clearing and shivered as the temperature seemed to drop. She'd been sweating her whole trek through the forest, but now the moisture clung uncomfortably to her clammy skin.

As she got closer, she saw that the clearing had been set up for a ritual, like Dahlia had said. Only Vivi didn't recognize most of the items here. There were candles, but instead of the shorter tapers the Ravens used for spellwork, tall cylindrical tapers ringed the blanket of dry leaves.

There was a cauldron like the one Etta kept in the kitchen, except the carvings around it didn't look like pentagrams—or any symbol she recognized. They were sharp and jagged, like letters from a foreign alphabet.

She shivered again, suddenly overcome by the same strange chill she'd felt looking at the doll in the archives. "Dahlia?" Her voice was barely a whisper now. "Where are you?" She took another step, and leaves crunched underfoot. Leaves, and something harder, snapping like a branch. Vivi glanced down and felt her breath freeze in her chest. *Bones.* She was walking across piles and piles of white bones. Small bones, like from a rat or a rabbit, and larger ones too. Femurs from something too big to be a small animal. Far too big . . .

Snap.

Another bone shattered right behind her, and Vivi's entire body went rigid except for her heart, which was beating like a wild animal trying to bash its way out of her chest.

"Vivian," Dahlia said from behind her. "So glad you could make it."

Vivi whipped around just in time to catch a glimpse of the older girl's twisted smile.

Then a spell hit her square in the chest, and the world went dark.

CHAPTER THIRTY-FOUR

Scarlett

Scarlett couldn't take her eyes off the shadow-girl before her. She swayed, the dark tendrils of smoky shadow forming and re-forming, the ruby pendant glowing red at her throat.

In the past, Scarlett had felt her magic crest like the water, but except for that one moment when she almost lost control while scrying for Gwen's intentions, she had never felt anything so powerful before. And looking at what she and her sisters had done, looking at this creation of magic and will, she felt a sense of awe.

She took a deep breath and let herself hope that the next step would work as well as the first.

"I'm coming with you," Mei said before Scarlett could say a word. When Scarlett opened her mouth to protest, Mei moved to her side. "Tiffany's my sister too."

Scarlett and Mei were the only juniors left in Kappa at the moment. Scarlett could understand why she wanted to come. Even if she didn't like the idea of anyone else risking her skin.

The other Ravens remained in a ring, eyes wide as they stared at the shadow-girl, who was still pointing at the doors. Pointing toward Tiffany.

"I'll come too," Etta offered. But Scarlett shook her head.

"We should *all* go. Ravens stick together; isn't that what you just told us?" Reagan crossed her arms, scowling.

"You need to stay here to keep performing the spell," Scarlett said. "I don't know how long the spell will last and I need to be able to follow her until I find Tiffany."

"Personally, I'm of the opinion *nobody* should go out there," Sonali said. "Let's at least wait until Dahlia gets back."

"I'm going to find Tiffany. Now." Scarlett glanced at Reagan. "This is something I need to do for me, not just for Kappa."

Somewhere in the back of her mind, she could hear Dahlia's voice: *You're not acting very presidential right now.* She wasn't. Running off into the night, leaving her sisters here without guidance? But she didn't care about the presidency or about doing what was proper.

She cared about doing what was *right*.

She and Mei traded looks. The other girl nodded, solemn.

"Shadow, trust me. Take me to Tiffany," Scarlett said.

Mei repeated her words, and the other girls followed their lead until their voices filled the air.

The doors swung open seemingly of their own accord and the shadow began to move toward them. The spell was working.

"Stay here, lock the doors, and don't let anyone but a Raven inside tonight," Scarlett told Mei, feeling her urgency intensify. This had to work. The shadow-girl had to find Tiffany.

Scarlett stepped out into the night, trailing the apparition into the backyard. She heard the door shut firmly behind her with a click.

Storm clouds had begun to gather, low and thick overhead. The muggy air felt like soup. She practically swam through it, following the shadow across the backyard, past the carefully cultivated hedge maze, right up to the edge of the woods that surrounded Westerly's campus.

The Spanish oaks creaked in the wind. Branches scraped together with a sound like broken violins. In the distance, thunder rumbled. Not close enough to rain yet, though the muggy air begged for it.

The shadow-girl beckoned Scarlett forward, pointing straight ahead, into the gloom beneath the trees. Fat tendrils of fog rolled through the woods underfoot. Scarlett could barely see the path well enough to keep her feet from tangling in underbrush and sprawling root systems. She picked her way behind the shadow-figure, who floated along in front of her, the ruby necklace glowing like a beacon.

After she'd walked a few paces, she peered over her shoulder. Already the lights of Kappa House were gone, swallowed by the trees. She could hardly see a thing. She pulled out her cell, tapped on the flashlight, and swept the forest floor for . . . what?

Tiffany's body?

Scarlett couldn't even let herself think it. It felt like a betrayal. *The scrying spell would have told us. It would have given us some sign if she was dead already.* Unless the shadow-girl was only leading Scarlett toward her owner's body.

She's fine. She has to be. In Scarlett's mind's eye, though, all she could see was Gwen. The horrible emptiness of her eyes. The smoke that poured from her lips.

The fog had thickened to a grayish-white mist now. Her shirt was soaked in sweat, sticking to her back, her chest.

And still the apparition, her pendant glowing, kept moving, urging her deeper into the woods.

She could hardly make out the figure in the swirling air, the shadow blending into the tendrils of mist. Her flashlight reflected weirdly off the clouds of fog, making it impossible to see through them, like high beams in a storm. Hell, she could barely even see her own hand.

The only thing drawing her onward was the glowing pendant, moving steadily in one direction, deeper into the bowels of the forest. Her heart hammered in her ears.

And then, without warning, the pendant vanished too. Scarlett cursed under her breath. Why had the spell stopped working?

"Tiffany!" She raised her voice as loud as she dared. The forest didn't answer.

She reached out in her mind for Tiffany. *Please, Tiff.*

When the shadow didn't reappear, she called out in her mind for Minnie, not expecting an answer but wanting one, needing her mentor desperately. *Please help me find her.*

She whipped around and around. She didn't even know which way she'd entered. And now she had no way forward.

Where was the shadow? Where was her friend? She held still, listening. But Scarlett couldn't hear anything. No crash of footsteps, no whispered voices. The longer she stood and listened, the more forest sounds came rushing in. The creak of the trees, and another hungry, long rumble of thunder.

For a split second, a bright flash lit the woods. Lightning. From the moment she'd stepped outside into the mist, Scarlett had wondered if she was the one causing it. Was the lightning an answer to her call for help? Or was it her losing control? Suddenly, Scarlett caught a glimpse of lights in the distance, far ahead.

Another flash illuminated a path through the woods toward the distant lights. A fire, she guessed, based on the way it flickered and danced, the red-gold flames cutting through the gloom of the forest.

Someone else was out here. Someone healthy enough to build a fire. *Tiffany*. Her heart practically exploded with hope.

I'm coming, Tiffany, she vowed, hoping her friend could sense her presence. She focused on that instead of on the fear that had begun to creep up on her. The nagging sense that *something was very, very wrong here.*

She kept pressing forward through the trees toward that dancing flame. Deeper into the unknown but closer to her friend.

Or what remained of her.

CHAPTER THIRTY-FIVE

Vivi

The first thing Vivi became aware of was something sharp digging into her side, like she'd fallen asleep on top of her phone. Then came the cold. She started to shiver, but the movement caused her head to rattle painfully.

A bolt of electric fear shot through Vivi as she jerked her head up, suddenly alert and frantic, but something stopped her from getting to her feet. It felt like invisible weights were attached to her arms and legs.

Vivi wrenched her head to the side and felt the scratch of stiff grass. She was still in the clearing, but the sky was pitch-black. The only illumination came from the flickering candles that'd been arranged in a circle around her. It should've been a comforting sight, but unlike the small tapers she'd grown accustomed to, these candles were thick and tall, scattered in an uneven pattern like bloody teeth. And the white bones she'd seen earlier were now carefully arranged around the circle, creating the effect of a ghastly crown.

Dahlia was kneeling a few yards away, smearing something in the grass. In the faint light, Vivi managed to catch a flash of red-stained palms. Her shallow breath caught in her chest when she realized what Dahlia was doing. She was painting a pentagram. In blood.

With Vivi at the dead center.

Heart pounding, she strained to sit up, but her wrists and ankles were bound together by an invisible force. She muttered an escape spell Scarlett had taught her, but when she tried to reach for her magic, the familiar buzz wouldn't rise to her fingers. She tried again, but the gesture felt empty and futile, like swiping at a phone that'd run out of battery.

"Oh, you're up," Dahlia said pleasantly, as if Vivi had just come downstairs for breakfast at Kappa House instead of regaining consciousness in the middle of the woods.

"Dahlia? What's going on?" It was foolish but there was still a tiny part of her that believed there could be a logical explanation for this. A hazing ritual that had gone just slightly too far. But then her eyes settled on Dahlia's throat, and a rush of fear swept through her.

The Henosis talisman dangled from Dahlia's neck.

"You wanted it for yourself," Vivi said faintly as Scarlett's description of the talisman came back to her. *To take another witch's power, you have to kill her.*

Dahlia shrugged. "I hope you know it's nothing personal. Not like it was with Gwen. The scarecrows . . . the tarot . . . she just wouldn't stop. She kept finding ways to make noise even with her mouth sewn shut. I had to get rid of her before she destroyed Kappa House and everyone in it."

"You *killed* Gwen?" In that moment, Vivi knew it was true, but she still couldn't keep the surprise out of her voice. Dahlia, the Kappa president, had *murdered* another witch.

Dahlia reached for something on the ground, then held up a rusty dagger with dead leaves clinging to the edge. "Yup, and I enjoyed it too. But it's different with you, trust me. I don't actually *want* to kill you."

"So don't. You don't have to do this." Vivi did her best to sound rational, even though she sensed that a desperate plea wouldn't have much effect on a girl who'd already killed before.

"I'm sorry, Vivi," Dahlia said sadly. "But you're the strongest Pentacles witch I've ever met." She ran her finger along the knife, flicking off the dead leaves, then took a step forward and placed the tip of the blade on Vivi's throat. "I need your magic. But I promise, I'll make this as fast and painless as possible." Dahlia paused and frowned. "Well, I'll make it fast anyway. I don't think it's possible to remove someone's beating heart without a *little* bit of pain."

The panic Vivi had been struggling to hold at bay shot through her, and she screamed, her voice echoing through the empty woods until it was drowned out by a peal of thunder.

Dahlia sighed and removed the knife. "Shout all you like. Nobody's going to hear you all the way out here."

Just keep her talking, Vivi thought desperately. The longer she stalled, the longer the Ravens would have to find her. "What do you need my powers for?"

"I need the magic of all four suits to perform certain spells. No more waiting for any pesky full-moon rituals. No need to borrow or beg my strength from others."

"So everything you said about sisterhood is bullshit, then? You don't believe that we're stronger together?"

"Sisterhood?" Dahlia's mouth curled into a sneer. "When I needed my so-called sisters most, no one was there for me. When I begged for their magic, they turned away. They left me no choice."

"The Kappas worship you. And even if we didn't . . . that would be no excuse to do this to *anyone*. What about Tiffany?" Vivi asked, bracing for the horrible truth. "Did you kill her? Did you take her powers?" The thought of dead witches' magic running through Dahlia's veins made Vivi's stomach turn; it was like imagining someone pluck out a person's eyeball and place it in their own socket.

"You know what? I think I've had about as much chitchat as I can handle." She snapped her fingers and Vivi's lips clamped together. Vivi tried to scream, but the attempt resulted in agonizing pain. She raised her arms as much as possible and awkwardly ran the backs of her bound hands along her mouth. Her lips had been sewn together with thick string.

"Now, just relax," Dahlia said in an almost singsong voice as she held the dagger over one of the candles. "It'll all be over in a minute. I just need to hold your heart long enough to complete the transfer. Then I'll kill you as quickly as possible. I have no interest in prolonging your suffering, I promise."

A wave of terror and nausea crashed over Vivi as she pictured herself splayed in the center of the pentagram, watching helplessly as Dahlia plunged the knife into her chest and removed her still-beating heart. Would she pass out from the pain? Or would she remain lucid as she bled to death, alone in the forest, abandoned by the sisters she'd let down?

She saw her mother getting the call from Westerly, an official saying he was sorry to inform her that there'd been an accident. A sob tore through Vivi's throat as she saw Daphne's face crumple, her mother whispering, "No, no, no," as she slumped against the wall. Spending the night crying on the couch, clutching one of the stuffed animals Vivi had left behind, the only piece of her daughter that remained.

She thought of her sisters, with whom she would never have the chance to make things right. And despite herself, she imagined Mason's face when he heard whatever version of the news Kappa decided to give. His mixture of anguish and regret about losing the girl who hadn't allowed him to love her.

Dahlia extended her arms as she tilted her head to the sky and began to chant in a language Vivi didn't recognize.

As her voice rose, the flames grew higher until the candles looked like torches releasing smoke into the air. Vivi watched with fascinated horror as the streams of smoke began to join and condense, forming the shape of three large birds with dark eyes and sharp beaks.

Ravens.

The birds rose into the air, then turned and swooped toward Vivi, smoke trailing from their wingtips as they descended.

She tried to scream, but again, no sound came out. She couldn't yell. Couldn't use her magic. She was helpless . . . and she was about to die.

The first raven landed on her stomach with surprising, chilling weight. *It's just an illusion,* Vivi tried to tell herself. *It can't actually hurt you.* But then the bird thrust its head forward, plunging its beak into her chest and piercing her skin. Another bird landed on her shoulder and began to peck at her chest from another angle.

Vivi wrenched herself from side to side, trying to scare them off, shake them loose, but their pecking only grew more painful and intense. With each strike, they dug deeper into her skin.

They were going to rip her chest open and expose her heart.

I call to the Emperor and the Empress, Vivi thought, screaming the words inside her head. *Help me with my distress.* It was a catchall spell Scarlett had taught her, a powerful invocation that could be used in any emergency. But without her cards or the ability to speak, there was nothing Vivi could do. She was far too inexperienced a witch to perform magic with just her mind. There was no way to break the magical binds Dahlia had placed on her.

Dahlia raised her arms higher and the birds' pecking grew more urgent. Vivi could feel blood spilling down the front of her shirt as the beaks dug deeper into her skin. The pain was already almost too much to bear.

Dahlia's chants had turned into a screech. She tilted her head back even farther, shouting straight to the dark sky. A jagged bolt of orange lightning sizzled through the clouds, and a moment later, a crack of thunder shook the ground. The air smelled thick and bitter, heavy with the choking smoke of wicked magic.

Another lightning bolt tore through the sky, and Dahlia's fingertips began to glow. She laughed and spun as her hair flew around her face. "I call to Death and to the Tower," she cried as she clutched the talisman. "Call home this witch and give me her power."

Something began to flow out of Vivi. At first, she thought it was more blood, but it was coming from places the birds hadn't touched. She tried to wrench her head around for a better look, but she was too weak to move.

She was dying, and Dahlia was taking her magic.

"I call to Death and to the Tower. Call home this witch and give me—" Dahlia went silent as the orange glow began to fade from her fingertips. She lowered her arms and turned, searching the dark woods for something to explain what'd gone wrong.

Another bolt of lightning flared above, and Scarlett stepped into the circle. Her dark eyes burned with fury and surging magic, and her skin seemed to glow from within. She strode forward to face Dahlia, unfazed by the grim accoutrements of wicked magic. "I can't believe it was you all along."

For the first time that evening, something akin to fear flashed across Dahlia's face. "Scarlett, hold on—"

Scarlett cut her off by raising her hands. The wind immediately picked up. Trees snapped and creaked as they rubbed against one another, and rain began to fall, softly at first and then suddenly much harder, coming down in sheets that doused the candles.

A moment later, the birds vanished, and Vivi exhaled in relief.

"What did you do to Tiffany?" Scarlett demanded.

Dahlia extended her hands, and the candles flared back to life, the flames leaping to double, triple their original height. In the firelight, her face took on a strange cast, as if it were bending and snapping out of shape. "You don't understand." Dahlia was shouting to be heard over the rain and the wind, but there was a desperate plea in her voice. "You have to let me explain."

"Explain?" Scarlett spat, her mouth twisted with disgust. "There's no way you can explain killing my best friend." She flexed her outstretched hands and Dahlia flew backwards.

The next moment, Vivi's rigid limbs went limp and the invisible cords binding her wrists and ankles vanished. By the time she rose unsteadily to her feet, she could feel power beginning to surge into her body, like water being sucked into a growing tsunami.

She felt the earth respond to the return of her magic. The ground trembled under her feet and the leaves began to shudder, as if quivering in anticipation of her call. But Vivi couldn't focus on anything except Dahlia's face, which seemed to be transforming.

Her nose shrank her eye and hair color shifted, her glamour was losing its form, her concentration pulled in too many other directions to maintain the mask.

Vivi gasped and Scarlett staggered backwards. Far above, one particularly ominous storm cloud reached a finger down, almost like a tornado. But neither girl noticed—they were too horrified by the sight right in front of them.

The sister staring back at them wasn't Dahlia.

It was Tiffany.

CHAPTER THIRTY-SIX

Scarlett

If Scarlett hadn't been witnessing this with her own eyes, she never would have believed it. But there was no mistaking who the blond, narrow-faced girl standing across from her was. Her best friend.

"What the hell's going on? I thought you were *dead*." Scarlett's eyes stung, though she wasn't sure if it was from the rain, her tears, or both.

"I know, and I'm sorry." Tiffany's voice sounded thin and almost contrite as it carried over the howling wind and the whipping of the tree branches. Wet leaves rained down on their heads, followed by loose sticks and branches. A tornado-like funnel swirled above them, roiling the debris in a whirling circle. "I had to make it look like I was the one missing so nobody would find her."

Her? Scarlett's confusion curdled into disgust as she remembered all the blood in Tiffany's room. If Tiffany herself was fine and had been walking around wearing Dahlia's face for days, then that meant . . .

"You killed Dahlia," Vivi said, apparently reaching the conclusion at the same moment.

"I needed her power," Tiffany said, still facing Scarlett. "If you'd just let me explain, you'd understand."

"Understand?" Scarlett's voice rose to a nearly hysterical pitch as she realized her best friend was trying to justify *murdering* their friend. Beautiful, brilliant, fierce Dahlia, who put her sisters before everything. Who'd stay up all night helping you brew a potion to calm midterm anxiety or drive four hours to get you if you got stranded in a freak snowstorm—even if said snowstorm was a product of your own foolish making. Dahlia, one of the most talented, committed witches in a generation, gone. Snuffed out as carelessly as a candle at the end of a ritual and with as little remorse. "There is *nothing* you could say that would make this okay."

"Oh, really? Okay, try this: I spent years listening to all those speeches about Ravens putting each other first, but when I really needed you all, no one was there for me."

"What are you talking about?"

"All I wanted was to help her." Tiffany's voice cracked slightly. "The doctors couldn't do anything more, so I found a spell in the grimoire. It was major arcana, something I couldn't do on my own, so I went to ask Dahlia if we could perform the ritual as a house."

Her mother. Of course. Scarlett's stomach sank as she remembered how thin Veronica Beckett had been at Homecoming. Tiffany had tried to put on a brave face, but Scarlett knew Veronica had been given a terminal diagnosis and had just a few more months to live.

"But Dahlia wouldn't even think about it," Tiffany continued. "She said it was an outdated spell created before we really knew how diseases worked and that it would 'mess with the natural order of things.' As if that's a good enough reason to *let my mother die*."

The pain in Tiffany's voice made Scarlett's heart cramp. She could only begin to imagine how her friend—and her friend's family—had suffered. But there were certain forces that even witches couldn't change, and death was one of them. "Would she want you to do this for her? Would she want you to become this?" Scarlett asked quietly.

Tiffany was drenched, her limp hair plastered to her face, but she radiated power. Scarlett could feel it emanating from her, filling the air with the pungent scent of rot. That was what happened when you contaminated your magic. Tiffany might've accumulated an unnatural amount of power, but it had come at great cost.

Another bolt of lightning tore through the sky, and for a moment all Scarlett could see was blinding white. When her eyes adjusted to the dark again, she saw Tiffany looking at her with a sad smile that made Scarlett's blood run cold.

"It's too late now," Tiffany said, stroking the talisman around her neck. "I've already collected the power of three suits. Mine. Dahlia's. And a Cups witch I met over the summer. All I need to collect is a Pentacles, and I'll be able to do whatever the hell I want." She turned to look at Vivi hungrily.

Scarlett stepped between Tiffany and her Little. "You're not going to hurt anyone else. Especially not her."

Tiffany raised a mocking eyebrow, then threw her arms to her sides and shouted into the rain, "I call to Death and to the Tower. Call home this witch and give me her power."

Scarlett started at the words of the spell, one she knew well but had never heard spoken aloud. It was the deadliest major arcana spell—one that required an entire coven to perform. Surely even the stolen power of two witches wouldn't be enough for Tiffany to do it on her own. But then the talisman around Tiffany's neck began to glow and a strange smell filled the air. The rain running down Scarlett's skin turned thick and sticky. She looked at her arm and gasped, then shielded her face and turned to the sky.

It was raining blood.

"Tiffany, no!" The thunder drowned out Scarlett's scream as a rush of wind struck her, blowing her off balance. There was a loud *crack* and she stumbled to the side just in time to avoid being hit by an enormous tree branch. The tornado Tiffany had conjured was stripping the tops off the trees. If they didn't find shelter before it touched down, they'd be flung into the air just like those branches.

"I call to Death and to the Tower. Call home this witch and give me her power!" Tiffany shrieked. Scarlett spun around and saw Vivi floating off the ground, her limbs as loose and powerless as a rag doll's. She seemed suspended by an invisible cord attached to her chest. No, that wasn't right, Scarlett realized with growing revulsion and horror as she watched a dark mass appear beneath Vivi's white T-shirt.

It was her heart.

"Tiffany, don't!" Scarlett screamed, but her cry was drowned out by another peal of thunder. "I call to Justice and Judgment, whose vision is long," she said breathlessly. "Set right to what is wrong." It was more a plea than a spell, an ancient appeal to two of the most powerful forces in the tarot. But it was also major arcana and required the magic of an entire coven.

The front of Vivi's shirt had turned red with blood, although Scarlett wasn't sure if it was from the rain . . . or from the pressure of her heart straining against her sternum as Tiffany did her best to tear it from Vivi's body.

Scarlett took a deep breath and shouted with all her might, *"I call to Justice and Judgment, whose vision is long. Set right to what is wrong."*

But the magic refused to heed her call. It was impossible. Tiffany was able to perform major arcana spells on her own only because of the stolen magic running through her veins, amplified by the talisman. Scarlett was no match for her. In a few minutes, she was going to watch Vivi die.

Something inside Scarlett shriveled. She'd never felt emptier or more powerless in her life. This was it. She'd failed Vivi. She'd failed Dahlia. She'd failed everyone.

Then she felt a pressure on her shoulder like the comforting weight of someone's hand. Scarlett spun around and saw no one, but the pressure only increased, sending a jolt of warmth through her. She felt her skin begin to buzz with a surge of new energy, the way it did when she cast spells with her sisters.

A moment later, they found her. Mei was the first to sprint into the clearing, Juliet at her heels. One by one, the Ravens streamed into the clearing, their confused or weary faces turning fierce as soon as their eyes landed on Scarlett and Vivi.

Tiffany let out an angry snarl, but Mei and Hazel took Scarlett's hands, and her fear drained away. She no longer felt the cold of rain-filled night air. She was no longer aware of anything except a growing surge of energy inside her, pouring into her from all directions. Scarlett's sisters were with her. She could feel the raw, unfiltered power of Juliet's magic and the steady stream of Jess's, understated but able to strike with surgical precision. She felt the tingle of Mei's magic, which felt cool and refreshing whenever she cast a spell. Scarlett even thought she could feel a trace of Dahlia and the intensity of her magic, which always gave off a faintly smoky scent, especially when fueled by great feeling.

"I call to Justice and Judgment, whose vision is long. Set right to what is wrong," she called again. This time, her voice didn't get lost in the roar of the wind. She was joined by a chorus of other voices that made the words sound deep and rich, the voices of her sisters.

"I call to Justice and Judgment, whose vision is long. Set right to what is wrong."

The storm clouds began to fray; a single bolt of lightning cut through the sky. Tiffany was illuminated by the flash, and Scarlett saw her face twisted in agony and her mouth open in a silent scream.

Tiffany was fumbling for the talisman that, while still around her neck, was floating in front of her, pointing toward Vivi. Then the chain went suddenly slack, sending Tiffany backwards and Vivi tumbling to the ground.

Scarlett directed some of her sisters' magic toward Vivi to stop her fall, but she was already floating a few inches above the ground. The blood seemed to be fading from her shirt, and the gruesome mass receded back into her chest.

Vivi's eyes opened as soon as her feet touched the grass. She bore no signs of having been moments away from death. In fact, she looked more alive than Scarlett had ever seen her. Her skin shone and her dark eyes seemed to glow as she said something Scarlett couldn't hear and raised her arms.

An enormous tree behind Tiffany began to sway as its roots shot up from the ground, reaching toward her like angry snakes. They curled around her ankles and dragged her down. But she barely seemed to notice—she was too busy fumbling for the talisman, which was starting to twitch and writhe. The chain around Tiffany's neck grew white-hot, and with each twist, it left burn marks on her skin.

The talisman began to glow even brighter and then, with a crack, it shattered, glass shards exploding in every direction. Tiffany shrieked, a sound more animal than human, then went limp as the whole clearing fell silent. The wind had stopped, the tornado disappearing into the darkness. The spell the Ravens cast had worked. They'd released the trapped magic from the talisman, setting to right what was wrong. But the force had clearly been too much for Tiffany to withstand.

Hazel fell to her knees, shaking with exhaustion; Jess doubled over and swore loudly while Sonali and Ariana ran to Vivi. Next to Scarlett, Juliet breathed heavily as she examined her outstretched fingertips, which had turned black, scorched by the surge of magic. But Scarlett stood frozen in place, staring at Tiffany, heart pounding as she struggled to catch her breath. Even from a distance, even with her face obscured by the shadow of the tree, Scarlett knew without a shred of doubt that her best friend was dead.

CHAPTER THIRTY-SEVEN

Vivi

Scarlett was the only person in Kappa House who slept much that night. As they staggered out of the woods, sopping wet and covered in dirt, Scarlett had collapsed against Mei, who'd then cast a spell to make her light as a feather so they could carry her back to the house. Vivi managed to walk, supported by a grim-faced Jess and a terrified-looking Ariana. As the sisters picked their way over roots and fallen branches, Reagan explained that the spell they'd cast to summon Tiffany's shadow had suddenly stopped working, and, fearing the worst, they had tracked Scarlett through the woods to the clearing.

The second they made it inside Kappa House, Scarlett immediately curled into a ball on the couch and, after a long pull of Etta's sleeping draft, fell asleep, though from the occasional noises she made and the look of pain on her face, it was clear her sleep wasn't restful. Vivi settled into an armchair and gratefully accepted the steady stream of tea Etta kept bringing. She suspected Etta had added a little something to the tea, because with every sip, Vivi felt her shock lessen, and her breath came just the tiniest bit easier.

As soon as Vivi could speak again, she gave the Ravens the

abbreviated version of events and shared the awful news that couldn't wait—Dahlia was also dead.

The entire sorority was squeezed into the living room, girls sprawling on the floor and perched on every free surface in a spontaneous vigil for the sisters they'd lost. The normally stoic Jess sobbed into Juliet's shoulder as her girlfriend stroked her hair. Hazel stared off into space, a faraway look in her eyes, while Etta and Mei sat on the couch, trembling as they whispered about how to deliver the horrific news to Tiffany's and Dahlia's families. Across from Vivi, Sonali and Ariana sat on the floor watching her anxiously, as if worried she'd get herself kidnapped right from under their noses.

Vivi tried to give them a reassuring smile, but she knew they'd have no trouble seeing through it. Tiffany and the Henosis talisman were gone. The immediate danger was over. But the losses had shaken Kappa to the core. Though it was hard to believe, their beloved, fearless president was gone. And while the pain over Tiffany's death would be far more complicated, it wouldn't lessen their grief over the sister they'd lost in more ways than one.

Marjorie Winter, Scarlett's mother, arrived around three a.m. Vivi wasn't sure if one of the Ravens had called her or if she had a magical means of knowing when her daughter needed her. Perhaps it was the latter, because shortly before dawn, there was another knock on the door, and this time, it was Daphne.

Somehow, Vivi wasn't surprised to see her mother on the front steps. She didn't even bother asking how Daphne knew what had happened. That was just her mother's way. She always knew. And for once, Vivi found that fact supremely comforting.

"You're okay," Daphne said with a sigh after she'd examined Vivi from all angles.

"More or less. Do you want to come in?"

Daphne hesitated a moment, then nodded. "I suppose it makes more sense than standing in the doorway until the sun comes up." She took a few cautious steps into the foyer, as if half expecting to be thwarted by some spell. She followed her daughter into the living room, but before Vivi could make introductions, Marjorie jumped up from the chair where she'd been keeping watch over Scarlett.

"Daphne Devereaux?" Marjorie said, rubbing her eyes.

"Hello, Marjorie," Daphne said. There was just a hint of frostiness in her voice, but when her gaze settled on the sleeping Scarlett, she asked softly, "How's your girl?"

Marjorie reached out and gently stroked Scarlett's hair. "She'll be okay in time."

Scarlett rolled over and slowly opened her eyes. "Mom?" she said groggily. "What are you doing here?"

Mei and Jess exchanged glances, then began to usher the other Ravens out of the living room. Vivi and Scarlett began to tell their moms what had happened, taking turns and filling in the gaps in each other's stories. "I'm so sorry you girls had to go through that," Daphne said, squeezing Vivi's hand. "This is exactly what I was trying to help you avoid, but I don't think I went about it in the smartest way."

"You did your best," Marjorie said crisply in an assured tone even Vivi would have trouble arguing with. "After what happened with Evelyn, what other choice did you have?"

Scarlett looked from Marjorie to Daphne, clearly startled. "Evelyn Waters? What about her?"

"Evelyn was my best friend," Daphne explained. "We'd been attached at the hip since freshman year, when we both joined Kappa. We both came from modest backgrounds, unlike some of the others in our pledge class, witches from old magical families." Daphne gave Scarlett's mother a pointed look.

Marjorie sighed heavily. "After all these years, you're still harping on this? You've *become* an old magical family, Daphne. Look how powerful your daughter is. You should be proud."

"You're right—and I am," Daphne said, coloring slightly. "But at the time, I didn't see how I could compare to witches like you, with your connections, or Evelyn, with all her natural talent. She was named president, a huge accomplishment, but she soon began to act erratically. I think the pressure might've been too much for her; she felt like she had to prove herself, demonstrate that she had what it took to be a real player in the magical world. But her spellwork couldn't quite keep up with her ambition. She was stretching her magic as far as it could go, and she grew frustrated. That's when she became interested in the talisman. Everything came easier to her when she was wearing it, and eventually, she became dependent on it. Almost addicted to its power."

"We didn't know exactly what was going on," Marjorie added, "but it was clear that something was very, very wrong, and whenever one of us tried to talk to Evelyn about it, she'd grow furious."

"When she learned that she was going to be removed as president, she just sort of . . . snapped." Daphne winced at the memory.

"I started to suspect that she was planning something terrible. She'd grown careless about covering her tracks, and I sensed she was planning to hurt the girl who'd been nominated in her place."

"Evelyn asked me to meet her at the beach one night," Marjorie said quietly. "I never should've gone alone, but she insisted, and she was still our president. A powerful one, at that."

"I followed them," Daphne continued. "Thank goodness, I arrived just in time. It took both of us to fight her off."

The older women fell silent.

"So, her disappearance?" Vivi asked after a long moment.

"It was just the story we told," Marjorie said wearily. "Evelyn died trying to kill us. She summoned a tidal wave onto the beach and we barely managed to escape before she was swept away herself. Daphne and I decided it was too dangerous to keep the talisman at Kappa. Someone else might be tempted to do what Evelyn had done."

"So I volunteered to take it, to keep it on the move. Away from anyone evil." Daphne placed her hand on Vivi's shoulder. "I'll admit . . . I was afraid of it. I blamed the talisman for making Evelyn so dangerous. I thought it might do the same to me or to anyone who came into contact with it."

"I'm sorry, Mom," Vivi said, her cheeks beginning to flush with shame and regret. "I shouldn't have taken the talisman. If I hadn't given it to Dahlia—or, well, Tiffany—maybe none of this would have happened."

Daphne shook her head emphatically. "No, it's my fault. I should have told you all this a long time ago. I thought that by keeping you ignorant and far away from Westerly, I was keeping you safe."

"Whereas I wanted to raise you and Eugenie to be stronger and smarter than I was," Marjorie said, facing Scarlett. "I figured if you were the most powerful witches in your years, then you'd never fall into the trap of idolizing the wrong person the way I did."

Scarlett grimaced. "No, I was just the girl who didn't notice her best friend had become a murderer."

"But once you learned who she really was, you did the right thing, didn't you?"

"She did," Vivi answered for her. Scarlett had risked her life to rescue Vivi. Whatever their differences, they were sisters. In some ways, her mother had been right—magic was far more dangerous than Vivi had realized. But even the evilest magic couldn't destroy what Vivi had witnessed in the clearing, a force more powerful than curses and tornadoes, more powerful than fear itself: sisterhood.

CHAPTER THIRTY-EIGHT

Scarlett

Two days—two long days—after her entire world had changed, Scarlett sat staring out her bedroom window, thinking the same thoughts that had been spiraling through her mind on repeat for the past forty-eight hours. How had she missed what Tiffany had become? How could the girl she'd danced on tables with, the girl who'd held her hand whenever Eugenie made her cry, be capable of murder?

And how, after everything Tiffany had done, could Scarlett still miss her? Still love her?

"Knock-knock." Vivi stood at the door, looking hesitant. "Just checking to see how you're doing."

Scarlett waved her in. "Is everyone circling? I can't seem to get out of this bed. Out of this room."

"Scarlett, I can't even imagine . . ." Vivi nodded. "Is that hers?"

Scarlett looked down. She was holding the elephant she and Tiffany had gotten from the antiques store the day after they'd met. "Yeah, I don't know why I'm holding on to this thing."

She threw the elephant in the trash, then turned her attention to Vivi, who looked at the trash for a long beat, as if she was considering rescuing the elephant. As if she could salvage some of the wreckage.

"I wanted to talk to you," Scarlett said. Even though she'd been consumed by thoughts of Tiffany, something else had been weighing on her too. She couldn't let things with Vivi stand the way they were before Tiffany had taken her.

Vivi braced herself, as if she knew what this would be about. Scarlett appreciated that she didn't protest or get defensive. She just nodded and drew up a chair beside Scarlett. Together they watched the morning sun slowly paint Westerly's campus yellow.

"It's about Mason," Scarlett started.

Vivi leaped right in. "Scarlett, I didn't get the chance to tell you, but I'm sorry. I should never have allowed anything to happen with him. It will never happen again. I know he's your ex, and I would never do that to a sister. There's no excuse."

"No, there isn't," Scarlett agreed. Then she sighed. "But I can't exactly blame you for screwing up when my screwup was so much worse." Her mind flashed to Tiffany. To the terrible, callous way she'd admitted to Dahlia's murder. *I needed her power.* As if it were that simple; as if it were just a matter of taking what belonged to her. Scarlett's eyes stung, and she blinked back tears.

"Your mom is right, Scarlett. You're not responsible for Tiffany."

"Maybe not, but I *loved* her. How could I not have realized how lost she was?"

"People aren't just one thing or the other." Vivi shrugged. "We're not just evil or angelic. She did terrible things, yes, but she did them out of love. That doesn't make them any better; we should still blame her. But just because we blame her doesn't mean we don't understand her. Finding out about what she did doesn't mean your love for her just vanishes. Love is more complicated than that."

Scarlett laughed. "Preach." She picked at her nails, now that her mother wasn't here to swat her hands anymore. "Feelings never really follow rule books, do they?"

"Hell no." Vivi managed a small smile.

Scarlett couldn't help thinking of Jackson, of the way he'd taken her hand right before they broke through Gwen's front door. Before everything spiraled out of control, there had been a split second when she'd thought *maybe* . . .

But her head was a mess. Whatever she felt for him was tangled up in adrenaline, fear, heartbreak. She'd need time to sort through it. For now, though, she could make sure others didn't have to suffer the same confusion.

"Look, Vivi, what I'm trying to say is . . . if I am honest with myself, Mason and I were over the second Harper died and I couldn't tell him the truth about it. That secret drove a wedge between us. And while we were apart last summer, he changed. It just took me this long to realize that I changed too. We want different things." Scarlett was a little surprised by her own honesty—and by the fact that it didn't hurt as much as she thought it would to admit it.

A sweet look of relief washed over Vivi's face. "And what is it that you want?"

"I want to be happy. I just have to figure out what that means for me. I spent my whole life trying to follow the rules. To be who my mother wanted me to be, who Dahlia wanted me to be, who I thought I wanted to be. But I have no right to force my rules on anybody else. Not you, and especially not Mason. So if you two have feelings for each other, then, well . . . you have my blessing to give it a shot. If you still want to, that is."

"You don't have to say that," Vivi said, looking uneasy.

"I know." Scarlett winked. "I'm just that big of a person."

As Vivi smiled with relief, Scarlett thought of how much she'd disliked Vivi at first. It was because she was a wildcard. Now she felt like she knew the girl before her almost better than she knew her other sisters. Even more surprising, she was starting to like her. She could see what Mason and the other sisters saw in her. The intelligence, the humor, the heart. Her remarkable effervescence despite being kept in the dark about her heritage for so long and despite everything that had happened to her the last few days. There was a freedom about Vivi, a lack of carefulness that she knew would appeal to Mason, who so desperately wanted to break free of everything that he was raised to be.

Even now, even after all that had happened, Kappa was where Scarlett wanted to be. Kappa was what she wanted to fight for. Kappa was what she wanted to fix. Still, she felt raw around the edges just thinking about Mason being with someone else. But looking at Vivi, she could at least understand it. She could see it. And she could let the poor girl off the hook.

Scarlett reached over and nudged her arm. "Don't think I'm

going soft, though. You might've survived Hell Week, but you're still my Little."

Vivi lifted her chin. "No one will ever think of you as soft. And I won't let you down. Trust me."

Scarlett's smile widened. "I do," she said. And she meant it.

When Vivi left, Scarlett pulled the elephant out of the trash and put it back on her dresser. Tiffany was gone. But Vivi was right. She didn't have to let go of what was good in her.

Campus life resumed a shockingly normal rhythm. But while Scarlett had sorted things out with her family and her sisters, she knew she still had something else to do. Something hard.

Scarlett had Jackson meet her at her favorite place off campus, a little bench overlooking the Savannah River.

"Hey, stranger," she said as she handed him a cup of tea she'd brought as a peace offering.

"She lives," he said as he sat beside her on the bench and took the cup.

"I texted you," she protested.

"I think I deserved more than a text message, Scar." He pulled out his phone. "'Guess you were right, I am the Final Girl after all. Will call you when I come up for air.'" He stared pointedly over the top of the screen. "That's hardly an adequate explanation, Ms. Winter."

Guilt pooled in her stomach. "I heard you came by the house. I'm sorry . . . I . . . It was just too much."

"I was so worried that something had happened to you." He scooted a little closer. "I'm sorry about Tiffany." The public story they'd put out had been that Tiffany died in the freak tornado that touched down just off campus. As for Dahlia, she'd been reported missing and was presumed also killed in the same storm. After all, the Ravens couldn't exactly explain that Dahlia had actually gone missing days before but had appeared to be wandering around campus looking perfectly fine.

"When the first report came in about the victim of the freak tornado, I thought it was you. I thought something awful had happened to you," he admitted, his voice gruff.

"The only thing that happened to me was a trip to the police station." She avoided his eyes. "As you can probably imagine, the cops wanted to talk to me. About a lot of things."

Jackson looked around to be sure that no one else was listening. "So what really happened? We found Gwen two days ago, and now . . ." He frowned, confused. "The police are saying she died from a gas leak."

"That's thanks to me." Scarlett caught herself picking a nail and flattened her palms against her thighs. Well. Thanks to her and Jess, the best Swords witch in Kappa now that Tiffany was gone. It had been easy enough for her to plant a few suggestions in the cops' minds to help them close the case. It didn't sit well with her, covering for what Tiffany did, but it had to be done. The Ravens' secret had to be protected. "I might've helped them come to some conclusions about things."

"And?" Jackson tilted forward, elbows propped on his knees.

"Scarlett, do you have any idea how crazy this has all been driving me? And then to hear the news about the tornado, I mean . . . that kind of coincidence doesn't just *happen*."

"No," she admitted. "It doesn't."

"Was it . . . you know, *witchcraft?*" he whispered.

When she nodded, Jackson looked at her intently. "Will you tell me what happened?" he asked. "What *really* happened?"

Scarlett had known he'd ask and she knew she owed him the truth. He listened and reacted to every detail with eerie calm: How Tiffany glamoured herself and killed Dahlia and Gwen and kidnapped Vivi too. How the Ravens had fought her off with their magic. How Tiffany had fallen. How they'd covered their tracks.

When she finished, Jackson took her hand and threaded his fingers through hers. "Scar, I'm so sorry. And I understand why you needed to cover it all up, but I have to ask: Where does Kappa go from here? I mean, the call came from inside the house. What if another one of your sisters decides a different talisman is worth killing for? Or just loses it on her roommate one day? What if—"

"There will be no more what-ifs. I can handle my sisters. This will never happen again," she said firmly.

"How can you be so sure?" he asked.

"I'm a witch," she said with a smile. "We know stuff."

He laughed. He didn't look entirely convinced, but he didn't press her. "Well, I'm just glad you're okay. I was so worried. I haven't been able to stop thinking about you."

His warm brown eyes caught hers and held them. And then he leaned forward. He brushed his lips against hers just once, lightly.

"I forgot to ask: Are witches allowed to kiss mere mortals?" he asked. "Or is one of us about to melt?"

In response, Scarlett cupped the back of his neck with her other hand and drew him against her. "If we're going to find out, we'd better do it right," she whispered. Then he kissed her for real. Soft and slow, the kind of kiss you could drown in if you let yourself.

But she couldn't. Not right now. Maybe not ever.

She'd broken the first rule of being a Raven. Of being a witch. *Don't ever tell.* Telling Jackson about witchcraft was a cardinal sin. She'd done it because he deserved to know about Harper. And because, somewhere, in the mess of all this, she'd developed feelings for him. Because he'd helped her when nobody else would've. But she couldn't risk making things worse.

The crisis was supposed to be over. They were supposed to be safe. But to use Jackson's analogy, the call *had* come from inside the house. Gwen. Tiffany. Even Evelyn, all those years ago. They had all been Ravens. Who knew how he'd react if he found out how powerful witches really were? Or that Kappa had trained murderers among its ranks? Jackson was already asking questions, and when he inevitably learned the entire truth of their history, who was to say that he wouldn't want to bring the whole house down? He cared about her; she could feel it. But his moral compass pointed more north than hers did. And why would he want to save the house that killed his stepsister?

She couldn't put her sisters at risk again, not like that. Her sisters were what mattered most in the world. At least, that was what she'd always believed—and she couldn't stop now.

With a heavy sigh, Scarlett pulled away. She scooped her tea off the bench and lifted it to Jackson in a *cheers* gesture. "Drink up," she said. "We have a lot to talk about."

He flashed her a smile over the rim of the paper cup. It was the most open smile he'd ever given her. Easy. Trusting. He swallowed a large gulp of the tea, then another.

She forced a smile and sipped hers more slowly. Hers was just herbal tea, after all. Chamomile to calm her nerves.

His, however, was a concoction Etta had spent years perfecting. One more sip, and Scarlett could tell she had him by the way his eyelids drooped and his breathing slowed. He wasn't asleep, not exactly. More just so relaxed, his mind so wide open, that anybody could easily influence him now.

Even a not-too-talented-at-Swords witch like Scarlett. She focused, drawing on the well of power her sisters shared with her. She reached into his mind with a whisper, a nudge.

In the end, it was even easier than it had been with the police. A few smoothed edges, and she made him forget it all. Gwen's wicked-magic spell, finding her body, the existence of witches . . .

Even their kiss. It would've felt wrong, somehow, to let him remember the kiss without any of the context that surrounded it. Whatever they were was based on him knowing the *real* her. Giving him any memory of their connection without magic would be a lie. She'd lost Mason because she'd never been honest with him. She couldn't go through that again with Jackson.

Her chest throbbed. Somehow, this felt harder than any of the other duties that had come before. Scarlett knew she was making the right decision. This wasn't Jackson's world. To protect him, he needed to remain oblivious.

Still, looking into his eyes, she couldn't help but wish for a few more minutes of this. The banter between them. The trust that they'd built up by running full tilt into danger together. She even wanted him to keep calling her the Final Girl, even though it brought to mind all the real-life horror that they had been through.

When Scarlett was growing up, Minnie had often explained the history of witches and the special power the Ravens had to share their magic with others. "It's a sacrifice to be a witch, to give yourself wholly to your coven." Scarlett had always taken that to mean that witches gave up a little of their autonomy to be protected and to be stronger, to do greater things as a whole. That was what it meant to be a part of a coven, to be a Raven. And it had never truly felt like a sacrifice; being a witch was the greatest gift she'd ever received.

But Scarlett realized she hadn't understood what Minnie meant. She'd never known what it felt like to sacrifice something she might really want to remain true to her coven. Until now. *Magic doesn't just give, it takes,* Minnie had said. It was her turn to pay.

She looked up as the rain began to fall. It wasn't just any rain; it was her rain, and every drop that touched Jackson was imbued with her magic.

Her heart thudded painfully against her ribs as she picked up his now-empty cup. All Jackson would know when he woke from this half trance was that he'd had a long conversation with Scarlett during which he'd learned the truth about his stepsister: her death really had been an accident. As for Gwen, she'd died from a gas leak in her apartment, just like the news reports all said.

It wasn't justice. He had spent the past two years of his life searching for answers, answers Scarlett had provided, only to wipe them all away. But it was the nearest thing to closure Scarlett could give Jackson, in the end. She hoped that even though the memory was gone, the peace would remain.

She reached down to rest a hand on Jackson's shoulder. "Don't worry, it'll be like it never happened," she whispered.

In another hour, he'd be just fine, if a little groggy. Until then, he'd remain dazed, staring out at the water, daydreaming. Yet when her hand touched him, he reached up, only semiconscious, and twined his fingers through hers.

Jackson looked at her with a quizzical expression. "Hey—Winter, right? Sorority girl?"

"That's me," she said with a smile that hurt her all the way to her heart.

Her throat stung with unshed tears. She squeezed his fingers gently. It took every ounce of her willpower to pry her hand from his and walk away.

CHAPTER THIRTY-NINE

Vivi

"You ready for this?" Ariana asked, squeezing Vivi's arm as they walked through the iron gates and onto the tree-lined brick path that led to the main quad. Westerly had generously offered the Kappas a weeklong break from their coursework to grieve their fellow students, and it was Vivi's first time back on campus.

"I think so. I think it'll be nice to have something else to focus on, honestly," Vivi said as she hoisted her heavy Kappa tote bag higher on her shoulder.

Ariana didn't have any classes today but she'd offered to walk Vivi to campus for moral support. "If you change your mind, Mei's organizing a group cleansing session in the greenhouse. Nobody would blame you if you decide to cut out of class early." They stepped onto the quad, which was bustling with busy, cheerful students, most of whom had never experienced anything more traumatic than receiving a B on an exam. "Seems a little unfair, doesn't it?" Ariana said, apparently thinking the same thing as Vivi. "While we were burying our friend, they were all getting drunk, ordering pizzas at two a.m., and contracting the occasional STD."

"Living the good life, you mean," Vivi said with a small smile.

"I'd get chlamydia a million times over if it meant bringing Dahlia back."

Vivi reached out and squeezed her friend's hand. "Now, *that* is the true meaning of sisterhood."

Ariana laughed and they continued on in silence for a few minutes. The energy of the crowds was both disorienting and a welcome change from the hushed silence that'd blanketed Kappa House the past week. Dahlia's death had hit everyone hard, especially the upperclassmen who'd known her best.

Vivi still didn't know how she felt about what they'd decided to do. Lying to the police felt wrong but the Ravens couldn't risk exposure by telling the truth—not that many people would have believed them. Maybe Vivi just needed to get used to all this. To having a whole part of her life she hid from most of the world.

Ariana walked Vivi to the front of the science building, gave her a hug, and then left to grab pastries and coffee to take back to the house. Her class didn't start for another fifteen minutes, so Vivi decided to wait on the bench outside rather than in the lecture hall, where she wouldn't be able to avoid the stares and whispers of her mostly kindhearted but still nosy classmates. By this point, everyone at Westerly knew that the Kappa president and another sister had died suddenly, and rumors were flying.

She was about to sit when a figure striding down the leaf-covered walkway caught her eye. It was a tall, brown-haired boy in a tan trench coat, the plaid-lined collar popped up against the autumn chill that had finally descended on Savannah. Vivi's heart fluttered as she took a few steps forward, trying to get close enough to call his name without shouting too loudly. "Mason," she said. He didn't turn around, so she broke into an awkward jog. "Hey, Mason!"

He spun around, startled, but when his eyes landed on her, his face broke into a grin. "Vivi." His familiar voice was as warm and rich as the hickory coffee she'd developed a taste for since moving to Savannah, but there were new bags under his eyes. Apparently, he'd had a rough week too. "How are you?"

"Hanging in there. Thanks for your message the other day." Mason had sent a short, thoughtful text telling her how sorry he was for her loss and letting her know he was there if she needed anything. It was a lovely, classy message, especially considering that the last time he'd seen her, she'd freaked out over their kiss and then sprinted out of the building.

"Of course. I'm glad to see you. Where are you going? Can I walk you somewhere?" Mason said.

"I have a class at ten in the science center, but you're welcome to walk me the—oh, what do you think?—ten yards if you want."

"How about we live on the edge and walk around the quad instead?"

"And risk being only five minutes early to class instead of ten? I don't know . . ." She trailed off with a smile and fell into step next to him.

"How have you been holding up? I still can't believe all the news. Dahlia and Tiffany . . ."

"It's pretty shitty, but I'm managing."

"I've been thinking about you a lot." He paused for a moment, then said, "I also texted Scarlett. We have such a long history, and I know how much she loved Tiffany."

"It was the right thing to do," Vivi said earnestly.

"Okay, good. I'm glad you girls all have each other right now. I'm sure it makes it easier, in a way."

"Yeah, in some ways. But it also makes their absence so much clearer, you know?" It was strange to gather in the living room without Dahlia's benevolent, commanding presence. No one seemed to know who was supposed to speak first or what to say. The sorority felt rudderless without its leader. "But at the same time, it has kind of brought the rest of us closer. It put a lot of things into perspective. For me, and for Scarlett too."

"That's good . . . right?"

"Really good."

They stepped in a pile of wet red and gold leaves, and Vivi went momentarily rigid as she remembered the dry leaves blanketing the clearing in the woods. And the candles, and the bones, and the blood. "Are you cold?" Mason asked, then, without waiting for her to answer, he shrugged out of his coat and draped it over her shoulders. "Is this okay?"

"More than okay," Vivi said, feeling safer and warmer than she had in a very long time.

"Good. I just . . . I don't want to . . ." He grinned and shook his head. "I'm not normally like this, you know."

"Like what? Unable to speak English?"

"Not normally, no."

"Well, if it makes you feel better, you should know that Scarlett and I talked and she gave me her blessing. She gave *us* her blessing."

Mason stopped in the middle of the path and searched her face. "So . . . you're saying she's okay if we . . ."

Vivi nodded and his smile stretched wide enough to show off the dimple that always undid her. But then he caught himself and his expression grew serious. "What about you, Vivi? What do *you* want?"

She considered this. She wanted a lot of things. She wanted to learn everything she could about magic. She wanted to find her academic passion and settle into life at Westerly. She wanted the type of romance she'd always fantasized about—dates in cozy cafés, browsing through bookstores, walking hand in hand across the quad at twilight when the gas lamps in front of the brick buildings glowed yellow as the moon. But she didn't want it with just anyone; she wanted it with *Mason*. She wanted to joke over his badly prepared waffles, and learn about the history classes he was taking, and hear about all the wild European adventures he'd gone on last summer. She wanted to be with him.

But she wanted her sisters, too. She wanted them happy, healthy, safe. She wanted them united, no matter what.

So she placed a hand on his arm and said, "One rule: my sisters come first. If Scarlett changes her mind and decides she's not okay with this after all, then it's over. Agreed?"

Mason nodded quickly. "Of course."

She smiled, unable to hold it back any longer. "In that case, you ask me what I want, Mason Gregory?" She reached up, slid one hand around the back of his neck, and drew his face down toward her own. "I want you."

This time when his lips touched hers, nothing held them back. His hands slid around her waist, pulled her up and against him so tightly, her feet lifted off the ground. Vivi knew a spell that would allow her to levitate, but at the moment, this felt like the best magic of all.

CHAPTER FORTY

Scarlett

Scarlett stood on the roof of Kappa House, stars like pinpricks scattered above her. The night air was cool and quiet. The moon shone brightly, the buttery orange of the harvest. And beside her stood Tiffany, wearing a loose white dress Scarlett had never seen before. Scarlett knew it was a dream, but it felt good to see Tiffany all the same. Tiffany turned and looked at the aviary, where the birds cooed and rustled softly.

"I think I was always like the ravens in the keep. Tied down," she said softly.

"I wish you had come to me," Scarlett said. "I wish you had talked to me. Maybe it would have all been different."

Tiffany shook her head. "I would always have chosen her. Be honest with yourself—wouldn't you have done the same for your mom? For Minnie?"

Scarlett went still, thinking. "Maybe part of me would have wanted to, but Minnie would have killed me before she let me kill another witch for her. So would my mom." A flicker of anger entered her words as the memory of Tiffany's actions washed over her once more. "You betrayed the fabric of what we are. Your mother wouldn't have wanted this; the cost was too high. It wasn't worth those other witches' lives. It wasn't worth *yours*."

Tiffany gazed at her as if carefully considering her next words. For a moment she looked unbearably sad and then she smiled.

"You were my best friend, Scar. But we never were the same witch." Tiffany walked over to the keep and tapped it. The ravens flew out, scattering across the night.

"Promise me something." Tiffany looked back at her suddenly.

"Anything," Scarlett said, but a part of her hesitated, hoping it wasn't something she couldn't do.

"Promise me you'll check in on her."

Scarlett's heart squeezed painfully. "You didn't have to ask. I will make sure we take care of your mom," she vowed.

Tiffany's eyes shone. "And something else."

"What?"

"Promise me that you won't let what I did stop you from being who you're supposed to be."

Before Scarlett could respond, a caw sounded overhead. Scarlett looked up to see a raven with yellow eyes circling. Her favorite one, Harlow. When she looked back to answer Tiffany, her friend was gone. Instead, a jet-black raven with blue eyes sat on the ledge. It blinked once at Scarlett and then, with a great flap of its wings, took off into the night sky, following Harlow into the darkness.

Scarlett awoke with Tiffany's name on her lips, the sun streaming through her windows. She was in her bed at Kappa House, and although she knew she'd been sleeping, she wasn't entirely certain that her conversation with Tiffany had been purely a dream. Scarlett hoped that her friend had found peace. That she was somehow soaring through the night like the ravens.

"Goodbye, friend," she whispered, hoping somewhere Tiffany's spirit could still hear her. And through her open window, she could have sworn she heard a single plaintive caw.

After dinner that night, there was a knock on Scarlett's door.

Vivi poked her head in. "It's almost time. I thought it might be fun if *I* helped *you* get ready for a change."

"I'd love that," Scarlett said. The younger girl approached and laid her tarot cards down on the table in front of them.

"I think you've proven you don't need those for every spell anymore," Scarlett said. Vivi smiled. Despite herself, and despite all they had been through, Scarlett could see that Vivi looked lighter. Happier than she had looked in the days before. She wondered if she had seen Mason. She wondered if they'd kissed already. If they were officially together . . . and then she pushed that train of thought aside. She'd begun to put Mason behind her, but moving on was never a linear process, and it didn't help anyone to dwell on the details.

"Close your eyes," Vivi commanded, and Scarlett could feel the tingle of magic as Vivi decorated her eyelids.

Scarlett cracked an eye open to peer out the windows. The full moon had just crested the trees in the distance, shedding a warm, yellowish light across Westerly's campus.

"Stop blinking so much," Vivi ordered.

She closed her eyes again, suppressing a smile. "My apologies."

"How am I supposed to glamour you properly for your first night as president if you keep moving around?" Scarlett could hear the teasing in Vivi's tone.

She grimaced. "Doubtful."

Her Little scoffed. They'd had this discussion about a dozen times already. "Please. Like there's anyone else we'd vote in after all of this."

With Dahlia gone, Kappa couldn't wait until next year to choose her successor. They needed someone to step up and fill her shoes now. Preferably before the full-moon ritual tonight, where they'd need an experienced witch to guide them, to lead the rite and channel the sisters' magic properly.

Once, Scarlett would've leaped at the chance. Now . . .

"I wasn't even president and I already messed things up horribly. I failed to notice my best friend going bad; I ignored you over petty crap with my ex when I should've been focused on Kappa problems." Scarlett had already gone down the "What if I'd picked up the phone when Vivi called me that night" path about a hundred times. "Not to mention I told an outsider about us," she added.

"You said you fixed that."

Scarlett hadn't admitted it to anyone else, not even Mei. But a few nights after she altered Jackson's memory (and after several mugs of Etta's infamous mulled wine), she'd admitted it to Vivi. In fact, she'd admitted a lot of things to Vivi. More than she ever would've pictured herself doing in the past.

"Yes, but it never should have happened in the first place," Scarlett replied, her stomach doing an unpleasant lurch when she thought about the moment she'd seen Jackson in the philosophy class they were both in this year. His eyes had stayed on hers for a second too long, and she wondered if somehow the spell had been broken. But then his gaze moved on and he'd said something snarky about social contract theory. As relieved as Scarlett was that the spell had held, the moment had been bittersweet. In spite of everything, she'd wanted him to remember their connection on some primordial level beyond memory. But that was silly and ran counter to her very actions. *You did the right thing,* she reminded herself. There was no other way.

"But you did the right thing in the end," Vivi said now, making Scarlett wonder if her Little might have a touch of affinity for Swords mind-reading magic after all. "That's what matters. But doing the right thing doesn't mean being a nun, Scarlett. Why can't you start again with Jackson? He doesn't ever have to know about before."

As Scarlett considered Vivi's words, she realized something. Even though it was Mason who had broken her heart, it was Jackson's kiss she couldn't forget, not Mason's. It was Jackson's lips that she could still feel on hers, not Mason's. But she'd had to give Jackson up, and unlike his, her memory was very much intact. She couldn't forget how he'd made her feel. But she was still a witch. And he was still a human. And she couldn't imagine being with him without telling him the truth all over again.

Scarlett shook her head. "It wouldn't be the same," she said firmly.

Vivi smiled sadly but nodded as if she understood. The two girls fell silent again as Vivi went back to work. Finally, Vivi tapped her shoulder. "Okay, take a look."

Scarlett cracked an eye open. Then both her eyes widened. The girl in the mirror looked both familiar and not. She had Scarlett's same brown eyes and deep brown skin. But her cheekbones seemed just a touch higher and sharper, her eyelashes longer, her lips a shade fuller—or maybe that was just an illusion thanks to the bright red color Vivi had given them.

Her curls were held up with dozens of glittering pins shaped like little fall leaves, burnt orange and garnet and peridot. Her hair fell in a cascade of perfect ringlets down her back to her black cocktail dress.

Normally the harvest-moon ritual was a time to celebrate the fruits of their labor before they buckled down for the winter. But tonight it'd be a more somber affair, honoring the cycle of life, death, and rebirth.

It seemed fitting, since Tiffany's and Dahlia's funerals had been held earlier in the week.

It also reminded Scarlett exactly how unfit she was to lead anybody, let alone Kappa House. Even if she looked the part, she didn't feel it, not inside.

"You don't like it?" Over her shoulder, Vivi bit her lip.

Scarlett shook her head. "No, the glamour is perfect, Vivi, thank you."

She rose and crossed her room to the balcony doors. Outside, she could already see their sisters in the backyard. Juliet stoked the bonfire, Jess at her side adding bundles of herbs to the wood at intervals. Those two hadn't spent more than a minute apart since everything went down.

Scarlett was glad they had each other. After these past few weeks, she wanted to hold tight to those she loved too.

Especially her sisters. Sisters who she couldn't bear the thought of letting down again. "What if you all vote me in and I just . . . what if I screw it up?" Scarlett's breath fogged the glass. She spoke so softly, she wasn't sure Vivi would hear.

But a heartbeat later, her Little materialized at her side. "I think the fact that you're so concerned means you're more ready than ever to lead."

Scarlett laughed.

"I mean it." Vivi caught her eye. "Great leaders are born of necessity, not certainty. We need you, Scarlett. More than ever. But if you stood here and told me you had no fears, that you were completely certain you'd be the best president the Ravens ever had, *then* I'd be worried. After all, we know what wanting power for power's sake looks like."

Tiffany.

Scarlett had spent so much time these past couple of weeks sorting through her feelings about her best friend. She'd probably always wrestle with them, because deep down, a big part of her still loved Tiffany. And seeing the way Tiffany's mother had crumpled at her funeral, weeping, had broken Scarlett's heart. She knew why Tiffany did what she did.

And that realization scared her. What if love led her down the wrong path one day too?

But no. If nothing else, witnessing what Tiffany had become—seeing her horrible end—had shown her what waited on the other side of wickedness, had shown her the consequences of the lure of untold power. Tiffany had taught her that much. Scarlett just had to believe she'd never forget the lesson, never repeat her friend's mistakes.

And in the meantime . . . Vivi was right. Her sisters needed her. Scarlett still wasn't sure she deserved to lead them, but if they asked her to, for their sakes, she would.

Kappa first, last, and always.

"I'm ready," she told Vivi's reflection.

Her sister smiled and reached for the door. "Good. Then go lead these witches."

Mei and Etta did most of the ritual setup, with Juliet's and Jess's help. The freshmen had pitched in too, baking the buttermilk loaves and mulling hot apple cider. Mei and Etta had prepared the altar, overflowing with apples and pears, rose hips and blackberries, winter melon and persimmons. It was a time for feasting, for celebration.

But they'd also brought over a chair and a small wrought-iron table from the greenhouse, and on the table they'd set a full plate of food and an overflowing cup of wine. They'd draped the chair with Dahlia's red ceremonial robes and adorned the table with red candles and some deep purple orchids Etta must have picked from the greenhouse. It was a symbolic place for Dahlia in their midst.

It made Scarlett's heart ache to see it. But she knew Dahlia would appreciate it. She'd loved Kappa with all her entire being. In the end, she'd given everything for them.

Scarlett wouldn't let her down.

Scarlett pulled out Minnie's tarot cards and laid them on the table alongside all the other witches' decks and began to speak.

"Sisters, thank you for gathering tonight." Scarlett eyed them one by one. Everyone had dressed for the occasion—they all wore black cocktail dresses, except Juliet, who wore an elegant black three-piece suit. The black served a dual purpose: Black for ravens. Black for mourning. And each woman wore her sorority charm on a simple chain around her neck. "The past few weeks have been a trying time for us all. We've suffered loss and betrayal. We've had one of our own taken from us well before her time." All the sisters looked to Dahlia's seat. "And we watched another break our deepest, most sacred vows."

For a moment, a heavy silence fell. Ariana broke it, sniffling softly; Vivi reached over and put an arm around her.

"We will not forget our sisters. Either their sacrifice or their mistakes." Scarlett drew a deep breath. "But the harvest is also a time of plenty. A time to celebrate what we still have as we prepare for the long, dark winter ahead." She stretched out her hands. Mei stood on her right, and she clasped that hand. Vivi took her left, her other arm still wrapped around Ariana.

One by one, the Ravens linked hands.

"Tonight, our ritual will renew the bond of our sisterhood. We will pledge ourselves to one another, share our magic and our loyalty both. But first . . ." Scarlett squared her shoulders. "We must decide on a new leader."

Traditionally, the exiting president nominated their first pick, and almost always, Kappa voted that person in. This time, however . . . "Mei?"

With a reassuring squeeze, Mei dropped her hand and knelt to pick up a bundle at her feet. Feathers. But not the pure white feathers they used to vote girls into the sorority. These were already a lush black, tinged with metallic green and purple.

Mei passed them around the circle to every Raven. While she did that, Scarlett explained.

"Any Raven may nominate a presidential candidate. Once we have all the nominations in, we will vote on our chosen sister."

When Mei reached Scarlett, she winked as she passed Scarlett her feather. "I nominate Scarlett Winter," Mei said before anyone else could speak.

"Seconded," Vivi spoke up from her left.

Scarlett bowed her head. She'd known that was coming, at least. "All right. And the other nominations?" The patio fell silent. She stared around the circle at each girl, expecting at least one other option. Maybe Jess would speak up for Juliet, or Etta for Mei?

But the only sound was the wind gently rustling the trees in the distance, tugging at the girls' skirts and toying with their hair.

Scarlett's throat tightened. Every Raven simply stared at her, waiting. As if she'd already been chosen. "But—" Scarlett started.

Mei interrupted. "Cast your votes in favor," she said. As she spoke, the feather in her fist tilted upright. It took on a brighter shine, ruffling lightly as, fiber by fiber, barb by barb, it transmuted into a gleaming metallic gold.

Slowly, around the circle, every other feather began to do the same. Vivi's transformed last, and her Little smiled, a proud glint in her eye, as she lifted her golden feather to Scarlett in salute. Everyone else mirrored her, until only Scarlett's feather remained.

The other girls watched her, clearly confused about the break in the ritual.

Scarlett took in her sisters, thinking about just how complicated it was being a witch and a Raven. She was getting exactly what she wanted, but in a very different way from what she'd always pictured. It wasn't a triumphant rise but an appointment born of heartbreak and necessity. But looking around the circle, with its gap where two sisters used to be, she realized that she was stronger than she'd ever imagined, and so were her sisters.

When Scarlett was preparing for rush, Minnie had told her, *You can be the most powerful witch in the world if you believe in yourself and you believe in your sisters. But being the best witch and being the best Raven aren't one in the same.*

At the time, she'd thought it was Minnie being Minnie. Minnie was so very good. But now, Scarlett saw the truth of Minnie's sentiment. Being a Raven had always meant being the best. But being the most powerful witch and being the best sister were not the same thing. The Ravens pushed one another forward constantly. The pressure of competition was what made them all their best, or so she thought. But what if she had stopped striving and taken time to notice what was happening with Tiffany? What if she had seen her friend hurting and then had stopped her from hurting anyone else?

There was a part of their history, a part of themselves, that they had failed to deal with all over again. How many witches had to die before they learned from their mistakes?

Scarlett looked around at each of her sisters. "I know how deeply I screwed up. How I put us all at risk. But if you trust me, I want us to become a different kind of sorority. One that values sisterhood just as much as it values power. I think we can do better. I think we can be better. I think we can make sure that what happened to Gwen and Dahlia and Tiffany and Evelyn all those years ago will never happen again. But only if we keep our eyes open. Only if we admit that there is a capacity for evil in each of us. I will accept this position if and only if you all want a new Kappa. One that doesn't ignore the evil but faces it. One that we can all be proud of. Now, I'll give you a minute, in case any of you want to change your feathers back."

There was a long pause. Jess tightened her grip on Juliet's hand. Bailey exchanged a glance with Ariana. Mei just stared at Scarlett, her expression unreadable. Finally, Vivi broke the silence.

"The only feather we're waiting to change is yours, Big," she said with a smile. The other girls nodded and grinned.

Surprised by the rush of emotion, Scarlett had to blink back tears. She cast one last glance into the center of the circle, where Dahlia's table sat.

I won't let you down, she silently promised her Big Sister. Then Scarlett lifted her own feather and let the golden barbs glitter beneath the night sky.

She looked from one sister to another. They had faced the evil and won. And there was nothing to say that they would ever have to do it again. Except history.

"I accept," she said, and she watched as the feathers lifted into the air, soared toward the center of the circle, and knit together to form a crown. Scarlett bowed her head; Vivi plucked the wreath from the air and carefully placed it upon her new president's head. When Scarlett lifted her chin, her eyes met Vivi's for a second before alighting on each of her sisters.

She felt their magic flowing through her. And she felt their magic around her. For the first time she felt like she truly understood what it meant to be a witch. The power. The sacrifice. The privilege. Vivi was right. She could do this.

She was a witch. She was a Raven. And together she and her sisters could do anything.

ACKNOWLEDGMENTS

Thank you to my friends, collaborators, and cheerleaders at Alloy who've made my writerly dreams come true: Les Morgenstein, Josh Bank, Sara Shandler, Joelle Hobeika, Viana Siniscalchi, and Romy Golan. And extra-special thanks to our editor Lanie Davis, whose wisdom, creativity, kindness, and immense storytelling prowess make her the most valuable witch in any coven.

I feel very lucky to be working with the fabulous team at HMH, especially Emilia Rhodes, whose keen editorial mind is one of the sharpest in the business. You believed in this project from the very beginning and your enthusiasm and clear vision inspired us to tell the best story possible. And thank you to Jessica Handelman for creating the witchy cover of our dreams.

A huge thank-you to the Rights People and all the foreign publishers who've produced such gorgeous editions of my books and allowed me to meet amazing people all around the world. Special thanks to Blossom Books, 20/20 Editora, and Éditions

Robert Laffont for their support, and especially to Fabien Le Roy for his help with my French spellwork.

I'm so grateful, as ever, to my staggeringly talented and endlessly encouraging writing group: Laura Bisberg, Michael Bisberg, Laura Jean Ridge, Matt Gline, Nick Eliopulos, Grace Kendall, and Gavin Brown.

And a second shout-out to Grace, along with Emily Clement, for accompanying me on a last-minute, whirlwind research trip to Savannah. There's no one in the world I'd rather drink cocktails and explore cemeteries with than you ladies.

Thank you to my Scholastic family, especially Olivia Valcarce for reigniting my love of tarot; Maya Marlette, for keeping me productive, sane, and making me laugh all day; and Shelly Romero, for bringing glam-goth vibes to the office and for her helpful, astute sensitivity read. Ellen Goodlett, thank you so incredibly much for your spells, witchy brain, and being part of our sisterhood. You are magic. And to my real family, especially my father, Sam Henry Kass, for making me a writer.

Benjamin Hart, thank you for your unwavering support and for bringing so much real magic into my life.

And the biggest shout-out of all to Danielle Paige. Thank you for this incredible opportunity and for helping me grow as a storyteller. I still can't believe I got to write a book with one of my favorite authors and one of my favorite people.

Kass Morgan

To my love, Chris Albers: You are magic. I love you.

To my family, Andrea, Daddy, Sienna, and Josh: I love you all so much; you are my heart. Sienna, I love you and all your magic!

To my goddaughter Fi: I love you to infinity. I can't wait to see what spells you cast.

To Annie, Chris, Fiona, and Jackson Rolland, my second family.

To Lauren Dell, my forever friend.

To Bonnie Datt: Thanking you and Nanette Lepore forever, friend.

To Daryn Strauss: There aren't enough texts to thank you, babe!

To Josh Sabarra: Thank you for almost two decades of love and support.

To Ellen Goodlett: Thank you for being an immensely talented member of our coven. You are a true Raven.

To Sasha Alsberg: Thank you for always being my cheerleader and my friend! I am so proud of you.

To my girls, Jeanne Marie Hudson, Megan Steintrager, Lexi Dwyer, Lisa Tollin, Sarah Kagan, Kristin Nelthorpe. And to the next gen of girls' night—Emma and Eli Brenner, Logan and Jasper Dell, Aidan and Colin Kennedy, Fritz, Julian, and Montague Sutton Nelthorpe, Daisy and Clara Muñoz, Connor and Samantha Wynne.

To my team at New Leaf: Thank you, Hillary Pecheone, Abbigail Donoghue, Jordan Hill.

Jo Volpe and Pouya Shabazian: Thank you for all the things.

To my assistant, Emily Williams, who keeps everything running and who is such a light.

To my *Guiding Light* family: You gave me my start and stuck by me all these years. Jill Lorie Hurst, Tina Sloan, Crystal Chappell, Melissa Salmons, Laura Wright, Jordan's Vilasuso . . . and so many more.

To Sasha Mote: Thank you for all the sweetness and support you bring.

To Kami Garcia: There's no one else I want to pull a heist with, and you know how much I love you.

To Frank Lesser: Thank you for being a sounding board and for being so prolific; you inspire me.

To Carin Greenberg: You are my friend and my oracle.

To Lanie Davis: After all this time I am so happy we found a spell to work together.

To Joelle Hobeika: Thank you for all your witchy guidance.

To Emilia Rhodes: Thank you for sprinkling your magic on our Ravens.

Thank you, Kass Morgan, for saying yes to being my sister witch, on the page and off. The first time I heard you tell a story, I was smitten with your voice and spirit. I am so glad we get to make magic together. I adore you, friend.

Danielle Paige